THE WEDDING WAS ONLY A
FEW DAYS AWAY

"Jerry, I can't... If it were just us. But there's father... And Sir Harald would hound us down. I gave my word. There's the house at Bressford and, and everything... I can't. If only I could..." To soften the refusal she put her hand on his arm.

Then they were in an embrace, mouth to mouth, his heart hammering in her body, hers shaking in his. Nothing frightening, nothing insulting in this; a shared moment of passion, part of the sunset's afterglow, one with the scent of flowers.

COPSI CASTLE

Norah Lofts

Writing as Juliet Astley

BANTAM BOOKS
TORONTO · NEW YORK · LONDON

*This low-priced Bantam Book
has been completely reset in a type face
designed for easy reading, and was printed
from new plates. It contains the complete
text of the original hard-cover edition.*
NOT ONE WORD HAS BEEN OMITTED.

COPSI CASTLE

*A Bantam Book / published by arrangement with
Coward, McCann & Geoghegan, Inc.*

PRINTING HISTORY

*Coward, McCann & Geoghegan edition / June 1978
2nd printing . . . . August 1978*
Book of the Month Club alternate / September 1978
Bantam edition / June 1979

*Bantam Books are published by Bantam Books, Inc. Its trade-
mark, consisting of the words "Bantam Books" and the por-
trayal of a bantam, is Registered in U.S. Patent and Trademark
Office and in other countries. Marca Registrada. Bantam
Books, Inc., 666 Fifth Avenue, New York, New York 10019.*

PRINTED IN THE UNITED STATES OF AMERICA

COPSI
CASTLE

On his wedding night Magnus Copsey said to his bride, "You bitch! A fine dance you led me. Now I'll lead you one!" He set about her with a riding crop.

She'd known that it would be bad; she'd lived in mortal terror of him for almost eight months; but she had expected the assault to take another shape. She was prepared for the rough sexual attack; a kind of rape, legalized now because they were married. She thought: You made the bargain and must stick by it. She thought: Don't scream; that is what he wants. She cowered, and dodged, tried ineffectually to grab at the stinging lash, failed and tried to protect her face. Your face is your fortune, my pretty maid! My face is my misfortune!

One cut of the lash curved round her breast; a searing pain, like a burn and blood soiled the pretty lawn nightdress trimmed with Aunt Hannah's pillow lace. The sight of it destroyed her fortitude and she thought: He once beat a horse to pulp! And desolate as her future might seem, she had no wish to die. So she screamed.

Just along the passage the young madman's father, alert behind a half open door, got to his feet, and called "Bolsover!" No need to shout; Bolsover had also heard the distress call. Unlike Sir Harald who had hoped for the best while fearing the worst, Bolsover had anticipated trouble and was prepared. He reached the room in which the girl was still screaming a little ahead of his master who had not been able to run since he was wounded at Waterloo, and saw at once that this was not time for half measures. In what seemed a single, dexterous move he pulled out and flung a net, similar to those used for

1

covering wagons conveying animals to market, but smaller and of far finer material. Entangled, Magnus struggled, became more entangled, gave in and stood cursing. Bolsover had just time enough to administer one swift, punishing blow, before Sir Harald limped in. Ordinarily, when obliged to resort to physical measures he did so dispassionately, a man doing his job like a machine; but tonight he thought: Little bit of a girl like that, and struck with venom! The blow silenced the railing voice by depriving Magnus of breath. The room was silent for a second, except for a little whimpering sound. The girl who had been Hannah Reeve that morning and was now, for better or worse, Hannah Copsey became aware of the thinness of her nightdress. Her nightwear until now had been stout calico in summer, flannel in winter; she moved a step or two and took shelter behind the hangings of the big four-poster.

They were new, very pretty, chintz with sprays of mossroses on a pale cream background. A little blood from the worst wound, or from the fingers she had held to it, remained for years, a pale brownish smudge, between two of the rose sprays; it seemed impervious to washing.

There was no need for Sir Harald to say, "Take him away!" Bolsover was already hustling his young master away to his own room where he planned to hit him again, for good measure.

Sir Harald, bitterly disappointed, swamped by a sense of utter failure, said in a manner which would have surprised all those who thought him a genial, even a kindly man:

"You brought this on yourself, you know. If you'd yielded an inch in the first place, none of this need have happened."

He'd been a womanizer in his time, before he married for love, before the wound which had lamed him had inflicted a deeper and secret damage, but he still had an eye for a pretty young woman, and he could never see anything particularly attractive about this girl upon whom his son had set his heart. Almost all farm girls, well fed, immune from smallpox, had a brief, blossoming time. Almost invariably they had smooth skins, good teeth, bright eyes and plenty of shining hair, and figures which in so short a time would thicken or shrivel. To Sir Harald's experienced eye there was nothing exceptional about Hannah Reeve, except a slight variation of coloring, pale hair and dark eyes.

Still, what had happened had happened, and he felt responsible, so he forced himself to ask:

"Are you hurt?"

"One cut is bleeding."

"I'll call my sister, she'll know what to do."

He meant the younger of the two under his roof. Christened Bertha she was more usually called Bertie, and she had her own room at the extreme end of the vast, sprawling house.

Leaving the so prettily redecorated bridal chamber, upon which Sir Harald's hopes had centered with such desperation and in which the recent scene had been the final disillusionment, he walked, carrying a candle in one hand, and regretting the support of his usual stick in the other, what he had always said was a quarter of a mile, if you counted all the ups and downs.

◄═══►◄═══►◄═══►◄═══►

Copsi Castle had retained its original name, though the family which had lived in it since 1071 had long borne the more anglicized name of Copsey. Its south and east walls, in places four feet thick, still stood, bleak and stern in winter, softened in summer by a multitude of climbing roses, wisterias, jasmines and clematis. Behind the walls people lived, not unlike birds nesting in a cliff face. To reach Bertie's apartments, Sir Harald had to climb six steps, walk through the Long Gallery, descend twelve steps, pass the rooms where his stepmother, his elder sister, a cousin of his mother's and a young relative of his all lay—sound asleep, he hoped—and then, slightly breathless from haste and agitation, face another ten stairs. He was relieved to see that Bertie's door was outlined in light. In fact as he reached it, it opened, and Bertie stood there in her manly old camel-hair dressing gown.

At the far end of the vast room that served her as

parlor, bedroom and office, french windows stood wide open on to a kind of terrace. Bertie's room looked out onto the big cedar tree, said to be six hundred years old. It was the favorite place for nightingales, and even from the doorway he could hear the icy, aching fountain of song falling.

"Bad?" Bertie seldom wasted a word.

"Bad! Worse than I expected..." The words he had come to say stuck in his throat. "He...struck her. Not badly, but she is bleeding. Not seriously, but I thought..."

The blessed thing about Bertie was that she didn't say things like *I warned you* or *What did you expect?* She had said what she had to say eleven years ago. Now she turned to a cabinet in which other women would have kept pretty things, china, ivory and jade, but which for her served as a medicine cupboard, and as she collected, for Hannah, what she would have used on a sick animal, she jerked a thumb at the big, cluttered table.

"Brandy there, Harald. Help yourself. You look as though you need it..." Before he had time to do more than pour a little, decanter chattering against glass, and take a sip, glass chattering against teeth, she was ready, stuffing things into the worn, sagging pockets, snatching up the oil lamp, and reaching out with her other hand for her own glass, in which about a tablespoonful of brandy remained, and tossing it down—a gesture as practiced as it was unwomanly.

"I'm ready," she said. Turning he noticed, tossed carelessly upon a sofa, the fine butter-yellow silk dress, the pale straw hat with the yellow roses which Bertie had worn at the wedding earlier in the day. She loathed what she called dressing up, but had made a concession to mark the occasion, little as she had approved of it. He thought, miserably: We did all we could!

At the foot of the stairs that led down from her room, Bertie turned left, avoiding the way to the Long Gallery and choosing a route which he had instinctively avoided, though it was, by a few yards, the shorter. It led past the room known as the King's Chamber. Henry VIII had slept there on two occasions, breaking his journey to

the shrine at Walsingham. Some years later the Copsey of
the day had been disappointed that Queen Elizabeth, on
her progress through Suffolk, had thought Copsi too far
off the road, and had chosen instead to stay at Long
Melford Hall. Later, when he heard that entertaining her
and her vast suite had well-nigh ruined her host there, he
had been relieved.

Beyond this grand apartment lay the rooms which
Sir Harald entered only when the servant who attended
them reported some damage and he was obliged to see
what repairs were needed. These rooms were traditionally
inhabited by the master of Copsi and his lady. Two
bedrooms, with a dressing room between them, and a
boudoir. In the bedroom Juliet had died, less than a week
after giving birth to Magnus. Twenty years and three
months ago.

He had virtually forgotten what she looked like, and
there was no portrait of her to remind him, and he did not,
in fact, wish to be reminded. That was why he entered the
rooms which she had so briefly occupied as seldom as he
could. He remembered her as the sweetest woman he'd
ever met, and their radiantly happy marriage had lasted
less than a year. Until he was between thirteen and
fourteen, Magnus, at his best, had sometimes shown a
fleeting resemblance to that sweetest of women, and Sir
Harald had always felt a pang at such moments. He was
glad that as boy grew into man the likeness, so mocking
and ironic, faded and if he resembled anybody it was his
ancestor of Stuart times, glowering and periwigged on the
wall of the Long Gallery.

Bertie hurried past the room where Juliet had
played the piano and arranged flowers and then tried to
capture their beauty and hold it forever in rather
wishy-washy watercolor paintings; past the room where
she had died. In the short time that Juliet had lived at
Copsi—20 December 1815 to 23 March 1816—Bertie had
been so extraordinarily pleasant to Juliet, with whom she
had absolutely nothing in common, that Sir Harald felt he
could never be sufficiently grateful. Grateful enough to
forgive her, after a short period of disapproval, for her
tactless, if well-meant advice, eleven years ago when

Magnus had roused her ire by ill-treating a pony.

"Face the truth, Harald. He's no good now. And never will be. What you should do is marry again and breed a decent boy." Despite Bertie's rejection of most feminine things, her liking for masculine ones, in her way of life, in her name, she *was* female and her brother, stiffly conventional in every way, found it impossible to explain to her that he might take as many wives as King Solomon was said to have had, and yet beget no child. Impotent as a mule was his own expression, used only in his own mind. When Bertie had been so outspoken he had taken refuge by pointing out that no other boy he bred, however decent, could inherit the title or that part of the estate which was entailed; and she had said that titles had never mattered to the Copseys, which was true. She also said that if he married again and had a boy and put Magnus under some kind of control, either in a private asylum or with a keeper here, she would leave all she owned to the second son.

Sir Harald evaded that issue by saying,

"Nonsense, Bertie. You're young yet. You'll marry and have children of your own."

"I think not. Father, bless his heart, made it possible for me to be independent, and so I hope to remain. . . ."

⬤━━◆━━◆━━━◆━━◆━━⬤

They were outside the room where Hannah waited, pressing a blood-soaked towel to her breast.

"You go along," Bertie said. "I can manage." She was sorry for him, in a way, such a deluded fool, deceiving himself and trying to deceive everybody else. She was sorry for the girl, too; silly little creature, flattered, dazzled by the prospect of one day being Lady Copsey. Bertie knew nothing of the bargain struck five weeks earlier in the parlor of a farmhouse known as Reffolds. She dealt with the cut brusquely but efficiently as she would have dealt with a similar wound on an animal. Lister with his antiseptic theories was as yet unknown, but since the days of the Good Samaritan who applied oil and wine to wounds, people had heard or learned by experience the adage: Something sharp, something soothing. She swabbed the cut well with vinegar and then plastered it with homemade ointment which smelled of tar, which was one of its ingredients. She had come prepared to put in a few stitches, but decided against it; it was not a deep wound, and in such young, healthy flesh would heal well.

She worked, and Hannah accepted her ministrations, in silence. Both had been taught how to behave: Bertie by her mother and then by a beloved old governess, Hannah in the stricter atmosphere of the Female Academy. Both knew how to enter, how to leave a room, to effect an introduction, pour tea gracefully and a dozen other trivialities which in sum made up the difference between civilized and uncouth behavior. But what had happened, in this room, so short a time ago, neither had been prepared for. What could one say, Bertie wondered, to a poor silly girl who had married a madman, and was already beginning to pay the price? And Hannah, who had stopped whimpering and had borne the stinging application of vinegar without flinching, was silent from shame, and from the impossibility of explaining. And although Miss Copsey was being kind, and deft in action, she was one of the family and naturally her sympathies would lie with Mr. Magnus.

Bertie applied the long strip of linen which would serve as bandage and also keep the brownish, rather smelly ointment from soiling anything the girl wore, tonight or tomorrow.

"There!" she said. "I don't think it will leave a mark."

"Thank you."

"You need another nightgown. I'll take this. Servants are such gossips."

Hannah knew about modesty of behavior. As Miss Copsey dealt with the bleeding slash she had kept her nightgown clutched about her middle. Now—and thank God for Aunt Hannah who had insisted that three of everything was absolutely essential—she could slip one nightgown over her head as she lowered the other.

Bertie said, with an awkwardness unusual to her:
"You know...This kind of thing may happen again."

"Next time I shall be ready. Tonight he took me unawares. I thought that once I had given in,...But I was wrong. I shall not be caught like that again."

Bertie looked at her young niece by marriage. Weight? Seven stone by the most charitable judgement, probably less. What chance did she stand? Even Bertie, tall and strong, hardened by an active life—the land her father had bequeathed her out of his unentailed estate was outlying, six miles from the castle, so she rode twelve miles most days in all weathers; she hunted during the season and shot a good deal—doubted whether now she could deal with her nephew. When he was ten she'd given him the only really good thrashing he'd ever had, apart from those at Eton, but not now!

"I think you would be unwise to provoke him." An understatement if ever there was one! "Your best way would be to shout for help. Or lock yourself in until he calms down. The fits seldom last long." And in between, apart from being as stupid as an owl, there was nothing to indicate...In fact Magnus could be charming when he chose. He'd probably been charming to this little nitwit. Bertie wondered what exactly she *had* done to provoke such a savage attack on the wedding night. Shown some maidenly modesty and reluctance most likely.

And there'd be tomorrow, and tomorrow, a whole series of tomorrows, a lifetime of them. Not my business. Bertie told herself, dissociating herself, as she had learned to dissociate herself from the squabbles between her sister and her stepmother, between one, or both of them, and one or both of the men who completed the family circle. As a child she had been sensitive, easily upset by any disagreement, but she'd learned to say to herself this does not concern me. The cultivated insensitivity soon became real. Sometimes she wondered whether her father had left her as much as he had in order that she could get away if she wished to. And sometimes she guessed that her dislike for women stemmed from having lived with two women who displayed almost every feminine fault with few or none of the supposed womanly virtues.

She stuffed what she had been using back into her pocket, folded the nightdress small, and said, "You'd better get some sleep."

Hannah did not speak, except with her eyes, wide and dark and distressed; they asked: Sleep, after this?

She had a lot to learn, Bertie reflected, a lot to endure, a long way to go. And nobody on earth could help her in any but the most superficial way. Still, what could be done, should be done. She reached into her pocket again and brought out a very small dark bottle, moved to the washstand and took the glass which topped the carafe, dripped six carefully counted drops of black, viscous fluid. She added water and swilled the mixture around.

"That should help."

Left to herself, Hannah went and lay down, moving gingerly. The bandaged cut was easier, some of the blows which had not drawn blood still ached and stung, but misery of spirit hurt more. Wave after wave of utter desolation swept over her. Not a shred of hope left, not a crumb of faith in God or man.

She'd had a pious upbringing and had once believed in prayer, though one of the mistresses at the Academy had tried to explain its limitation as a mitigation of circumstance. There were the laws of Nature, she said, and only a miracle could suspend them; ordinary people could not expect God to interfere with the laws of Nature—which were actually His own—simply because He was importuned. Hannah had not been warned by this argument. She'd prayed, first with full faith, and then with rising doubt, that Father might get better. It would take a miracle to cure him, but only a small one; people did get up from beds to which doctors had condemned them for life; even the laws of Nature decreed that some injuries should mend. Father had remained as he was, helpless from the waist down and Hannah's faith had faltered, faded, died away like an untended fire. The prayers, once so fervent and full of faith, became mere words. And lately the rational explanation about the laws of Nature had been made to seem ridiculous. It might be a law of Nature, and therefore a law of God, which decreed that a man who had fallen from the top of a stack should be incapacitated for the rest of his days, but what law, of Nature or of God, could possibly have arranged what had happened to a harmless, dutiful girl like Hannah Reeve? A girl whose latest prayer had been: God give me strength to go through with it.

She lay for some time and then something extraordinary occurred to her. It was like a dream, but she was not asleep. She proved that to herself by sitting up in bed and lighting a fresh candle from the one burning down. She was not dreaming; she was awake here, in this dreadful room, but most of her was elsewhere; in the little house in Bressford which had been part of the bargain. In actual life she had gone over it once, when it was empty and bare. Her mother expressed her disapproval of the whole affair by finding fault with the house itself, calling it dark and poky and asking where would the dresser stand? Now it was all lightness and brightness and full of flowers, all highly scented, all unfamiliar. She seemed to be alone there, floating rather than walking from room to room. Then she heard a voice, recognizable as Aunt Hannah's, speaking from some hidden place. It said, "You see we were right! They are happy here." She rather wished that she could see them, witness their happiness, but not being able to do so in no way diminished her own sense of happiness or well-being. She thought: So long as they're happy. Nothing else matters.

Upon that thought she fell into genuine sleep.

><=>■<==><■<====><■<=======><■<=====>

In his own room, just along the corridor, Sir Harald sat down in the chair in which he had waited, with hope, with apprehension, and said to himself: God, what did I ever do to deserve such punishment? What more could I have done?

The answer to that came in Mrs. Reeve's rasping, brutal voice: You should have had him locked up! Years ago!

With the last hope dead, and with all the tomorrows to face he was almost forced to admit his error; but his excuse presented itself immediately: he had Copsi to

consider. Consider it now then and squeeze out what
comfort you can. . . .

━━━━━◆━━━◆━━━◆━━━◆━━━

Copsi was his first love and apart from Juliet—
though of course the two were not comparable—his only
one. He'd been born there, second son, as his very name
indicated. Firstborn sons were always named Magnus;
second sons, Harald; if a third came along he was Robert;
if a fourth, he was Ralph.

A man simply called Copsi had ruled in the Orkneys
when William the Conqueror took England. It took a
little time for the news to reach him, but as soon as it did,
he hurried down to England to pay his allegiance, and
then, secure of his tenure, hurried back. But in his train,
which he had made as impressive as possible, there was
another Copsi, son, brother, cousin, nobody knew now
nor ever could know. He had borne the name of Magnus
and had elected to stay in England and share the rich
pickings. William knew a good man when he saw him and
had entrusted Magnus Copsi to build a castle on what was
virtually a peninsula, land between the mouths of the Rad
and the Wren, and to exercise feudal rights over the area
as payment for protecting it.

That had been the beginning and there was not, the
Copseys claimed, any other tenure in England which had
passed, in unbroken succession, from father to son.
Perhaps in early times because nobody envied it enough
to take action. In theory and on parchment, in *Domesday
Book* itself, the acres dominated by Copsi Castle sounded
impressive; but much of the land, especially near the river
mouths, was marshy, unproductive in a wet season; there
were stretches of sandy soil, so light that when a good east
wind blew, as it often did, a whole crop, seemingly well
rooted, could be blown away. There was also Monkswood, dense, intractable remnant of the primeval forest
which had once stretched between Humber and Thames.

On the whole the Copseys had been steady,
home-keeping people, exercising what ambition they had
on improving their land and beautifying their castle. In
the course of time they threw up a maverick or two,

frivolous and profligate; the Magnus to whom James I had given one of the early baronetcies had been a courtier and had died in debt, his title having cost him dearly in "loans" to the King. *Not* an example to be followed. Nor was that of a rabid gambler who had committed the iniquity of selling a hundred acres on the outskirts of Wyck, land which his successor tried to buy back, but could not, since the Rad Brewery and some other commercial buildings had already risen on the site.

Sir Harald had grown into boyhood without realizing the depth of his affection for Copsi and the way of life that it represented; he only knew that as a child, after any absence, short or long, he returned to Copsi with joy, convinced that his home was the most desirable place in the world. It could never be his of course, unless something unthinkable happened to his brother Magnus, to whom he was also much attached.

Most schoolboys suffered from homesickness which wore off after a time, he was perpetually homesick during his time at Eton; counting the days to the next holiday, and towards the end of each half being careful with his money, so that he could hire a post-chaise which would travel through the night and thus give him a few hours extra in the precious place. He often compared Windsor Castle unfavorably with Copsi: it was too big and impersonal to be lovable. Later in life he felt the same lack of enthusiasm about such diverse manmade things as the Knights' Castle in Malta, the Pyramids in Egypt, and the Taj Mahal in India.

Second sons almost invariably went into the army and Harald Copsey was the last man to break with tradition. As a soldier he was reliable and conscientious, indisputably courageous, but more popular with the men than with his fellow officers. No specific reason; he was a damned good fellow, but a bit of a sobersides, never, in fact, quite belonging, a bit over-inclined to treat other ranks, and even natives, as though they were tenants to be protected, not exploited. He had indeed once done a very unorthodox thing—argued hotly with his colonel about a deduction from the troopers' poor pay in order to meet the expense of some unnecessary, frivolous change in uniform. He'd been well snubbed, of course, but he had scored a kind of moral victory, saying, "Then, with your permission, sir, I will defray the expense myself."

He could afford to do so, for an aunt on the maternal side had recently left him all she had; a neat little manor house, two hundred acres of sheep-run in the Cotswolds, and a certain income of eight hundred pounds a year.

He went to view his inheritance and though grateful for it and the independence it conferred, decided that he could not possibly live in a countryside so alien, so different from Suffolk with the wide skies and the wide landscapes, open vistas interrupted by nothing bigger than a clump of trees, or a church spire. At Gayton-on-Wold, he felt shut in, restricted, homesick; he could never settle there.

He was reaching the age, and was now in a position to think seriously, of retirement and of marriage. Napoleon was safely caged up in Elba; peacetime soldiering seemed to offer little prospect but boredom. And his brother Magnus who had succeeded in 1812, made him a generous offer.

"There is the Dower House, Harry. Except as a threat to hold over two quarrelsome old women it serves no useful purpose. It's yours whenever you want it. And if you felt the need for occupation, you could always lend me a hand."

It was as near as a privileged elder brother could come to offering to share his inheritance with his junior and Harald was touched.

"I'll think about it. Thanks, Magnus." It was a proposition that needed thought, attractive as it was on the surface. It would mean—and he was clear-sighted enough to see it—his becoming a kind of glorified agent, lending a hand, then assuming responsibility, but never making a decision. Of late his visits to Copsi had been rare and brief, but his managing, cherishing eye had seen several things to which Magnus seemed to be oblivious; things which he would have wished otherwise and would have changed, if only . . . He cut that thought off abruptly. It smacked of disloyalty to his brother, who, if he had a fault, it was that he was too easygoing, with a far less managing nature than his own. Magnus had never learned the need to be managing; since leaving Eton he had been subject to no discipline; everything handed to him on a plate. Disloyal! Ungrateful!

But there the thought was; and perhaps it would be better, after all, to retire to the place that was indisputably his, thanks to Aunt Sophie, refurbish the house which at the moment was being looked after by caretakers, and turn his serious attention to sheep-farming.

Overnight he had almost made up his mind, but, leaving early in the morning, he turned in his saddle and looked back, as he had done so many times before. It was late February and the elms in the avenue were budding and reddening, and a few wild daffodils had broken into flower. Against the brightening morning light Copsi stood, stark and stern, stripped of its summer finery, its history written in its face in the various windows, some very old—heavily arched Norman; Tudor mullions, casement, sash, oriels, bays—and above them rose the chimneys, candy twisted, crowstepped, plain. All part of Copsi, all part of himself, and he thought—I belong here; nothing else will do for me. Better be agent at Copsi than lord of the manor at Gayton-on-Wold. A curious thought, a bit of psalm chanted unthinkingly, struck him: I had rather be a door keeper in the house of my God than to dwell in the tents of wickedness. Quite ridiculous! He had not been obliged to choose between good and evil; simply between two places.

Having made one momentous decision, he was called upon to make another and another.

In March 1815, Napoleon had broken out of Elba and was in France again, with old soldiers flocking to him in thousands. No time for a good, experienced soldier to hand in his papers; no time for a sensible man to get married. However, he fell in love with an obscure, not even very pretty girl called Juliet Evett, as wholeheartedly as and far more consciously than he had fallen in love with Copsi.

He was no innocent. Young and relatively poor, he had taken pleasure where it was to be bought for the first year or two. Then, tall and good-looking, splendid in uniform, he had been welcome as an escort, sometimes more. When his windfall fell, he had even become an eligible man, possible catch for sisters and cousins. After all a place, a small property and a steady income was not to be sniffed at in these hard times.

The bought girls were agreeable, but the business was over and done with in an evening; and those with more serious intentions made as little real impression on his mind. He was twenty-eight and had never met the woman with whom he wanted to live day after day until death did them part; the same face across the table. And then abruptly, what had always seemed to hold the possibility of unmitigated boredom assumed the look of security and happiness ever after.

Juliet was the daughter of the Rector of Gayton-on-Wold, a querulous hypochondriac, nephew to an earl and secretly resentful that his family had not done more for him. Now that Harald had decided to sell his property and had come west to make the necessary arrangements, there was one slightly disputable boundary to be settled and it concerned the Rector because if affected the tithe. So Harald was asked to dine, met the head of the house, ate one of the worst meals he had ever had in his life, pitied the girl, then admired her, and fell in love.

They were married in May; her father performed the ceremony in a state of temper more suited to Black Mass than any real religious rite, and in June they were in Brussels, Juliet wearing her wedding dress for the second time, at the Ball which was to become famous because from it so many men were called away—and so few returned.

Captain Harald Copsey was one of the survivors—though his dancing days were done. He spent his convalescent time in a pleasant little château near Leaken where Belgian and English ladies—Juliet among them—played at being nurses without doing much that involved a real rolling up of sleeves, any real soiling of the hands. Juliet was different and the ladies sensed the difference. They put upon her. She seemed not to notice, but her husband did. He resented it fiercely; she was by birth related to a noble family, and by marriage connected with a family which if not the grandest, was one of if not the oldest in England. But in the eyes of the great ladies she was just Mrs. Copsey.

He said, "My love, as soon as I can hitch myself about on a crutch, we'll go to Paris."

In his thigh no bone had been broken, only muscles and tendons torn, and—a determined man—he was soon able to dispense with his crutch. And for the first time in his life he was, as he put it, fairly well off. Aunt Sophie's house and all appertaining to it had been sold by a clever agent to one of those nabobs, coming out of India with a fortune.

The Allies were in Paris and the gay city was *en fête*, crowded with visitors, all eager to be entertained. There were a multitude of pleasures in which even a man with a limp and a pregnant woman could partake: concerts, operas, theatre shows, picture galleries, and the shops. Oh, the shops! And the delight of buying beautiful things for a girl who had hitherto had so little, and was so grateful. October and November sped away. The baby was expected in March and it was time to think about homemaking. He had never yet given Magnus a firm answer about the Dower House which would need repairs and redecoration; it had not been occupied since his grandmother's death. Soon he must make up his mind, and now he had something else to consider—Juliet's extreme meekness, the ease with which she could be put upon. Would she be happy at Copsi? The Dower House was within easy walking distance of the Castle and the two quarrelsome old women to whom Magnus had referred— their elder sister and their stepmother—were both still pretty spry; both were aggressive; both would attempt to involve her in the running feud which had gone on for years and which could find fresh fuel in the most trivial thing.

He said, "Darling, we have to decide where to live and think about settling in. We can afford a decent house and small estate anywhere in England. You say."

He was—and he knew it—being disloyal to Copsi

where even as a kind of agent without any real power, he could have used influence.

"Wherever you choose, Harry. I should prefer *not* to be near Papa. That may sound undutiful, but if I were within reach....I chose Mrs. Gull from a number of applicants, and I am sure that she is a good housekeeper and has, moreover, nursing experience . . . But I feel that if I were available, every time he had gout. You know..."

He knew and hastened to assure her that wherever they chose to live would be well away from Gayton-on-Wold. At the same time he hoped that she would not settle for somewhere within easy reach of London. He rather feared that since she was at heart what he called more townified than he was himself. She really *enjoyed* things that bored him and which he only endured for her sake. Music to him was just a noise and all operas seemed ridiculous; sometimes he fidgeted, and then she changed from rapt attention to immediate concern, asking him in a whisper if his leg hurt; would he like to go? And often, viewing pictures, wonderful, famous pictures but meaningless to him, the dear girl would sense his withdrawal of interest and blame his leg, saying that they had seen enough for today.

Now, when the matter of where they should live was becoming urgent, she showed the same understanding, asking quietly,

"Would you not prefer somewhere near Copsi, of which you are so fond?"

"Did I ever say so?"

"Not outright. But when you speak of it your voice changes, as it does, my dearest, when you say my name. Also, once or twice you have talked in your sleep. Always of Copsi . . . Once you seemed perturbed because counting the windows outside and the rooms inside, didn't match."

"It was a game with us. With Magnus and me. We never got it right. It is no ordinary place."

"But you are fond of it? Would like to visit occasionally? So why not look for a settled home, somewhere in the vicinity?"

"Magnus offered me the Dower House. It would

suit us well in many ways. But—.."

"But what, dearest? I assure you that no place could be less convenient or more difficult to run than Gayton Rectory."

"Oh, it is not that. Mere inconveniences can be easily overcome. What deters me...I have a sister, the oldest of us all. She made what was called a good marriage to a Frenchman...He went to the guillotine; she escaped, with some jewels, sewn into her corset, I believe. Naturally she came home to Copsi, only to find that my father had married again. A woman of about the same age, and unfortunately of very similar nature...They cannot agree upon any single point. My other sister, Bertha—she is quite different—once summed the whole thing up: if one wishes a window open the other wishes it closed; if one wants a log on the fire, the other wishes it removed. Nothing is too trivial. They'd fall upon you like vultures, feigning friendship, each seeking allegiance. And then if you failed to satisfy—and I assure you nobody possibly could—they'd combine against you. Not for long, but long enough to make you miserable. No, the more I think about it the more I see how unworkable it would be."

"But if you were happy, dearest, I could ignore such petty things."

"I doubt it. Even Philippa..."

"That is Magnus's wife?"

"Yes. You'd think to look at her that she hadn't a nerve in her body. A very solid, stolid young woman. Magnus himself told me that even she was upset by conflicting advice about her baby and how to bring it up. Neither of them has had a baby, by the way, so of course they both know everything." He grinned and Juliet gave her little low, tinkling laugh. "Magnus was obliged to say that if either of them mentioned the baby again he'd send them to live in the Dower House. As for Bertha—we call her Bertie—they led her such a dance that now she lives almost entirely apart and only comes to the family table on special occasions."

"Could we not do the same? Especially if we had our own establishment. How old is the baby?"

"He was a year in... Bless me, I clean forgot his birthday. It was July."

"We'll take him something from Paris. From that beautiful toy shop in the Rue de Rivoli. Perhaps a rocking horse. It would be rather pleasant to think of another little Magnus and another little Harald growing up and playing together—and counting Copsi's rooms and windows. Would it not?"

It was a pleasant thought. But he looked at her dubiously. She was twenty-five, but now happy and properly dressed, looked younger, despite the thickening of her figure. In many ways she was more knowledgeable than he was; about music, about pictures, about books, but she was so yielding, so anxious to please that he felt fiercely protective towards her. On the other hand she had lived with that horrible old father and somehow retained her sweetness of nature and a capacity for enjoyment.

Finally he compromised.

"Look," he said. "In his last letter Magnus said that he hoped we'd spend Christmas at Copsi. Suppose we do that. You could see the Dower House, and the family, and then we could decide. Any my dear, you must be completely frank about it. Consider your own wishes for once, not mine. Admittedly, I am fond of Copsi, but with you I shall be happy anywhere."

Within hours of this, his final repudiation of Copsi, the place reached out and claimed him for its own.

It was an express delivery letter, addressed in Bertie's unmistakable hand, addressed to... there it was, plain as print, Sir Harald Copsey. That could mean only one thing.

❖❖❖❖❖❖

Juliet wept for people who were no more than names to her. And to Harald, genuinely shocked and grieved, she tried to apply comfort by recalling what she remembered of a typhoid outbreak at Gayton. "People may suffer at first, but they lapse into delirium and then unconsciousness. They didn't *know*—towards the end. Darling, I am sure I am right. I remember that Papa was sent for and refused to go—to one family. He said it would be futile since the woman who was dying wouldn't recognize him or realize *why* he was there. And he had had a good deal of experience...."

There was another interpretation to be put upon that refusal to risk infection, but Sir Harald did not mention it. He accepted the well-meant words, and in his turn tried to comfort her. She broke into fresh tears when the rocking horse, already crated for the journey, was delivered; she said, "Oh dear, that poor little boy..." And he found a panacea. He said, "*Our* child will use it. Juliet, we must look to the future."

Looking to the future was, in fact, the only real comfort. What had happened was a tragedy, but it had given him what he realized—shuddering away from the fact but obliged to face it—he had always wanted, Copsi. For his own. For his son, and his son's son. And in his heart he did not doubt that he would be a more able custodian than his dead brother, so easygoing, so slack about so many things. All the little things which on his brief and infrequent leaves he had noticed and regretted, all the things he had intended to mention, with tact and caution had he become unpaid agent, now depended upon him alone.

Their homecoming was necessarily muted. Mourning and Juliet's condition forbade any entertaining yet there always seemed plenty to occupy Sir Harald and his wife. He derived enormous pleasure—not completely untinged by guilt—in showing her everything in and out of doors.

"I swear, darling, I never consciously envied my brother in my life. I understood the situation from the first and we were the best of friends. I never even *wished*...But now...Well, nothing can alter things. I always loved the place and now I love it more than ever."

"I fully understand," she said, perceptive as usual. "Rather like a hat, if that isn't too trivial a simile. You see it in a shop window, you admire it, you know it would suit you, but you can never have it because of the price. Then, by sheer accident you have it and like it even more because it belongs."

His love of the place showed in his knowledge of it, its history. He had stood unmoved before masterpieces of art, yet he seemed to know something about every picture that hung in the Long Gallery—even if were only to say that about such and such a one nothing was known: "Quite anonymous, poor chap!" He seemed to value them indiscriminately and they were a heterogeneous collection, ranging from a splendid Holbein to amateur water colors—the kind of thing she produced herself, or rather worse. "That is a view from the lake. Painted by my great aunt Lydia. She was considered to have great talent, but she died young. Consumption... Now this, almost the same view, is a Gainsborough, done before he was famous. I think Lydia's compares well, don't you?" It would have been churlish to contradict.

"And that, surely, is a Romney."

"Yes, my mother. There is quite a story about that. She and her father were in London when a great fuss was being made about some picture he'd done of a Lady Hamilton. My grandfather thought my mother much more beautiful, so he took her along and said, "Paint a decent woman for a change!" Romney said it would cost him a thousand guineas and my grandfather said, "Never mind that. Get to work." And the sad thing was that when it was completed everybody who saw it thought it was yet another Lady Hamilton. And that so infuriated my grandfather that he would never have it hung in *his* house and my mother brought it with her when she married."

And somebody had hung it between an engraving of Copsi, sinister in black and white, and a drawing in red chalk, an economical sketch in a few light lines of a horse.

Somebody should really take this Long Gallery in hand and rearrange things. She'd do it, she thought, when she had more energy and had rearranged more vital things; for frankly the standard of housekeeping at Copsi was appalling. There *was* a housekeeper, aged, doddering, who confessed that she didn't see so well as once she had done. Among the things she had failed to see were a number of unpaid bills, and the filthy state of the kitchen, and the number of people who seemed to scuttle about, performing no recognizable function.

"And now, I'll just show you our mystery picture. Then you must rest."

The mystery picture was actually no picture in the usual sense of the word. It was a painted panel of the wall of the main staircase which rose, shallow stepped, slightly sagging between the great hall and the landing off which the Long Gallery, the King's Chamber and some other rooms opened. But there were other stairways—eight in all—and this one was seldom used.

"There," Sir Harald said. "What do you make of that?"

Nothing; no picture. Just a dark panel in which dead colors, dark olive green, black, chocolate brown seemed to shift and shimmer. There was a somber resemblance to that gorgeous material known as shot taffeta, of which she had one beautiful dress, capable of changing color with a movement, green or lilac.

"*Is* it a picture? Really I must confess... I see nothing. Perhaps the light is wrong. At Gayton, in the church, there were pictures. Cromwell's men splattered them with whitewash. Others followed suit, but sometimes, just sometimes, in certain lights one could see. Vaguely, of course. Once I saw what I am sure was the miracle of the loaves and fishes."

"It *is* a picture. With a story. Try from this angle."

She glanced at him and saw him looking at her with a kind of anxiety. Did he want her to see it? Was he anxious that she should not? Was it some kind of test? Perhaps one could not qualify as a member of the Copsi family unless one could see behind the blurred, smudged surface. She might have pretended, had she known what he wished, and what to profess to see.

"Did you ever see it?"

"No. My mother said she did. Magnus and I often tried to, but never could. We'll go this way. It's nearer for the dining room." He took her arm to help her down the stairs.

"What is the story?"

"We've never been a political family," he said. "Perhaps that is why we're still here. Loyal in sympathy, of course. The Civil War just missed us. The Copsey of the day was an old man, his son—he'd married three times—a mere child. But we were visited, once, by Cromwell's men, and there on the wall was the portrait of Charles 1. It couldn't be removed, so it was hastily painted over. Afterwards attempts were made, only partially successful as you see, to remove the extra paint."

"How very interesting. Of course, it must have dominated the hall."

She looked back, and this time she saw it, as clear as though it had been painted yesterday; the grave, inscrutable face under the wide-brimmed, feathered hat; the lace of the collar and cuffs, creamy white against plum-colored velvet.

"Now I see it!" she said, quite excited. "It's beautiful!"

"You're pretending. Or seeing what you think you should see—knowing the story." She glanced at him again and understood that this was what he *wished* to think. Why? Agreeable as ever she said lightly,

"Of course I am. Pure pretense."

Possibly because Charles Stuart had come to such a luckless end some superstition was attached to the picture—those who saw it were out of luck. He hoped to God that she had been pretending.

━━◇━━◇━━◇━━◇━━◇━━

Sometimes, even in January and February, there were fine, mild days, and then he took her, in a little low phaeton, drawn by a steady pony, around the estate, to the farms and holdings which made up the two villages, Copsi Major and Copsi Minor. The larger village had the church, but the smaller one, on the river, had not only the mill, but a tiny wharf at which coal barges unloaded. The farms had descriptive names—Rookwood, Cowfield, Squirrel's Hall, Reffolds, Marsh End near the river, Warren Place where the land was sandy and rabbits abounded.

Everywhere they were welcomed civilly, but with a

touch of reserve. Sir Magnus had been loved, for his go-easy behavior cut both ways. He might not mend roofs very promptly, but he never increased rents, or busybodied about suggesting newfangled things. Sir Harald could not actually be regarded as a stranger, having been born here and paying visits afterwards; but he could not rightly be regarded as one of *us*. Very few of *us* ever ventured much farther afield than Bressford and Wyck. Also he'd been a soldier and though East Anglians made the best soldiers—old Cromwell had known that—soldiering as a trade was distrusted; too much inclined to lay down the law. Yet there were two families in the village who had sent sons, armed with long-bows to Crécy, with the Harald Copsey of the day. He'd been killed, so had young Reeve and young Smith; the family up at the castle had paid for all the bodies to be shipped home and buried, the Copsey inside, Reeve and Smith outside, the church.

The new young Lady Copsey was, of course, a complete foreigner, out of the West Country it was understood; but she looked amiable enough and seemed disposed to be pleasant. (Years and years of acting as unpaid curate at Gayton had trained Juliet in the right word. Her father had often offended people and it had been her job to soothe and she had learned that the best way was by admiring something, however small. What a pretty pussy! Gracious, how William is growing! I have never seen such a beautiful geranium! Such remarks went a long way on the road to reconciliation.) Here, so far as she knew, there was no need to conciliate, but she aimed to please; and succeeded. Harald was pleased with her. Darling you charmed them all; even that terribly deaf old woman at Rookwood *looked* as though she understood you.

Almost without exception the women in the villages wished her well in the approaching confinement. Many of them thought ahead, and rather looked forward to the time when, not bound to the phaeton, she could make a proper visit, sit in the seldom used parlor and take a cup of tea and see other things to admire, a cherished teapot, a few silver spoons, a sampler or a bit of patchwork.

Inside the castle things went with surprising smoothness, too. Both Old Lady, as Lady Copsey had been known since Philippa had become Lady Copsey, and Madame le Beaune had been considerably sobered by the disaster which had snatched away not only Magnus, Philippa and the child, but several servants and even Doctor Fordyke—old enough, as Madame le Beaune said, to be immune to anything. That blow struck home, for he was very nearly their contemporary. Deaths of those younger than oneself could be fairly easily dismissed—the young were sappy, the young took risks; death with people considerably older than oneself could be faced with a certain fortitude—nobody could expect to live forever; but when death struck within one's own decade, it was different. A shared feeling of vulnerability temporarily halted the running quarrel and for six weeks or so Juliet felt that Harald had exaggerated when he warned her about the squabbles which might involve her. Then, mainly for lack of other occupation, and because the belligerent spirit had revived, the squabble broke out again, with her and her love of flowers as its center.

Copsi, like many households of substance, had hothouses, one devoted to flowers and pot plants, the other to the production of vegetables out of season; the only unusual feature about the flower hothouse at Copsi was that it sheltered a remarkable rose which might almost be called an evergreen rose, for though it dropped its leaves after the fashion of all deciduous plants they were so quickly replaced—and buds followed—that it was known as the Everlasting Rose. Its flowers were pale yellow and its foliage more bronze than green. It was enjoying a brief resting period when Sir Harald showed his wife around, but he assured her that within a short time she would have roses. She had said "How wonderful!" and was prepared to wait. Even in January and early February there were flowers, some grown inside the hothouses, lilies and carnations and a few brave little things, snowdrops and primroses, even a daffodil or two, outside.

On the bad days—too wet or too windy to allow a drive—Juliet arranged and then tried to paint various posies. She liked the wild things better, but, brought in from the cold, they wilted before she could really recapture them.

She had an easy pregnancy, actually too much concerned with Harald, so wounded and weak, and then so anxious to enjoy himself and see that she enjoyed herself, that most afflictions had passed her by, or been ignored. But...women did die in childbirth; it was the most hazardous occupation in the world, and she, who had never taken a fancy for some out-of-season food or indulged any whim or temper, had an urge to leave something—as well as a son—to Copsi. She wanted something to be hung on the walls of the Long Gallery; something that could be pointed to, with pride, in years to come. My mother, my grandmother, my great-grandmother painted that: she had talent, but she died young...She knew it was a foolish fancy, directly attributable to her condition, but it persisted and she painted away happily for hours, delighting in the plentiful supply of good stout paper, and the very best watercolor paint, of both of which she had been deprived hitherto.

It was with surprise and delight that she greeted Old Lady Copsey, one bitterly cold morning in February. She carried a sizeable bunch of the yellow roses and said, with complacency,

"I gathered them myself, Juliet, despite the weather. I have always held that daily exercise is the secret of good health. Not of course that you, just at present, could be expected..." The words were spoken amiably, but held just a hint of rebuke. Lady Copsey thought Juliet looked pale, and who could wonder? The boudoir was decidedly overheated and both its tall windows were firmly closed.

Juliet said, placatingly, that if the weather cheered up in the afternoon she might take a turn in the garden. She then admired the roses and thanked Lady Copsey for the thoughtful gesture. She even invited her opinion as to which vase would display the flowers to best advantage, the blue or the brown? She forebore to mention that anyone living in Copsi Castle had no need to venture out in search of exercise and fresh air: long stretches of frigid, draughty passages and so many stairs lay between the occupied rooms, and although the Long Gallery had two fireplaces they did little to heat an apartment the size of a small church.

After due consideration, Lady Copsey said, "I think the blue. It would provide more contrast. The foliage has a brownish tinge. I will fill it for you." Glad to escape from the stifling room, she went along to the housemaid's closet at the end of the corridor, took down the blue vase and drew water from the tap.

"There you are, my dear. I leave the arranging to you."

The door opened and there was Madame le Beaune, dressed for an Arctic expedition. She wore a long sealskin coat, fur-lined boots, fur-lined gloves and had her head swathed in layers of a lacy woolen scarf of her favorite blue—a color which had suited her when she was young, but which now made her eyes look somewhat faded. Faded as they were they could sparkle with indignation, and they did so now at the sight of the roses.

"So!" she exclaimed. "That is what happened! I positively *forbade* Thomas to touch them. I intended to cut them *myself* this morning and bring them to Juliet. And despite the abominable weather, I held to that intention, as you see. . . . What a sly trick to play. You had absolutely no right."

"As much right as *you*!" Lady Copsey retorted with spirit. They were back in the well-trodden arena. Their relationship had been doomed from the first. Lydia Monkhouse had hardly found her way around Copsi, become accustomed to her new name and her title, and learned that in some ways the path of the second wife was not easy—too many comparisons—when Madame le Beaune arrived. Disturbances in France had interfered with the postal service and she did not know that her father had remarried. She had plainly come home with the intention of resuming her role as elder daughter of the house. The rivalry, the spite had started then. And now involved even a bunch of flowers which had, after all, reached its rightful destination—but by the wrong hand.

"Your right I fail to see," Marie le Beaune said. "My mother brought that particular rose from Southbury when she married. As she brought so many things." A nasty dig, for the mother of Marie, Magnus, Harald and Bertha had been something of an heiress, whereas the second Lady Copsey had come empty-handed, bringing, as Madame le Beaune often said, nothing but a pretty face and a bad temper.

This squabble, beginning so simply, became too complicated for Juliet to follow but she watched and listened with dismay. She had lived until her marriage with sarcasm, scolding, easily-provoked irritability, self pity, and, once she had accepted Harald's proposal, downright denunciation of ingratitude and betrayal; but this cut and thrust of vituperative words between antagonists equally matched was new to her, and quite shocking. She made one feeble attempt to intervene.

"Please don't quarrel about the flowers. I have them and I am deeply grateful to you both." A mistake. Momentarily halted from a recollection of past grievances, old insults, both ladies looked at the flowers and Marie le Beaune said,

"And look how you cut them, you ignorant woman! Such long sprays! A waste of young shoots. Every one of these buds would have flowered if left on the bush. Now it will be bare for a month."

"I took into consideration Juliet's wish to paint them. Just a few blooms, cut short, would have been almost like primroses."

"So! Now you profess to know about painting! Very true! About painting—your own face—you know all that is to be known!"

The small frustrated artist in Juliet took a step away and reflected how closely the two old women resembled one another now, when enraged. So far as she knew there was no blood kinship, but they did look alike. Both fair, both fading, both resorting to every competitive artifice. In fact neither was truly *old* as age went, but both had been pretty in youth and both resented, fought against, the diminution of prettiness which the years brought. It was pitiable. They had no husbands, no children.

She thought: Suppose I outlive Harald, and live on

here in suffrance with nothing to keep me alive but a quarrel between my son's wife and me, or Bertie and me? What a hideous fate!

It was the first time that she had ever faced the fact that everybody must grow old and lose contact, lose faculties, lose the hope of better things to come, a hope that kept the young, however miserable their present condition, alive and active and which, in her case, had been fully justified. Without that what was there? Heaven with its everlasting joys or Hell with its everlasting pains? The truth was that she no longer held any firm-rooted belief, having lived so long with a skeptic, disguised as a clergyman; a man who had been forced into the Church, as, in another family, he might have been forced into the army, the navy, the wine trade or wool. The Church provided him with a meager but certain living, a decent house, some status in the district, but its teachings meant almost nothing to him and affected neither his behavior nor his tastes which were classical. He enjoyed making a neat translation and occasionally, for lack of other audience, would try one out on his daughter who, being as he said so incurably stupid, often missed the point. But now something, perhaps not correctly remembered, but exactly fitting her mood, returned to her: Day follows day, and though we do not hark; suddenly the dark one calls. Calls and we follow; by that road or this, into the universal silences.

It was too much, she gave way to tears, and although that halted the quarrel for a moment, another bad mark was ticked up on the invisible but relentless scoreboard which both kept.

Juliet had, after that, no wish to paint the roses. In fact she never wanted to see a yellow rose again; and since in saying that the bush would be bare for a month Madame le Beaune had been indisputably correct, the painting she had planned could never have been made, even had she wished it.

<hr>

Sometimes, when a woman was so narrow-hipped and a baby so big-headed, a doctor would crush the eggshell thin skull and thus make the delivery, but young

Doctor Fordyke was optimistic and hoped that such a desperate, barbaric measure would not be necessary. Lady Copsey was not exactly built for child-bearing, but she was young, well-nourished, patient, brave.... In the end he was obliged to resort to his forceps and the baby, a boy weighing at least eight pounds, was hauled into the world and handed over to the midwife who could remember what she thought of as better days. Days when doctors scorned confinements and things were left to people like her. She thought, sullenly: I could have done better with a well-soaped hand!

She probably could have done, for a well-soaped hand would not have carried the infection which an unsterilized metal instrument did. (Young Doctor Fordyke lived long enough to be old Doctor Fordyke and to read about antiseptism and the virtues of carbolic.)

In low moments, Sir Harald reflected that he had never gained anything without a commensurate loss. Now he had his heir, Copsi had an heir, but he had lost his wife, the sweetest woman in the world. He always thought of her as that, even when he had forgotten what she looked like; though he scrupulously remembered her birthday, their wedding day, and the day of her death. And having had two of her pictures framed and glazed he hung them with his own hands, just under the blazing Holbein. One was a saucer-shallow bowl of primroses, the other a spray of pussy-willow, the gray catkins just powdered with yellow pollen. For a time he could not bear to look at them, once they were hung, because they recalled so sharply and painfully their few happy days together at Copsi. Nor could he contemplate occupying the rooms he always thought of as hers.

But, inch by inch, day following day, grief died its natural death and he must busy himself with what remained: Copsi which needed a great deal of attention and expenditure, and the boy. A precious child, in any circumstance, the firstborn, the heir; in the circumstances a thousand times more precious—the only child of my body, and Juliet's child.

Not that the boy was to be or ever had been spoiled in the ordinary sense of the word. Sir Harald had foreseen the possibility of the two old women carrying their rivalry into the nursery, and, as soon as the boy was conscious of people as people, competing for his smiles. There must be none of that. Bertie could be trusted; she would take little interest in the boy until he was old enough to learn to ride. She had, however, consented to act as godmother at the quiet christening—so different from the one Sir Harald had planned—and therefore there was the *likelihood* of her property coming back to the estate. She was twenty-seven, and although she much preferred the company of men to that of women, she had never, so far as anyone knew, shown any particular interest in any one man. Besides, just now, as after any war, there was a dearth of eligible men.

To his elder sister and to his stepmother, Sir Harald placed the nursery virtually out of bounds. Even while the baby was too young to be spoiled, there was the danger of their contradictory advice confusing the nurse, a woman whom he had chosen with great care. She was a local girl, daughter of the tenant at Rookwood Farm, and she had gone at an early age into the nursery at Fowlmere Manor, where she had successfully reared a whole brood of young Barringtons. Mrs. Barrington said she could not speak too highly of Miss Sawyer, who, by the way, liked to be called Mrs. All housekeepers and most cooks enjoyed the same technical status.

At Copsi Mrs. Sawyer's task was easy. Magnus was an exceptionally healthy baby. Unlike many, anything he could eat he could digest; he cut his teeth without trouble; and even the vaccination against smallpox, in which Sir Harald was a strong believer and about which Mrs. Sawyer had her doubts, resulted in less than two days' mild fever.

Nothing, in fact, ailed Master Magnus, except, as he advanced into his second year, what his nurse regarded as a nasty little trick of holding his breath when he was in a temper. He'd go quite black in the face; a state frightening to the inexperienced, but Mrs. Sawyer knew the answer. A sudden, smart, but harmless smack, on the hand, on the bottom, took a youngster by surprise and made him gasp and then draw a new breath in the ordinary way.

Sir Harald was a wonderful father. He installed himself in a room very near the night and day nurseries—a situation which most fathers would have avoided. He looked in every morning, regular as clockwork, and if not prevented, again just before, or just after lunch. Then, in the evening, at about six o'clock, there was a little family gathering in the library which by good fortune, was just below the nursery floor. There Sir Harald, having finished his day's work, was presented with Mrs. Sawyer's day's work, a clean, sweet-smelling, plump, amiable child, who sprawled and gurgled in his father's arms, or on the big tiger-skin rug, and Lady Copsey and Madame le Beaune, absolutely forbidden to criticize or advise, drank Madeira and nibbled little biscuits which bore the same name. Mrs. Sawyer was always offered, and occasionally accepted, a small glass of wine; she refused just often enough to prove that she was no wine-bibber and accepted just often enough to show that she had a certain right. It was a nicely-judged performance. Sir Harald, who somewhere along the road had lost what he called his sweet tooth, drank whisky and water.

He knew, though nobody else did, exactly when his sweet tooth had failed him. It had been in the July following Juliet's death. He'd been a bit off his fodder ever since, but he was recovering and a dish of raspberries, fresh from the garden, powdered with crushed sugar had revived his appetite; then the taste reminded him: last year ... and here am I guzzling like a hog, while she will never taste anything again.... Ever since then anything sweet had sparked in him that same misery of remorse, and he sedulously avoided the occasion for it. Every hostess in the area, entertaining Sir Harald, a most ostensibly eligible widower, recognized his little foible and bore lightly on the sweet course, concentrating on the savory.

It was concerning a sweet biscuit however, that one of the happy little family gatherings in the library came to grief. Magnus, eighteen months old, strong on his feet, a great credit to Mrs. Sawyer, wanted a piece of Lady Copsey's. She said, "May I?" Sir Harald reflected that there was nothing like giving a firm order and seeing it obeyed. He indicated that she might give the child what remained of her biscuit. Mrs. Sawyer disapproved. Such tidbits blunted a child's appetite. Master Magnus's supper, a lightly boiled egg and some bread and butter cut into fingers, would be served as soon as they returned to the nursery. Then of course Madame le Beaune must put in her spoke. "May I?"

"Well, to be fair. But only half of what you're holding, Marie."

He knew he was breaking his own rule; in preliminary talks with Mrs. Sawyer she had mentioned her dislike for haphazard feeding and he had agreed with her. But between the two women he had always tried to exercise impartiality.

Madame le Beaune broke the biscuit which fell into two uneven portions, the smaller of which she gave to her nephew. He gobbled it and reached for the other piece. Sir Harald and Mrs. Sawyer spoke together; he said, "No more, Marie," and she said, "Madame, *please*; he won't eat his supper." Madame le Beaune held the piece of biscuit well out of reach and Magnus had what everybody except his nurse thought was a fit. He screamed with rage and then seemed to choke, his face going crimson, then dark purple.

Neither of the Ladies had seen him in this state before; and Sir Harald had only once heard screams like this coming from the nursery, and although he was there in almost no time at all, they'd stopped before he burst in, all anxiety and concern. On that occasion he found nothing wrong. The precious boy was on his nurse's lap, partially tipped over her left arm. She had just administered the smart smack on the bottom that had caused an intake of breath. To the doting father she said,

"It was nothing sir. Just a touch of wind...."

If she ever entertained any thoughts about what such fits of temper in so young a child indicated, she never spoke of them. She regarded them as she would have regarded attacks of hiccoughing. She knew how to deal with them and now, under the eyes of three shocked adults who were thinking about convulsions and all the other myriad things which lay in wait for the young, she moved from the background to the foreground, administered the smack which had never failed to work and which worked now. Magnus drew in a long breath and was restored.

That smack however had not been delivered with quite the usual calm and almost medical attitude. Mrs. Sawyer was mortified; she felt, as all good nurses felt when a charge misbehaved, that she had been let down. For the first time there was an element of ill-will in the restorative smack. But it worked. The three agitated adults could also breathe freely again. Mrs. Sawyer lifted the child and said, "I'll take him away now."

Lady Copsey said, "That was entirely your fault, Marie. Dangling the biscuit. Even a dog would have expected it."

"And may I ask who started the whole procedure? Harald distinctly said—and anyone not in need of an ear trumpet could have heard—Mrs. Sawyer objected to haphazard feeding and he agreed with her. Am I not right, Harald?"

"I am *not* hard of hearing. Admittedly sometimes I do not hear *you* very distincly, because, after all these years you persist with that ridiculous French accent. Sheer affectation."

They were well away and would go on for an hour. Their wrangling, so long as it did not immediately affect him or his, did not try his nerves, hardened to battle noises and rowdy nights in the Mess. He had made it clear to them that they were not to involve Juliet in their squabbles and on the whole they had behaved very well. Tonight, being honest with himself, he knew that he was to blame.

He rose, a bit stiffly, out of his chair and leaving them to pursue their quarrel until the dinner gong rang, went upstairs. Because there was something he must see to; something he did not like. Mrs. Sawyer hitherto so completely trusted, had delivered that smack with a certain venom.

Like the Great Duke under whom he had served, Sir Harald believed in corporal punishment, but only to an extent; with really recalcitrant cases where other means of persuasion had failed, or where the King's Regulations demanded it. About smacking a child of such tender years he was prepared to expostulate.

Magnus was being fed fingers of bread and butter dipped into egg yolk. He gave his father a smile and for a moment resembled his mother. Then he concentrated on his supper. A more placid scene could hardly be imagined. The door to the night nursery was open and the nursemaid was emptying the slops.

"If you wouldn't mind waiting a minute, sir. There's the white still to eat." She took a silver teaspoon, and scooping small portions, continued to feed the child. Then she called, with the voice of authority,

"Ruth, you may put Master Magnus to bed this evening. Wash him first; he has egg on his face." In delegating the duty she was conferring a favor.

Then, because if there must be a battle one might as well fire the first shot, she said,

"I expect it is with regard to that smack, sir."

"Yes. I was surprised. I understood that you did not favor smacks for the very young."

"Nor I do. But I know from experience that for that kind of fit—and for hysterics—a smack is the only cure."

"What kind of fit, Mrs. Sawyer?"

"Sheer bad temper, sir. Even when he was a tiny mite Master Magnus could be very fractious if things weren't exactly to his liking. Lately it's got worse. It's dangerous for a child to hold his breath until he goes black in the face. A smack makes him draw breath. Besides, he must learn. "She was not going to be shaken, or argued with. The Bible said it. A man diligent in his business can stand before kings. And that applied to women, too. Also the Bible said that a child should be trained in the way he should go. "I had something of the same thing over at Fowlmere with Master Philip, but by the time he was two it was all over." Mrs. Barrington, recommending Mrs. Sawyer had remarked not only upon her honesty, cleanliness and such desirable qualities, but upon her absolute devotion: "I veritably believe, Sir Harald that if she were out with a child and a bull charged she would defend it with her life."

"I merely thought, Mrs. Sawyer, that you smacked him rather hard. He is still very young."

"When it started—that'd be about nine months ago—just a tap was enough. It is no longer enough. I think people fail to realize that for his age Master Magnus is exceptionally big and strong." Her honest mind added—and willful. "We don't want him bringing on a *real* fit, do we? Or being unmanageable by the time he's three?"

"Of course not. Most certainly not. I'm sure you are right. I think the best thing is to avoid the occasion." No more biscuits with the Madeira in the library.

Sir Harald had been and still was extremely busy; some of the things which, riding round with his brother on his brief visits, he had observed and deplored, subjected to closer scrutiny, had shown themselves to be mere froth on a great wave. If he wanted to be, as he intended to be, a model landlord, with a model estate, there was a great deal to be done because so much had been neglected. Even the little coal wharf at Copsi Minor was dwindling into disuse, for the simple reason that the river dredging had not been done.

All repairs, all innovations were costly, prices had risen phenomenally since the turn of the century, and the taxes imposed to pay for the late war were exorbitant. As somebody had said, there was now a tax on everything that moved, horses, carriages, gigs and man servants; and on many things which did not move, such as windows and hearths. Sir Harald had no intention of bricking up a single window or of dismantling a single hearth; Copsi must be preserved intact. He did reduce his staff of men servants, several of whom, as Juliet had observed, held no particular office and served no particular purpose, but were there because from time immemorial it had been the custom that the man who carried water could not be expected to carry wood or coal, and that the one who cleaned windows was exempt from all other duties. It was almost as bad as India, Sir Harald reflected, and vastly more expensive. He was careful and considerate; the old were pensioned off, the young transferred to other, more productive work. He reduced his male staff to one butler and two footmen and a general handy man. Maid servants were not taxable.

He was spending the money which he had inherited because he did not wish to increase rents. He regarded this expenditure of his legacy as an investment and was reasonably certain that by the time young Magnus inherited all would be well, every roof watertight, every field productive and the little port thriving. Once the river was cleared not only coal barges had easy access, fishing vessels came too and since they brought fish well in excess of local demand, he'd instituted a fish-curing establishment. Ugly, of course—all industrialization was ugly but he planted trees, mainly poplars, quick growing. They made a screen. And one day they, too, would be a source of income. Their wood was much in demand for papermaking. If Magnus planted a new tree for every one he cut down, in time to come he would have a steady source of income. In addition to all else.

Copsi came first, but Sir Harald did not neglect his civic duties; he took his brother's place on the magistrates' bench, on the Board of Guardians, on the Bressford Hospital committee. On all he was far more active, everyone agreed, than Sir Magnus had been; but he entertained far less and some of his hospitality took forms disappointing to his female neighbors who had begun to make hopeful little schemes when Juliet had been dead for six months. A man in his position and with a young child to rear, was in positive need of a wife; and the range of young women was wide. He couldn't be much over thirty, so that there would be nothing outrageous in his marrying sixteen-year-old Victoria Collins from Thorn Grange.

On the other hand, he was thirty or over, and a very *settled* kind of man, eminently suitable for Mrs. Barrington's younger sister, robbed of her fiancé by a battle nobody remembered much now, Waterloo having been so much more conclusive. Unfortunately her name was Juliet, but that was only a slight drawback; she had another name, Diana, and could use it during her protracted stay in Suffolk. But Sir Harald had entirely the wrong idea about returning hospitality, very seldom giving an intimate little dinner party, inclining more to *mob* entertainments: a concert in the Great Hall, where the acoustics were poor, though the buffet supper was excellent; a garden party in midsummer. At least fifty people. It gave a girl or a young woman no *chance*

Except in certain areas of the mind, where Copsi and where the boy were concerned, Harald Copsey was no fool. He saw the bait offered, and even Bertie said he should marry again. But he had no intention, no wish to do so; and the long glass in his bedroom gave him, from time to time, information as inevitable as it was unwelcome. Gradually the eunuch was consuming the soldier. Something remained, though much was lost. It was the same with animals. The best draught horses and the best oxen—they were still used on many farms—were castrated late, after they had acquired the shape, the weight of stallions and bulls. More risk was involved than was in the neutering of young animals, but it was a compensated risk. Those which survived were the more valuable because of their rarity. And he had survived, but his condition was rare; in the full flush of manhood he had been emasculated. Thank God it had not happened earlier, when even his voice could have been affected; it was bad enough as it was—no hair on his chest; shaving every day more a ritual than necessary performance; and a really troublesome tendency to obesity which he tried to counter by hard exercise and spare diet. When he could he missed lunch altogether and he always rose from his own dinner table feeling that he could have eaten the whole meal over again. But, as he said, when his sister and his stepmother fussed, he had a lame leg and to overburden it would be unwise.

In a curious way, disgusting as he sometimes thought his condition, there were times when he saw its advantages. With sex dead a man could devote energy and emotion which would otherwise have been squandered, to the job in hand. Whoever imposed celibacy on

Catholic priests, had hit upon that truth. Left, as he could well have been, a whole man, subject to the lusts of the flesh, susceptible to women, he could not have been so wholeheartedly devoted to Copsi, or to his son.

***

He had been master of Copsi for three years when he received a letter from William Orde, a man somewhat dimly remembered as a cousin, in the first or second degree, of his mother's. It made a simple appeal to a fundamentally simple man. And another, more subtle appeal to a subtle man. Cousin William's house in Portman Square had burned down and he was homeless. Not penniless—even the house had been insured with the Pelican Insurance Company. Cousin William could afford to live anywhere, but he had happy memories of Copsi and the neighborhood and would like to come and stay while he looked around for a place in which to settle down. "I was never meant for town life," Cousin William wrote, "but circumstances compelled me to it. Now, with the loss of my house and the compensation, and what my business in the City will provide when sold, I shall be a free man."

Sir Harald wrote back enthusiastically. Plenty of room at Copsi, Cousin William was welcome to stay as long as he liked.

Cousin William, considerably younger and more spry than could be expected, came and stayed, and stayed and stayed. He brought with him his own manservant, a person of marked versatility, able and willing to act as footman when one extra was needed. If Cousin William had ever intended to look around for a place of his own, he soon abandoned this intention; he settled into some disused rooms, installed several articles of furniture and presently offered to pay for his keep, a suggestion which Sir Harald utterly repudiated; so they compromised. William Orde's city connections included a partnership in a wine importing business; he would supply all that was needed in the way of liquor, except ale.

Sir Harald was delighted by Cousin William's decision to make Copsi his permanent home. It was a compliment to the place. And it afforded him some masculine company without the bother and expense of formal entertaining. It provided Lady Copsi and Madame le Beaune with something new for which to compete, and presently, when the most discreet enquiries revealed the fact that Mr. Orde was not a poor relation but a man considerably endowed with worldly goods, it diverted some of the matchmaking activities. Mr. Orde might be forty? Forty-five? but he'd worn extremely well, was witty and charming and something of a ladies' man, epithets which certainly did not apply to Sir Harald, good man that he was.

Cousin William had been settled in for less than a year when he began to show some concern for a young man rougly as closely related to him as he was to Sir Harald.

"He was never a strong boy, Harry, and personally I don't think two years in Italy did anything for him. I was against it. But my cousin, his mother, was a pig-headed woman and believed in his artistic talent. I'm no judge of course, the whole thing is a closed book to me. All I know is that he came back from Italy looking worse—and with some damned funny ideas. However . . . when I lived in London I tried to keep an eye on him, see he had a square meal now and then, gave him *carte blanche* at my tailor's. Money . . . you might as well throw it in the gutter. His mother's dead now and he seems to be in a poor way. Would you mind if I asked him here—say for a month? A bit of a holiday. . . ."

"He'd be very welcome. Plenty of room here. What's his name?"

"Winthrop. Jonathan Winthrop."

"A good old Suffolk name, William. And there is a belief, you know, that to get back to your roots, your native air, is a tonic. I must say I never felt so vigorous as I do here."

"I feel the same. And Harry, I have no wish to impose on you. I'd pay, you know."

"William, I told you before, when I start letting lodgings I'll put a notice out. . . . If Jonathan stays a month and feels under any obligation, he can make me a portrait of the boy. It's time he was painted; he's growing fast."

Ignorant as he was, and admitted to being, about art and all that appertained thereto, Cousin William felt a stab of doubt. Nothing he had seen of Jonathan's work promised the picture of a three-year-old child which a doting father would want. The boy was pretty in a strictly orthodox way, golden curly hair, blue eyes, pink and white complexion. The baby chubbiness had vanished and even the little snub nose was shaping up into muscle and bone. A pretty boy who would lose prettiness with every year and who might, or might not, emerge as a handsome man. The point was that Jonathan, though he talked volubly about beauty seemed to have no sense of it. No woman he ever painted was one an ordinary man would have looked at twice, emaciated, haglike, with their hair in disarray. And his trees all seemed to have been struck by lightning or dying of decay. He claimed to paint what he saw, in which case one could only feel sorry for him and think that his eye was as much disordered as his liver or his lungs or whatever it was made him so delicate.

Jonathan duly arrived and was accommodated in the empty rooms just across the passage from Cousin William's. Sir Harald felt, at first sight, something too faint to be called dislike, call it a mild distaste. The thought occurred—if I'd had him in the army! But then the most avid recruiting sergeant would never have offered him the shilling, knowing that he had not what the army called *the makings*. A good deal could be done with drunks, with boys from the slums who merely needed a few good meals, even with rogues and jailbirds. Hadn't the Great Duke himself called the army mere scum? But Jonathan Winthrop was outside all ordinary categories; slender as a young girl, willowy and drooping, too much hair, and exceptionally long white hands with which he made gestures as he talked. But civil, but engaging, grateful. One of his first acts was to thank Sir Harald for being so understanding in providing him with such a wonderful studio; a thing with which Sir Harald had nothing to do. The rooms just across the corridor had been chosen because it was convenient for Cousin William's man, Peter, to serve them both.

When Sir Harald's first involuntary recoil had died away he found himself oddly in sympathy with his new guest. Something—God alone knew what—had emasculated that poor young man from the start; even his voice was light and fluting. And his admiration, what he called his adoration, love at first sight, for Copsi was an overwhelming element in his favor. He painted Copsi twice, from differing angles, before he set about making a portrait of Magnus. It was necessary, he said, to soak himself in the atmosphere, because Copsi and the child whose heritage it was were in fact indivisible. It was not a sentiment which Sir Harald would have expressed, but once it was put into words, he saw the truth of it.

Meanwhile Jonathan made himself agreeable, or disagreeable to Lady Copsey and to Madame le Beaune. "That shade of blue, dear lady, is a trifle too harsh. It obscures you. Blue in any case is a *cold* color. You are susceptible to cold, are you not? Yes, I thought so when you insisted upon closing the window. I think something warmer, a shade of rose or violet." And he said, "I have been studying you, my Lady, and have come to the conclusion that your hair should be dressed higher. The chignon, I know is fashionable—though less so than it was. I think that brought up, and coiled...."

Naturally such individual attention which neither aging lady had enjoyed for some years, charmed them and had an emollient effect upon family life which now centered very largely around the dinner table since the little gatherings in the library had ceased. The child, once the center of sycophantic attention, was at three, altogether too much. He'd pulled Lady Copsey's pearls until the string broke and the beads showered on to the floor, he'd deliberately jogged Madame le Beaune's elbow as she lifted her glass so that she spilled a glassful of Madeira into her lap; he'd been rather slow in learning to speak, but once started seemed never to stop, so that conversation was impossible; he brought down unsuitable toys, such as his hobby horse and ran about on it,

bumping into furniture and people. What had been quite
pleasant little sessions became a torment and first one
lady and then the other began to excuse herself. For once
they were in full agreement; such boisterous behavior
should be checked at once and dear Harald was making a
rod for his own back. Imagine what such a naughty boy
would be like when he was six!

Some kind of family solidarity compelled Madame
le Beaune to say, "Personally, I think Mrs. Sawyer is to
blame. After all she has the child all day. Harry only has
this hour with him, and naturally regards it as playtime."

"Your brother," Lady Copsey began. Sir Harald
could be Harald, dear Harald, poor Harald, or Harry,
with various prefixes, but when he was "your brother" it
was a sign that the Copsey family as a whole were about to
be criticized. "Your brother, after ten years in the army,
retired with the rank of Captain. Probably because he was
a poor disciplinarian."

"One rather wonders," Madame le Beaune said,
looking thoughtful. "So far as I know Harald was never
involved in a mutiny." And Lady Copsey's brother, a
captain in the navy where the word implied far higher
rank than in the army, had been involved in the sailor's
mutiny at Spithead.

◆━━━◆━━━◆━━━◆━━━◆━━━◆

In fact Sir Harald was—always had been—against
the spoiling of his son. He did say, "Magnus, that was
naughty! Say you're sorry." He said, "Don't interrupt."
He said, "A little less noise." He said all the right things,
but without any real force behind them. Part of him might
deplore the naughtinesses and the noise, but a far greater
part of him rejoiced because the boy was so lively. His aim
to be a model landlord had brought him into close touch
with his tenants and once the river was dredged and the
little wharf was busy he also had casual contact with a
wider circle, so he heard about deaths, all too frequent,
and barring accident, mainly concerned with the very old,
or the very young. And though a family like the Cowpers
at Cowfield might be commiserated with over the loss of a
boy and a girl through scarlet fever, they had two boys

and three girls left, and might have more. His situation was different. He had only this one son and boisterousness was a reassuring sign. Honest man that he was, he was however forced to admit that an hour with his son was a long hour; and he, like Madame le Beaune, reflected that Mrs. Sawyer had the boy all day; so he excused her from attendance in the library once Magnus was old enough not to have the little mishaps to which even the best trained children were subject during the first two years.

"He will be safe with me, Mrs. Sawyer, and I am sure you have plenty to do."

Mrs. Sawyer welcomed the respite. As Madame le Beaune had remarked, she had the child all day and he gave her more trouble than all the Barringtons—including Master Philip—had ever done. Coming up to the age of three, he no longer went almost black in the face with temper; the rage now turned out, not in. Crossed in the slightest way—and one never knew what would provoke him, so one could never be prepared—he lashed about, kicked, bit, seized the nearest thing and threw it.

Mrs. Sawyer still administered smacks, harder and harder ones, but they no longer served their therapeutic purpose. And the threat, seldom used but direfully effective at Fowlmere—I shall tell your Papa—was quite useless here. Mrs. Sawyer, struggling with a very difficult child indeed, was struggling also against her own sense of failure. She'd been so successful, taken such pride in her success, and now this! In an oblique way, bandaging Ruth's leg, very swollen and bruised from an attack made when the poor girl had her hands full, emptying the washbasin into the slop pail, Mrs. Sawyer said, "Between you and me, I sometimes wonder.... Is he quite right in the mind? It was a very difficult birth. Perhaps some injury may have been done to the brain." Mrs. Sawyer was excusing her failure. To herself and to the girl who said,

"You mean daft? He ain't daft. He knew just when to come at me. Tell you the truth, if I hadn't had my hands full, I'd have fetched him a good clout."

Mrs. Sawyer seized as so many people did, and were

to do, on the trivial and told Ruth that if she ever wished to succeed in the world she must avoid the use of *ain't*.

❮━━❯❮━━❯❮━━❯❮━━❯❮━━❯

So now it was June and the perfect day which Jonathan Winthrop had waited for dawned clear and bright; all was ready for the portrait. Great trusses of wisteria, the frailer but more encroaching growths of honeysuckle and early roses made a perfect background.

"He should, perhaps, have some toy to amuse him," Jonathan said. So the rocking horse was hauled down. The rocking horse bought in the Rue de Rivoli for another little boy who had died of typhoid fever; directly attributable, Sir Harald was sure, to the terrible state of the Copsi drains. Quite soon after his homecoming he had called in some people who called themselves sanitary engineers, and they had overhauled the whole system, discovering in the process no fewer than seven cesspools which had been covered in when they were full. Copsi had virtually been standing over a sewer. Now, the oldest building in Suffolk, it had the most up-to-date plumbing and drainage, including two bathrooms.

❮━━❯❮━━❯❮━━❯❮━━❯❮━━❯

When all was ready, Magnus was brought down. He wore his brand new miniature sailor suit which, since Trafalgar, had been every little boy's best wear. It was so acceptable, so almost a uniform, that it did not strike Sir Harald as incongruous that a soldier's son should be painted as an able-seaman.

"Now look," he said. "Cousin Jonathan is going to make a picture of you. A beautiful picture to hang with all the others. You must do exactly what he tells you, sit still or stand still. If I hear that you have been good, you shall have some sugarplums." He lowered his voice and instructed the artist. "Not more than ten minutes at a stretch, Jonathan. He is very young."

Mrs. Sawyer and Ruth hovered in the offing with orders not to interfere, but to see that the tedium was broken every ten minutes and to take Magnus for a walk, or play a game with him between each two sessions.

No artist ever had a less cooperative model. Magnus had already fallen into the habit of starting eight out of ten sentences with the words *I want*. I want to sit on my horse. I want to come down. I want to go to the privy. I want to see what you're doing. I want to paint, too. By the end of an hour, punctuated by little walks and little games, Jonathan's patience, never his strong point, was exhausted; two more ten minute sessions and he was almost gibbering; and he was much relieved to be able to say to the nursemaid, "You may take him away, my dear. I have the essentials."

Sir Harald's first feeling when he saw the result of Jonathan's two days' work was stunned bewilderment. Copsi was unmistakably Copsi, at its best, all aflower but with its bones showing; the tower which linked the two remaining wings, and a bit of the battlements here and there standing out, with the chimneys, above the flowery tide. But it stood high and well into the background, as though it floated on air; not unlike the cities which on occasion could be seen in the sky when clouds piled up to great stairways and towers and turrets and steeples, even mosques with domes and minarets. In the foreground, made to look larger by the diminution of Copsi, was Magnus; again indisputable and completely recognizable. Golden hair like a halo, blue eyes; damn it, the man had even caught the change in nose and jaw which marked the end of babyhood and the beginning of boyhood; and every detail of the clothing had been most faithfully reproduced. So why did he hate the picture on sight? Wish it had never been painted?

He and Cousin William had been privileged by being allowed the first viewing, and Cousin William seemed to have nothing to say. Sir Harald remembered that William was some kind of relative to Jonathan and had brought him here, seemed to be fond of him. So instead of making a statement he asked a question.

"Well, William, what do you make of it?"

"I'm no judge, Harald. It looks to me more or less—accurate. More than that I can't say. A bit, well, shall we say fanciful? But that is Jonathan's way."

Sir Harald fixed upon the obvious fault. Where was the rocking horse? It had been hauled down from the day nursery and set out in the sunshine, had reminded him of things better forgotten.

"He left out the rocking horse," he said. And that explained why the child looked—to put it mildly—so ill-tempered. Deprived of his toy!

"Oh. Yes, so he did." Cousin William brought his mind to bear rather ponderously on this omission. He realized that Harry wasn't much pleased with his protégé's work. "He could paint it in, I expect. I'm sure that if he'd known you particularly wanted a rocking horse...."

"I did *not* particularly want a rocking horse," Sir Harald said, quite testily. "I wanted a picture of Magnus, with Copsi in the background."

"Well, that's what you've got, isn't it? I mean, if I'd seen this in any shop window, I'd have recognized it. Wouldn't you?"

"I don't know. Both the other pictures he made of Copsi were so good. Here the place looks as if it were floating on air—and cut out of paper into the bargain. And he hasn't got the boy right, either. Bad tempered looking little brat! No I'm not much taken with it William, there's no use in pretending that I am."

A pity! Because if Harry had been pleased and proud and shown it off there would have been commissions from other parents, or grandparents, and though William Orde was willing to share his last penny with his young near-relative he knew how much the younger man valued his independence, and how highly he thought of his own work. Soothe him down!

"I'm sure that when Jonathan knows that you are disappointed, he'll try again."

"Not for all the tea in China, William, my dear," Jonathan said, his fluting voice almost shrill. "Nobody can ever *know* what I endured in the *short* time when I was obliged to ask him to sit or stand. Fidgety, yes, one *expects* that with children. It was the sheer *malice* which appalled me. I *hope* you won't think—I don't consider that I *am*—unduly sensitive, But I *assure* you that though it was a warm day, positive cold *shivers* ran down my back from time to time. Really, I was *astounded* that what emerged looked so *human*."

"That may be the point," William Orde said. "What Harry wanted was an angel child."

"Exactly. At least you understand."

The degree of understanding that existed between the two men, so utterly different, was astounding. William Orde, though he had lived in London for more that twenty years, was an outdoor man, a countryman. He was a good shot, a keen rider to hounds, washed in cold water even when hot was available. He'd slipped into Copsi and this corner of Suffolk like a native born, merging with the landscape. But between his coming and the arrival of Jonathan there had been a gap in his life which nobody could quite fill; not Sir Harald, though in many ways their interests were identical, not any woman, though he liked Bertie's company while totally disapproving of her way of life. He'd missed Jonathan and lost no time in bringing him to Copsi. That their relationship was of a concealed homosexual nature, he would have violently denied, as would Jonathan. They were distant relatives, and close friends, able to communicate and understand across a seemingly wide gulf which was not in fact wide.

"Sooner than *subject* myself to such an *ordeal* again, I would go back to Soho," Jonathan said.

"That will not be necessary. Poor Harry expected an angelic child, and a rocking horse. He'll come round. And the women will have their say."

Lady Copsey said of the picture, "Very nice! I never painted myself and therefore should not set up as a judge, but I know a pretty picture when I see one. Yes, in my opinion, a very nice, pretty picture."

Informed by some mysterious instinct—for Sir Harald had arranged that they should view the picture separately, in strict order of precedence, Madame le Beaune said something almost equally wrong.

"I never painted myself and therefore should not set up as judge, but it seems to me to be out of proportion. A most lifelike portrait of Magnus, that I will admit, but of Copsi, no! Neither big enough nor strong enough."

"You think it a good likeness of the boy?" Sir Harald asked, a trifle anxiously.

"Yes, indeed. Excellent. In *your* place, Harald, I should suggest painting out Copsi and substituting a plain background. A sunset sky, perhaps."

Bertie, inspecting it in her turn, stared for some time without speaking. Then she said,

"You don't care for it, Harry? I think I know why. It isn't a real portrait, either of the boy or the place. It's this new idea, symbolism. I must say that young man has more talent than I thought."

"And what exactly do you mean by symbolism?"

"Oh dear! Hard to say exactly.... Showing the essence of a thing rather than its actual form."

"I don't understand what you're talking about." He doubted whether she did, either. If that bad-tempered brat was the essence of Magnus, he was a Dutchman.

His well-meant suggestion that Jonathan should have another shot, making Copsi look a bit more solid and Magnus a bit more amiable, was cursorily rejected.

"*Quite* impossible, dear Cousin. The picture may not have won *general* acclamation—that is so often the way! I regard it as my best work to date. Any attempt to repeat it would be *futile*."

A place was found for the picture in the darkest corner of the Long Gallery where it hung for many years in obscurity. When in the middle of the twentieth century it was "discovered" it caused quite a sensation, a genuine example of early Jonathan Winthrop, that pre-Pre-Raphaelite.

Sir Harald's disappointment with the picture did not result, as Jonathan had rather feared, in any hint that he had been at Copsi long enough. Such a suggestion would never have occurred to Sir Harald who was actually gratified that five people, each of whom could have lived elsewhere, chose to make their homes in the place he loved so dearly. Anybody who had taste enough and sense enough to wish to live at Copsi was welcome to do so; and had he been the head of a more prolific family he'd have been open to further exploitation.

Magnus was four when Mrs. Sawyer slapped him for the last time. Nursing a heavily swaddled right hand and wearing a woeful expression, she tendered her resignation.

"I can't tell you how sorry I am, sir, but he's more than I can handle. You see, I've told him, time and again, not to tease that poor cat, but he *would*, so I gave him a bit of a slap and, sir, he bit me! Right through the side of my hand." She looked pale, had been crying not long ago, and might cry again at any moment. Sir Harald told her to sit down, and poured her a glass of Madeira. He had a vague memory of hearing that human bites could be dangerous; or was it monkeys?

"Have you had it seen to, Mrs. Sawyer?"

"Oh, yes. I told Ruth what to do. It's throbbing a bit. Nothing much. I mean it was more the shock. When you think, four years and I've treated him as though he was my own. And then to do such a thing."

"It is most regrettable. I apologize on his behalf. I shall speak to him very severely."

Speaking was a waste of breath, she knew it if he didn't.

"So you'll take my notice for the end of the month?"

"Oh come, come, Mrs. Sawyer, no need for that! A burst of temper is surely not so unusual. As I said, I shall speak. I promise you it shan't happen again."

The threatening tears brimmed and fell.

"It's the failure.... After all these years. ... Nurserymaid and nurse since I was twelve, sir. Delicate ones and difficult.... and never before...."

How would it look? How would it sound? I had to leave Copsi because Master Magnus *bit* me.

Sir Harald shifted his lame leg, took a sip of his whisky and tried another approach.

"There is no need to *leave*, Mrs. Sawyer. Possibly I have overlooked the fact that the boy has outgrown the nursery and needs a governess. But there will always be room for you here, some easy job...."

He wasn't very clear as to what it might be. He had got rid of the housekeeper about whom Juliet had mildly complained and replaced her by a very efficient, strictly honest woman, who if she had a fault, could be accused of nepotism; almost all the household staff were in some way related to her. But there were spheres outside the kitchen, surely. Little sewing jobs, or making lavender bags.

"I'm sure you mean well, sir, but I shouldn't be satisfied with a tiddly job. I'm not all that old, yet. No need to worry about me. I shall find a post...." With a child—with children—who could be controlled and would grow up to be a credit to her. And indeed there was one in the offing, for Miss Victoria Collins had married and was expecting.

Sir Harald, already making tentative enquiries about governesses, was determined to see that Mrs. Sawyer left Copsi on a wave of goodwill which would obliterate the unfortunate incident of the biting.

He had scolded Magnus more sternly than he had ever scolded him before, demanding an apology. But even as he did so he had a disconcerting thought—this quite charming little boy was not the one who had inflicted the bite, or swung the cat by the tail, or, come to that, done many other things, witnessed or reported. *That* boy was something alien...something, well, one must not give way to fancies and think that when the boy was provoked something else took control.

He found the perfect parting present for Mrs. Sawyer, a beautiful little watch, with a true-lovers'-knot pin. The back of the watch, the part which would show, was of blue enamel, with the words—*Remember the Giver*—showing through, in the silver of which the watch was made. A really elegant, and rather expensive parting present, and Magnus presented it with grace, saying exactly what he had been told to say: "Thank you for all you have done for me. I hope you will be happy wherever you go." As Mrs. Sawyer was always the first to say, there was a *nice* side, when he cared to show it.

After that there were governesses who came and went. Another room along the rather empty corridor was furnished as a schoolroom and the one beyond as a most comfortable bed sitting room for the incumbent of the moment. Despite his careful choice—youngish women who enjoyed outdoor life rather than the indoor, die-away, bookish sort—despite the comfortable room and a social recognition very seldom accorded to governesses, and despite the fact that they were ten a penny, not one stayed long. They left for a number of reasons, each valid on the face of it—a chance to go abroad, quite irresistible, a sick mother, a distaste for country life. "But Miss Boyd, when I engaged you you said you liked, preferred, country life." "Yes, that is so; but I did not realize that Copsi was so isolated." Or so cold, or so windy, or so this or that. Only one, the sixth or seventh, not young, not a professed country lover, but engaged because she was so clever, fluent in three languages, had the courage to say,

"Sir Harald, I propose to leave because I am wasting my time here. Your son is incorrigibly *stupid*. And as Schiller said, so rightly: *'Gegen Dummheit kämpfen Götter selbst vergebens.'* You wish a translation?" Poor man he looked utterly confused. "It means in simple English, 'Against stupidity the gods themselves battle in vain.' I have battled, Sir Harald. I had great hopes. Some predecessor of mine had taught him to read and to write. I was hopeful . . . But four months have seen no progress. None at all. And as I say, I feel that I am wasting my time. And not only mine," she raised her head and gave Sir Harald a direct, defiant look. "That of young people willing to learn, capable of benefitting from instruction. I trust I have made myself clear."

"You have," he said in the brusque way which showed her that she had given offense; but she had herself been reared on and had tried to transmit to her pupils, the simple adage: "Speak the truth and shame the Devil!"

After the governesses, tutors; far more expensive, all most carefully chosen, all, sooner or later, proving to be inept. But it was one of them, a rather standoffish young man, who offered a clue worth pursuing. The word he used was shocking and offensive, nevertheless it was worth thinking about.

"It has occurred to me to wonder, sir, whether it may not be a form of epilepsy."

"Epilepsy? Have you ever seen my boy fall to the floor, writhe, foam at the mouth?"

"No. And to be honest I have never seen anyone in an epileptic fit, but...."

"Well I have. On several occasions. A most distressing sight. Why on earth you should suggest...."

"*But*, as I was about to say, sir, I have read about things I have never seen and I have read that epilepsy takes various forms. Not necessarily the commonly called fit such as you were describing. Alexander the Great is said to have suffered from it; Julius Caesar...many notable men. In fact Hippocrates called it the sacred disease. Other writers refer to it as the Commanders' disease, and...I can see the connection. In a catagenic state the victim of the fit is insensitive to pain, completely reckless as to consequences and afterwards has little, or imperfect memory of what happened during the interlude. I have kept careful note, sir and I have consulted my father, and my brother, both medical men, both well-esteemed. It occurred to me after the incident...Mrs. Barrington's chairs. You may recall it."

Sir Harald recalled it only too well.

A boy must of course have some social life, consort with his people of his own age, learn how to act as host, and as guest. Sir Harald began to give children's parties, one in winter, one in summer. They were very popular with his young guests. They all came from substantial homes but there was nowhere to compare with Copsi for a game of Hide-and-Seek, and even if the summer party took place on a rainy day there was room in the Great Hall and the Long Gallery for activities usually associated with out-of-doors.

In return Magnus Copsey received invitations and, since nothing occurred to provoke him, behaved remarkably well. He was seven when he attended what Mrs. Barrington said would be her last completely juvenile party—her youngest child, Angela, was now twelve, and Philip, long since outgrown his difficult stage, was a supercilious Harrovian. Mrs. Barrington had tended to cling on to the children's parties because they were a relatively inexpensive form of entertainment. Some mothers brought their own children and stayed, sharing the substantial tea; fathers drifted in towards the end of the party and were given sherry and biscuits, and so, for a time, the Barringtons had fulfilled their obligations.

At all children's parties—not only at Fowlmere—it was an unwritten rule that in competitive games such as Musical Chairs the older, bigger children should give smaller ones a chance, so on that memorable afternoon Magnus Copsey found himself competing with one other boy, also about seven years old, for possession of the last chair. The other boy won the game and what happened next was unbelievable. Magnus Copsey moved to the place where the chairs which had been removed from the game stood haphazardly. He took one of the frail, gilt and lacquer chairs in each hand and banged them violently together. He did it three times, so six chairs were ruined. "Which was bad enough," as Mrs. Barrington confided to Lady Collins, "but the look on his face was worse. Quite—malignant." Naturally this reminded Lady Collins of what that excellent nurse, Mrs. Sawyer, had once told Victoria. It had sounded almost unbelievable at the time.

The story went the rounds and led to some speculation which wronged Juliet. Nobody had known her; she came from a far place; she was an Evett wasn't she? Yes, related to Lord Heston. Perhaps the Evetts were given to fits of uncontrollable temper; no Copsey ever was, at least so far as anyone could remember; old Sir Magnus, young Sir Magnus, Sir Harald, all decent ordinary men.

Mr. Barrington was capable of ill-temper himself, and he said the young thug should never enter his house again; a verdict with which Mrs. Barrington readily agreed since this was to be the last of the juvenile parties.

Sir Harald apologized almost abjectly, and said he knew a cabinet-maker in Wyck who could repair the chairs, make them as good as new. "Or better," Lady Collins said in confidence to her husband. "Those chairs were so fragile; I never sat on one without feeling apprehension."

Magnus apologized. He was sent, armed with a bouquet of the Everlasting Roses, to say that he was sorry, very sorry indeed.

That there could possibly be some physical explanation for what happened to Magnus from time to time, must be explored. Leave no stone unturned!

Doctor Fordyke, the first to be approached, thought little of it; but then Sir Harald thought little of Doctor Fordyke and privately blamed him for what had happened to Juliet. His accusatory thoughts were vague, interference too soon, interference too late, a fatal bungle anyway and if only old Doctor Fordyke had been there, things would have gone otherwise; but that, of course, was a private opinion and he had never voiced it.

At Sir Harald's request, Doctor Fordyke examined the well-grown, handsome boy and could find no signs of any physical defect. He had heard of, read of, cases where a forceps delivery had inflicted a brain injury which evidenced itself in some impairment of function. None of that here. As for epilepsy in a concealed form, a thing which Sir Harald mentioned with obvious unwillingness, that was plain nonsense. You might as well talk about concealed smallpox!

The truth was, Doctor Fordyke thought, that the boy was completely spoiled: the only young person at Copsi; two old doting women, one young one, his father, two other men—if the younger could be called a man. No mother. The diagnosis was easy, the prognosis certain. But the prescription—a damned good hiding—would not be welcomed and there was absolutely no reason why Sir Harald should not take his problem and his guineas to a good friend of Doctor Fordyke who had set up practice in Norwich....

Passed on, from Bressford to Norwich, and from Norwich to London itself, feeling more and more foolish, exhibiting a boy in the prime of health and asking to be told what was wrong, Sir Harald persisted until one physician, more percipient than the others, put his finger, he thought, on the nub of the matter. There was nothing wrong with the boy; it was the father who needed help, and reassurance. Both supplied in good measure.

"We all change, Sir Harald, and there may now be some scientific support for the old superstition that each seventh year makes the change obvious. The ages of seven, fourteen, and twenty-one are landmarks of growth and change. Your son has had his seventh birthday. Has he suffered a so-called fit since?"

"Not to my.... Yes, one."

"You will find, I think, that that was the last. One must not be *too* greatly influenced by mere dates; a month or two, earlier, later.... Changes do take place, witness the shedding of baby teeth, usually completed at or around the age of seven; the change of voice, at or around the age of fourteen; full maturity at twenty-one.... The man—quite the most helpful and comforting that Sir Harald had encountered so far—thought to himself; and twenty-eight, with full maturity tipping over; thirty-five with even the biblical span of years half run; forty-two when middle age settled in and the decline began. He was forty-three! Gather thee rosebuds, and guineas while ye may!

Much heartened, Sir Harald returned to Copsi and nothing much happened for quite some time. Then, Magnus and Bertie had their memorable row.

Until then, Bertie, making no secret of the fact that very young children had small appeal to her, had been very good, in her own way. She'd offered to teach the boy to ride and had supplied the miniature pony; had lifted the boy into and out of the saddle, run about, and then ridden for a week or two with the leading rein in her hand. Magnus was soon independent of that and was, Bertie said, shaping up well.

Whether she had, or had not heard about Mrs. Barrington's chairs was doubtful, for she had cut herself off at the earliest possible moment from women, and women's chatter; she lived almost apart from the mainstream of life in the house. She was doing for her vastly inferior heritage what Sir Harald was doing for Copsi—but she'd had a start on him and at one point said, "Harry, I'm beginning to make money while you're still laying it out. Let me at least pay for my board and lodging." He said "Nonsense!" to that. What was her lodging? A room nobody wanted. What was her board? Far less than any servant regarded as his or her due. It was indeed rather difficult to see what she lived on, up and away before breakfast and back so late. "Oh, I eat a ploughman's lunch. No need to fret about me." Both

Lady Copsey and Madame le Beaune envied her figure, or, to be exact, her waist. Both as the years bore down and years of easy living took their toll, had a little trouble with corpulence; fair enough in the case of Madame who never willingly took any exercise at all; grossly unfair to Lady Copsey who walked every day and never lolled as Madame did. The ideal measurement for a waist was eighteen inches when a girl was eighteen; then with each increasing year an added inch, up to the maximum of twenty-four. After that, in most cases drastic corseting was a necessity. It was irksome to see Bertie in her thirty-second year still slender as a girl without, as was so often the case, being emaciated or prematurely wrinkled. But then, almost everything about Bertie was, or had been, irksome to two such strictly conventional women. Eccentricity, permissible in a man, was deplorable in a woman. However the scandal of her way of life—which extended to occasional riotous parties, all male, and very mixed in status—had long since ceased to surprise or shock.

<hr>

When the miniature pony was outgrown, Bertie supplied another, bred by herself at Sheppey Lea.

"You'll be able to go much farther afield now," she said. "You can ride round with your Papa occasionally. I might even take you to my place one day."

"When?"

"When I say."

Sir Harald had, of course, taken the boy with him on a number of occasions, usually in the gig. He wanted Magnus to see the property and the people—and the people to see him, so big for his age, so handsome. Such outings had not been wholly successful. Nothing interested the boy for long, and he was easily bored, restive, and to a busy man a bit of a nuisance, interrupting any conversation, however serious, always trying to draw attention to himself; always wanting something. The truth was that from infancy onwards, Magnus, when in his father's presence, had been accustomed to receiving full attention and still expected it.

Perhaps he sensed that he had no such hold on his

Aunt Bertha. While she was teaching him to ride the times
were chosen to suit *her* convenience and no amount of
cajolery or show of temper had any effect. She was
interested in teaching him to ride properly and there her
interest ceased. Once, when he had deliberately tried to
attract her real attention by disobeying all her instructions, she'd simply said,

"All right. If you want to ride like a sack of potatoes,
ride like a sack of potatoes. But not on *that* pony! Try a
cart-horse."

He was too young and too stupid to handle a word
like *impervious* but he knew that Aunt Bertha was
different from all the other people with whom he came in
contact; and he was slightly in awe of her; so on the whole
they got on well together and she kept her promise of
taking him to Sheppey Lea which was disappointing. For
some reason, because he had never been taken there, it
had sounded interesting and rather mysterious, but it was
just like other farming places and far less interesting than
the wharf at Copsi Minor where everybody was always so
concerned lest he should fall into the water. There he had
indeed been the center of attention, words of warning,
guardian hands outstretched.

None of that at Sheppey Lea, where Aunt Bertha
immediately became busy with something or other and
when he said, "I want my lunch..." said, "Don't
interrupt." She was talking to a man about something. He
tried again after a minute or two. "I want to go home."
Aunt Bertha said, "All right. You know the way," and
went on talking to the man who did give a moment's
attention, just long enough to say something very silly,

"You know, young sir, if you put on such a scowl
and the wind changed, you'd have that ugly look for the
rest of your life."

Then the talk went on and Magnus hung about,
waiting for his lunch which was entirely unsatisfactory,
simply bread and cheese. Both were excellent of their
kind, the bread new and crusty, the cheese just ripe, but
not hard. Magnus ate it, but with a languid air which
signified disapproval. At home such marked lack of
appetite would have attracted some notice but Bertie

cheerfully ate her ploughman's lunch and ignored him.

"I don't want any more."

"You're not obliged to eat it. It's a free country."

He lacked intelligence but had as compensation a considerable amount of cunning which warned him against the next move, certain as it usually was—I'm going to be sick. If he said that now she would probably say, "Go outside, then."

He stared with disfavor around the little room, the parlor of the foreman's house, dedicated to Miss Copsey's use most middays, otherwise reserved for very special occasions. It was low and dark, heavily beamed and oak paneled, the only relief from somberness a few bits of pottery—cheap fairings—on the narrow shelf over the fireplace.

"This is an ugly room, don't you think, Aunt Bertha?"

That at least made her take notice, but in the wrong way. She said,

"Sh! It is Mrs. Fowler's holy of holies. You may *think* what you like—as I just said it's a free country; but you must learn not to be too critical, Magnus. Or at least not to *say* hurtful things. Well, if you've finished. . . ." She looked at her watch—nothing like such a pretty one as he had presented to Mrs. Sawyer—and said,

"I am going to look at the sheep. Do you want to come with me, or would you rather go home?"

The outing, which had sounded so promising and meant a morning with no lessons, had dwindled down to nothing. As most things did. He was too young to realize—and in fact never did realize—that devoted egoism was the surest road to boredom.

"I'll go home," he said. After all Aunt Bertha's sheep were just like everybody else's.

When a turn in the road and a clearing in the trees brought Copsi into view, he realized that he had made a mistake. Mr. Burrows, his current tutor, took lessons very seriously indeed, and had eyes, or spies, everywhere. Magnus had only to set foot in the castle or its grounds and there would be Mr. Burrows, fussing about him like an old hen, talking about making up for lost time, dragging him off to the schoolroom. Downright disobedience or defiance was unwise since for some reason Papa seemed to think highly of Mr. Burrows and always sided with him. This had not always been the case, either with the governesses or tutors. Magnus always *knew*. The person in charge would get angry and say: "Very well, I shall report this to your Papa!" Sometimes nothing resulted, sometimes a mild scolding. But with Mr. Burrows it was different; when Magnus angered him, Papa was angered, too. Magnus did not stand in awe of his father but he preferred to be on good terms with him since he was the giver of presents, and, if forced to it, the witholder of privileges.

Well, he could defeat Mr. Burrows and stay free for the rest of the day—as was only his due, since he had been granted a day's holiday. And what a holiday! He swerved aside and rode into the paddock in which Bertie had fitted some jumps of varying height. She had strictly forbidden him ever to go there without her; but she was up at Sheppey Lea, staring at sheep. She'd never know.

Magnus had hardly left before Bertie felt a pang of guilt. Harry had been so very peculiar about Magnus riding at all; so timid, so reluctant, so nervous. He'd had doubts even about the miniature pony. "Don't you think the boy's a bit young?" She'd said, "Good God, Harry! If anything he's too old. Should have started a year ago. And the thing's no more than an animated rocking horse."

About the change of mount, Sir Harald, still despite his stiff leg an intrepid rider to hounds, a man who had been a soldier, was even more dubious.

"It's rather a big pony. Hardly a pony at all, Bertie."

"He's a big boy. On Midget his feet were practically dragging on the ground. You can't change horses every six months."

"I'm not sure that I wish him to jump."

"Then how's he going to hunt? Don't you want him to hunt?"

"Of course.... But I don't want him to take any risks."

"All right. Wrap him in cotton wool and label 'Fragile, Handle with Care.' It's all one to me." Despite the disclaimer, she was a little put out. She knew that she was not a very good godmother, disliking children as she did and being as near a freethinker as made no difference: but she had seen herself making up for it as far as possible, by seeing that at least the boy rode well.

Then her flash of peevishness passed; she saw her brother looking distressed, knew that she had been a bit rough-tongued.

"Look Harry, I trained Perkin myself, with Magnus in view. At three feet he's safe as a rock. And when you're young you fall—if you fall—like a feather. It's old men who break their necks. And what could be a better ending?"

"Well—all I ask, is keep an eye on him."

She had kept an eye on him so far. Now she had sent him off on his own. Nothing in the world could happen to him on the six mile ride back to Copsey; it was clear flat road, bright daylight still. But suppose something did? Harry would never, never forgive her. She thought, rather irritably, that Harry had turned into a nervous old woman where the boy was concerned, and that such a state of mind was contagious. Here was she, canceling her visit to the sheeprun, that part of Sheppey Lea of which she was most proud since it had been reclaimed literally from a waste of near-derelict land, all bracken and gorse and coarse grass. The ten years of her careful, indeed inspired management, had brought the land back into cultivation. She'd read somewhere that goats would eat anything; they would even eat a plant which made cows abort and many cow-keepers had a goat running with their herds. She'd bought twenty goats and let them fend for themselves and they'd eaten everything even remotely edible. Then the sheep had moved in, with its golden foot as the fanciful expression went. Bertie was proud of her flock and more than a little fond of the man, who, with the help of a dog, looked after it. That he was slightly mad, claimed to have seen fairies dancing in a ring on the close-nibbled turf which the goats had cleared and the sheep had kept low, and that he believed that there were wolves in the dense forest which flung out an embracing arm to the north east and thus protected the sheeprun in the worst of winter, Bertie found not ridiculous but entrancing. It was true that on the now almost lawnlike surface of the sheeprun, there was, exactly where Joseph had claimed to see fairies dancing, a complete circle of deeper green, and not as her sceptical thought was, clover or any natural though rather misplaced growth; it was simply a ring where the ordinary grass grew greener.

"And, I swear, Miss; no sheep'll go near it. Nor the dog. So I scythe it down from time to time; and they 'on't even *eat* it. All thass good for is the Beltane fire, midsummer night."

Eccentric herself, Bertie enjoyed Joseph's oddities; even his regular setting of wolf-traps along the edge of the tree belt. He never caught anything—wolves had been exterminated in Henry VIII's time. But his belief that he might one day find one, like his belief in fairies, enabled him to pursue a calling, so lonely, so remote from all human contact that few men could have borne it. She made regular visits and was always welcome because she listened to his tales. Today was her day for going and she had hoped that Magnus would go with her, and possibly, just possibly, be fascinated by the old man.

Today, because of her conscience, she felt that she couldn't go; so she sent a message by a boy renowned for his fleet-footedness. "Tell Joseph I can't come today, but I will tomorrow. For certain." It had always astounded her that living his curious, almost timeless life, the old man knew one day from another, but somehow he did.

Then, just as she was ready to leave, Fowler her foreman appeared and said he'd got something he wanted to talk over with her, it wouldn't, he said, seeing that she was about to mount, take more than a minute. In fact any talk with Fowler took more than that, he was so slow-spoken, given to long thoughtful pauses and tiresome repetitions. So she did not overtake Magnus on the road; nor did she see any ominous sign of his having come to grief by being unsupervised. Hating to admit it even to herself, she felt relieved when a turn in the road and a break in the trees brought Copsi in sight. And then, in a few seconds, something else was in sight, too . . . She did not wait to enter by the paddock gateway but set her horse to the hedge and was upon Magnus like the wrath of God.

━━━◆━━━◆━━━◆━━━◆━━━

"Hurt him? Of course I did. I meant to. You know me, Harry, I'm not sentimental. Horse needs a whack it gets it, but to see Perkin, the gentlest, best-mannered... God, I could have killed the little brute."

"Do you realize, Bertha, what you might have done? Jerking him out of the saddle as you did, and holding him suspended while *you* flogged him? He might have choked."

She looked, not penitent, complacent. "I didn't know I was so strong." And in fact had someone suggested to her that she should lift such a lump with one hand, and flog it with the other, while still perched in her own saddle, she would have said it was impossible. But she'd done it. Just as she'd done... oh, too many things to remember; all things which her delicate, almost frail build would seem to refute. Jonathan Winthrop who longed to paint her and had never been allowed to do so, once described her as a butterfly made of whalebone, and he had not meant it either as entirely complimentary or entirely derogatory.

"The fact is, Harry, Magnus has been asking for a sound good hiding. It fell to me to give it. I hope it taught him a lesson. Otherwise he's never going near an animal of mine. I can tell you that."

Sir Harald had no wish to fall out with Bertie. For one thing she'd been kind to Juliet, during that brief, happy time; for another she was his sister in a far more positive way than Marie was—though Marie must be valued too, since for all her Frenchified way, she had chosen Copsi. But Bertie was company, sympathetic with his schemes, knowledgeable about farming. Cousin William's love of country life was concerned wholly with the sporting side; Bertie, could talk about foot-and-mouth disease, swine fever, liver-fluke. Often, after dinner when the old ladies, William and Jonathan had settled down to play Whist and the boy was safely asleep,

Harald would go across to Bertie's room and drink her brandy while they talked. At other times, she would visit him in his library. He preferred that, for there was something about her huge, cluttered room which made him uneasy because it offended his military sense of order, and he could never, for the life of him see why with so many unoccupied rooms she should use this for all purposes. He'd mentioned the matter once or twice, but she said, "I like it this way. It saves a lot of walking about and everything is to hand."

It would never do to quarrel with Bertie, yet she must be made to see that though the boy had been at fault in losing his temper, she had done exactly the same thing.

"It was certainly a severe thrashing. The boy will bear marks long after the welts on the pony have vanished."

"There you miss the point, Harry. The pony is probably ruined. Set to a jump too high for him and knowing his rider to be inexperienced, he very properly refused and was cruelly beaten. He may never face such a jump again. And quite apart from that...", she was aware that she was being cunning, "there was the downright disobedience. I'd told him never to go into that paddock without me. I knew how reluctant you were to let him jump at all."

She had no wish to quarrel with Harry; she appreciated their easy, almost laconic relationship as much as he did.

"Yes, there was that—and I should have punished him myself."

"How?"

"There are ways—without resorting to violence."

Bertie's greenish-blue eyes sparkled with malice. "No pudding for a week? No sweets for a fortnight? Surely you know how futile... He simply goes creeping round to one of the old women—whichever is in favor—and gobbles himself sick."

"That I certainly did *not* know. It must be stopped at once. I shall issue strict orders."

Poor fellow, he still, after all these years, thought he was in the army.

For a minute her fondness for her brother warred

with her principle of not getting involved, and fondness won. She said,

"I may offend you, Harry. Only son and all that. Understandable. But unless somebody, soon, gets the upper hand, you are going to have an unmangeable boy to deal with. A poor outlook for you. *And for Copsi.*"

The last three words were trigger words. Sir Harald had not been blind—though he would gladly have been—to the fact that Magnus had taken so little interest in the place, its people, its history—all the things which Sir Harald had found so engrossing. By various means Sir Harald had tried to make a recruit for Copsi. In the church where a Copsey lay, in chain mail, his legs crossed, and a little dog at his feet: "He was a Crusader, Magnus. You know about the Crusades?"

"It was a war."

Sir Harald, at or around the same age as his son now was, had heard the bugle calls, seen the standards flying. And hadn't the man here rigid in stone been one of the great host who every morning and every evening had cried, "To Jerusalem!"? To him the whole thing had been a thrilling story, though of course it must have been told him by somebody, though he had no memory of the telling. It had been part of him for as long as he remembered, but the son of his body seemed not to have inherited this, whatever it was. That his own feeling for the Crusader had not been derived from Sir Walter Scott's *The Talisman,* he could be sure. He had read the book and found it rather tame. All similar attempts to interest Magnus in the most honorable record of his family had been similarly disappointing; the boy had no imagination. And that was a thing you either had or hadn't, like red hair. Nothing to be done about it!

"I'm seriously considering sending him to school, Bertie. He is rather young. But it would rid us of tutors. What do you think?"

"An excellent idea. And the sooner the better."

❧━━━❧❦❧━━━❧❦❧━━━❧❦❧━━━❧❦❧━━━❧

Eton was well equipped to deal with most boys, athletic, dreamy, academic, stupid, cheerful, morose; it had generations of experience behind it and had become

more than a school, a world of its own, though in no sense
an isolated world. Compared with that of most other
educational establishments the regime was free and easy.
As an earlier Provost once explained to a parent who
actually protested that his son was allowed too much
freedom, "My lord, I did not adopt this profession with a
view to becoming a jail keeper."

Sir Harald was not one of those men who would
have said that his Eton days were the happiest of his life;
he'd been so homesick for Copsi all the time. Apart from
that, however, he'd been reasonably happy, made friends,
enjoyed some lessons, loathed others; hunted butterflies
with one of his friends who later became a naturalist and
disappeared in the South Pacific, and with another, when
he was sixteen, visited an afternoon brothel in a Windsor
back street. That the place existed and that some boys
frequented it were facts not unknown to the authorities;
but it was well under control, the house being owned by
the College, the three girls guaranteed free of disease. It
was system which Harald Copsey had staunchly advocated for the army—especially in India where syphilis was
rampant; but his was a humble, almost solitary voice,
easily quelled when his colonel said it was the equivalent
of licensed debauchery.

Now he was almost sure that he was doing the right
thing in sending Magnus to school, if only because it
would teach him to get along with boys of his own age and
kind. Just at the moment there were, unfortunately, few
such in the neighborhood. One thing was certain, the boy
would not be homesick, as he had been, for Copsi.
Magnus would never be, as he had been, short of pocket
money, painfully saving up for that night ride in a
post-chaise. He thought that Magnus might well enjoy
himself. Two things about which he had heard—bullying
and homosexuality—he discounted, having met with
neither himself, except in the army—other ranks, of
course, and drawn unfortunately from poor, rough,
ignorant people. Recruiting sergeants could not be too
choosy, so that there were a few, but surprisingly few,
distasteful incidents. Nothing like that at Eton!

Magnus received this turn in his life with that same

dismaying lack of interest. Was he indeed incorrigibly stupid, as some governess had said? Poised on the point of decision, hoping that he was right, thinking it possible that he might be wrong, Sir Harald would have given way had Magnus said something even so simple as: "I don't want to leave home." Just six words and Sir Harald would have relented, but they were not spoken and he felt a qualm; had he, in his anxiety to make the place seem not unattractive, made it sound over-attractive? Would the poor boy have a shock? Issue a little warning!

"I can't say what the food is like now. In my day it was bad. But you'll have your tuck-box. And there was a place in the High Street, called Annie's ... I remember she used to cook bacon and eggs and sausages. A sound breakfast, any time of the day, for fourpence. I don't suppose she's still there, but there'll be a similar place, I have no doubt."

"Annie's," Magnus said, showing his first spark of interest. "I'll remember that."

Almost irritably, Sir Harald remembered a tutor saying that the boy's great failing was inability to distinguish between the important and the unimportant. He also remembered that in his rides around villages, Magnus had distinguished between farms and holdings by what the woman of the house had to offer. Squirrel's Hall meant gingerbread, Marsh End currant bun, Cowfield blackberry wine...

━━◆━━◆━━◆━━◆━━◆━━

Eton, under it's mild and civilized surface—even riotous demonstrations in favor of this, in disapproval of that, were tolerated—had a tough hard core which did not give up without a struggle. Had Magnus's condition been curable by what Bertie called a sound good hiding, he would have been cured. He had several, most of them through delegated authority; prefects—and it was a tale often told, how Palmer had been savaged by young Copsey; it had taken three other prefects to pull him off. Handed on, handed up along the escalation of authority. Reason, sweet reason was tried and everything failed. Eton, despite its wide scope, was not equipped to deal with lunatics who every now and then needed a strait jacket. Send him home! Only one old master, creaking in voice as well as joints said, "Such a pity! I remember his father. Most inoffensive boy. Spent a lot of time hunting butterflies, if I remember rightly."

The expulsion practically coincided with Magnus's fourteenth birthday and almost against his better judgement Sir Harald hoped that the magical change which the man in London had mentioned might come about. And such a hope seemed to be justified; the boy seemed *glad* to be home. Uncomplainingly Sir Harald paid fifty pounds for the damage wrought in the frenzy which resulted in expulsion—Magnus had heaved a bench through a stained-glass window. The school experiment might, on the face of it, appear to be a failure, but it had done something if only to make the boy appreciate his home.

There followed two years of happiness. Magnus developed some interest in the estate, asked intelligent questions, listened to the answers. He was simply a boy who had developed late and had carried on into boyhood the childish rages of babyhood. Even Bertie admitted that he *seemed* to be greatly improved, and, withdrawing her disapproval, resumed her attempts to make a good horseman of him. Soon he was hunting regularly, virtually taking his father's place in the field, for Sir Harald's injured thigh which had healed so well, and of which he had taken so little notice, was now beginning to trouble him. It grew stiffer and often ached with a low grinding pain. He was still capable of riding his acres and of following hounds on a short run. More than that he could not manage. Bertie said it was rheumatism which often attacked at the weak points. She mixed him some fierce liniment.

Another change during these two years, and a fortunate one from Sir Harald's point of view, was the acquisition of new neighbors. An Anglo-Irish family named O'Brien moved into Axworth Grange, only two miles away if one took a short cut through Monkswood. The house had been unoccupied—except by a caretaking family—for many years because Brian O'Brien had inherited a far bigger, and he thought better, estate called Barrymore in Roscommon. There, for something over twenty years, he had tried to be a conscientious landlord, living on the spot, pouring in his resources, at one time considerable, for he owned, as well as Axworth, a house in Piccadilly and two shops in Edgware Road. Inexorably and ungratefully, the Roscommon estate had swallowed them all and in the end he accepted the necessity to retrench, and the best way to do it was to let Barrymore go, leaving an agent to wrest out what rents he could and pay himself out of the proceeds. After all, he had eight children to consider

On one occasion he said to Sir Harald, "You fought the French. I had to fight the potato. The worst thing that ever happened to Ireland was the potato. They'll dig for a bit in Spring, throw in the potatoes, then sit on their hunkers and wait. I've bought seed corn, out of my own pocket, peas, beans. Believe me or not they fed it all to the pigs. Speaking of pigs. . . . You see, until my uncle, God rest him, died and left me all he had, I'd lived in Dublin. Meant for the law. I was horrified to see hovels, men and women bedding down alongside pigs. I built houses, decent little houses, parlor, kitchen, two bedrooms, and they moved the pigs in. I swear to you, Copsey, if they could have got a pig to climb stairs they'd have had them in their beds. And me, ruining myself to improve things. So I left them to it. They can coop fowls in the bedrooms for all I care. But I often think: God help them if the potato ever fails."

"As it well could," Sir Harald said. "I have proved and some of my tenants have proved that land put down, year after year, to the same crop, fails in the end. Most of my people understand that now."

"Mine never did. And last December. . . . Not a thing one wishes to remember, but it is true. I found in the parlor of one of my nice little new houses an old woman, very old, a child aged about ten, and a pig in bed together. All fevered. I drove the pig out. The old woman lived, the boy died and *I* was blamed. The pig had supplied heat. You understand? So I was a murderer. Then the maiming of my cattle started. . . . And I gave up. When you cannot leave a cow in a field or a horse in a stable without bloody bloodshed, it's time to withdraw."

To the best of his ability Mr. O'Brien was deploying his forces in an effort to recoup the family fortunes. His eldest son was already in France, learning to judge and buy wine, which his second son, younger by a bare thirteen months, would sell in the Edgware Road shop. Then came a girl, very beautiful and quite wild; and then two boys, Ross, just a few months older than Magnus, and Barry, a few months younger. They became Magnus's great friends. One or both spent a good deal of time at Copsi, and Magnus was always welcome at Axworth. All seemed well.

From the point of view of somebody deeply concerned with crops, the year 1832 was a wonderful year, a mild moist spring so good for root crops and for hay, and then, in June, setting in with hot sunshine. Just what was needed. Even the fish curers over at the wharf were rejoicing, hanging up the gutted fish on lines, like a washerwoman dealing with laundry.

Sir Harald, after a happy afternoon, rode home, took a tepid bath and changed his clothes, went down to the library and poured his whisky. Neither of the old ladies would join him this evening as they had gone to Fowlmere to take tea with Mrs. Barrington; therefore he could smoke a cigar, a pleasure he usually deferred until after dinner. Both his sister and his stepmother often said that they had no objection to smoking, but one would cough, very delicately and on a note of protest, the other would wave a hand to disperse any small gust of smoke which approached her.

The younger of the two footmen came in.

"There's a Mrs. Webling asking to see you, sir."

Thomas, like all well-trained servants, made a nice discrimination between people; *a Mrs. Webling* was a grade below *Mrs. Webling*, and a grade above *a person*. The name meant nothing to Sir Harald but he was quite accustomed to receiving calls from people unknown to him.

"All right, Thomas. Show her in."

A small woman, decently dressed in black, but with—yes—something oddly aggressive about her. He felt immediately that she had not come to ask a favor of him; she wasn't the wife or mother of a poacher, or a mother wanting her son got into, or out of the army, or somebody who thought that because he owned so many houses he could provide any homeless person with a roof. And he was glad, for he had a kindly streak.

"Good evening, Mrs. Webling. Do sit down." He indicated a chair near his big, meticulously tidy desk, and abandoning the low leather chair near the window where he had been enjoying the seemingly incongruous scents of his cigar and the roses nodding by the sill, sat down behind the desk.

Mrs. Webling sat down, bolt upright and seemed for a moment to be taking stock of him, and of his surroundings. Then, just as he was about to say "And what can I do for you?" she spoke in a voice surprisingly low and pleasant.

"It's about my daughter, Sir Harald, and your son." She paused. "He's put her in the family way."

It was wrong, he thought, to speak of one's heart rising or falling; it was one's stomach. His gave a little lurch downwards, but his mind snatched it back into place. Only to be expected, he thought. He remembered that tolerated near-brothel in the Windsor back street. Inevitable as cutting teeth. Done in the right place, with the right woman, nothing to make a fuss about. But at the same time, almost alongside this tolerant thought, a warning bell rang and when he spoke his voice was cold and hard and defensive.

"Such an accusation needs proof, Mrs. Webling."

"I know. I also know there's no redress by law; even if he stood there and admitted it. But it wouldn't *look* well, would it? We're very respectable and nobody could call my Katie flighty. Quite the opposite. . . . But she did go to this fair and I can only think that she was drunk. We're total abstainers so she'd never touched anything of that sort, a glass of wine'd send her silly. So it happened. A lot of them together at first, then pairing off in the dark behind the booths."

Disconcertingly, her tongue flicked, more of a

motion than was needed to moisten her lips and Sir Harald who, after all, had been around a bit in his day, took time to think—What about *you*, twenty years ago? The action was definitely salacious.

"As soon as I knew," the low, pleasant voice went on, "I asked *who*? At first she wouldn't say. In the end she did. So there we are. I thought the best thing to do was to have a word with you."

"I see." He was already thinking about money. Fifty pounds? No law demanded it, because paternity could never be proved; still, he wished to be *fair*. Having a baby and caring for it cost time and money. On the other hand he had no wish to appear simple and easily persuaded. "And what am I supposed to say, Mrs. Webling?"

"Yes or no to what I have to suggest, sir." She moved, leaning forward slightly. "There's a young man I know who'd marry Katie straight away. He's served his apprenticeship at the saddler's in Bressford and he'd like to set up on his own, in Wyck, but that'd cost money. I've never been able to save anything; I've two younger than Katie and I was left a widow nine years ago. But if I could get my hands on a hundred pounds...."

He'd been thinking fifty very generous.

"That is a great deal of money."

"To *some* people." She looked around the room again. "Rape isn't a very nice word, sir; and when a young gentleman is known to be a bit wild, and the girl strictly brought up and never had a word against her, well, rape is the only explanation, isn't it? It takes away some of the shame, if the girl is known to be forced. And there is another way of looking at it. There are some men, decent men, who if they see wrong being done, the more especially by a young gentleman to a poor honest girl, they're not above taking the law into their own hands."

Sir Harald had known it to be done; no farther away than Radmouth. The captain of a fishing vessel had been accused of killing a young member of his crew, but there was little hard evidence, once hearsay was discounted; not enough to justify passing the case on beyond the magistrates' court. But that skipper had not returned from his next voyage. He'd fallen overboard. Then he did return, a corpse washed up, identifiable by the tattoo patterns on his arms and shoulders, and so smashed about that there was hardly an unbroken bone. Understandable if he had tossed about amongst rocks—but there were no rocks between Radmouth and the fishing grounds where his accident occurred. This was the most recent case of men taking the law into their own hands that he could recall, but there were others. (Nobody had ever quite explained how a very deadly small snake, a krait, had got into the bed of a very unpopular sergeant when the regiment was at Barrackpore.)

Once he began to think in this fashion a hundred pounds seemed less of a sum. He unlocked the bottom drawer on the right hand of his desk and took out the money in the notes which still did not seem to him to be real money; paper money, like income tax, and other taxes, had been war-time measures, but once introduced they were here to stay.

Mrs. Webling accepted the money without thanks; she said, "I am sure this is the best way, sir. Good evening."

———————

Except where Copsi was concerned he was a man of limited imagination, but in a way this did concern Copsi and he could imagine a little boy—his grandson, for the idea that the baby might be a girl never occurred to him—a little boy, ostensibly son of a saddler, growing up with Copsi in his blood, perhaps coming to deliver a saddle or a set of harness, and staring, being entranced.... Really, Sir Harald told himself, this is the extreme of sentimentality! Yet the thought persisted; his whisky had no taste, his cigar had died, and for the first time he found himself really angered with Magnus. Hitherto he'd been exasperated, worried, hopeful, despairing but not downright plain angry. He did not examine closely the reason for this change of attitude; he was puzzled by it, remembering how eager he had always been to find some excuse for far less excusable behavior. Deflowering a girl behind a booth on a fairground might not be exactly praiseworthy behavior, but there was nothing so unusual about it. And now he came to think about it, what was so very decent a girl doing at the fair at all, unescorted, drinking with strangers, staying until the end? There was in fact far more excuse, far more reason for what the boy had done than there was for many things he had done in fits of rage—heaving a bench through a window, for example. Yet now he was angry with his son and made up his mind to speak severely, very severely indeed.

No opportunity occurred before dinner; Magnus only just slithered into place in time for the meal. Nobody noticed that Harry was more silent than usual; Lady Copsey and Madame had brought news from Fowlmere and were happily quarreling about it. Angela Barrington, now aged twenty, was engaged to marry Sir Walter Hilborough, three times her age, but rich.

"I was so astonished," Madame le Beaune said, "that I almost dropped my teacup. I always thought of Mrs. Barrington as a *fond* mother. What hope of happiness can that sweet girl have, married to a man old enough to be her father?"

"Every hope," Lady Copsey said. "My husband was considerably my senior and we were happy." She ate some asparagus and said, as though by afterthought, "Sir Walter has no children by his first marriage." Everybody at the table knew what her remark meant. Cousin William who approved of marriage for other men, said,

"Well, good for him. Stonehurst may yet have an heir."

Jonathan Winthrop planned a picture—Three Witches. When the two old ladies were thus engaged in planting darts they did look like witches, alike enough in their mutual spite to be sisters. He'd thought so before; but he needed a third, and of her he had just caught a glimpse this very evening, a small woman, all in black, being driven away in a hired vehicle. Nothing noticeable, except the expression on her face: *gloating*. Now, he thought, I have them, all three.

"I want a word with you," Sir Harald said, coming out of his unnoticed silence to address his son in a brusque, cold way; not saying Magnus, not saying my boy.

Even Magnus noticed and looked startled.

"Yes, Papa."

Nobody actually said, what is the matter *now*? but the question ran about the table, conveyed by glance, sly, avid, knowing.

Magnus enjoyed another reprieve. Just outside the dining room door the second footman said,

"Mr. O'Brien, sir. He wished to wait. He is in the library."

Sir Harald welcomed the idea of talking the matter over with a man who had sons of his own. He would not, of course, go at the subject like a bull at a gate, indeed the less said the better; but he intended to touch upon the subject of lads getting into mischief and hear what O'Brien had to say. It would help, he thought, to get the thing into perspective, which he needed to do. He was still astonished by the effect the incident had had upon him. At table he could hardly bear to look at Magnus—ordinarily the light of his eyes.

There was no reticence about Brian O'Brien; after an exchange of greetings, the offer and the acceptance of brandy, he said,

"Have you had an old hag here?"

Oddly, the very sight of his friend, the so typically Irish face, the wide mouth so ready to grin, the blue eyes so ready to sparkle, had brought yet another change of heart; already, in his own eyes he looked a fool. A hundred pounds indeed!

"Old hags," he said, "pester me regularly."

"This was no ordinary one. You'd remember her did she cross your path. I took the notion she might try you next; so I came over hotfoot with the warning word."

"That was friendly. What warning?"

"I've been through this hoop once before—with Francis, the one that's now in France. *She* didn't know that; she thought Ross was my eldest. And twenty pounds she was asking because my wicked boy had as good as raped her innocent virgin daughter at the mid-May fair. Oh the killing shame of it, such a decent, poor girl!" The grin spread, the eyes twinkled. "D'you know what I said? I said: 'Ma'am, it's my boy who should have twenty pounds for teaching your daughter to keep off fairgrounds.' That took the wind out of her sails, I promise you. But I thought to myself, failed with me, she might try you: your boy being just the right age, and you without the experience that I, God help me, have endured."

"That was very friendly." But something needed to be defended: dignity? Naïveté? Plain simple-mindedness? Copsi's good name?

"Suppose the woman's tale had been true? Or you'd been dealing with the situation for the first time . . . ?"

"There was a first time. And worse. It was away in Roscommon, and the girl was not only young and decent, but practically a nun, which brought in more than being poor and decent exploited by the rich, but something downright dangerous. I well remember the day. I went out and whistled up Francis and asked him, point blank. Now," the confident father said, taking a sip of brandy and savoring it, "one thing with my boys I can be sure of. Angels they are not; liars they are not. From the time they're knee-high they know I'll take anything but a lie. Murder I'll forgive and they know it, but a lie, no! Francis, on that occasion, didn't lie, he told me the truth and I looked into it. The girl was a cheap whore, her so-called mother, her pimp. It was the blackmail and the intimidation that put the butter on their bread. That time," the happy man said, "you could buy yourself clear for five pounds. But that was in Ireland where a pound was as good as five elsewhere. Which reminds me of another thing. . . ." Mr. O'Brien, since coming to England and settling down in Axworth, had become aware of the difference between his own volatile, Celtic nature and that of his stolid East Anglian neighbors. Born and bred in Dublin, a very English city, he had little Irishness about him, no marked accent, just a turn of phrase now and again; and he'd slipped into Axworth and its surroundings like a hand into a glove. But he had found. . . . Exactly what? A mental slow-footedness; a think-before-you-speak, ponder-before-you-laugh attitude which at times he had found trying. He'd once put it into vivid language to his wife: "Light a fire under their bellies and budge them you will not. The fellow will say "I smell smoke" and look around for the origin of it." So, in dealing with his neighbors Brian O'Brien had learned not to be precipitate. He had been precipitate himself, racing over to Copsi to warn Copsey who, dull dog that he was, seemed not to comprehend what he had escaped. The old black-clad hag who had tried to dun him for twenty pounds might well have raised her price if she had come to Copsi. So, conscious of having done Sir Harald a favor, and aware that of all the slow-moving, clod-footed East Anglians Sir Harald was the worst, Brian O'Brien moved carefully.

"Did you ever take this thing they call the Grand Tour?"

"No. I went straight from school to the army. And of course there was the war which put the Continent out of bounds."

"I've been giving it some consideration. I never had it. They say travel broadens the mind."

"I'm no judge. I've been as far west as the Sugar Islands, as far east as India, but in the army of course; much the same wherever you're stationed." He remembered being homesick for Copsi all the time. And had his mind broadened? He was acutely aware still of having been duped, in this very room, this very evening.

"Barrington was saying the other day he thought highly of it. It meant selling a few acres, but well worth it," Mr. O'Brien liked Sir Harald but felt more akin to Mr. Barrington whose circumstances much resembled his own, a big family and a shallow purse. "So I was thinking, it'd be cheaper if we combined and sent the three boys together. Ross is for Cambridge eventually, but not until Michaelmas next year."

He paused, expectant and hopeful while Sir Harald thought before he spoke. Possibly his visitor that afternoon had been a fraud, but the situation might arise again and wild oats were best sown away from one's own back yard; the company of the O'Brien boys could only be beneficial. How enviable for a man to be able to rely so completely on the veracity of his sons!

"Yes," he said. "I'm entirely in favor. Of course I must see how the boy feels."

Mr. O'Brien thought: Bad policy, man! Thank God, I've got mine so in hand that if I said they were off to Timbuctoo on Saturday, they'd *go*. But I suppose it's different with only the one.

"Visiting what they call the château country will be cheap, anyway," he said comfortably. "Francis has a house in Bordeaux and friends all over the place. So if your boy consents to have a treat that most would give their ears for, will I ask Barrington the name of his bear-leader, or will you?"

"Bear-leader?"

"It is a name given to men who conduct the cubs around. Barrington thought highly of his. A great scholar and yet a man of the world."

Sir Harald found himself hoping—and yet feeling ashamed of the hope—that Magnus would take kindly to the proposal. To think of the boy's absence for several months on end with relief, was surely slightly wrong. He loved his son, didn't he? Until this evening when he'd found himself hating him. School had improved him, hadn't it? Foreign travel might improve him still more; and wasn't this Grand Tour something which O'Brien had said, with a sarcastic note in his voice, most boys would give their ears for? Hadn't Barrington actually sold land in order that his son might enjoy such an advantage? And Sir Harald was reasonably sure that to send Ross and Barry abroad would call for some sacrifice on O'Brien's part. There, of course he could be helpful; if Magnus went, he would insist upon paying a full half, not a third of the cost. In fact the whole thing was an admirable idea and why he should be of such divided mind about it, he simply could not understand.

Magnus, consulted, took to the idea with a show of enthusiasm, somewhat rare in him.

"Why, yes, sir, I'd like that. Phil Barrington never stopped talking about what he'd seen and done."

"We—that is Mr. O'Brien and I—are hoping to obtain the services of the same man who went with Philip."

"Good." Phil Barrington's account of his Grand Tour rather indicated that the man of the world often took ascendancy of the scholar: a bullfight in the south of France, a spectacular horserace somewhere in Italy, a lot of gambling everywhere, a lot of girls as good as naked who danced and pranced and then were auctioned off, the highest bidder to be the buyer for the night.

In the warmth of his son's approval and acceptance, Sir Harald's doubt about his decision and its validity, melted away and he threw himself happily into the preparations and the plans for the Grand Tour which was to begin in mid-September—a time which, except for Easter, was the best time for Paris; a week there and then they would go south, as swallows did. They should be in Naples for the great festival of Saint Januarius, when the saint's blood liquefied before an adoring multitude. Easter in Rome, and Whitsun in Venice where they would witness the symbolic wedding between the city and the sea, when the doge threw a wedding ring into the water.

Then, in early September something happened which convinced Sir Harald that it would be not only desirable, but wise for Magnus to be elsewhere for a while. Partridge shooting started in September and since the boys would not be here for the pheasants, Sir Harald made rather more of an early shoot than he would ordinarily have done. The light was tricky especially towards the end of the day, long level, almost blinding shafts of light, temporarily blinding. Magnus missed an easy shot and a young underkeeper laughed. Then Magnus shot him.

Everybody said: accident, accident, most unfortunate, but accidents do happen. Magnus himself said it was an accident; but Sir Harald knew better. He'd been near enough and in a position to see, in the tiny space between the shot that missed and the shot that found its mark, that look of ungovernable fury which he had hoped never to see again.

Fortunately the young man was not fatally injured and fortunately he was a Copsi man, so the thing could be smoothed over, with apologies, with full pay while off work and a shilling or two extra for invalid foods; but Sir Harald was too close to his villagers not to sense an undercurrent of animosity; muttering talk which stopped short as he approached, smiles less ready than usual, and when produced, less sincere. And then there was the painful interview with his headkeeper, related to the underling in several ways, by kinship three or four times, by marriage at least twice.

"I'm sorry to tell you, sir, Jim don't aim to come back. His time was out at Michaelmas and he say he's going a-navvying."

"He can't do that!" Sir Harald was genuinely shocked. Navvies were the men who were building the iron network of rails which Sir Harald was not alone in thinking was ruining the countryside. They were men without homes, without any allegiance—except to the gang leader who hired them; they were outside the law, positively worse than gypsies. The work was hard and well paid, and most of the wages went in drink, and then there were bloody fights between men armed with shovels and pickaxes. As the rails crept forward decent people in the vicinity were as alarmed as though an army of barbarians were expected to invade. Lock up your fowls—the navvies stole with impunity, safe in the anonymity of their state and the certainty that even the ganger would support any alibi, not wanting to lose a worker. Lock up your womenfolk—gangs of men, mainly unmarried, constituted a very real threat.

"Worse than going into the army," Sir Harald said. "A soldier is under discipline and stands some chance of emerging at the end of his time honest and clean and law-abiding. The navvy, unless he dies young, becomes a pest."

"I done my best to talk him out of it," Bateman said. He was a large, solemn man who took his job and himself very seriously. "So did his mother, sir. She's frantic, poor woman. She said she hadn't nursed him all these weeks just to see him go off and kill hisself with overwork and drink and the pneumonia. I took the liberty of saying I'd ask for a raise, sir, shilling a week, maybe. But he's set."

"Well, I'm very sorry to hear it, Bateman. It'll be the ruin of him."

"So we all think. But time we was arguing, Jim said something that I ain't sure I oughta repeat, sir; but that do go towards explaining."

"Tell me. Surely you know by now you can say anything to me."

"Well, sir...Jim claims 'Mr. Magnus shot him deliberate, because he laughed. And he wasn't laughing at *him*; he was laughing because Mr. Frisby's dog what he'd been so boastful about, was up to such antics. And Jim said: 'Think forward a bit,' he said, 'and ask what life'll be like serving a master that'll shoot a man like he was a rabbit.'"

Perfectly true; but Sir Harald was not prepared to admit it. Offensive measures were the best defensive measure and, feeling uneasy, he made tentative steps on a number of fronts at once.

Half-jocular. "Jim's looking rather far ahead, isn't he, Bateman? I'm good for thirty years, I hope."

"We all hope so, sir. With all our hearts."

Point blank denial. "Jim is wrong in thinking the act deliberate. I know. I was there. He is even more wrong in spreading such an untrue and malicious tale."

"I wasn't, myself, in a position to see, sir. Jim was. *And he wasn't alone.*"

Cajolery. "You were right, Bateman, to promise a raise. His hiring ended, as you say, at Michaelmas. So I stand by that. And another thing. Since he is so forward looking, he will soon be thinking about marriage. In Copsi he can at least be sure of a cottage."

"I did point that out, sir."

"Well, if you've done your best, and I've done my best, he must go. But I'm very sorry to think of a Copsi man becoming a navvy."

The underkeeper was not the only one to go that autumn. Two young men went to sea; one emigrated to America, and one joined the army. It was, perhaps, significant that they were all Jim's contemporaries, and cronies.

His own son was footloose in Italy, but Sir Harald was not hypocritical in thinking it a great pity that five young men, born and bred in Copsi, should desert the home place. He felt sorry for them.

Magnus wrote—not as often as Sir Harald could have wished—but with fair regularity. His letters were singularly uninformative; how many miles traveled between one stopping place and the next, what the inns or the lodgings, what the weather was like. No more. For real information Sir Harald depended largely upon Mr. O'Brien whose sons wrote shared letters, long, slightly incoherent, inky. "They've both got the gift of the gab," he said, deprecating what he was proud of. It was in fact from Mr. O'Brien that Sir Harald first learned of a change of program.

The bear-leader, whose name was Garnet, had so successfully mixed his roles, scholar and man-of-the-world, as to see a unique opportunity. Ross O'Brien must return to England, being due for Cambridge in early autumn; no such urgency concerned Barry and Magnus. Mr. Garnet had rightly assessed the financial situation; young Copsey was the one with the money. That he was also the most troublesome and the least appreciative, Mr. Garnet was prepared to overlook—if only he could get, expenses paid, to Egypt. By way of Greece and Cyprus. Magnus was all in favor of prolonging the tour; ruins and history bored him, he had no eye for scenery, no real interest in local customs, but he enjoyed traveling and the sense of freedom which resulted from being here today and gone tomorrow; and he enjoyed what he called the highlights, particularly as he so often acted as host. Old Garnet would often say, "What do you say Copsey? Can we *afford* an evening out?" Magnus was shrewd enough to see through this pretense of making him, in theory, the joint keeper of the communal purse, but it put him into a splendid position. Sometimes he would pretend to consider the matter, keeping them all in suspense.

They were in Venice, at the Lido, when Mr. Garnet very tentatively suggested prolonging the tour. Venice was the penultimate stop. Only Naples to come, and the thought of turning back to the north for the summer and taking one of the jobs—coaching backward boys or doing some hack work for a publisher—settled on him like a cloud. Bear-leaders were never properly occupied in summer, parents thinking that hot weather in foreign places was very dangerous.... To dispel the cloud he drank freely of Magnus's wine and through another cloud said, "I wish...."

Ross O'Brien who had inherited his father's impervious head for wine or any other drink, said,

"I must go back. And I doubt very much whether my father could affort to spend any more on Barry."

Mr. Garnet, slightly drunk, knew what Mr. Garnet had realized, sober. Mr. O'Brien was his real employer; he was the one who had got in touch with him, talked Sir Harald into letting his boy make up the threesome. Mr. Garnet had met Sir Harald only twice and had guessed that, left to himself, he would never have thought of sending his son abroad, and though he had made the decision, entertained some doubts about it. He reasoned that if both the O'Brien boys went home at the prearranged time, young Copsey would go too. So he worked out a neat financial arrangement which would certainly appeal to Mr. O'Brien and not be likely to daunt Sir Harald. The nub of his argument was that this tour had been so very successful because the boys had been company for one another on those occasions when he was pursuing his studies. "Even on a familiar tour a man in my position must read a good deal, and since Egypt is unknown to me, I shall have much to read. So, my dear sir, if you would allow Barry to accompany us, I should regard him a companion for Magnus, and see that his expenses were minimal."

Mr. O'Brien went to chat over the suggestion with Sir Harald, who, as was only to be expected, said he'd like to know how Magnus felt about it.

"I had word from mine by the same post. Ross is only sorry he can't go; Barry is all agog. But facts we must face. Unless you're prepared to share, it is not feasible."

"I don't know about Greece, I've never been there. Or Cyprus. But there's nothing to see in Egypt except sand and flies and blind beggars."

Such a statement astounded Mr. O'Brien who had a lively mind.

"But the Pyramids were one of the seven wonders of the ancient world!"

"So was something—a kind of lighthouse I was told—at Alexandria. Nothing to see of it when I was there. No, I'm against Egypt. It had the seven plagues in biblical days, now it has ten, not counting the sand and the flies. We lost a lot of good men between Alexandria and Suez."

"Fighting?"

"No, damn it. Sickness. Things you never heard of. Things I don't want to remember. . . . No, I draw the line at Egypt. And if you don't care to tell Mr. Garnet so, I will. I'm agreeable to Greece, if that is so important. Cyprus I don't know and have heard nothing bad of. Egypt, no."

With such a compromise Mr. O'Brien and Mr. Garnet had to be content. By a careful manipulation of funds available, and by traveling in rather humble ways, which did not suit Magnus much, Mr. Garnet managed to squeeze in a visit to Leptis Magna, a forgotten place, simply crying out to be excavated; fishermen spread their nets to dry, women spread laundry on the tops of lordly columns and arches, deep sunk in the sand. Oh, if only, Mr. Garnet cried within himself; if only he had money and time. . . . But both ran short and by Easter of 1835 he was facing the prospect which he had cleverly dodged at Whitsun of the previous year.

So, just after his eighteenth birthday, Magnus came home. He'd grown a good deal, both in height and width of shoulder; apart from that, and the fact that his hair had darkened from light golden to dark blonde, he seemed to have changed little. And once again he seemed glad to be home. Sir Harald, so glad to see him, alive and well and if changed, only for the better, made the curious error of saying, at the dinner table, how nice it was to have somebody young about the place again.

That affronted everybody by implication. Lady Copsey and Madame le Beaune bristled; Cousin William snorted into his wine and Jonathan, having no consoling looking glass to consult, studied his hands as though searching for signs of age, brown blotches, prominent veins.

"You seem to forget, Harry, that the epithet 'old'

was applied to me to distinguish me from Magnus's wife—and from poor Juliet. It was premature. I am barely twelve years your senior." She would like to have added that she could still walk two miles, a taunt to Marie, but it would also be a taunt to Harry and his honorable wound. There was no need for Marie to speak; everyone knew that she and Lydia were so almost exactly contemporaries as to celebrate their birthdays in the same week.

"Age shouldn't be reckoned by birthdays," said Cousin William who was sixty-two. "It's largely a matter of how you get about. And whether you enjoy your food." He tackled his saddle of lamb with renewed gusto.

Magnus, upon whom all attention had centered since his return, resented the diversion and hunted about in his mind for some arresting thing to say; a sentence beginning, "When I was in Crete...." None of those present knew anything about the place, so they would listen at once. The trouble was that he didn't remember anything much—at least not anything fit for their hearing!

"Well now that you are back, my boy," Sir Harald said cheerily. "we must liven things up a bit. How about a ball on May Day?"

"I should like that," Magnus said.

The Great Hall at Copsi made an ideal ballroom; adjoining it was the big dining room, only used when several people were expected—that would be the supper room; from the half landing the stairs branched, to the left the Long Gallery, to the right the drawing room, also seldom used nowadays, both excellent sitting out places and both large enough to contain a few card tables for those who did not dance. The smaller, family dining room could be at the service of those who wished to smoke. Sir Harald, with an old soldier's eye for terrain, was satisfied, but he noticed that with the exception of the small dining room which was in everyday use, all the apartments could do with a thorough good cleaning. The place looked a bit dingy and dusty. It lacked.... Skip that thought! He had a perfectly good housekeeper and plenty of maids, and it

wouldn't hurt either footman to mount a ladder and dust
the tops of things, trophies of the chase and bits of armor
on the walls of the Great Hall, tops of pictures in the Long
Gallery. He thought, with a flash of irritation, there are
three women in this house! But as with the nursery, all
that time ago, so with the house, he had been obliged to
forbid his stepmother and his sister from exercising any
control except over their own apartments; they'd
contradict one another's orders just for spite. As for
Bertie, she lived a life apart and her own room showed
how thoroughly undomesticated she was.

The thought that the house needed a châtelaine led
on to the thought that Magnus, though too young to
marry yet awhile, would one day have a wife, and since
long engagements were now the fashion, it was not too
early to begin to look round. In the immediate
neighborhood the field was rather thin: two Collins girls,
one about eighteen, one rather younger; both nice girls
but neither pretty. Nothing actually wrong with their
faces, but.... It was amazing, Sir Harald reflected, how
two eyes, a nose and a mouth could be so arranged as to
make for comeliness, or the reverse. Rosemary O'Brien
promised to be a beauty, with very blue eyes and a wealth
of black hair. A bit on the young side, but there was no
hurry. There were the Bradfords over at Southbury. Sir
Harald's mother had been a Bradford, but the place had
passed to another branch of the family, so the relationship
was slight. And that was about all. Still, he told himself
comfortably, there was no need to choose a local
girl—though he would have preferred it; and thanks to his
careful management, there was no need to look for a girl
with money. Things would work out all right.

He was reasonably sure that the fit of fury in which
Magnus had shot the underkeeper had been the last; just
as the loudest crack of thunder and the sharpest shaft of
lightning could sometimes mark the end of a storm. If
Magnus had been in any way troublesome, Mr. Garnet
would not have wished to prolong that tour, and after
Ross O'Brien came home and Sir Harald was dining at
Axworth, he had—he thought rather skillfully—brought
the talk around to the matter nearest his heart: "Well now

Ross, pander to a father's feelings for a moment and tell me about my boy." Ross had responded with all the right things suppressing an account of how, in a *maison tolerée* in Nîmes Magnus had appeared to go mad because none of the available girls pleased him and he'd seen one who did, flitting across the landing. The madam's plea that the girl was already bespoken had not appeased him at all; he'd begun to tear the place apart, starting with a huge chandelier. It had taken Ross and Barry and Mr. Garnet—called from his own pleasure—to control him; and the bill for damages was the equivalent of twenty-five pounds, absolutely iniquitous considering the rate of exchange. But Magnus, of course, had paid. Mr. Garnet had taken the whole affair in his stride, being a man of vast experience; Ross and Barry had privately speculated as to *how* Magnus had managed to jump high enough to reach the chandelier at all. They agreed that any horse able to make such a jump in proportion to his own height would be a miracle; and Magnus himself said he could not have done it in cold blood. Mr. Garnet had said that another evening like that and they'd have to stop short at Rome because the money would give out and Magnus, fully recovered, had said quite amiably, "But it was *my* pocket money, sir; not out of the general fund." The two were by that time so confused that Mr. Garnet wished not to pursue the subject.

Of all this Ross said nothing. And within Sir Harald, time had already begun its healing work; he could no longer be absolutely dead certain that he had seen that devilish look on his boy's handsome face half a second before the keeper was shot. The light was tricky and he was a man who, his fellow magistrates sometimes complained, was a bit too ready to give any man the benefit of the doubt.

Like the good officer that he was at heart, Sir Harald knew that orders must not only be given but must be seen to be obeyed, so, having ordered a thorough cleaning to be done, he made his tour of inspection and was well satisfied. He began on the ground floor. Supper room spotless; even the walls, covered some time ago with fluted crimson silk—a sure harborer of dust—had been thoroughly brushed, the furniture gleamed with polish. In the Great Hall all was clean, too; though there were a few vacant spaces. Some of the antlered, or fanged heads had been too old to sustain a thorough brushing. "Just fell to pieces in my hands. It was the cobwebs held it together," the footman said.

Well, Sir Harald thought, it was a pity, but nobody except himself would notice. He turned and went to climb the stairs towards the landing where the stairs parted and the blank, ruined panel-portrait of Charles I was supposed to stare down, dominating the vast hall. He wasn't thinking about it or about the mystery as to why some people could see what lay under the smother and some could not; he was actually thinking about the Long Gallery where he must avoid, or quickly pass by, two things—Juliet's two small water colors commemorating all she had ever known of Copsi, a few pale spring flowers, and the portrait which Jonathan had made of Magnus.

Facing this ordeal of avoidance he climbed a few steps and then saw in the panel, as clearly as if the painter had only just laid down his brush, the grave dignified face of Charles I.

His first thought was that in the process of what he had ordered—a thorough cleaning—somebody had managed to remove the obliterating layers of paint. He even thought—a vast improvement! Then he mounted another stair and it was gone, all the rich color simply submerged.

He said, aloud, "Well, I'll be damned!" and stepped backwards and downwards. The panel remained as it had always been, a mass of smears, dark green, black, brown. Those who believed the story about the panel and those who had claimed to see the picture always said that it was a question of light; but the light had not changed as he mounted one step.

As he stood there, bewildered, and to be honest, a little apprehensive, remembering the old story, his sister Marie rustled out from the Long Gallery and said,

"I *thought* I heard somebody. I rather feared it

might be Lydia, bent on interference, as usual."

There had been a dispute as to which of the old ladies should arrange the flowers and Sir Harald knew that they were completely incapable of making a joint effort so he had suggested that one should decorate the Long Gallery, one the drawing room. But which was to do which? Two women with whom dispute had become a habit could quarrel over even so small an issue, and Magnus—much in favor of the ball—had said, "Why not draw lots?" That had worked admirably; chance was a thing not to be contested. But there were endless, most enjoyable squabbles ahead, for though May was a month of full bloom in woods and hedgerows there was, not a scarcity, but a shortage of garden and hothouse flowers.

"I was just looking," Madame le Beaune said, "at where I should position my flowers. I have decided upon one bowl at the very far end. I am superstitious, as you know, Harry, and I think it unlucky to bring lilac or hawthorn indoors. So I shall not have much to arrange, except the tulips and sprays of the Everlasting Rose."

There! She'd got her claim to that in first. When dispute arose, as it most certainly would, she could say to Lydia: "But I spoke to Harry, almost a week ago."

Of her chatter Sir Harald really heard only the word superstitious; superstition was for the ignorant, yet he had felt something, not when the picture appeared, but when it vanished, which proved that its emergence was not due to cleaning. But then to believe the hoary old story was as stupid as his stepmother's refusal to allow lilac—now at its best—into the house. Or to cross your fingers when somebody said the Devil or Satan or, as country people still did, Old Scrat; or throw a pinch of spilled salt over one's left shoulder, or avoid walking under ladders. All rubbish!

It was all rubbish, but it left him with just enough feeling of apprehension, to think about the way the staircase sagged. It had always, so long as he could remember, had a slight slant and it had never in his time been subjected to much strain; when he gave children's parties his young guests had scampered up and down, but children weighed very light; suppose, just suppose, that at the end of a dance a number of dowagers and their charges mounted the stairs together and it was too much. Catastrophe indeed!

However, the estate carpenter, a reliable man, having made a thorough inspection, said that the staircase was as sound as a rock as well as being as old as the hills. "If you ask me, sir, that went a bit lopsided in its early days. Two sorts of timber used, some seasoned, some not, and the unseasoned shrank a bit. But you can rest assured there ain't no danger. Like I say, sound as a rock."

No catastrophe occurred. The ball was a resounding success and resulted in a good many invitations during the following weeks. The ball had been Rosemary O'Brien's debut; she wore the traditional white muslin dress, and with her wealth of hair coiled into a chignon looked very pretty indeed. Sir Harald was not alone in thinking that it would be an admirable match.

It was a happy, peaceful summer and the crops were good.

Then it was September and one morning, making his rounds, Sir Harald visited Reffolds, eager to see how the tenant there, a man named John Reeve—a very good fellow indeed—was experimenting with a kind of barley new to Copsi. It produced a particularly hard grain, much favored by brewers, but it had one disadvantage; it was a late-ripening crop and if September brought much rain, as it often did, it failed of its purpose.

Scything had begun in the dark brown field and three men were at work, John Reeve himself, his permanent hired man and another, one of those rather unsettled, but versatile fellows who moved from job to job and was tied to none; he'd shear sheep, thatch a house, work in the fish-curing sheds, build a pigsty. It was a thousand pities, Sir Harald reflected, not for the first time, that Reeve had no son. He'd had one, a very promising boy, but he'd died of scarlet fever. Mrs. Reeve had never fully recovered from the blow; after fifteen years she was still unsmiling, seeming to have a grudge against the world. Sir Harald was accustomed to hearty greetings wherever he went; invitations to step in, out of the heat, out of the cold, to sample and approve home-brewed ale, homemade wines of many varieties, to ake just a bite of plum cake or ginger bread. He had never et foot in Reffolds and knew Mrs. Reeve only as a small, neat, pale, civil, but unfriendly woman, reputed to be the best butter-maker in the neighborhood. John Reeve he iked, a big hearty man, who on the only occasion when he sore subject had been mentioned—something to do with a renewal of lease—had said, "Well, I always hold hat when one door shuts another opens. My brother has our boys, I might take to one of them; or Hannah might marry a likely lad. In which case, I trust, sir, you'd give consideration."

"No doubt about that," Sir Harald said heartily, hoping that Hannah might even marry a cousin; there had been Reeves at Reffolds almost as long as there had been Copseys at Copsi.

On this glorious September morning, John Reeve aid down his scythe, stepped over the ditch which divided barley field from lane, and wiped his wet forehead on his forearm. "Good morning, sir."

"Morning, Reeve. It looks very well. Just the weather for it, eh?"

"Couldn't've been better," the man agreed, but with no smile, none of the look of satisfaction to be expected from a man who had taken a risk and won.

"And it looks set fair for two or three days more," Sir Harald said. He had three ways of foretelling weather; a proper barometer, a bit of seaweed hung up on the wall outside the door most generally used at Copsi, and his wound. The three did not invariably agree, and when they differed he was inclined to favor the verdict of the seaweed which turned limp and damp some good twelve hours before rain, dry and rigid when good weather was on the way; the barometer, perhaps because it was indoors, was slightly less readily responsive, and his wound might ache for other reasons. This morning all three foretold good weather and Reeve should get his chance crop in, home and dry, and very profitable.

But the man looked ill at ease, unsmiling, wiping his forehead again, this time on a handkerchief, red, with blue and yellow horseshoes in the pattern.

"I'm obliged to ask you something, sir. And it's a bit difficult."

"Come on man, out with it. We know each other well enough by now, I should hope."

"It's no ordinary thing, sir.... It's like this. My Hannah went to stay with a schoolfriend of hers, out beyond Axworth. Light land and harvest very early this year. So Mr. Wentworth had a Harvest Horkey. The young gentlemen from Axworth looked in—you know the way they do, and Mr. Magnus was with them.... And he took a kind of fancy to Hannah, so much so that she left the dancing in the barn and went back into the house.... But that wasn't the end, as it *should've* been. She's at school, as you know, and, well, I'll put it bluntly since there's no other way.... He's been pestering her there for a fortnight. Miss Drayton don't like it, and Hannah don't like it. Once he said he was her cousin and was shown into the parlor. Hannah went down, all unsuspecting, and there was a bit of fuss. Then he started sending things, flowers and gloves and scent. All in a fortnight. And they go walks, the girls, two by two, every afternoon; they go to church every Sunday. He's always hovering, making Hannah conspicuous like.... There's some that'd like it, or make a joke of it, but Hannah ain't made that way. Not shy, exactly, but modest. So she wrote and asked would I speak. No offense meant; we all know what boys are."

So far as he could remember Sir Harald had never pestered anyone. John Reeve had; it had taken quite a bit of pestering to get Martha to marry him. Nobody would believe it now, but she'd been a very pretty girl with plenty to choose from and some a notch higher than a tenant farmer. But he'd pestered her and he'd won, and except for the death of the boy and the survivor being a girl theirs had been as happy a marriage as most. But this kind of pestering was different; its aim, if it had an aim, was seduction, not respectable marriage.

"You were right to ... draw my attention, Reeve. I'll see that it stops." The words were correct, but there was a change in his manner, far less friendly; some offense had been taken, though none was intended. Well, it couldn't

he helped, Reeve thought; something had to be said, and
he'd put it as mildly as he could; no details; no attempt to
convey the real fright which had been in Hannah's letter.
'Dad, I'm terrified of him. I'm afraid he'll do something
awful. I think he's mad. He might shoot me, like he did
Jim Bateman." Reeve had not mentioned his slight
predicament over the letter; two letters really—the usual
ordinary weekly dutiful one intended for them both, and
the one inside another, smaller envelope with sealing wax,
and the words "Dad only. Personal." It had begun with
the words: "Please don't say anything to mother, she'd say
it was my fault." He'd read so far, folded the sheet, so
closely written and knowing that he must say something,
forced a smile and said, "It's about your birthday
present." Martha had accepted that, merely saying, in her
rather bleak way, that birthdays, once you were over
forty, were best ignored. He had then gone to the privy
and in the dim light there, read the rest of the letter and
been shocked, and touched by the final appeal: "Please
Dad do something. Miss Drayton is so much annoyed. I
might have to leave."

It was true that the little girl had always looked to
him for support, even for company. Martha was a very
good mother, but for a long time she'd seemed to hold it
against Hannah that she had survived the fever which had
killed Johnny; nothing much that you could fix on,
certainly no unkindness, but a bit sharp, a bit like God in
the Psalm, extreme to mark what was done amiss. And it
was Martha who had insisted upon sending Hannah to
Miss Drayton's. "She is growing so spoiled, being the only
one." Another reason for sending Hannah to school was
the idea that she should become a governess—Martha
had been a governess in Bressford before her marriage.
"But teaching one's own child is very uphill work. And
she's always wanting to be out, with you. Besides, times
change, and French is all the rage nowadays." John Reeve
had not particularly wanted to part with his lively, pretty
little girl, he'd miss her; and he certainly did not want her
to become a governess. But he'd cross that bridge when he
came to it. After all, what was a governess but a kind of
servant, working for wages?

Still, the fact remained that a tenant was a tenant
and it was better to keep on good terms with your
landlord. So he said, almost humbly,

"A word would be enough, sir. If you'd be so good
as to point out that Hannah ain't the playful sort."

"I know what to say," Sir Harald said; telling one of
the brashest lies he had ever told in a singularly honest
lifetime. He sat there, a big, portly man, astride a big gray
horse, confident, sure of himself, lord of all he surveyed,
and inside himself the coward lurked, quivering. He knew
what he *should* say; what any decent man, confronted
with such a situation, *would* say: "Stop pestering a decent
girl; there're enough of the other sort about, surely to
God." But he dreaded being obliged to say anything
which would upset the happy, friendly relationship which
was at the same time so delicate. He was not afraid of his
son, perish the thought! But . . . there was a lot of truth in
that statement, so often ridiculed: This hurts me more
than it hurts you. Time and again, ever since Magnus was
very small, it had been true. Whenever he had spoken, as
he put it, severely, he had been the real sufferer, losing
something that mattered to him—a mixed thing—his
son's approval, his confidence in his own judgement, the
dream image of Magnus which he had erected and
sustained, often in the face of difficulties which nobody
understood and nobody could share. He looked back and
saw that from the time when Magnus had bitten his
nurse's hand, it had been one compromise after another:
like trying to drive a team of wild horses on a thread of
cotton.

The thread broke that evening. They were in the
library; days were drawing in and the lamps were lighted;
in a day or two fires would be needed towards the day's
end, even this evening felt slightly chilly.

"Magnus, I have something to say to you. It
concerns a girl—Hannah Reeve."

"Yes, I suppose you were bound to hear, sooner or
later. I mean to marry her."

For what seemed a long, dreadful moment, Sir
Harald thought he had been taken with a stroke. He
couldn't move his jaw or his tongue, so he was speechless.

tight band around his chest prevented him from
eathing. He could think, though, panic-stricken
oughts about a stroke having rendered him speechless
d helpless; horrified thoughts about what those five
mple words implied. Then he could speak, and gasped
t,

"You—don't—mean—that."

"I do. I made up my mind the minute I clapped eyes
a her. In Wentworth's barn."

"But why? Why? With all the dozens of suitable girls
out."

Had Magnus bothered to explain—and been
onest—he could have explained exactly why. The
termination to have this particular girl had not come
on him at first sight as he had just said; he'd been
tracted to her then, thinking her the prettiest girl there;
t the feeling, whatever it was, had only come upon him
en, singling her out and asking her to dance with him
r a fourth time, he had been rebuffed. She'd said, very
ietly, "No, Mr. Copsey. You must distribute your
vors more evenly. Dance with Alice." She'd taken a step
vay and a little to the side, so that she was half behind a
e buxom wench who was looking at him with an
pectant expression and had one hand already out-
etched. Then when that dance was ended, the girl he
anted had vanished. And desire set in.

He was accustomed to getting what he wanted,
en he wanted it. Bit by bit, over the years, people had
ven in to him, fearing, he knew, the violence of his
mper. He had practically no self-control and no real
telligence; he was the center of his own universe. Even
on had taught him nothing and about the only thing his
rand Tour had taught him was the value of money; he
no paid the piper called the tune. He had cunning, which
mistook for cleverness.

Cunning now provided the answer to his father's
zzled question.

"I fell in love, I suppose." His limited mind had a
ste for, and a memory for, gossip and from the talk of
e old ladies he had learned long ago that his father had
ved his mother and married her despite the fact that she

had no money. So that was a clever thing to say.

"Well, it is to be hoped that you will fall out again. I would be entirely unsuitable. I've nothing against th Reeves, good hard-working honest folk, but give th matter a little thought, Magnus. Think of Copsi."

"What about it?"

"It'll all be yours, one day."

"I know."

"Well, then, can you imagine this Hannah Reeve—worthy girl no doubt. But mistress *here*!"

Such an exercise of imagination was beyon Magnus; but he said something which only afterward struck Sir Harald as being sinister.

"Yes, if I can't get her any other way."

At the time it sounded simply stubborn an headstrong, and all that Sir Harald realized at th moment was that this serious talk, like so many other had ended in deadlock. His one comforting thought wa that Magnus was young, subject to the kind of infatuatio which had struck a good many young men; somethin that would wear off, given time, and enough distractio

Then, within a week, attention must be focuse upon the Reeves again. The wonderful, late-ripenin hard-grained barley was being loaded. John Reeve stoo in the wagon, receiving and stowing the sheaves as fast a the two other men could heave them up. The load ha reached a height where balance and sure-footedness wer needed and he was about to say, "That'll do," when he fel His regular hired man said that he thought a wasp ha stung the horse and made it give the little start which upse its master's balance. He lay prone in the stubble, flat o his back, and as the two men dropped their pitchforks an ran to him, he said,

"All right, boys. No harm done." Apart from th thump as he landed, he felt nothing at all, but when h attempted to scramble up it was as though he had no leg

"Gone a bit numb," he explained. They rubbed h legs, tried to set him upright. "Grab hold of me, maste Heave ho and up we go!" Useless. It was like trying to set sawdust-stuffed doll on its feet. In the end they took th field gate off its hinges and carried him up to the house. A

e entry of the yard he said, "Stop. Don't want to
ighten the Missus. I'll try again now." He tried, they
ied until the sweat poured down.

"All right," he said, "carry me in. It'll wear off. I ain't
roke anything." Broken limbs were painful, made
rating noises, sometimes assumed strange shapes.

By this time Mrs. Reeve had heard the voices and
ame to the kitchen door with her butter stamper in her
and. At the sight of her husband, prone on the gate, she
ave a stifled cry. Before she could even ask, he spoke in
is usual calm, controlled voice.

"It's nothing, Martha. I just had a bit of a fall and
ıy legs went numb. It'll wear off."

She was a practical, sensible woman and saw the
npossibility of getting a heavy man, on a gate, past the
end in the stairs. When John's father was carried out for
he last time, the coffin had had to be practically upended.

"Bring him into the parlor, and lift him onto the
ofa," she said.

The parlor at Reffolds was altogether superior to
he one in the foreman's cottage up at Sheppey Lea which
Magnus had called ugly. It was larger, the ceiling beams
vere whitewashed over, and those in the wall covered
vith pretty, rose-patterned paper. The round table in the
enter was covered by a rose-colored cloth of chenille and
ll the furniture in the room was good. Martha Reeve,
aving been a governess, knew more about such things
han the average farm wife.

The men put the gate on the floor, then lifted their
naster onto the slippery horsehair sofa, placing him in a
rone position again, but he, anxious about Martha, said,

"No, set me up. I'm all right—except for my legs."
hey pulled him into a sitting position which neither was,
or looked very comfortable, since the head of the sofa
urved back. Martha slipped a cushion behind his
houlders. John said,

"Thanks, lads. Now you get back to the carting. I'll
e out as soon as the numbness wears off."

Martha busied herself for a minute or two making
ertain that nothing was broken, and then suggested that
nevitable panacea, a cup of tea. Drinking her own, she

watched him. His hands were very steady; the fall hadn'
even shaken him. He told her how the accident hac
happened and Sam's theory about the horse having beer
stung—he didn't want her to think he'd been clumsy or
careless. The black marble clock on the draped overmantel ticked away and after a quarter of an hour she
ventured to say, "How is it now?" He attempted to move
one leg, then the other, to turn a foot, flex a knee; it was
still as though he had no legs.

"They ain't come round yet," he said. "But they
will."

"Well, just lie still. I'll get back to my butter. Call if
you want anything." She had regular customers in the two
Copsis; people who had no cows; she even salted down a
few tubs of butter for sale to the coal barges and little
fishing smacks. She had known, when she married John
Reeve, that the one skill she had—teaching children—
would find no market in this out-of-the-way place, so she
had set herself to learn something by which the income
from a sixty-acre farm could be augmented. And because
she understood basic principles, and was by nature a
perfectionist, her butter was better than most.

Presently, in the parlor, the stricken man felt the
want of something which Martha couldn't supply—at
least she could, but he wouldn't want her to. She was his
wife, they'd bedded together successfully and she had
borne two children, but in his fond eyes there was still
about her a daintiness, the kind of superiority which had
drawn him to her in the first place. Never, in almost
twenty years, had he allowed her to carry the swill pail to
the pigs for instance. So this was unthinkable.

He shouted and she came quickly.

"Call Jerry," he said, choosing the odd-job man
rather than the permanent help because, if a man must be
shamed in his own eyes and those of another, it was better
to be in the eyes of somebody who, as soon as that barley
was safely in, would be off and away, rather than in the
eyes of somebody with whom he must work every day of
the week hereafter.

And he had made the right choice. Jerry came in
swinging a bottle from one hand.

"I guessed what might be needed."

"A fine state to be in," John Reeve said, when what was needed had been used.

"It happens," the young man said, as lightly as one might speak of a sneeze. "It happened to me once. I was young and silly and shipped out of Radmouth on a ship bound for the Gold Coast. There I had fever. It wasn't my legs I lost, I was lost altogether. Out of my mind. But I had good mates and when I came to myself I was clean and decent. Somebody'd even changed my shirt."

"It's an hour and a half, now," John Reeve said, eying the clock. "I'd hoped to be out by now."

"Well, give it the rest of the day. And a night. And then if it's no better, I'd suggest calling a doctor. Would you like me to take your boots off?"

Boots off, boots on; it made no difference. Dead from the waist down. And just suppose....

No, he couldn't face it! The prospect was too terrible. He shuddered away from it. Terrible things did happen; he was no fool, raking his memory he could recall a number of seemingly slight accidents which had proved fatal, a dog bite in Bressford market place, a nick of a scythe, a toe pricked by a fork.... An endless catalogue of men in their prime being carried off by something that might be expected to kill a child perhaps, but not a grown man who'd never ailed in forty years of life. And who ever heard of a simple fall taking away a man's legs?

Martha looked in and said, "Any better?" and he tried again, desperately, but with no results. She said, "Then I'll bring you your dinner. But before that.... Do you want...?"

"No. Jerry saw to it."

"There was no need to call him, my dear. No need to by shy with me."

She was a woman who had always been rather sparing with endearments since the little boy, her darling, her sweetie, her little love had died, and the *my dear* touched him. Made him all the more determined not to be a nuisance to her, not to disgust her. To please her he ate what she had brought, all neatly set out on a tray, including the mustard which he liked with boiled beef....

"And if you are not better by tomorrow I shall send for Doctor Fordyke," she said, therefore showing how different she was from the average village woman, who would do almost anything rather than resort to the physician. They had their own methods and medicines, handed down from a time when there had been no doctors in country towns. Only when the old methods and the homemade remedies failed was the doctor sent for, and since by that time most cases were beyond his aid, sending for the doctor was almost tantamount to a sentence of death; but Martha was different. As the day wore on this difference in her, hitherto a desirable thing, and something to be cherished, began to bother him and when the time for the end-of-the-working-day meal came round, he refused to drink anything—surely that way he could avoid embarrassing them both until the morning. The men stopped work at sundown and Jerry, without being asked, brought the bottle, and it was used while Martha brought down a proper pillow, a blanket and a quilt, for the evenings were chilly now, even after a fine sunny day.

After that she lighted the lamp and sat down with her knitting—a bad choice of occupation, since she was knitting the warm woolen socks which he wore in winter. Every click of the needles asked the same question: *Will he ever need them?*

She had not been in love with him when, at last, she married him. She liked him, a very different thing. There was a number of men whom she had liked and did like, but the only one she had ever loved in the high romantic fashion was young Doctor Fordyke who had had no eyes for her. Still, she had not lacked suitors, some, like the new apothecary at Wyck who needed a wife who could at least read, and the curate at Bressford, who, when he obtained the hoped-for living, would need a wife who was socially adept yet capable of keeping house on a shoestring. But she had chosen John Reeve, tenant farmer, barely literate, because, if you couldn't have somebody you adored, it was as well to have somebody who adored you. And John's adoration was unmistakable.

Years of living together had made her more appreciative of his quality; kindness itself, indulgent, understanding, admiring. Other men of his kind would go to market from time to time, and if what they had to sell made a good price, drink to celebrate; if a sale disappointed them they'd drink to drown their woe; John Reeve went to market and on a good day, or a bad one, came home sober, with some offering, a book, a piece of sheet music, a bottle of scent. She realized that since the little boy's death, which must have hit him just as hard as it did her, she'd changed; grown, if not exactly old overnight, harder and colder, gloomy, with a grudge against life which was so bitterly unfair. Other children had scarlet fever, and less devotedly, less intelligently nursed, survived. Hannah had survived. . . . And even the change which the loss had brought about, John had faced with kindness and tolerance and good humor.

So, now was the time for her to do something for him!

The marble clock—a wedding present from the family where she had been governess—struck nine which was bedtime for farm people who must be up early in the morning. On the last stroke she pushed her knitting needles into the ball of gray wool and said, in the brisk, businesslike way which some people called dour, and some sour,

"Look, John. Anything Jerry Flordon can do, I can do; and make no bones about it."

"I hate it, I loathe it," he said miserably.

Nine o'clock and he'd been carried in and left there, a helpless hunk, shortly after eleven. Ten hours. And no improvement. God! God! How could he bear it? How could she? And what of the farm?

◄━━━►◄━━━►◄━━━►◄━━━►◄━━━►

Sir Harald heard, rather late than evening, that Reeve had met with an accident and first thing in the morning turned his horse's head towards Reffolds. It had never been his favorite place and now, what with what Reeve had said, and Magnus had said, he wished it at the bottom of the sea. But it was his duty to call and inquire;

offer help; most of all suggest a visit from the doctor, a step which so many of them were reluctant to take. He was quite prepared to ride into Bressford himself and make the request. He was also prepared, despite his distaste, now, for the very name of Reeve, to dismount, visit the victim, assess the damage for himself and say a few encouraging words.

He had no chance; as he approached the house the front door opened and Mrs. Reeve stepped out. There was another subtle difference between Reffolds and most of the other small farms where it took two strong men to force open a front door which had been closed since the last funeral, wedding, or christening.

Whatever looks she had once had had faded, in the literal sense of the word; hair, once fair, quite gray, face the color of parchment, even her lips were pale as though constant compression had rendered them bloodless. Her figure was spare and very upright, and she was more neatly dressed than farm wives usually were so early in the morning: the traditional print work dress, gray sprigged with white, very clean very well-fitting. Little gold studs glinted in her ears.

She was civil enough, making a slight curtsy, unlike the usual bob, and saying, "Good morning, sir." But there was no sycophancy—a thing to which he had become so accustomed that he never noticed its presence, only its absence; and there was none of the everything-will-be-all-right-now-that-you-have-come, to which he was also accustomed.

"I was extremely sorry to hear about your husband. What exactly happened?"

"He fell from the top of a half-loaded wagon."

"Anything broken?"

"Not so far as I can ascertain. His legs have gone numb."

"I'd suggest that you send for the doctor."

"I have already done so."

"I see. Well, Mrs. Reeve, do you think your husband would care to see me?"

"I am sorry. It would not be convenient just now."

It would be very inconvenient, for in the front parlor

John and Jerry Flordon were having their first struggle with the bedpan.

He knew her, of course—he knew all his tenants—but not well; she was not what he called one of his cronies, nor had Reffolds ever been what he called one of his ports of call. He knew that the loss of her son had turned her sour and unfriendly, but this morning a feeling of vicarious guilt made him see a personal hostility in her manner, easily attributable to his son's pestering of her daughter. Was this a fit time to mention it? He decided that it was, since the poor woman, anxiously awaiting the doctor's arrival, must have enough on her mind. With awkward sincerity, he said,

"And I'm sorry about my son's behavior. Believe me, it had neither my knowledge nor my approval." He added, knowing the weakness of his position, "It won't happen again."

He saw the controlled composure of her face break up into an expression of surprise. Her lips parted slightly and her eyes widened. Rather fine eyes—if you cared for dark ones—deep brown, very large and with exceptionally clear whites, exceptionally long, curved lashes.

It occurred to him, just too late, that he had been mistaken. Reeve hadn't told her about the pestering. And indeed what man would confide in a woman whose ramrod figure and shuttered face showed such an utter lack of sympathy with any kind of human frailty?

"I am sorry, Sir Harald. I have no idea what you are talking about."

"No matter! No matter! Nothing to bother your head about. Well, I very much hope that the doctor can do something and that your husband will soon be on his feet again. Let me know if there's anything I can do—or anything you need."

"Thank you," she said. "That is very kind."

He turned his horse and trotted briskly away.

Young Doctor Fordyke—the name still clung to him, though he had ceased to be young a long time ago—knew all about bones. He had been one of those fortunate medical students who could afford to buy a skeleton, skillfully wired together. Known as Old Adam, the dry, rattling framework of what had once been a man had shared his sitting room all through his student days. Less fortunate fellows had often dropped in to compare Old Adam with diagrams in their medical books.

A prolonged examination of this stricken man convinced him that no bone was injured; he had not fallen on his head and caused an injury to the brain which might explain his present condition. He'd never lost consciousness or suffered any symptom of concussion. The only conclusion—and it was a sad one—was that he had injured his spinal cord, that still somewhat mysterious mass of nerves and blood vessels which, in a living man, ran through the hollows of the vertebrae. In that case there was nothing to be done, except to hope that the injury would be self-healing.

In the cheerful, noncommittal manner cultivated by all the best doctors, he said, "You may have to stay in a bed for a while. Quite possibly the fall bruised a bone, which is worse than bruising flesh. On the other hand recovery may be as sudden as the disability was. We must hope for the best." He thought rather miserably that a broken bone could have been set, a gangrenous toe cut away, a hemorrhage staunched, a pain mitigrated, but here was nothing to be done, except wait upon time. And although he had spoken of a while in bed, making it sound a fairly light sentence, he felt that Mrs. Reeve should be prepared.

He'd known her for a long time, ever since she was Miss Allsop, governess to the Wheeler children in Bressford. Mrs. Wheeler had been completely useless, a spoiled hysterical woman, so when one of the children fell ill, as they did fairly often, having been born in India and therefore unduly subject to what the English winter could inflict, it had been the governess who had acted as nurse. Admirable, competent, and as pretty as a picture, silver gilt hair and beautiful eyes and an apple-blossom complexion. He'd found her very attractive, but he was in no position to marry; his father had treated him very well, very generously during his student days and was now exacting his pound of flesh in servitude, ill-paid, but at the end of it a good practice. Judging by the old man's state of health, it would be some years before his son was in a position to marry, and no man with any sense of honor would make advances which might take ten years to come to anything; nor would he compromise a young lady by making advances of the other kind. So the one faint glimmer of romance which had flickered over his mundane life had come to nothing. She'd married, had children, sent for him when the scarlet fever struck, and gone quite distraught when the boy died. From that time until this morning he had not seen her and was bound to admit that he could have passed her in the street without recognition. A nasty reflection upon what just living could do to people.

"I must confess, Mrs. Reeve," he said, standing by the front door, just out of earshot of the parlor, "I can neither explain nor alleviate your husband's condition. I only wish that I could. He may make a spontaneous recovery—the first sign will be pins and needles in his legs; or he may—and I think I should warn you—be permanently disabled."

"I see," she said, seeing the grim prospect confronting her; seeing also the man with the paunch, the scanty fringe of sandy hair who had once represented all beauty, all desire, stalking through her waking thoughts and through her dreams.

"Keep him cheerful, as far as possible. And his weight down." She looked so slight, so brittle, and the man on the makeshift sofa bed was heavy and might, without exercise, grow heavier. "I'll look in from time to time, and of course, if you need me, send."

"Thank you."

She saw him off and went back into the parlor, mustered the smile which, seldom used, had the quality of all rare things, and said,

"Well, it looks as though you will be bedridden for a day or two, and you might as well be comfortable. I'll get the boys to bring Hannah's bed down."

She was set on her course, resolute cheerfulness; and he was set on his, gloom and suspicion.

"What else did he say, out there?"

"I've just told you, a few days in bed. And when the feeling comes back it may be like pins and needles."

"Well, let's hope to God it'll be tomorrow. I can't lay about here, useless. There's that barley to get to the maltings. There's the ploughing. There's a hundred things. . . ."

"Worry won't help. You just take things quietly for a few days."

"You said a day or two, now you say a few days. Which do you mean?"

In less than twenty-four hours their roles had been completely reversed; he'd always been the cheerful one, optimistic to a point which she had thought silly, getting over even Johnny's death. Now she must at least feign hope.

But that evening, when the lamp was lit and all was settled and she went to the rosewood chest of drawers in which she kept all her knitting and sewing materials, she did not bring out the winter socks, choosing instead a piece of needlework, a red flannel petticoat for Hannah, measured and cut out during the summer holidays but not yet stitched upon, since it would be a Christmas present.

Conversation between them had always been easy enough, though limited in scope, confined to trivialities. He'd never cared for books and was practically incapable of entertaining an abstract thought. He liked to tell her what he had done during the day, what he planned for days ahead. Now, poor man, he'd had an empty day, and would have perhaps an empty one tomorrow. It was almost with relief that she found a topic.

"Sir Harald called this morning. It was while Jerry Flordon and you. . . . So I did not ask him in. But he said a very peculiar thing to me. Can you think of any reason why *he* should apologize to *me* for his son's behavior?"

"Did he?"

"Yes. I remember his words exactly. He said, 'And I'm sorry about my son's behavior. Believe me, it had neither my knowledge nor my approval.' And when I said I didn't know what he was talking about, he said, 'No matter,' and rode off."

"Well, it was something I tried to keep from you. I didn't want you fretting. Nothing much; it was just that Mr. Magnus has been pestering Hannah a bit."

"Pestering Hannah! How did you know?"

"Hannah said so in that letter—the enclosure, you'd call it."

Had he told her about it earlier, she'd have rapped out a few remarks criticizing even the fact that Hannah had written to her father rather than to her. She'd have said things like going behind her back, being in a conspiracy against her. And she would most certainly have blamed Hannah, saying that men didn't pester girls without some encouragement. As it was she thought these things without saying them, and simply asked,

"And where on earth did he get a chance to pester her?"

"It started when she was staying with Alice Wentworth. They had a Horkey and he and some friends looked in to join the fun."

Martha thought: Oh yes, and Hannah made eyes at him! And for that you are partly to blame! For it was a fact, she'd noticed it with her own school-fellows and with her pupils; the girls whose fathers spoiled them were always the ones who grew up thinking that they'd only to look at a man to get whatever they wanted; in fact it would be safe to say that all flirts cut their teeth on their own fathers.

Such things could not be said to a poor helpless man.

"People do get a bit wild at Horkeys, especially when there's barn dancing. But I should have thought Mrs. Wentworth could have been trusted to see that everybody behaved themselves."

"Our girl behaved herself. She went back in the house. But that weren't the end."

"What happened next?"

"He went to the school, saying he was her cousin. And he's been sending presents. Hannah said Miss Drayton was proper upset and might ask her to leave."

"That *would* be a disgrace." All the more so because Miss Drayton was a bit of a snob and hadn't wanted to have Hannah in the first place. Daughter of a small tenant farmer. Martha knew that it was only her own superior speech and manner that had prevailed over prejudice. And now of course Miss Drayton would be saying, "What could you expect?"

"So I reckoned. The day I got the letter, I spoke to Sir Harald and he said he'd put a stop to it."

"He said the same thing to me. But it's a known fact that he has no more control over his son than he has over the moon."

An idea occurred to her. The disgrace of expulsion could be forestalled. The perfect excuse lay there on the bed. Martha thought rapidly as she laid the two edges of the second long seam together ready for tacking. She'd tacked the first as they talked, her fingers moving automatically. Now, as she tacked the second seam, she thought: He would not object; he didn't want her to go to school in the first place, and thanks to Magnus Copsey's behavior, he would see nothing ominous in Hannah's withdrawal. The girl was fifteen and a half, old enough to be helpful. Martha had planned on her staying at school until the end of next summer term, but no matter; she could bring her books.... And when she was sixteen and a half—about this time next year—she'd be old enough for her first post as governess.

Martha desperately wanted Hannah to become a governess in, naturally, a *nice* family. She'd held two posts herself, the first a bad one, where she had been very unhappy and lonely, poised between the family and the servants and apparently scorned by both. But she had been very happy with the Wheelers, occupying a position second only to that of Mrs. Wheeler herself, and indeed, in any crisis, superceding her mistress.

At the end of a silence which John Reeve feared might end in a tirade, she said quietly,

"Well, I have been thinking the thing over and I think Hannah would be better at home. *We*,"—that was a cunning touch—"could at least see that she wasn't pestered."

"She did say she was scared," he agreed.

Martha folded her work.

"I'll write to Miss Drayton now and send Jerry in with the trap in the morning. He can bring her home."

It did occur to her, as she moved the lamp and opened the flap of her writing desk, and began to turn over in her mind the dignified phrases which were to be set down in her exquisite handwriting, that what with one thing and another, she seemed to be becoming rather too greatly dependent on Jerry Flordon, that completely unreliable fellow. But the only alternative was Sam Archer, who, to put it mildly, was dead stupid and clumsy as well. Fairly well-meaning, fairly hard-working, but more like a cart horse than a human being. Yesterday morning, had she chosen him to go and call the doctor it would have taken her ten minutes to explain where to go, what to say. She could excuse his stupidity—it was the result of in-breeding, cousin marrying cousin and an occasional bit of incest over a long spell of time. And sometimes, when John, comforting himself for the loss of his son, said that he hoped Hannah would marry one of her Thetford cousins, Martha had felt otherwise, visualizing grandchildren, defective in some way, nothing like Sam Archer, of course, but slightly deaf, short-sighted, dim-witted.

Miss Drayton, knowing nothing more than that Hannah's father had had an accident and that she was needed at home, broke the news as gently as she could, and organized the swift packing and the removal. Hannah, at last seated by Jerry Flordon in the trap and headed for home, felt that she had just emerged from a whirlwind.

"Now," she said, "tell me exactly what happened?" Ever since Miss Drayton had called her from the French class, used the word accident and said that Hannah was needed at home, a terrible fear had consumed her. She'd done wrong in writing to her father; he'd gone and done something rash and Mr. Magnus had hurt him in some way.

"He was on top of the wagon, loading, Sam and I were pitching to him. And he fell. He didn't break anything, but he's lost the use of his legs. Numb and useless from the waist down."

"Has the doctor been?"

"Yes. Yesterday morning. Nothing to be done, he said, except wait and see what time could do."

She began to cry. At first, shocked and feeling half-guilty, she'd been unable to cry.

"I thought you'd better *know*," Jerry said, some apology in his voice. "I mean, if you'd just walked in. . . ."

"Oh, yes. At least I am now—prepared." She went on crying and mopping her eyes with a silly little handkerchief, about seven inches square, lace-edged.

"He's in no danger. No pain. And there's always hope."

He'd broken the news too abruptly, and now there was something wrong with his last words, for she said, between two gulps,

"But *you* don't think—much of a hope. Do you?"

"I didn't say that. Here, take this. It's clean." He handed her a huge handkerchief, silk, gaily colored, the kind of handkerchief favored by snuff-taking gentlemen because linen stained so easily. "Mop up and try to stop crying. You'll do him no good if you go in looking like a funeral, will you?"

"No," she snuffled into the fresh handkerchief, "there is that to think of. . . . How is he, apart from his legs?"

"Very cast down. And who wouldn't be? But the sight of you'll cheer him up. That is if you can muster a smile."

"I'll try."

His practical, almost offhand manner was just right, Hannah realized; no pity, which would have made her cry harder; no evasion, which would have made her suspicious of the worst. The fact was—even Mother admitted it—whatever Jerry Flordon did, he did well. Mother was not a wholehearted admirer of the man; she would have regarded the silk handkerchief as an affectation. Mother liked things to fit and Jerry fitted nowhere. (Actually Martha's faint—very faint—resentment of the hireling had a deep, secret root; his manner, his speech, all underlined her failure to make her husband less rustic. She'd tried, in the early days, and given up in the face of his placid, amiable impenetrability whereas Jerry Flordon, after two fishing seasons spent in the company of an ex-Naval officer, a disgraced man, who had preferred life at sea, even on a humble trawler to life on land, had acquired all that Martha had failed to instill by example, by gentle admonition.)

Mopping and blowing, regaining control, Hannah said,

"I am so glad you were there to help."

"Yes, it was lucky. I had a few days to spare and your father had this late barley. But I'm due at Yarmouth the day after tomorrow."

"Must you go?"

"I gave my word." No more to be said, then, except as the house came into sight,

"Do I look all right now?"

"A bit pale. Give your cheeks a rub." She was a pretty little thing, but with a prettiness that depended largely on color, on contrast.

"Better?" Hannah asked, having knuckled her cheeks.

"Yes. It'll do him good to see you."

At the kitchen door he jumped down and handed her to the step in exactly the right way, his lean brown hand conveying a kind of confidence.

"I hope everything will be all right," he said. And Hannah said, "Thank you, Jerry. Thank you for everything."

John Reeve was pleased to see his daughter and took a stance, far from sincere.

"It's nothing much, dearie. I just stunned my legs a bit. Even the doctor said the use could come back as sudden as it left."

As though to mock him the black marble clock struck. Every time it did so it sent a pang to his heart—another hour gone and here I lie helpless! The damned clock marked the receding tide of hope.

Dinner was roast chicken; it always was when Hannah came back from school, roast chicken never being served there as the portions were too difficult to assign fairly. It looked and smelled delicious but nobody ate much. John was thinking about the pan—the less intake the less output. Jerry Flordon who managed so well would be gone the day after tomorrow, and nothing, nobody, not even Martha could make Sam Archer handy. Willing—but you might as well depend upon an ape. Martha and Hannah were concentrating upon seeming cheerful in a markedly uncheerful situation. Just two days of enforced inactivity, and of worry, had already changed the hearty, always healthy and fundamentally carefree man.

Mother had changed, too, Hannah reflected. Curious! Never at any time that she could remember had Hannah known Mother other than glum, prone to take a gloomy view, ready with a sharp word, the rebuke, the fault-finding. A *good* mother, indisputably, but not fond. When Hannah first heard Mrs. Wentworth address Alice as *darling,* she'd been astounded and envious. One would have expected Mother to be, in this crisis, resentful and sour, acting as though life—and Father, its instrument— had done something else to spite her. The reverse was true. Mother was still brisk, but in a far nicer way.

"I'll deal with the dishes," she said. "You two have a game of checkers."

It was Father who was bitter now,

"Yes. I could just about manage a game of checkers."

The relentless clock struck two. His hand poised for the next move, John Reeve reckoned the hours of his infirmity and Hannah thought of the girls dressing and mustering for the daily walk. And it was Miss Drayton's day.

❬━━❭❬━━❭❬━━❭❬━━❭❬━━❭

Miss Drayton believed in fresh air and exercise, and in taking turns, so far as possible, with mere routine.

"We will go along Priory Lane, across the Haberden and back by Ivy Street," she said, and all the girls, lined up, two by two, gave inaudible groans. Quite the dreariest walk of all; no shops, hardly any people.

The line of girls had harldy turned into Priory Lane before a horseman passed them, wheeled around, rode back, bending low and scrutinizing each face. Miss Drayton recognized him—young Mr. Copsey, who when the term was only two days old, had come to the school pretending to be Hannah Reeve's cousin and been admitted to the parlor.

Miss Drayton included vigilance among her duties and on such occasions the parlor door was left ajar and a responsible person sat in the anteroom; that evening it had been Miss Drayton herself. Hannah had entered the room, the young man had spoken and Hannah had run out again, all in less than a minute. From the parlor came the sound of curses and a crash, then the visitor, his face a mask of fury, had pushed past Miss Drayton, stately in the doorway, and out of the house. On the parlor floor lay Miss Drayton's much-cherished Dresden rose bowl, irretrievably smashed.

A shock. An even greater one to learn that the caller was Mr. Magnus Copsey, the son of Sir Harald for whom Miss Drayton had a great respect—both were active in good causes. With some girls Miss Drayton would have doubted the story, but Hannah had always been regarded as honest, if high-spirited, and there was Alice Wentworth to confirm the identification with the story of the Harvest Horkey. Plainly Hannah had behaved impeccably. Then gifts had begun to arrive, and the pestering had continued. Now here he was, glaring at the girls and coming towards Miss Drayton as she walked at the rear, seeing that the younger girls did not lag. He turned his horse so that Miss Drayton was pinned between it and the railings. She remembered how Hannah had said, "I am terrified of him." She was apprehensive herself, but she kept her head.

"Sybil, take charge. Girls, keep moving."

Magnus asked in the most arrogant way, "Where's Miss Reeve?"

"She is no longer at the school."

"I said *where*?"

Copsi—but that was where this dreadful young man lived. God must forgive a lie.

"She has taken a post."

"Where? Can't you answer a plain question, you old bitch?"

He really looked as though he might strike her with his crop or make the horse crush her against the railings. She thought: Not London! Such people are familiar with London.

"Bristol." Bristol. The Avon. "Avonmouth Terrace."

"God damn you!" Flogging the horse he galloped away. Miss Drayton straightened her hat, drew some steadying breaths and hurried to join the girls. How terrible for poor Sir Harald!

***

At Reffolds Magnus had not been mentioned and Hannah dreaded the moment when he must be. She imagined the afternoon walk and his lurking, saying, "Where's Hannah Reeve?" Somebody would say that she had gone home. Then he'd come. And even this different Mother would say that Hannah must have encouraged him in *some* way. There'd be no Alice to support her. True, Father could say that she had written and complained. But was he in a state to be bothered with such things? Was Mother? Oh God, with all the thousands of girls there are in the world, why must this happen to me?

In the morning there was a letter for Martha. Recognizing Miss Drayton's writing, Hannah had a second of nausea.

"Finish the frying. Remember he likes his eggs turned over. He is being ridiculous about the needs of Nature and imagines that by starving himself...."

She opened the letter neatly and made a sound, not quite a laugh, almost a bark.

"Well done, Miss Drayton! You may read it."

Miss Drayton was not a waster of words. She said she was sorry about the accident and hoped that there would be a swift recovery. Then, "I do not know whether Hannah has confided in you concerning Mr. Magnus

Copsey. She appears to have behaved discreetly. This afternoon he accosted me and demanded to know where she was. I thought it wise to mislead him and gave an invented address in Bristol. Yours sincerely, Agatha Drayton."

"It was not my fault," Hannah said, falling back into the defensive attitude habitual with her when dealing with Mother. "I never even *looked* at him, after that first time."

"I know." How? How much? "Don't fret. It'll wear off. He's just a spoiled child, all agog for the thing out of reach." It was a succinct, shrewd assessment of the situation, but Miss Allsop had had experience with children, spoilt and otherwise.

Sir Harald also hoped that Magnus's infatuation would wear off, but had experience of the deadly obstinacy the boy could display when it came to a matter of attaining his own ends. He did not reopen the subject with Magnus but, feeling the need to talk it over, went across to Bertie's room to tell her the shocking thing that Magnus had said. He expected her to be caustic rather than sympathetic; she was neither, she was shocking too.

"Would it be such a bad thing, Harry?" It was an astounding choice but it sent her nephew up a notch or two in her estimation. She would have judged him to be incapable of anything but self-love. "The Reeves are a decent, *old* family. The girl has some education. It could be the making of him."

"Bertie! You amaze me. You remember our mother. My Juliet.... Can you seriously consider this Hannah Reeve, a small tenant's daughter bearing *their* title? I'm no snob, thank God, but...."

"A respecter of rank."

"Very well. Who isn't? I *know* you consort with cattle merchants, auctioneers, attorneys. All very democratic! But you'd never dream of *marrying* one."

(I would! If he hadn't been married, with two children when I first saw him.)

Bertie shrugged. "I'm not well versed in the matter of love, but if one believes what one reads, it can work marvels. There's another aspect, too. He might have landed you with somebody a damned sight worse."

"I know that! Quite beside the point. This is bad enough. Bertie, think of our lineage. I cannot allow my only son, heir to Copsi, to marry a farm girl."

"Can you stop him?"

"Damn it all, Bertie! You know I can't. That hoary old threat—cut off without a shilling. I can't even use that. He's bound to inherit."

Miserably he accepted some brandy. Excellent brandy. He sometimes wondered whether she didn't number a smuggler or two among her heterogeneous acquaintances. He wouldn't put it past her. The spirit loosened something in him and presently he said,

"There's another thing I don't like about all this. The girl seems not to welcome Magnus's attentions. She complained to her father."

"She probably doubted his intentions. She sounds sensible."

"And that isn't all. When he said he'd marry her, he said *if he couldn't get her any other way.*"

"Not very loverlike! But you can't buy her for him for Christmas, can you?"

"Bertie, I wish to God I could. Not as a wife, of course."

"You shock me!"

"I shock myself. But facts must be faced. A jolly good roll in the hay and the whole thing would be over and done with." What a coarse thing to say to a woman! Somehow with Bertie one tended to forget.

"She doesn't sound the hay-rolling kind. Have you ever seen her?"

"Not recently. She used to follow her father round. Leggy little thing with a mane of hair—straw-colored. Great eyes.... Reeve, by the way, has had an accident." He told her about it and Bertie said,

"Poor chap! I hope not another Charlie Felton case. Oh, of course it was before your time. I always think of you as having been here forever. Charlie Felton took a toss and his horse rolled on him. He never walked again. His people dragged him around London, and to Bath.

Useless. In the end he shot himself and I don't blame him."

Sir Harald looked at his sister and wondered whether this Charlie Felton had been her secret tragedy. Before his time meant a time when Bertie was young, beautiful and much sought after.

Bertie poured more brandy and presently Sir Harald felt able to say,

"Well, one must hope for the best, I suppose...."

Bertie felt able to say, in her curious, offhand manner,

"Harry, to change the subject completely—I have decided to build myself a house up at Sheppey Lea."

She'd sensed that he would take this decision badly and she understood why. She shared his passion for the ancestral home, scorned herself for procrastination. It seemed idiotic, having achieved personal and economic freedom, to be tied to a place; to mind about leaving the cedar, said to have been brought as a sapling from Lebanon by a Crusader; the lake, around which in Spring thousands of daffodils bloomed; the maze, dark and mysterious; this huge room with its vaulted ceiling. But they were not hers, could never be hers. And the time had come to move on. And now seemed the time to tell Harry, when, fussed about other things, he would not fuss. But he did. He said,

"What on earth for? Because of what I said about Magnus getting married? Forget it. It may not happen—for years. And even when it does, *whoever* he marries—I'm good for years. And even when.... Well we must all go, of course. Even then.... It's your home, Bertie. Nobody would want this." He gave a disparaging glance about the cluttered yet somehow ordered room. "If you need more space there are empty rooms on either side. I've told you that before."

She turned flippant. "Harry, please, allow me every little woman's little dream—a home of her own. I don't want to be one of the old ladies. And there's a practical side to it too. The day will come when I shan't feel like getting up at dawn and riding six miles in order to oversee things."

Rational, sensible, but awful. Everything seemed to be breaking up under his feet.

"Copsi won't seem the same."

"Nothing is ever the same, Harry."

"I know. What beats me is that all change seems to be for the worse."

In the morning Magnus said, "I'm going to Bristol for a few days."

Sir Harald thought: Good! Change of scene often had a therapeutic effect. The choice of destination rather puzzled him, but for once Magnus condescended to explain.

"On the Grand Tour we met a man. His father has something to do with ships. He said Bristol was a fine place and he said visit him any time."

"Splendid! If you feel so inclined, invite him back. The birds have done well this year. There'll be some good shooting."

The low cunning which served Magnus Copsey in the place of intelligence smirked to itself. Bring *him* back. Bring *her* back! She'd been coy or shy or scornful, but a few days in a menial job, a post as that old hag had said, would have brought her to her senses. She might even be glad to see him. She would be glad to see him. And then the fun would start!

Bristol had grown very rich and bloated on the slave trade, only recently abolished, and like all fast-growing things had done a bit of sprawling; but there actually was an Avonmouth Terrace, the address that had slipped into Miss Drayton's mind in a moment of controlled panic. At the hotel somebody directed Magnus to it, saying that it was only a few steps away, just round the corner by the barber's shop.

The terrace consisted of eight tall, stucco-fronted houses with basements; the kind of places where people were likely to be employed. The one at the end employed a manservant, very precise and superior. Magnus's uninventive mind could produce only one question—the one which mattered to him.

"Is Miss Hannah Reeve working here?"

"Not to my knowledge, sir." Apparently, from his clothes, his voice, a gentleman; and up to no good! one of that vaguely defined body known as *followers,* which the best households did not allow.

"Oh. You're sure?"

The man servant was at heart a red-hot Radical and had been very active in the Bristol riots during the altercation about the Reform Bill. He was a good servant because alongside his feeling that Jack was as good as his master, ran the belief that Jack should earn his wage. But there was no reason why, simply because he served, a young gentleman who'd never done a day's work in his life should question his word, saying: You're sure? in that extremely offensive way.

"I am sure. We have had no changes of staff here during the last six years. But if you doubt my word, sir, perhaps you would care to ask Mrs. Parkinson." And she'd give you the right-about-turn, my lad.

"No," Magnus said, seeing in an interview with Mrs. Parkinson, whoever she was, merely a waste of time.

All right! the man servant thought with delight, driving the knife home,

"If I may suggest, sir, if you are enquiring about an *employed* person, the area door is the proper place."

One down and seven to go.

Mostly pert parlormaids tossing their streamers and ogling.

"Oh no, sir. No Hannah Reeve here; I'm sorry."

Once another manservant, old and shuffling, so bent over that he looked as though he had lost sixpence.

"No. We don't have no wimmin here. The Colonel don't like 'em. No more do I."

Once a very sprightly young woman, dressed for the street.

"I don't know," she said, "we're always chopping and changing. What was the name, again? Hannah Reeve. I'll soon find out." She opened a door to the rear of the hall and shouted. Her voice resounded as though from a cave, but all Magnus heard was Hannah Reeve; echoing, echoing.

The young woman came back and said, "No I'm sorry. Our new maid—she came yesterday—is Anna Green—and she's cook's niece."

Seven down and one to go.

At what was number eight—and would have been had the houses been properly numbered—was a dead house. He had not, of course, taken the advice about going down to the area doors; after all he was Magnus Copsey of Copsi. But at this last house, having heard the jerked bell jangle, and no answer, he was seriously considering demeaning himself and going down the basement stairs when the door at last opened, about six inches, and held in place by a stout chain. A voice, female, slightly shaky, said,

"What do you want?"

Behind the six-inch aperture there was darkness.

Once more the question: Is Miss Hannah Reeve working here?

"Working here? Nobody works here, now. I cannot afford...."

She was one of those old people to whom age had brought fear of penury; she was rich, even by Bristol standards, but she had convinced herself that she was poor and when potatoes went up a farthing a pound she would do without. The twin fears of her life were burglars and rising prices; to defeat the former she kept all her valuables in the vault of her bank; about the latter she could do little except do her own shopping, shuffling her way to cheap shops in poorer areas. For this reason she was of more use to Magnus in his predicament than anyone else in the terrace.

"There's another Avonmouth Terrace. Very poor place. It's a disgrace that our name should be used like that. We may be poor, but we've always been respectable."

"Where is this place?"

She knew, and was willing to tell, but her directions were enormously complicated and intelligible only to one who already knew the way. She said such things as, "not the corner where there *is* a crossing sweeper, the next one where there *isn't*." And, "There's a short cut through the yard of the King's Head." Magnus soon grew impatient with her, and without a word of thanks turned and left her still talking. Very peculiar behavior, she thought, and a terrible fear assailed her. It had been known for a gang of housebreakers to send somebody to spy out the land. What better cover than a handsome, well-dressed, well-spoken young man inquiring after a nonexistent servant? Well, she had emphasized her poverty. But perhaps he didn't believe her. She'd better make sure of the shutters. Lighted only by the rush-dip which she found cheaper than lamps or candles, she made her way from darkened room to darkened room, before retreating to the basement where the windows were barred, to keep followers out and wanton maids in. She felt safer there.

Magnus found his way back to the busy street in which his hotel stood, and there hired a hackney cab.

"I want to go to Avonmouth Terrace."

Suits me, the driver thought; five minutes walk away, just round the corner by the barber's shop and up a slight rise. But that was not the kind of thing you said to silly young toffs. You said, "Right away, sir. Thank you, sir." Hopes of such an easy journey were quelled when the young toff said, "And I don't mean this one. I mean the other one." Before he'd lost all hope of following the old woman's directions, he had listened and could now add, "It's near some sort of cheap market."

"I know it, sir." The driver's wife did her shopping there, and a very good market it was. He resented the word *cheap*.

This Avonmouth Terrace might be, in the opinion of one eccentric old woman, a poor place, but it was in fact a place that figured largely in the daydreams of many good citizens and their wives. It was a row of twelve very narrow houses, squashed into small space, but with a patch of front garden and a longer strip at the back where laundry could be dried and where children could play. With a bit of a kind of awning between the back door and the privy and the coalhouse, such houses were highly desirable and as a rule obtainable only by those with steady incomes; people who worked for the railroad, or the Post Office.

Avon was in Bristol an almost magic word, freely used. It did not matter to the speculative builder that the only view of the river could be enjoyed by somebody sitting astride the roof and that in fact the only view, in the ordinary way, was the blank wall of a warehouse.

Magnus began to adjust himself. There had always been things about which he was quite sure, and other things which when tested, proved uncertain. He knew now that he was liable to lose his temper, but when he was angered everything went a bit misty and afterwards any reference to what he had done, any scolding, even any punishment had seemed unreal.

He struggled with the unreality; yes, he had been angry at not finding the girl amongst the other girls. So perhaps he hadn't listened very well. A post, the old hag had said; or had she said looking for a post? This was the kind of house in which relatives of the Reeves might live.

"Wait," he ordered.

He changed his question; nobody in such tiny houses would employ a servant. "Is Miss Hannah Reeve staying here?" No. No, I'm sorry. No, never heard of her. No. One well-meaning woman, hearing the toff's voice, seeing the broadcloth and the cab, volunteered the information that there was another Avonmouth Terrace. Over on the other side.

"I know. I've been there."

Because of the warehouse dusk fell early in this humble street and by the time Magnus had asked his question nine times doors opened upon lighted interiors and the scent of food being prepared—onions, herring—reminded him that he had had no lunch. He'd spent the night and breakfasted well, at a coaching house along the road, driven hard, reached Bristol, and skipping a meal, set out on his hunt. Now hunger added itself to frustration. The pretty dream he'd had, snatching Hannah from servitude, taking her back to his hotel, ordering a slap-up dinner, with wine—always a help to seduction—began to fade. After the twelfth rebuttal he went back to the hackney carriage in a very bad mood.

"That old bitch foxed me," he said, not caring whether the driver understood or not.

"You looking for somebody, sir?" An unnecessary

question, for the answer was obvious. For what other
reason should a young toff go to twelve doors making the
same inquiry? The houses were so narrow that the
question at number twelve was practically as audible as it
had been at number one.

"Yes." The low cunning came into action; just as he
was about to say "my sister" and concoct some tale about
her running away, he realized that his name was Copsey
and he'd been inquiring about Hannah Reeve. So without
denying his identity he could not claim her as sister. So,
what to say? His uninventive mind gave only one answer.
The truth. Why not?

"It's a girl from our village. She ran away.... And
I'm *sure* the old hag said Avonmouth." His distress,
though selfish, was genuine enough; so was his bewilderment. He was at his wits' end. But it was not sympathy
which provoked the driver's offer; it was a desire to make
money from what was plainly a country bumpkin dressed
up as a young toff.

"It's a common enough name around here, sir."

"What? Hannah Reeve?"

"No. Avonmouth... Crescent, Street, Avenue. I
could name you half a dozen. More, if you take in the big
separate houses. Tell you what, sir. Why don't you hire
me for the day tomorrow? Say a quid for the round trip."

"All right."

"With a bait for me and the nag." Press the
advantage home, and hold another suggestion in
reserve....

The horse had a good day next day, no hurrying,
nobody wanting to get from here to there in the shortest
possible time; just a leisurely amble about the city, with
frequent halts, and a good dinner of oats.

At the end of a day's abortive hunt—and the cab
driver was very ingenious, even hinting that the word
might be *haven,* he tested the ground.

"What sort of girl was she, this Hannah Reeve, sir?"

"Pretty. Very pretty."

"Well, sir, meaning no disrespect but whoever told
you the address must have got it wrong. And a girl up
from the country, a pretty girl, could've gone to a different
sort of place altogether."

Even Magnus's blunt mind understood the leer.

"No. She is a very decent, respectable girl."

"Maybe. But if she was straight from the country she could have been snatched. I've known it happen. Poor innocent girls, the younger the better."

By this time he had taken the young man's measure. Without Copsi behind him Magnus lost stature and was just a young man with plenty of money and only one idea in his head. Just asking to be exploited.

"I know all the places and all the madams, clear down to Tiger Bay. But it's early yet. Tell you what, sir. You and me and the nag take a bit of supper and a bit of a rest and then we'll go the rounds. That'll be two quid, night work always being extra."

He was being truthful in saying that he knew every brothel—unless a new one had opened overnight—and if he calculated rightly in some place his young toff might find this Hannah Reeve, or better still, forget her, hire a girl, spend a lot of money on bad champagne and earn his cabdriver a bit of a bonus.

The man underestimated Magnus Copsey's dedication to himself and what he wanted. That evening the brothels in Bristol had the experience of being visited by a customer who wanted none of their wares—a pity because he plainly had money. He'd varied his question again. "Have you a Miss Hannah Reeve here?" Given the same old answer, "No," he said he'd like to see for himself. Men's vagaries were catered for as far as possible and most houses were tolerant at first, then hostile when it became plain that he was only looking, and did not wish even to drink while making his inspection. One madam believed that any man who refused a drink was already drunk and decided to play a trick on him.

"Hannah Reeve," she said meditatively. "Well, you know, sir, some girls change their names as easily as they change dresses. What is she like, the young lady you want? Pretty, no doubt."

"Yes. Very pretty."

"Tall or short?"

"Short."

"Dark or fair?"

"Oh. Fair. Very fair. Lots and lots of hair, silvery hair."

"You wait here, sir. Take a glass while you wait. On the house."

"I just told you. I don't want a drink."

She was a bulky woman but she was nimble on the stairs.

"You, Fanny," she said, selecting the girl who most nearly fitted the description, "there's a client downstairs, dead drunk and looking for a girl. You're Hannah Reeve for tonight. Got that? Hannah Reeve."

"And what's his name?"

"Just call him dearie. Look pleased to see him. Show him a bed and he'll fall sound asleep."

It sounded an easy assignment.

She had made a good choice. In this deliberately dimly lighted place and at a little distance, the girl did look like Hannah, but as she came closer, smirking, calling him dearie and saying how nice to see him again, the deception was obvious. He seized her by the hair, lifted her by it, shook her by it. "You bitch. You bloody whore!" A certain amount of manhandling was expected and permitted, but there were limits. Not only was the pain unbearable, but she could feel her hair, her precious hair, coming away from her scalp. She screamed and the man who was never out of earshot during business hours, and whose motto was "Act first, question later," hurtled in and with a single punch to the jaw, laid the madman out cold. The madam appeared and said,

"Get back upstairs, Fanny. You played your part and shall have your share."

It was a rich haul; fifty pounds at least, a heavy signet ring, a gold watch and chain.

"The usual place," the Madam said. "And give him one on the back of the head so it looks as though it was done from behind."

━━━◆━━◆━━◆━━◆━━━

Magnus's driver waited and waited. His horse with two exceptionally good meals inside it, slept standing up. The man dozed intermittently and was roused once, somewhat sharply and told to move his vehicle to make way for a closed carriage. He too had eaten exceptionally well that day and drunk a good deal of his favorite beverage, porter. So he was somnolent, and it was not until the chill of late night in early autumn finally struck him that he roused again, and fully. Aware of loss. He'd lost his customer. Possibly while he was moving his vehicle, or during one of his snoozes, his unusual customer had either found what he wanted and stayed, or come out and tried another house. Which? No means of knowing. This whole area was riddled with them. There was even a belief that some houses were connected with secret passageways by which a redhead, or a Frenchie, or a mulatto, not immediately available in one establishment could be summoned from another.

In any case the driver had no redress and he took his loss philosophically; he'd had his pound for the day's work, two good meals for himself and his nag. Mustn't grumble. In any case who was there to grumble to? Except the horse.... And he saw nothing incongruous between the words, "Come up, Boy, we'll go home," and the plying of the whip.

***

Magnus woke in the place where he had been dumped, a narrow foul-smelling alley between some back fences and a tanyard. His mind fumbled about, in this direction and that. He couldn't remember getting drunk, or falling down or having a fit of temper, or anything else that might account for such a headache, such an ill-all-over feeling. He pulled himself to his feet by clutching at the fence. It was growing light. Morning. What time? He felt for his watch, it wasn't there. His money! Also gone. What a plight! The alley lurched about a bit, then settled, and as it did so his consciousness settled, in the way it had, upon one thing. Hannah Reeve. Around the name other things began to cluster; yesterday's futile hunt ending with the girl who looked like Hannah but was not. He could remember feeling disappointed and furious. Nothing beyond that. But he could remember who he was, where he was, and why, and the name of the hotel where he was staying.

The alley debouched into a side street which in turn debouched into a thoroughfare where already there were some people about. Of a pale thin boy taking down some shutters from a shop front, he asked, "Which way to The Swan?" The boy told him, thinking: "He's had a night of it, lucky sod."

Magnus was dimly aware of the fact that the stink of the alley was with him. He must have lain in a drain all night. Well no matter, he had a valise of clean clothes at the hotel. The loss of his possessions did not concern him much. In all his life he'd never been short of money and therefore valued it lightly.

Life was stirring at The Swan, too. An old woman was scrubbing the floor, a young porter polishing brass. To the porter Magnus said,

"I've been set on and robbed. I want a bath. I want some coffee. I want my breakfast."

Neither then nor later did he attract much sympathy. Young gentlemen who went, flaunting their wealth, into rough parts of the city were asking for trouble—and usually got it.

The room assigned to him was part of what had once been the attic floor, and the hotel stood high. Bathed, reclad, and having had his breakfast, Magnus went and stood by the window and looked out at the view which in his hurry and preoccupation he had formerly ignored. Now the size of the city impressed him, evoking not admiration or awe but disgust. To look for one girl in a place this size; hopeless! What he must do was to get back to Copsi and wring the truth about her whereabouts from her parents. They must know. And he should have thought of that before setting out.

But to get home he needed money. Well, he must borrow some.

He was genuinely shocked when the owner of The Swan, servile in manner, rocky in intention met his demand, "I want fifty pounds," with the ridiculous statement that he made it a rule never to lend money.

"Why not? Isn't my word good enough? I'm Magnus Copsey."

"It is apt to create ill-feeling, sir."

The landlord had slightly more feeling about what

had happened to one of his guests; such incidents were all too frequent and gave the city a bad name. He was sorry that it had happened, not particularly sorry for the young man to whom it had happened. Nor was he much perturbed about the money the young man now owed him. For the silly young simpleton had a horse, worth at least eighty guineas and a good gig worth fifty secondhand and from the moment that the landlord learned of Mr. Copsey's mishap both had been under guard. The law operated severely against landlords, insofar as they were held responsible for what happened to any animals or vehicles or goods on their premises, but in a case like this even the law would be on his side. But it would be better to avoid such a confrontation and he suggested trying a bank. "Which bank do you favor with your custom, sir?"

"Spear's," Magnus said after a moment's reflection.

That hesitation and the fact that the landlord had never heard of Spear's, led to a deepening suspicion. There were men who were knocked down and robbed, the more shame to the new police system; but there were also cases of pretense and fraud, often concerning well-dressed, well-spoken men with lordly manners, like this one.

"There is no branch of Spear's bank in Bristol, sir."

"That's all right. There wasn't in Naples, either. But I got my money all right."

Full of confidence, but on foot, because he lacked enough to hire a conveyance for ten minutes, Magnus tried four banks. The old, well-tried I *want* worked, up to a point. "I want to see the manager," got him in; but "I want fifty pounds," brought him up against what he thought was dead stupidity. In this alien, barbarous place the name Copsey meant nothing and Spear's very little. And when he said, angrily, that in Rome, in Naples, even in Cairo, he'd been able to get all the money he needed, they said, "Yes, by pre-arrangement," and a lot of other silly things, like waiting three days so that letters of credit could be exchanged.

It did occur to him that this was something Mr. Garnet had always dealt with—was paid to deal with. He'd have given a good deal to see Mr. Garnet now. But he was alone; robbed, penniless, rebuffed. But not without resources. He had his horse and his gig and his wits of which he thought highly. He went back to The Swan and struck one of those bargains pleasing to both participants.

"Look. I thought I wanted fifty pounds, but less will do." He'd asked for fifty because it was a good round sum and about what he had been robbed of. But twenty surely would hire post-chaises and overnight lodgings. He explained, painstakingly, "I want twenty pounds, to get me home. You keep my horse and gig. In pawn. For what I owe you and the twenty pounds you lend me. The minute I'm home, I'll send a man. He'll bring what I owe and the twenty pounds. All right?"

"No. The horse'll need feeding and the gig'll take up space. Say a pound a day. And I'd like it in writing, sir."

Magnus traveled by night as well as by day, as his father had often done in his eagerness to get back to Copsi; but Magnus's aim was not the castle—indeed if things went as he wished he would go no nearer home than Reffolds. He arrived in Wyck at about nine o'clock in the morning, visited a barber, had a quick breakfast at the Station Hotel and then went to the bank where he drew out a hundred pounds. He then hired a horse from a livery stable. What he did next would depend upon the information he could extract from Mrs. Reeve, or from Reeve. Sir Harald had mentioned Reeve's accident, but as always with things which did not directly concern himself, Magnus had forgotten immediately. He now rather hoped that Mrs. Reeve would say that Hannah was in Bristol, because then he could go back to The Swan and fling some money at the landlord. Fling it on the floor and watch him grovel for it.

Hannah was upstairs giving the bedrooms their weekly turn out. She was back in her own pretty room with the sofa as bed; about the last thing Jerry Flordon had done at Reffolds was to carry up the sofa—with a little hindrance from Sam. When it was in place, Hannah standing by to say where she wanted it, he remarked that it didn't look very comfortable and would be better without the padded back and the bulging curved roll at its head. "I'll take them off for you, if you like; it'd give you a good two inches more width and about six in length."

"I don't think Mother would like it much; it matches the parlor suite."

"When you get your own bed back, I'll fix this up again." Privately he thought that Hannah would only get her bed back when John Reeve went to his grave. Any condition that had lasted four and a half days couldn't be regarded as a temporary numbness. "I'm a handy carpenter," he said.

"All right, then. It would be better."

On this Saturday morning Hannah leaned from her own window to shake out a duster. Then she tore downstairs and into the kitchen where Martha was rolling pastry for an apple pie.

"It's Magnus Copsey. Coming here. Mother, don't tell him I'm here. Make up some tale. Please. I'm so scared of him."

She certainly looked frightened.

"I'll deal with him," Martha said grimly. She removed her apron and dusted her hands on it. Then she went to the front door, opening it just as Magnus was trying to decide whether to approach from the front or the back. He wished to please and he knew the mechanics of being pleasing when he wished.

"Good morning, Mr. Copsey." Martha said in her grandest manner. "You have called to inquire about my husband? How very kind. I'm afraid I cannot ask you in. My husband had a poor night and is asleep now."

She had not seen him close to since he was a child. Sir Harald gave a party for tenants each Christmas in the Great Hall and until Johnny's death soured her, she'd attended, much as she had disliked being classed with—no other word for it—peasants. Sir Harald's idea of a party for tenants was archaic; gallons of beer and the kind of food one would give men straight from the plough. All the men became a little drunk and made coarse jokes and the woman had no conversation—except children. She had talked children, until death robbed her, and made her a recluse.

It was with a little start of surprise that she saw Magnus Copsey as a handsome young man. Not

unlike . . . but this was no time to think about Johnny and
what he would have looked like, had he lived.

Magnus said, "Yes. I'm sorry about your husband,
Mrs. Reeve. I hope he will soon be better. But what I want
to know. . . ." A change came over his face; it was like a
cloud coming across the sun's face on a summer day and
making everything, a whole landscape, utterly different in
less than half a minute. "Where's Hannah?"

She was ashamed of herself for being frightened,
after so long a time of certainty that she would never feel
anything again, not joy or sorrow or fear, but she was
frightened, thinking how isolated Reffolds was; how she
was alone here with a scared girl and a helpless man. Sam
had gone to the mill—one of the simple errands with
which he could be trusted. Anything might happen. . . .

The fear was not evident; she braved the glare in his
eyes and said,

"Why is my daughter's whereabouts of interest to
you?"

She was going to be awkward. Well, he could be
awkward, too.

"That's my business."

"On the contrary, mine. Hannah is very young—not
yet sixteen. Any business you have with her, Mr. Copsey,
concerns me."

His slow mind took some seconds to find an
acceptable reply.

"I want to talk to her."

"I understand from my daughter's behavior both at
Mrs. Wentworth's and at school, that she has no wish to
talk to you. In such a situation, a girl's wishes must be
respected."

"I never had a chance. But I want to talk to her. I
mean to talk to her."

He shifted his glare to the house and her fear
sharpened. He was quite capable of thrusting his way in.
She could no more stop him than she could a mad bull. So
placate, placate.

"Then you must wait until she comes home. And
then you must talk to her in my presence."

"Where is she?"

"I am not sure."

"Don't you lie to me."

That was impolite, but she let it pass.

"Hannah has an aunt who thought it was time that she should make the acquaintance of some distant relatives. And when I say I am not sure where they are at the moment, it is the truth. They set out from Radmouth by sea, and whether they went north to Hull, or south to London, depended upon which ship sailed first." She sounded calm, sensible and convincing.

"When'll she be back?"

"Probably not before Christmas."

He believed her; she could tell by the sulky, childish expression of disappointment which replaced the mad glare.

"First it was Bristol; now Hull or London."

"Bristol was part of the itinerary, but towards the end."

"Damn all," he said, and wheeling round, kicking the worn old hack into something resembling a gallop, rode off.

Thank God, she thought, that the parlor now had only one window. It had once had two, John said, but when the window tax was imposed the one at the front, the smaller one, had been bricked up. She hoped to get back into the kitchen, recover her composure, but John called, "Martha!" and when she opened the parlor door, asked, "Who was it? I heard a horse."

"Somebody who wanted Squirrels' Hall and had been misdirected. Are you all right?"

He knew what she meant; did he need the detested bottle, the even more detestable pan.

"Yes, I'm all right."

"Then I'll get back to my pie."

Once he had counted hours, now it was days. This was the second Saturday; soon he would have been here for a fortnight! And Sam was worse than useless, so the whole humiliating business fell on Martha. He did his best, eating and drinking very sparingly—if he could do so unobserved, tipping a cup of tea into the plant pots on the windowsill.

He owned a gun. Every farmer did, for although

tenants were not allowed to shoot game, they could shoot vermin, which included pigeons and rabbits. His gun stood where it had always stood, just inside the kitchen door, and after each humiliation, he thought that if only he could get to it, or have it brought to him, he'd blow his brains out. Alive he was worthless, just a stinking burden; dead, barring a few clauses, shipwreck, or suicide—and he could make it look like an accident—he was worth two hundred pounds of the Pelican Insurance Company's money.

He'd made one attempt to get his hands on his gun, saying that at least he could clean it; and Martha said she'd lent it to Blount of Marsh End. He did not believe her any more than he believed her when she said she didn't in the least mind emptying slops. It was a peculiar thing but lose the use of your legs and everybody behaved as though you'd lost your senses as well.

Hannah was not in the kitchen, but after a minute or two the larder door opened an inch and she peeped out.

"Has he gone?"

"Yes. I just managed to fob him off. I've gained a little time. Perhaps long enough for this crazy whim to pass over. One can only hope so. I think he is crazy. I think he could be dangerous. And I have condemned you, my poor girl, to hiding in the house until Christmas. You see, I said...."

She reported what she had said and Hannah repeated that she had done nothing to warrant such persecution.

"I believe you. In fact I think it accounts for it. He is so accustomed to having everything he wants that anything not instantly attainable acquires a special value.... All the same, I think it would be as well if you went to stay with your Aunt Hannah, for a time at least. Sam is inclined to gossip. And in Radmouth you would be able to go out."

This was a remarkable turnabout on Mother's part, akin to the change which took place when Mother went from the kitchen to the parlor. For a long time something of mystery had surrounded this sister of Father's, the aunt after whom she had been named. Country people had an expression, referring to children. "Little jugs have big ears." Hannah had been a very little jug, with very big ears and a lively curiosity which had little to feed upon, grownups having the exasperating habit of cutting short a conversation, even a quarrel whenever a child appeared. Aunt Hannah at one time had come to Reffolds for a week each June; she had pretty clothes and always smelled very sweet; she brought presents—most of Hannah's toys, her doll, its cradle, a miniature teaset, had been gifts from Aunt Hannah; for Father she brought tobacco and things to drink; for Mother books or rolls of stuff to be made into clothes.

Then there had been a terrible row. Nobody shouted, of course, but it was a row. "So unfair to John," Aunt Hannah said. She said, "Young." She said, "Time enough for half a dozen more if you pulled yourself together." Mother went to the bedroom and had no supper; and Father said "no right to speak to her like that. You never had a child."

After that Aunt Hannah didn't visit any more. And then, Uncle Frank, on one of his rare visits, had said something about Hannah beginning to go blind. Not very blind, just beginning.... Mother, naturally behaved correctly. She said, "Hannah and I had our differences, about many things. But blind! Poor thing. John, you must write and offer her a home."

Uncle Frank said, "We did, soon's we heard. But she's all right. Yes, in the end they did right by her.... Tidy little house, I understand, and a maid to wait on her. And she ain't blind to the point where she can't write or do her lace."

***

And now here was Mother suggesting a visit, saying, "You'd like that, wouldn't you?" It was the first time that Hannah's wishes had ever been given much consideration in this house and she was unused to making decisions— she'd made one, in the Wentworths' barn, but that was different. Purely personal. And look what had resulted from that! What she really wanted was to go back to school and not be pestered. Like many children whose home life was not completely happy, she'd liked school. But Miss Drayton wouldn't want, wouldn't have her back now. And Mother was obviously scared too; wanting her elsewhere.

"It might be best," she said reluctantly. "But how do I get there? Without his knowing? I know Jerry fetched me home safely—but *he* was still watching the school then. He may be watching here. Now."

"I think not. I told him...he seemed to accept. ...But of course one never knows with somebody so demented. And this is England," Martha said angrily, "the country of the free! We might as well be living in the Middle Ages, or in the middle of Africa. *Your* father spoke to *his* father—and he a magistrate! There should be a law. Something should have been done when he shot Jim Bateman. And would have been if anybody else had done it....Stop crying. Your father will notice. He mustn't be worried. That beyond all." She lifted a saucepan lid and said, "Now we've let the potatoes boil to mash. Strain them off and mash them properly, with a knob of butter. I'll think of something. Leave it to me."

But that evening, before she lighted the lamp in the parlor or the candle in the kitchen, she drew the curtains close. People in lighted rooms were sitting targets.

Later, supper over, the bottle used, the guard against bedsores applied—Hannah naturally dismissed before such jobs were undertaken—Martha, keeping her manner and voice light and cheerful, approached the subject of Hannah's going to Radmouth, emphasizing the advantages, almost ignoring the real reason.

"It is so dull for her, being confined to the house, and with nothing much to do. And Hannah used to be good company."

Every now and again he had the feeling that he must oppose her, just a little. He still loved her, was entirely dependent upon her, and in a way grateful, but unless he asserted himself from time to time, he'd become like a child, or like one of the plants on the windowsill, well looked after, but of no importance.

"I reckoned it was partly Hannah being good company led to the breach."

"Well, that's all over and done with now."

"I'd sooner she went to Frank's."

Martha almost said, in her old sharp way, "Well, I wouldn't." It was indeed difficult to imagine Hannah there; Frank was much like John, decent enough, but he'd married a woman of absolutely no refinement who, if she had ever had any notion of mere cleanliness, had abandoned it in the face of difficulties, one careless man, three rough boys. The house was definitely malodorous, reeking of many unpleasant smells, manure and sweaty feet being the most prominent.

"They haven't much spare room."

"Hester could turn her sitting hens out of the parlor."

"And if anything it's even lonelier than this."

There, he had shot his small bolt in support, of independence.

"Well, if Hannah'll have her and if you think it'll be all right."

"I'll write and apologize and beg her help in a difficult situation."

"And how're you going to *get* her there?"

"I'll find a way."

Yes, and tell me about it afterwards, when it's all settled! I don't count no more!

"God," he said violently. "I can see now where I made my mistake. When I got Hannah's letter, I shouldn't have talked to Sir Harald. I should have taken my gun and laid in wait, and shot that young bugger the next time he started pestering."

"Then they would have hanged you."

"And I'd have been glad."

"John you shouldn't say such things. You haven't been abed a fortnight yet. If you'd caught smallpox you'd...."

"Been on the mend, or dead," he interrupted harshly. One thought followed another. "And if you did lend my gun to Blount, you get it back. And let me see how he's kept it. You know how people are with things they borrow."

"It'll have to wait until I can fetch it myself. You know what Sam is. He'd come back with a pudding basin."

She mustered a smile—and really sometimes a smile hurt.

❮━━❯❮━━❯❮━━❯❮━━❯❮━━❯

"There you are," Martha said, standing back, "he could sit in the same coach and not know you." Such a disguise was possible because Grandmother Reeve, as far as her means and her husband's indulgence allowed, had been very dressy. And because John Reeve was sentimental about the past and about belongings, Martha had used one half of the huge old wardrobe in Grandfather's room as a linen cupboard while in the other half there had reposed, well guarded against moth, a number of things which were not suitable for giving away to the poor, and which could not, without giving offense, be burned. Amongst them was a poke bonnet, an article which had been fashionable only briefly, because the huge brim made any charm of feature practically invisible, the wearer's face looking like a pale blur at the end of a long dim tunnel. In its day it had been the only poke bonnet in the two Copsis and envious women had called it Mrs. Reeve's coal scuttle. Grandmother Reeve had also owned something more practical; a long, voluminous cloak, warmly lined with rabbit fur; and the very early start on a morning of early frost justified the wearing of such a garment.

"I'll drive you to the Gibbet Crossroad, and if the early coach is punctual, see you on to it. Should there be a delay I must leave you; I cannot be away more than an hour. Sam is so inept! What would I not give for Jerry Flordon—or somebody like him. Somebody with a bit of gumption. But they're all employed elsewhere. Never mind. We shall manage. And I am sure that time will solve both problems. That besotted young man will take a fancy for somebody else; and your father will be either better—or resigned."

❮━━❯❮━━❯❮━━❯❮━━❯❮━━❯

John Reeve did not get better, nor did he become resigned. He worried about the farm routine, repeatedly urged Martha to try to find better help than silly Sam who couldn't even plough a straight furrow.

"John, I have tried. It isn't like the old days when there was nothing but the land; boys can find work down on the wharf now."

"No winter wheat," he groaned. "No barley. Ruin staring us straight in the face."

Martha knew—she gave it back stare for stare every night of her life—but she managed to speak cheerfully.

"It's early days to speak of ruin, my dear. I've two calves ready for market and that huge white sow has ten young. We'll manage until you're about again."

There were times when, loving her, grateful to her, dependent upon her, he could have killed her. Kill!

"You never got my gun back, did you?"

"No. Did I forget to tell you? Blount offered me three pounds for it. And since it was so old, and you not wanting it just at the minute...."

Not a word to him!

Up at the castle, Sir Harald allowed himself moments of hope. Magnus came back from Bristol, explaining his penurious state by saying he had lost money at gambling and Hannah Reeve was not mentioned. Diversion was plainly the right thing and there was plenty of that just now; shooting parties, and all the festivities of Christmas and the New Year. Magnus behaved very well, dancing with girls, pretty, not so pretty, even plain, but never, alas, seeming to take a fancy to any one of them.

Immediately after New Year the usual bad weather set in, somewhat worse than usual, heavy snowfalls, blocking roadways and lanes. For five consecutive days no movement was possible.

Even Sam Archer, loyal though stupid, failed to get to work and Martha—so dainty, and like all town-bred women so timid with even the mildest cow, was obliged to deal with the stock. John would have preferred Hannah to do it—she was bred to it. But Hannah was at Radmouth.

Hannah was at Radmouth with the aunt for whom she had been named, and all things considered, she was enjoying herself. Aunt Hannah lived very comfortably indeed, in a neat snug house, tended by a stout, middle-aged, vastly efficient maid named Minnie. Here, for the first time in her life, Hannah enjoyed the luxury of a fire in her bedroom and breakfast in bed. And Aunt Hannah herself was something to enjoy. Old, of course, but slim and upright, very well dressed, most fastidious, sweet-scented. The only evidence of her increasing blindness was the fact that nothing in her rooms must ever be moved, if things were left in the proper place she could feel her way about. And her obsession about eating tidily. Plying her table napkin, focusing her remaining sight upon the bodice of her dress or on the tablecloth near her plate she said, "I have the utmost horror of becoming slovenly."

She asked Hannah to describe herself. "And no need to be modest, my dear. The Reeves were always reckoned handsome and your mother was comely."

"Well, some girls at school said I was pretty." And look what that brought on me! "I have a lot of hair, the color of straw."

"Silver-gilt sounds kinder." Aunt Hannah had had much practice in saying the pleasing thing.

"And my eyes are like Mother's, but flecked. Rather like this sherry, with flecks, some darker, some lighter."

"Very attractive! Complexion?"

"I'd say fair. And I don't have spots. Or freckles."

"They are things to avoid."

(Minnie, asked to give her opinion, privately, said, "Pretty enough; but, madam, not a patch on you when you was young.")

Aunt Hannah wanted to know about the accident and said with real feeling.

"I wish I could help, but I am in a curious position. A very dear friend, thinking blindness implied helplessness and imbecility, provided for me in a way that he believed would save me from being taken advantage of. This house, for my lifetime, all my bills paid by a lawyer, and a nice little nest egg for Minnie if she stays the course.... So I cannot help."

"Mother could manage, in a way, I think.... If only we could find a good man." (If only Jerry Flordon hadn't felt that, his word given, he was under an obligation to go

trawling herring!) "I could work, too. I'm not scared of
cows. I was learning to milk one when I was about
eight.... But Mother wanted me to be a governess ... and
I did enjoy school. The thing is governesses don't earn
much, do they?"

Nor, the elder Hannah thought, do dressmakers'
apprentices—in fact they *paid* for the privilege of sewing
themselves blind in airless rooms. She felt, even at this late
hour, a wave of gratitude toward the young man who had
rescued her and at the same time ruined her, made her a
kept woman, set her feet on the downward slope as the
moralists would say. She was willing to admit that she had
been fortunate—but clever, too. And she hadn't done so
badly. She did not regard her blindness as a punishment;
it had been incipient, in the headaches as she bent over the
infinitesimal stitches. As it was, she had yielded, become a
bad girl, saved blindness for the years when everybody
had some affliction. And she had enjoyed herself and
helped a lot of other people to enjoy themselves. And now
she was, if almost blind, very comfortable and lively
enough in her mind to take an interest in things outside
herself. More than could be said by most people. She was,
in fact, a woman who had learned to live with herself and
with the essential human predicament—and to treat it
lightly.

When, as was inevitable, Hannah confided her own
problem, the aging courtesan became thoughtful. At first
hearing it sounded like a repetition of her own story; but
Hannah insisted that Magnus Copsey terrified her. "He
has such a savage temper. There're all sorts of tales and we
know for certain that he once shot a keeper when he was
in a rage."

Aunt Hannah was not unduly shocked; she knew
that all gentlemen were prone to lose their tempers, but as
time went on and she came to *know* Hannah and
understand her—using her natural perception, reinforced
a little by the particular sensibility of the blind—she
decided that the girl was more suited to marriage than to
the role of mistress. There was a good deal of her mother
in her. She wished she could help towards marriage by
providing a dowry and could actually have done so had

she been prepared to sell her jewelry, but the very thought of such action was depressing. Some of the pieces had genuine sentimental value, all were tangible evidence of success. In her easy way she'd think that Hannah was very young and she herself might well be dead before marriage became imminent; one day she'd make a will, and leave her treasures to Hannah.

Magnus went to Reffolds just before Christmas.

"Is Hannah back?"

"No, Mr. Copsey. I am not expecting her until after Christmas."

"A pity. We are having a ball and I wished to invite her."

Martha thought: A likely tale! But at least he had been civil and gone away without fuss.

He came again after Christmas and in a different mood.

"Damn all! You said *after* Christmas. This *is* after Christmas. You're lying to me."

"I am not in the habit of having my word doubted," Martha said in her sternest manner. "But since you do doubt it, come in and see for yourself."

Undeterred by her manner, he swung himself down from the saddle, and searched the house in a most thorough way, up into the attic where apples were stored, the larder, the dairy. He muttered to himself. Plainly demented. The hunt ended in the parlor where John Reeve lay. A resumption of civility there. "Good day to you, Reeve. Sorry to see you still abed. Let's hope the New Year brings better luck.... For us all." Then eccentricity, to say the least of it, again. "I must look under your bed."

"Hannah ain't there if thass what you're thinking." John Reeve sounded surly. He had indeed begun to blame this young whelp not only for Hannah's absence at a time when she could have been useful, but also for his accident. Lying here with nothing to do except think, he had had some peculiar thoughts and had come to the conclusion that worry about Hannah had made him careless. If his mind had been wholly on his job he'd have kept his balance better and wouldn't now be in this state.

"Then where is she?" Magnus demanded, rising from his knees.

"How'd I know? I don't count no more. No more than them plants on the windowsill."

At the front door, in a very nasty way, Mrs. Reeve said, "Well, I hope you are satisfied."

Magnus's impulse was to hit her, straight across her jeering mouth but he thought better of it—oh, much better, because he was so clever!

"You lied to me," he snarled. "Lie on lie. You'll be sorry for this!"

***

John slept in the parlor, with the door open, Martha slept in the room they had once shared, with the door open. The last thing she said to him every night was, "Call if you want me, my dear. I shall hear." He had been very good, had never called, until tonight. Now he called urgently: "Martha! Martha! Come quick!" She was quick because she was always prepared: she kept a candle—the kind used in nurseries—always burning so that should he call she did not have to fumble about in a minute of darkness, making a light; her dressing gown lay on the foot of the bed, her slippers within reach. Within seconds, the slow-burning candle in her hand, she was downstairs and in the parlor. But she had had time to think: perhaps the miracle has happened! The urgency of his voice justified the supposition. But it was not that! "Something burning," he said. "Can't you smell it?"

Now she could and ran into the kitchen where she had left the day's wash airing before the dying fire. Perhaps a spark.... No, everything in order in the tidied-away-for-the-night kitchen; but the smell of something burning was growing stronger and a flickering light, bright, dim, brighter. She tore open the kitchen door. Thank God not the pigsty or the cow byre, but the barn on the other side of the yard. The hay which was to keep the cows alive and yielding through the winter. Nothing to be done. And even as she looked, with desperation, down came the snow, the best ally a helpless woman could have against such an enemy. She watched the white curtain fall, smelt the odor of burning change to smoulder, and presently was back in the parlor with the comforting lie. "I left the damp kindling wood a little too near the fire. No harm done. It was the scorching of green wood that made such a stench." Poor man he must not be worried, but she was almost frantic; the words, "You'll be sorry for this," kept ringing in her ears. She wished to be just but the coincidence was too ominous to overlook. She knew that fresh hay, stacked before it was properly dry, could heat spontaneously, but this was seasoned stuff, lightly heaped. And apart from the willful damage and waste there was something creepy in the thought of anybody, let alone a crazy man, prowling about, unseen, unheard in the darkness. She felt nervous and vulnerable. The need to tell somebody was strong and whom could she tell except Hannah?

Aunt Hannah could not see the expression of dismay or the sudden pallor; but she heard the sharp intakes of breath and sensed the distress and asked quietly, "Bad news?"

"Horrible! That wretched man has been pestering Mother, asking where I am, searching the house, and she *thinks* setting fire to the hay.... She may just *think*, I *know*. Nothing too vile. And she's helpless. He's the landlord's son.... Weren't things bad enough without this? Honestly, Aunt Hannah, awful as it sounds, I sometimes think that I'd have done better to let him rape me that night at the Wentworth's. I have to be here, not at home where I could be useful; Mother's being crazed...."

"Steady, dear, steady," Aunt Hannah said. "It's bad, but panic never helps. Read me the letter in its entirety." Hannah did so. "I see," Aunt Hannah said. "No positive proof that he fired the hay. Well, we'll see. Give me my frame, please."

She had devised the frame when her sight was better. It looked like a musical instrument, thin taut wires across a light, strong frame. They guided her hand so that she avoided over-writing one line with another. Using the frame, a quill cut thick and the blackest possible ink, the older Hannah could still write a legible letter; but writing was an exercise she hated, ink being as dangerous as gravy or soft-boiled eggs, and ink spots more difficult to erase.

She wrote very slowly, pausing now and again to choose the right cautious word and to reflect that twenty years ago the now pompous, important man to whom she was writing had been a very scared, muddle-minded young man whom she had helped out of a very tricky situation. He owed her something, and she had never until now made any effort to collect the debt, or by word or glance, to remind him. Now she did, in the gentlest possible terms, saying only, "For my sake Walter, do something if you can." It was both an appeal and a challenge.

The office of lord lieutenant of a county was a very ancient one, and like many other things had been whittled away with the passage of time. He was still expected to act as host to his sovereign, to be responsible for raising the militia and all other defensive measures in time of war; he was, in theory, the source of all law and order in that he chose the justices of the peace—with the exception of certain mayors in certain towns who automatically became, during their term of office, justices. It was to this aspect of the matter that Lord Hornsby indirectly referred in his extremely diplomatic letter to Sir Harald—"In these changing times, my dear Copsey, when all authority is being challenged it is essential that those vested with it should not be open to criticism."

Sir Harald read the letter with astonishment, with mounting fury. The vagueness of it was infuriating. "I hear from various sources...." *What* sources. "Conduct not entirely desirable...." What conduct? In what way not desirable? What the Hell did the man mean? And that veiled threat! Sir Harald recognized it as such; Lord Hornsby practically said that a man who could not keep his own son in order was not a fit person to sit in judgment upon others. Blasted upstart! Probably didn't realize that Copseys had been justices of the peace ever since they were invented.

That hideous sensation of being threatened by a stroke returned and he admonished himself to keep calm. He must hear what the boy had to say. So far as he knew Magnus, apart from taking his inordinate fancy to Hannah Reeve, had behaved very well lately. He'd gone to Bristol and lost a lot of money—but all youngsters gambled. He'd like to talk to Bertie who had the most extraordinary way for hearing things, but on his way back to the castle—where this letter awaited him—he'd seen Bertie, half dead from lack of sleep on her way to bed after two nights in the lambing pen because her shepherd didn't like to be alone with the new breed of ewes, expecting every lamb to be born with two heads. She'd be asleep now. Had Lord Hornsby's seat not been at Withinstone, about as far from Copsi as a place could be and still be in Suffolk, he'd have gone there and confronted him, asked him what the devil he meant. It was just possible that Magnus's declared intention of marrying that damned girl had somehow drifted across the county; but even so such a letter would not be justified; most families had a misalliance tucked away somewhere.

"I want you," he said to Magnus when the port had gone round once. In the library he handed across the letter: "Read that! And tell me what it means."

How slowly he read! Governesses, tutors, Eton, Mr. Garnet and the Grand Tour, and he read like a boy who'd had three months at a charity school.

"I don't know." Magnus contrived to look both innocent and sulky. "What does the man mean by conduct not desirable?"

"That is what I am asking you."

Magnus appeared to search his memory. It couldn't be to do with setting fire to that old bitch's hay; nobody knew about that, he'd been too cunning. No accomplices, and if ever accused, a good alibi.

"I've got a bit drunk at Pepper's a time or two. And I've spent a night at Old Mother Hubbard's." Mrs. Huppert, in slightly different circumstances, could have been regarded as a bawd, but she was known to be the widow of a poor clergyman, left with three pretty daughters, all very flighty, joined sometimes by relatives, female, pretty and flighty and all much addicted to the giving of parties which went on till all hours. Knowledgeable young gentlemen dropped coins into an ornate vase that stood on the hall table.

Sir Harald said bluntly, "Drinking at Pepper's and whoring at Mrs. Huppert's could hardly account for a letter like this. Look here, Magnus, I must *know*. I have to make some sort of answer."

"I don't know what this is all about. What've I done? I got a bit drunk at Pepper's and I spent a night...."

Oh God, give me patience!

"Did you, by any chance, tell anybody that you meant to marry Hannah Reeve?" He spoke the name, so far sedulously avoided, with supreme distaste.

"No. How could I? I'd look a fool, wouldn't I? Not even knowing where she is. I never had a chance to ask her. But I will. I'll marry her."

Exasperated beyond control, Sir Harald said, "You will not!" and then instantly undermined his case. "Unless you wish to starve. You're bound to inherit, but I'm under no obligation to give you a penny, or to house you. You'll have nothing until I'm dead—and I'm good for twenty years."

All right then, die now! When Magnus flew into a fury it was truly blind and thoughtless. No thought about what would happen if his father were found dead, in his own library, his skull cracked by his own decanter.

Sir Harald, who in his day had known hand-to-hand fighting, grabbed Magnus's right wrist in such a paralyzing grip that the decanter fell from the suddenly flaccid fingers. At the same time he dealt his son, his only, his beloved son, a resounding clout on the jaw.

Bertie and several other people would have it that the blow was delivered years too late but it was effective. Magnus in a rage might be insensitive to pain, but he was susceptible to shock. The speed with which his father had defended himself, disarmed him and retaliated, took him aback. Sir Harald was shocked, too, both by the attack and the ferocity behind his own blow. They stared at each other in silence for what seemed a long time, then Magnus turned and went out. Sir Harald entertained the idiotic idea of following and apologizing, but the sight of Lord Hornsby's letter stiffened him. It was all very well to think: I provoked him. One must think: I was provoked first. And the damned letter must be answered. Not just yet, his hand was not steady enough.

Some whisky remained in the decanter; he poured a

stiff drink and drank it with deliberate slowness, switching his mind from the recent scene and concentrating upon composing a letter which would be civil, but not servile. It must also convey rebuke.

Since your Lordship did not see fit to name any of the various sources, and since close inquiry *here* has revealed no misdemeanor on the part of my son, I can only conclude that any report your Lordship chose to believe must have been grossly exaggerated.

Other stinging little sentences came to him and he was surprised at the ease with which he composed, and also by the fact that the whole thing reeked of the army. Cut out the words "my son" and it was Captain Copsey writing to his colonel, defending Trooper Smith from some unspecified charge and himself against being called a slack disciplinarian. It struck just the right balance between respect for rank and confidence in his own opinion.

He was pleased with the letter, but when it was written and he read it through he halted at the words no misdemeanor. The falsity leaped out at him. A boy who would attack his own father. . . . And with such a look! Sir Harald remembered the sheer malevolence of the look which Magnus had worn when he took aim at Jim Bateman.

After some time his almost infinite capacity for self-deception where Magnus was concerned came to comfort him. The thought that he and Juliet had bred a monster, a potential murderer, was too horrible to be entertained for long. The boy just lost his temper too easily. Bateman had provoked him; he himself had provoked him and when you came to think about it, coolly and calmly, there was something childish, almost pitiable about the boy's reaction on both occasions. So guileless. In the morning he'd apologize for taunting Magnus—and then, he was prepared to bet, Magnus would apologize for losing his temper; and he'd say, genially but firmly: "My boy, you must learn self-control. Do you realize that if you had cracked my head you'd have hanged?"

Almost invariably they breakfasted alone together. Magnus's face was lopsided and discolored. His attack was immediate and aimed at the heart. Before Sir Harald could say anything, Magnus said,

"I've been thinking about what you said last night." Not about what had been done! Sir Harald remembered that somebody, governess? tutor? had once said that Magnus's great weakness was an inability to distinguish between the important and the unimportant. Years ago. No matter.

"I spoke in haste and I am prepared to. . . ."

"There are men, in London, who'll lend money on expectations. Maybe you didn't know. Somebody told me. So if you do what you said and leave me to starve I shall go to London and borrow. How about that?"

Sir Harald's good resolutions took flight. Almost choking on a mouthful of scrambled egg, suddenly turned to sawdust, he said,

"You young fool! You could do it. But vultures like that charge two, three hundred per cent. Get into their clutches and you'd end with nothing but a title and a lot of litigation. The Chancery and the money-lenders would fight over Copsi like two dogs at a bone. It'd be the end. The end of Copsi."

"I don't care about Copsi—except to live in. What I want is to marry the girl I choose. And do as I like. If not I shall go to London. And you'll be to blame."

It was a pleasant morning, but the sunshine, the feeling of spring about to break, did little to lift Sir Harald's spirits as he jogged gently around his estate. In addition to everything else distasteful he felt that he ought to visit Reffolds—a place he had avoided. He was a conscientious visitor of the sick, enjoyed being hearty and hopeful and helpful; but poor Reeve's case was different and he had never liked Mrs. Reeve. But he'd go this morning, nothing could make him feel worse!

When he turned into the lane which led to the house, with the Reeve acres on either side, he momentarily forgot everything except that he was a landlord who had been shockingly remiss in his duties. This year the necessary hedging and ditching had not been done, so rain and the melted snow had not drained away properly; the arable acres had not been ploughed, last year's stubble and this year's weeds matted the fertile fields. Except for some cows in a soggy pasture and a drift of smoke from the chimney of the old house, it looked like a deserted, derelict farm. He should have foreseen this and done something. Bad, very bad! Then as he rounded the house and entered the yard, the old bonfire stench assailed him and he saw charred wood around and over the barn door.

Mrs. Reeve, neat and trim—and grim—as ever, came to the kitchen door. She invited him in, not cordially as other farm-wives did, but civilly enough. The kitchen was speckless. He knew some where hens pecked and dropped turds, or a sick piglet, an orphan lamb might be cossetted by the fire—somehow they seemed more welcoming.

"And how is your husband?"

"No better. And still far from resigned."

"Poor fellow. I feel I have been neglectful, Mrs. Reeve. I see the work has dropped into arrears."

Naturally she took that in the wrong spirit.

"I tried to hire a sensible man as soon as I realized that John's disablement was not temporary."

"I'll send along a couple of men to clear up a bit. It's rather late for planting, I'm afraid."

"That would be very kind, Sir Harald." What an unyielding, unfriendly woman!

"I see you've had a fire in your barn. Not serious, I hope." Something stirred in her face then, a slight shifting below the surface.

"It was. Very serious. I lost all my hay. Only the snow saved the barn itself."

"Dear me. Have you any idea how it started?" Surely an innocent question, and in the circumstances almost routine.

"I have no real evidence."

As though coaxing an unwilling witness, he said,

"But you have some suspicion. Tell me. Arson? A very serious offense."

"I can accuse no one. All I say is that I see a link between your son coming here in the morning, questioning my word that my daughter was not in the house, searching it, riding away making threats, and the fire starting in the middle of the night."

Now he saw it all. This woman, before she married, had been a governess and some governesses maintained links with former employers. And alongside this flash of insight was the horrible thought that she might be right—a boy who would try to kill his father would not hesitate to fire a barn.

"I only wish, Mrs. Reeve, that you had seen fit to bring your grievance—your *supposed* grievance—to me, rather than complain to Lord Hornsby."

"Lord Hornsby! How could I complain to him? He is unknown to me. And I could hardly complain to anyone—having no proof."

By this time John Reeve was growing impatient; he'd heard a horse, and then a mumble of voices, going on and on. So he called, "Martha," and rang his little bell.

"You will see him?" Martha asked. "He leads such a dull life."

"I came for that purpose."

In the dark short passage which connected the kitchen with the hall out of which the parlor opened, Martha said,

"Please, don't mention the fire, Sir Harald; he has enough to fret over." She sounded quite human for once, and somewhere in that short passage she had undergone a metamorphosis, throwing off her grimness and saying, almost gaily,

"Look dear, a visitor for you. Sir Harald."

As she opened the parlor door the sickroom smell hit her and humbled her. She'd battled against it, with soap and water, with burnt lavender and genuine lavender water, with sprigs of rosemary, crushed, and the window open whenever the weather allowed. But there it was, the apparently incompatible odor, and as she closed the door on it, Martha thought: It is the very smell of failure!

John Reeve was not aware of it because it had built up, day by day, around him; and Sir Harald, although aware, was more concerned by the vast change in Reeve's appearance. It was incredible that a man obviously well-cared for and suffering from no wasting disease, could have suffered such a decline. Under the smooth patchwork quilt his legs were no more than broomsticks and against the dazzling white pillows his head was a skull, the bones just covered by skin the color of tallow, and the eyes expressive of nothing but despair.

Sir Harald was always at his best when he could *do* something. Momentarily—and mercifully—self-forgetful, he was glad to be able to say that he was sending some help along. "Just to tide you over, till you're up and about again."

"That'll never be, sir. I know now." Automatically he glanced at the clock. Once he had reckoned in hours, then in days, then in weeks, and now it was in months.

"Now, now, that's no way to talk.... Tell me, have you seen Doctor Fordyke lately?"

"He've looked in. Well-meaning. Useless."

"Well I wouldn't go quite so far as that, but the fact remains that a country doctor can't be expert at everything. I tell you what I propose to do—find you a specialist. On nerves. It must *be* nerves, your bones are all right."

"Better if I'd broken something, or even lost a leg. I could've fed pigs with a wooden leg. And ploughed. And harried Sam Archer about. The way I am now, I'd be better dead."

"No!" A lost of firsthand experience with death had made Sir Harald value life. He was fairly regular at church—church parade, setting a good example—where he stood up and declared with the rest of the congregation that he believed in the resurrection of the body and in life everlasting, but he had never seriously examined such beliefs. "No, Reeve, you must not think that. You must cling to hope, and to life. I'll see what I can arrange."

For a little while after leaving Reffolds, his plans to help, his sense of duty performed or about to be performed, bore him up, then he thought about his son and depression blotted out the bright day. He must talk to Bertie.

"She's up at the house, sir," said the first man he asked and for a second Sir Harald's mind groped. House.

What house? Then he remembered Bertie's idiotic idea about a house of her own. He had never referred to it in the intervening months and he hoped she had forgotten it. "Up the sheeprun, sir," the man said helpfully. Sir Harald left the ploughland and the pastures, the houses and outbuildings, orchards and trees behind and emerged into a stretch of country as desolate as his mood. Sheep-nibbled turf as far as the eye could see, here and there a stunted, wind-bent hawthorn, and at the edge of the plateau where the land dropped away in a chalk cliff to the river, Bertie had chosen to build her house. Of gray brick, a material he detested, it was so much colder looking than weathered stone.

Bertie had had no difficulty in finding labor; everywhere the walls were eaves-high and at one end the roof rafters were being laid. Men swarmed about like bees. But despite the cheerful clangor and the voices and the sunshine there was an innate cheerlessness about the place. What would it be like in dead winter, with a nor-easter blowing?

Bertie came briskly down one of the ladders. She wore her ordinary working clothes: a frieze skirt, short enough to expose more than her ankles, and a scruffed old sheepskin coat. She was bareheaded and her hair, in color much like his own—in a horse it would be called bay—was a mass of short curls. It had been cut off when she had scarlet fever, years and years ago, and then for a brief time there was a fashion of short hair, copied from the French, of course. Now as outdated as the ruff, but it suited her and she stuck to it. She looked, of course, like nothing on earth, like nobody else on earth, yet you'd never take her for other than she was, a gentlewoman, a Copsey.

"Hullo," she called, "come to see the lambs?"

"No. Something I wanted to talk over. You were too tired last night."

"I have a favor to ask you. Come in and you'll see what I mean."

Close to, she could see the distress signals on his face. More trouble. Poor Harry!

They went in through what would one day be a doorway, just a gap now, as were the window openings on each side. The room, roughly of the size of Bertie's room at Copsi, was just a shell, the gray walls not plastered yet. Raw, horrible. And the view from the windows, surely the bleakest in the world: the slow-moving river, the marshes, and beyond them the sea. Imagine this, after Copsi!

"Sit down," Bertie said, indicating a pile of planks. "I have sandwiches enough for four, and...," she dived into the pocket of the dreadful old jacket and produced the kind of flask which men—never women—carried when hunting. The planks were to serve as both table and chairs; the sandwiches, wrapped in a napkin, lay there ready.

"We can't talk here, with all these men about."

"It's time for their dinner. I don't know why, but I seem always—in whatever company—the only person with a reliable watch." She pulled it out from another pocket. Not a pretty lady's timepiece; a big ugly, workmanlike watch. Having glanced at it she snapped her fingers—amazing what a sharp sound those seemingly delicate fingers could make, and somewhere a man shouted. Peace descended.

"What is it, Harry?"

"Almost too horrible to talk about, but Bertie I have to talk to somebody or go out of my mind. And I know I should not burden you. This," he looked about the bleak place, "is *his* fault, too. If he'd been...well...friendly and ordinary, you'd have stayed at Copsi, wouldn't you?"

"And been next generation's old lady? No, Harry. I always had something of this kind in mind. I dithered, convert one of the farm houses or build.... Then I decided and I am glad. Now tell me. What has happened?"

"Bertie, last night he tried to kill me." In all the world there was no other person to whom he could have made that simple statement. And even Bertie who might have been expected to stay aloof, dispassionate, dropped her sandwich to the floor among the shavings.

"God!" she said. "Not that. Why?"

He told her everything. Lord Hornsby's letter, the scene in the library, the threat this morning. And Mrs. Reeve's suspicion.... He ended by saying in a tone of misery that cut Bertie to the heart,

"I don't know what went wrong—where I went

wrong. I've loved him all his life—more; you begin to love a child before it is born. And now..... When I think of what he's willing to do to Copsi. It makes my whole life seem so futile. Unless...." Even to Bertie he hesitated to mention an idea that had snaked into his mind.

Outside the gulls wheeled and screamed. Bertie rose and gathering the remains of this dismal picnic meal, threw them out of the window opening. With her back to him—to make it easier for him to overcome his hesitation—she said, "Unless what, Harry?"

"There was a child.... You said yourself that the Reeves were decent people.... It may sound heartless and vile, but honestly, Bertie, if the succession were assured, I'd have him put under restraint."

"He certainly needs a keeper. More than he does a wife, by the sound of it." She scowled thoughtfully for a second, then almost smiled, as though she had reached some kind of satisfactory conclusion. Yet her next words were not optimistic. "Would they agree, *now*? They have sent the girl out of reach. And arson is, to say the least, an unusual form of wooing."

"They may not realize that he intends marriage."

"That is true. Things do look better through a wedding ring. Well, you can but try. What worries me, Harry, is *you*. If the slightest thing goes wrong and angers him, he could make another attempt."

"I shall be on my guard, now." He had actually no fear for his personal safety; he had been a soldier and a fearful soldier was useless. Everything, training, tradition, behavior, was aimed at inculcating the certainty that nothing could ever happen to *you*. A thousand might fall to right or left, but you'd be all right.

Working toward the idea she had had while she scowled, Bertie said,

"And there's nothing to stop him going to London and working havoc. I know who could help, though. The very man. He'd stand guard over you and keep a strict eye on Magnus." She gave a slight grin and her crystal blue eyes glinted with malice. "A very strict eye. Magnus is in Bolsover's bad books already. Magnus committed the cardinal sin of kicking Bolsover's dog. We must bear in mind that Magnus can be very charming when he wishes and always has plenty of money. But he won't get round Bolsover by cajolery, or bribery, or, come to that, brute force. Bolsover is an ex-pugilist."

Sir Harald had nothing against boxing, properly organized and supervised. During his army days he had arranged fights; they provided cheap, on-the-spot entertainment and often settled a grievance which, left to rankle, could lead to worse things. He did, however, object to prize fights where two ruffians were hired to kill or maim each other, watched by unruly, bloodthirsty mobs. In his capacity as magistrate he had often forbidden such meetings. A futile gesture, as the promoters just moved to an area outside his jurisdiction; however it showed where he stood.

"I hardly think that would be suitable."

"You'd better see him before you judge."

"Where is he?"

"Here. Carrying a hod."

She led the way out and around the house. There were several ladders, and at the foot of one lay a large dog of no recognized breed. A kind of lurcher.

"She never stirs," Bertie said. "Here comes Bolsover." The dog rose. "No need to decide now. Take a look, have a word, then think it over."

The man came briskly down the ladder; his figure was spare, taut, youthful, younger than his face which was weathered and hard and which bore, surprisingly, no marks of its owner's former trade; no crooked nose, lumpy jaw, cauliflower ears, uneven eyebrows. He just touched the lurcher on the head and was off to refill his hod when Bertie called.

"Yes madam?" Voice a surprise, too.

"This is my brother, Sir Harald Copsey. He used to take an interest in what you call the Fancy. So when I mentioned your career...."

"Oh yes...."

Of the three Bolsover was the one most at ease, though he had most reason for immediate apprehension. This was the father of that objectionable young sprig whom Bolsover had treated to the old one-two and laid out cold. And though, of course, you never knew with women, Bolsover thought he knew what was in Miss

Copsey's mind; he hadn't worked for her long but he had developed great respect for her and gathered that what she meant by this quite unecessary and irrelevant introduction was that he would be wise to make himself scarce—up the ladder, over the roof, down another and away, thus avoiding charges; assault and battery, grievous bodily harm . . . and the man a magistrate!

A trifle awkwardly, Sir Harald said,

"I must say, you appear to have guarded your face remarkably well."

"Oh, I could take care of my face, sir. *I* could take care of myself. Pneumonia ruined my bellows."

"You seem to be active."

"Good for eight or nine rounds. Who wants that?"

"I see."

Bertie said, "What Bolsover would really like is a job as valet—or something of that nature."

"Any experience?"

"Not lately, sir. I know the drill. I used to help my father. He served Lord Byron for a time—as valet and sparring partner."

"I see. Well, I'll bear it in mind. Good day to you." Bolsover's peculiar facility to foresee a move before it was made, a kind of mental antennae, informed him. Nothing to be feared from that quarter and maybe even a flicker of hope. He returned to his hod-carrying. Bertie walked with Harry to his horse.

"Well?"

"I was quite favorably impressed. But Bertie, if he is expecting a post as a valet. . . . I never employed one, as you know. And I should find it . . . well, rather difficult to explain what his actual duties would be."

Bertie thought: Oh, God give me patience! I could hit you over the head with a decanter! Then compunction set in and she said,

"Look Harry, how would it be if I talked to Bolsover and made everything as plain as possible? It would be easier for me than for you."

"I'd be everlastingly grateful. Would you?"

And then, as he actually had his foot in the stirrup and was bracing himself for the now troublesome business of mounting, he, who once could do a perfect vault-mount, withdrew his foot and justified Bertie's belief that Harry was rather special.

"I was forgetting," he said, "you said you had something to ask of me. A favor, you said, and I've talked of nothing but myself."

"It was nothing. . . . I just thought I'd like some of the stone from Copsi, some of the ruins, carved bits, for my fireplace."

There was plenty of it. What remained standing of Copsi was only a fraction of what had been, while the parts fallen in disuse, into delapidation, into ruin had been made use of; there was hardly a building in either of the villages, hardly even a pigsty which had not at some time been built of, or mended up with, a bit of the castle stone. Yet much remained, greened over with moss, humps in the garden and the park.

"Need you ask, Bertie? Of course, take what you want. And I would like you to have those two tapestries from your room. And, oh, anything else."

"Thank you, I'd like to have a bit of Copsi here."

He saw then that she was as sentimental about the place as he was and he felt sick, imagining how things would have been had Magnus been ordinary, dependable. Bertie would not have felt compelled to move from the place she loved and spend the rest of her life in this desolate spot. She might say what she liked about having planned to build, the fact remained that she had only taken the decision when she heard about Magnus's choice of wife.

He gave a vast sigh and Bertie shot out one of her fragile-looking hands and grasped his wrist.

"Try not to worry too much, Harry. And look after yourself. If I were you I wouldn't let Magnus near Reffolds until something has been decided. He might do something else—silly."

Even the use of that harmless word was a slight comfort.

"Bless you, Bertie. Where should I be without you?"

━━━━━━━━━━━━━━━━━━━━━━━━━━

Aunt Hannah awaited with some eagerness the result of her letter to Lord Hornsby. He had acknowledged hers by return of post: a brief, but friendly, if rather evasive letter, saying that of course he would do what he could, for the sake of old acquaintance; at the same time it was rather a difficult situation and he could make no definite promise. This letter she had painfully deciphered herself, using her magnifying glass; she did not wish Hannah to know about her intervention until it bore fruit.

Now Hannah had a letter, almost certainly from Copsi and in a minute or two Aunt Hannah would know.

"How terrible!"

"What, my dear?"

"Magnus Copsey wants to *marry* me!" The old woman's vanity gave itself a congratulatory hug. Good old Walter had certainly brought influence to bear! "And I'd as soon marry the Devil!"

"Of course." Aunt Hannah had long ago learned that open opposition defeated its own ends. So did blatant curiosity. She applied herself to the tidy consumption of her breakfast. Presently Hannah said,

"Mother says it is for me to decide."

"On all but one subject your Mother is a very reasonable woman."

Hannah tried again. "I'm so scared of him."

"Yes, so you said. Of course Lady Copsey might find him less intimidating."

"Lady Copsey." Hannah thought of the old lady who took such long walks, in the villages, in the woods. Then she said, "Oh, of course; but I should find that poor consolation for marriage to a man I hate—and who hates me."

"Now that *is* interesting. Do men usually propose marriage to women they hate? Unless, of course they are heiresses. . . ."

"Actually *he* didn't propose. Sir Harald did—to Mother."

"How very confusing," Aunt Hannah said and laughed, the little tinkling laugh with a hint of mockery in it.

"You know what I mean, Aunt Hannah. *Through* Mother. And Sir Harald has been very kind. Lent two men to clear up, sent a load of hay and promised to get somebody from London to see if anything can be done about Father. But . . . well, Aunt Hannah, it isn't a kind old man I'm asked to marry, but a horrible young one."

"One of life's little ironies," Aunt Hannah said. "I never liked to seem inquisitive, Hannah, but I have sometimes wondered—are your affections engaged elsewhere?"

"You mean am I in love with anybody? No. And what difference would that make? I just hate and fear Magnus Copsey." But all unbidden the figure of Jerry Flordon flashed, a just-glimpsed picture, across her mental vision. Kind, helpful, understanding—and absolutely reliable.

She reread the letter and said, unhappily, "I can't understand Mother. She *knows* how I feel. She sent me here to be safe. And now she writes so . . . well, as though it were something that needed thinking over; as though there were something to decide and only I could do it."

"You should think yourself fortunate. Hundreds, thousands of mothers would have jumped at the chance and decided for you."

"I suppose *you* regard it as a chance." There was a touch of scorn in Hannah's voice.

"It would be so considered. I can give no opinion. I have never been married. I *can* say that your mother was right in leaving the decision to you; and in saying that you should think about it. Minnie says it is a fine morning. If I were you I should take a good walk."

"The funny thing is, apart from Sir Harald's promise to find another doctor for him, Mother doesn't mention Father at all. But perhaps she wouldn't worry him with it, yet. One thing I do know, when he does hear about it, he'll be on my side."

※※※※※

At Copsi Bolsover had slipped into an anomalous position. He took some meals in the servants' hall, but he was inclined to ask for sandwiches, or a bit of something on a tray. He slept in a bedroom near Sir Harald's and Mr. Magnus's. He was supposed to be a valet, but he didn't work much. His valeting largely took the form of criticizing the way in which Sir Harald's clothes had been kept. "I've seen a tent better mended," he said of a shirt.

And that remark offered a clue to his past and a reason why he now enjoyed a near sinecure. Long ago he'd been in the wars with Sir Harald, perhaps even saved his life. That could explain, but it did not mollify. His sleeping place was held against him; so was his freedom to come and go as he wished; the fact that he could go down to the stable yard and pick the horse he wanted; his manner, arrogant; and his horrible dog which bore the entirely unsuitable name of Lily. Wherever Bolsover went, Lily went as though attached by an invisible string about four inches long. At table Bolsover gave her bits—the choicest bits—from his plate and then let her lick any gravy or fragments. It wasn't healthy; nobody could say it was healthy.

The housekeeper, long ago installed, and in this place which had no real mistress a woman of unchallenged authority, said, "If you persist, Mr. Bolsover, I shall complain to Sir Harald."

"Do that," Bolsover said and there was something about his voice and his glance, steely gray, that warned her that she would be wise not to.

Bolsover was enjoying himself immensely. He had been quite truthful when he had said that his father had served Lord Byron and that he had helped. In an age which believed in child labor, there was much that a little boy could do. There was also much to observe, to envy and to emulate. Bolsover's father died when he was eleven, just too old for the workhouse authorities to worry about him, too young—and at the time, too small—for proper employment except as a page boy, or as the miniature groom, the "tiger"' who sat bolt upright, with folded arms, at the rear of a gentleman's carriage. Both occupations were overcrowded and only entered by way of influence. Bolsover experienced some very hard times. There was, however, a way out of dire poverty for a likely young man who knew how to use his fists. It was not what Bolsover would have chosen, yet he was suited to it, having intelligence as well as aptitude, and being animated by a cold ferocity rare even in the brutalized world of the prize ring. Contrary to general belief, the fellow who did the fighting seldom made much money; the real pickings went to the promoters and to those who made lucky bets. Many fights were rigged but Bolsover was too proud to agree to be beaten, even for that extra five or ten pounds.

Most prize fighters shared a single ambition, to save enough to take a pub. Bolsover's was different; he wanted to be a country gentleman on a very small scale, a house, a garden, a few acres of pasture, a cow, a few pigs, some poultry, and above all a good horse. This modest ambition he failed to attain partly because his tastes were extravagant and because he believed that he still had years to go, so penny-pinching could wait. Many of his kind trudged from meeting to meeting, slept in ditches or under the shelter of stacks; Bolsover traveled by post-chaise, or hired a horse. Other men might lodge in low ale-houses, but for Bolsover the best hostelry within reach was just good enough. Other men got themselves encumbered with women and children; Bolsover avoided such traps, though he liked women of the more expensive kind. He was also fond of clothes and was known as Dandy Dan, Daniel being his Christian name.

Despite his way of life he had saved fifty pounds when a broken rib—not the first he had suffered—brought on pneumonia and ended his career. He had lost, and forever, that invaluable thing, staying power. He had also lost, as he discovered when he recovered consciousness in a workhouse hospital, his fifty pounds and all his belongings, even his clothes.

Now, after another wretched period of real penury, he had hit lucky. And he was using Copsi for precisely the purpose for which it had been built—keeping watch. One apparently leisurely, actually brisk walk about what remained of the castle had shown Bolsover which windows overlooked which ways of egress, which of the several staircases led most swiftly to the stableyard. Magnus, whom Bolsover had been hired to watch, stood no chance at all.

Magnus was a bit confused about Bolsover whom he recognized, as he did Lily. He understood that his Aunt Bertie had brought him into the household, possibly because of the damned dog. Bertie was mad about animals—she'd once given him the worst flogging of his life, far worse than anybody at Eton could manage,

because he had ill-treated a horse. Magnus could see that
Bertie had only to say, "Poor man, poor dog, do
something for them," and Father, soft as grease where
everything except his own son was concerned, would
hasten to do something. Father was the enemy; and very
soon Magnus saw that Bolsover was his spy.

Father said, pretending—and suddenly Magnus's
whole world became peopled by pretenders—that it
would be as well if Magnus did not go to Reffolds again.
He did not know about the firing of the hay; had he done
he would most certainly have mentioned it. Magnus had
been too cunning for him there! Father said it would be
better for him to talk to the Reeves, and that *sounded* all
right, but it seemed to have come to nothing. Just another
deception. Everybody in a plot against him.

Once Magnus set out for Reffolds, meaning to
cajole since Mrs. Reeve was so stubborn and stupid that
she couldn't heed a warning. He got half way there, and
then, out of the bit of Monkswood that flung a kind of
arm around the edge of the cultivated land, Bolsover
appeared, mounted, of course, and with his damned dog
loping alongside the horse.

Magnus believed that he was not afraid of anybody
and to a certain extent it was true; indulgence and
privilege, his belief in his own cunning had bred
confidence in him. But in his heart he did fear Bolsover
who had knocked him down flat, and seemed to be on the
lookout for a chance to do so again. That was absurd of
course; if Bolsover did that he'd lose his job. Still, it was a
fact that he had done it once, and yet been given a job. It
was also absurd to think that there was something
uncanny about the way in which Bolsover always seemed
to know where he was going, as now, bursting into the
lane between Magnus and Reffolds and saying,

"You know you're not allowed there," nodding in
the direction of the farm.

"I don't take orders from you. Get out of my way."
Magnus half raised his crop, uncertain whether to strike
the insolent fellow or the horse he rode, make it jump so
that he could pass.

"I wouldn't try it," Bolsover said in a tone all the
more menacing for being so quiet. "Lily'd have you out of

that saddle before you could say knife." It was true. Lily was already eying him, her amber eyes greened with hatred. "You leave this to your father. He's doing his best; God knows why."

"I was intending to make a friendly call," Magnus said attempting dignity.

"Umm. Set fire to the house?"

Now what possible reason could the fellow have for saying *that*. Nobody knew. Who could know? Momentarily muddled, Magnus swung his horse round and rode off.

There was a plot against him and the center of this plot was his father, pretending and lying, saying such things took time. How about shooting him? That needed a gun. And now at Copsi the guns were not only in a locked stand, but the door of the gun room was locked, too. Never mind, people sold guns. Being cunning, being crafty, Magnus left Copsi by the road that led to Bressford, though he intended to buy the gun at the new shop in Wyck. He rode as far as the crossroads, still called the Gibbet, though people were no longer hanged there, and then swung left. Very clever! So clever that he actually succeeded in buying a gun and was coming out of the shop when there was Bolsover. "I'll carry it for you, sir." Bolsover was sparing with his terms of respect; he had never called Magnus "sir" before, but the gunsmith who had accompanied his customer to the door and all the people passing by—the gunsmith had set up shop in the busiest area—could hardly know that. And while Bolsover reached out his left hand to take the gun, his right was ready, and just behind him was Lily, ready too. Magnus handed over the gun.

Sir Harald was, as Bolsover said, doing his best. He was a proud man who had never been conscious of humiliation; he'd accepted his position as second son—that was the law; his lack of promotion in the army had been easily explicable, not enough money, not enough influence and not enough of the sycophant touch. Even his impotence which had so greatly affected everything, had not humiliated him; it was an honorable wound which had deprived him, just as others deprived men of limbs or eyesight. But he did feel humiliated when circumstance forced him to go, cap in hand, as it were, to arrange a marriage between his son and a tenant's daughter. And Mrs. Reeve, that grim, dour woman, did nothing to help. She did not even look surprised when he spoke the words that almost choked him.

"Mrs. Reeve, my son wishes to marry your daughter. I am agreeable. I trust that you and your husband will be agreeable, too."

"It will be for Hannah to decide."

He allowed himself a flash of temper. "That is nonsense, Mrs. Reeve. You know as well as I do that marriages are arranged every day—between parents. It would be grossly irresponsible of you to allow such a momentous decision to be made by a girl—how old?"

"Hannah will be sixteen on St. Patrick's day."

"Old enough for marriage."

"Old enough to decide whom she should marry. She is terrified of your son."

"A little girlish timidity," Sir Harald said, sticking up for his own. "He may have been—precipitate, but did he ever hurt or damage her in any way? Or offer an insult? I assure you, my son's intentions towards your daughter are serious and strictly honorable."

"I will write and tell her so. As I said, it is for Hannah to decide."

"Or, perhaps your husband. . . ." After all, the man of the family, the direct tenant, the girl's father, should have some say.

The terrible woman went and stood by the door that led into the passage, assuming a defensive pose; completely ridiculous.

"No," she said. "I will *not* have John bothered with something that may come to nothing. I will write to Hannah and tell her to think."

He couldn't very well push past her, in her own house.

A little cog engaged in his mind. *Her* house? Whose house? He could forget certain things, some names, some dates, all men were prone to such lapses; but he loved

Copsi and all that appertained to it with such a consuming passion that every detail of leases, subleases, tithes, could be more instantly called to mind than they could be found in his tidy files. Reffolds—five years, expiring at Michaelmas this year. He thought: If that chit of a girl. . . . Bring pressure to bear. . . . The idea was obnoxious and he put it away.

Nothing had been decided hastily; it was some days before one of the men whom he had lent to get Reffolds into some kind of shape brought a note from Mrs. Reeve. "Dear Sir Harald, I enclose my daughter's letter which arrived this morning. It speaks for itself." He could hardly be said to read the letter, he absorbed its gist at a glance, cursed, and then read it in detail.

"Dear Mother, I have done what you said and thought hard and long. Aunt Hannah thinks walking helps, so I walked, but since no amount of walking could change my mind, all I've done is wear out shoe leather. Aunt Hannah is so anxious not to influence me that she will hardly talk about it; but she gives herself away now and then and I feel that actually she is in favor. I have counted the advantages, but I am not brave enough; even the thought appalls me. And now, Mother, we have the future to think of. I cannot stay here, idling time away. Perhaps Miss Drayton would help to find me a post."

So far the letter was very neatly written. Then in a scribble that could have come from another hand, "Mother, I can't. I'd sooner be one of those girls who gut herrings and put them in barrels. Give Father a kiss for me."

Outmaneuvering Mrs. Reeve was simple. Sir Harald dismounted at a short distance from the house, made a stealthy approach and tapped on the parlor window. Now that the weather was better, John's bed had been pushed much nearer the window, so that he could open and close it as he chose. It also made easier the job of tipping an unwanted drink into one of the potted plants; sometimes he even managed to throw food out of the window. He now opened it and said,

"The front door's locked, sir. If you wouldn't mind going round the back...."

"I wanted to have a word with you—in private, Reeve."

John knew what about—that doctor from London who'd poked and prodded and asked a lot of questions, but said very little. But the news was bad, if Sir Harald didn't want Martha to know!

"It's all right; she's in the dairy."

Moving like a thief, Sir Harald entered the house and got himself into the parlor. He looked at Reeve and felt a pang of compunction; that pared-down face, those hopeless eyes.

"He didn't hold out much hope, did he?"

"Oh, that so-called specialist," Sir Harald said, jerked back to the realization that there were other problems. "He is pessimist, Reeve. We'll ignore him and try again. I'm afraid that Doctor Fordyke is rather out of touch and cannot recommend the best of the up-to-date men. But it was on another matter that I wanted to talk to you. I hope *you* at any rate will be pleased to hear that my son wishes to marry your daughter."

"Marry!" In one word John Reeve managed to express the very essence of feudalism. For centuries Copseys and Reeves had lived alongside in mutual respect; a Reeve had gone with a Copsey to Crécy; good landlord, good tenant, but each in his place, generation after generation, but always the great, unbridgeable gulf... now crossed with one word.

Yet, when after a stunned silence John Reeve spoke, what he said had nothing to do with all this.

"Hannah's scared of him."

"Yes. So I understand. But I assure you, quite unnecessarily. He's young, you know, and clumsy. As a matter of fact, Reeve, I've never known him to show any interest in any girl before and now he swears that if he cannot marry Hannah, he won't marry at all. Then where should we be?"

In the same boat. Copsi without a Copsey, as Reffolds had been all these years without a Reeve. And the one Reeve, the last one, with no legs.

As though catching this vagrant thought, Sir Harald said,

"Quite apart from this, important as it is, there is Reffolds to consider. It's running down, you know. And even if a cure is found for you—as I sincerely hope it may be—it is doubtful if you could work quite as you did before."

"If I could just get my legs back, I'd work, sir."

"What I should really like to do, Reeve, is set you up in a small, comfortable house, probably in Bressford, and make you an adequate allowance so that you could employ a good manservant."

A natural enough suggestion, John Reeve thought. If Hannah married young Copsey it would hardly do for her father to be working in his shirt with dung on his boots. That thought was quickly followed by another: How wonderful it would be to have a man to deal with the bottle and the pan! There was a third thought, too: How Martha would enjoy to return to town life. He pictured her, neatly dressed, doing some leisurely shopping, going to the theatre again, to concerts; enjoying the company of educated people.

"And there need be no sense of obligation," Sir Harald said, sounding kindly, yet driving his point home. "You'd be part of the family."

"If only Hannah wasn't so scared...."

"A little natural timidity, Reeve. The boy is impetuous and lacks experience. I'm sure that once the thing was arranged, he would treat her with consideration and respect."

"I should hope so."

"Then are you agreeable?"

"Oh no. Thass not for me to say, sir. Not without talking it over with my missus, *and* with Hannah."

"Of course." Sir Harald suppressed a feeling of irritation. "I think it would be a good idea if Hannah came home and you had a good straight talk. Where is she?"

"At Radmouth, with my sister."

"I could send the carriage for her. Tomorrow?"

"Maybe I oughta have a word with Martha first."

Once again sir Harald choked back his irritation. Poor man, so entirely dependent upon that cold, hard woman, formidable in any circumstances.

"Yes," he said, "talk it over and let me know about the carriage."

They had been married for almost twenty years and never had an open quarrel. Differences of opinion, and the great grief—Johnny's death—which might have brought them closer but had set them further apart, little secret resentments which dripped acid without apparently affecting much the rock-hard foundation of their marriage. Both knew, without consciously thinking about it, that to squabble, to exchange harsh words, even blows, as some people did, would have been an acknowledgement of having chosen badly; the plain, simple farmer choosing a governess with airs and graces, the woman of education marrying a barely literate man. Such an admission would have been possible to neither, both in their way proud people and well aware of the virtue of the other. Mutual respect. And it had worked well—until now. And even now there was no shouting, no abuse. Some quiet, deadly words.

John said to Martha, "So you knew that marriage was intended. But you didn't tell me, did you? I suppose you think that because I've lost the use of my legs, I've gone daft."

"I wished you not to be bothered. Sir Harald talked to me and I wrote to Hannah, saying nothing except that the proposal had been made and that she must decide. She replied. She said, no, and I sent her letter to Sir Harald."

"Without letting me so much as see it."

"I wished to spare you."

Presently, at the end of a long, tangled talk, Martha said to John,

"I see you have been won over. Very well, let her come home and tell you how she feels. But she will not come home in Sir Harald's carriage. That would give altogether a false impression."

"Then how'll she get home?"

"As she went, by coach. And I will meet her. That is, if she decides to come home."

"You'll write and tell her not to."

"That is a totally unworthy accusation. You shall read what I write and give it to Silly Sam to post."

––––––◆––––◆◆––––◆◆––––◆◆––––◆––––

In the parlor she had sounded firm and confident; had written the letter, given it to John to read—he read very slowly—but he had said,

"All right; you put it fair and square."

Then Silly Sam had taken the letter and trudged off with it.

Afterwards, alone in the kitchen, she had one of those little breakdowns of spirit which afflict those habitually self-controlled and self-dependent. She felt so completely isolated, and helpless, and defeated. She sat down by the table and put her head in her hands. To have cried would have been a relief, but no tears came. The present crisis was bad enough, but it was taking place against a background which spelt ruin; no harvest this year and how could they keep going on the butter money, hard as she worked? They were living expensively, too, since she could not go shopping in her usual, careful way; the butcher brought meat to the door and there was a van which supplied other necessities, but such service was reflected in the prices.

She had lost faith in prayer when Johnny died; had prayers availed he'd have been alive today. She did not believe in miracles. It was with angry desperation that she thought: Oh, God, for a little real help!

And there it was. Jerry Flordon at the kitchen door.

"Good afternoon, Mrs. Reeve. May I come in?"

She had seldom been so glad to see anybody in her life, but the gladness was tempered by the realization that since the upper half of the door was open, he must have seen her in the posture of helplessness, and also by the possibility that he had just looked in on his way to somewhere. Still, if he'd just tend John for one evening; the bottle and pan routine would be difficult now that there was anger and resentment on both sides.

"Do come in. When did you get back? You're early this year, surely. I was just about to make a pot of tea."

She was endeavoring, by talk and bustle, to deny her attitude of despair.

"I got home yesterday; about two weeks early. How is Mr. Reeve?"

"No better. We had a specialist from London the other day. He did not hold out much hope."

"Well, I just looked in to see if there was anything I could do."

"About a hundred. How long can you spare?"

"Until the herring start again. And I've squared them up at home."

It was rather difficult to associate a man with such a taste for roving with any settled place of habitation; but Jerry had a mother, crippled with rheumatism, and a sister, a widow, who looked after her in a slatternly way. She'd had three small children when she came back to Copsi Minor to live; she now had six. It was a scandal but nothing could be done about it. Jerry supported them all and the rent was regularly paid; the lease granted old Mrs. Flordon security of tenure during her lifetime, and if public opinion or any other pressure forced the sloven and her brood out, who'd look after the poor woman?

"Take a cup through, will you, Jerry? It'll do him good to see a fresh face."

He was gone so long that she had time to drink two cups and was feeling better by the time he came back and began to talk. As usual, sensibly.

"I've been thinking, Mrs. Reeve. It's too late now for a cereal crop, but the land is in good heart. You could grow vegetables. They'd sell like hot cakes down at the wharf. Anything green and fresh. There'd be time for peas, beans, carrots—and potatoes, of course."

It was the kind of farming which farmers in general despised; farmers were notoriously bad gardeners. If a farm had a productive garden it was due to the woman of the house.

Martha said, "If you are to be here through the summer, that would be an excellent idea. Sam can't plough, but he can dig and with you to oversee...."

A small worry stung her.

"Did my husband say anything about Hannah?"

"Only that she was away, but coming home soon."

That was good; she had been rather afraid that John might have blurted something out, and until things were settled one way or another, the less said, the better. She would warn John about that.

"If she decides to come home, perhaps you could fetch her. She's at Radmouth."

"Of course. And if you decide to go in for vegetables, I could buy seed at the same time. Radmouth is more go-ahead than Bressford or Wyck."

Aunt Hannah, still being scrupulously neutral, did say one thing which Hannah thought at the time rather coarse, but remembered afterwards.

"I'm quite sure, my dear, that you have nothing to fear. *Nobody lets anything happen to a brood mare.*"

Precisely what Hannah was determined not to be. She was going home to have it out with Mother, whom she suspected of changing her mind at the mention of marriage, and with Father—sure to be on her side—and then she was going to seek Miss Drayton's help in finding a post. If she could find one, however poorly paid, she could send all that she earned home, for she would need no clothes, nothing in the way of toilet articles for years and years. Aunt Hannah had been so generous, saying, in her curious, offhand way that she would never wear this or that again, and if Hannah could contrive. . . . And as a parting present she had given her a dressing case, a wonderful affair, all cut glass and silver topped bottles and containers, fitting into slots in a leather case. "A very useful traveling companion," Aunt Hannah said, "but my traveling days are done now, the poor thing would only pine away in the attic." She had also given Hannah a string of pearls.

"They are genuine, my dear, none of this modern fake rubbish. But the catch is difficult. Minnie does fumble so. So I never wear. . . . . They'll serve you until you have something far better."

As Hannah had written, Aunt Hannah *did* give herself away now and again. Nevertheless, they took a fond parting from each other. "Goodbye, Aunt Hannah; thank you for having me. I have enjoyed myself—and learned a lot." "Goodbye, my dear, I hope all goes well with you. Write when you have time." "I will, I promise. And I will come to see you, too."

━━━◗◖━━━◗◖━━━◗◖━━━◗◖━━━

Now, here she was, perched up beside Jerry in the old familiar trap, going home again, but perhaps only for a short time. Everthing depended upon Magnus Copsey; whether he would take no for an answer and turn his attention elsewhere or turn even nastier, if that were possible. In the treadmill that her mind had become since the proposal was made, vague fears of some kind of devilish revenge had played a part; so had the thought of being rich, able to do something for her parents. Sometimes she actually thought: I'll do it! Then deep-seated repugnance would come over her and she knew that she could not. Glancing sideways now at Jerry Flordon, not nearly so handsome, a good deal older, and not at all rich, she wouldn't think twice about it.

"How do you think Father is, Jerry? Mother didn't say much in her letters."

"Well, he's still the same in himself. But not quite so down-hearted as he was when I left. Terribly thin, though."

"You've gone thin, too." She was the first person to notice that; to his family it was enough that he, the provider, was back with money in his pocket, and two able hands to make and mend; to Mrs. Reeve he was, fat or thin, just somebody to share her load.

"We had foul weather. Five days when even the galley was flooded. Cold water and hard tack'll get the suet off."

She had remarked upon his appearance; could he mention hers? She had changed in some indescribable way. Become—yes, elegant was the right word. Out of the pretty little girl, the pretty schoolgirl, an elegant young woman had emerged.

For this change Aunt Hannah was responsible. As one could not live in close contact with a sweep without some of the black rubbing off, so one could hardly live side by side with a woman who, though almost quite blind, still knew how to make the best of herself—and of everybody else—without something, an unconscious imitation, taking place. The way Aunt Hannah held her head, defying the double chin or the so-called dowager's hump; the way she used her hands to express things without words, the way she modified her voice, said serious things lightly and frivolous things seriously, were all transmittable. Jerry almost said: And you've grown very, very elegant, but thought he better not; it sounded too familiar. So he talked about his plans for Reffolds in this extraordinary year. "Winter cabbage," he said, almost gloatingly. "There're times when any sailor would give an ear.... I've eaten scurvy grass, and seaweed in my time. Nobody in the Copsis seems to have woken up to it yet, but there's a ready market, right on the doorstep." He talked about his plans with a rather touching enthusiasm and the treadmill in her mind went round and round. Presently it occurred to her to wonder if any gossip about Magnus Copsey and herself had leaked out. Apparently not, for in reply to her question about village news, Jerry said there was nothing much; two people, both old, had died in the hard weather, somebody had had a baby. Just the ordinary village chat. Then she thought that it might not be a bad idea to have an absolutely dispassionate opinion and she said,

"Jerry, if I told you something very secret, you wouldn't tell anybody, would you?"

"You should know me better. Go ahead, tell me."

"Magnus Copsey wants to marry me."

"Marry? Now surely you don't believe that. Hannah, he's daft. Even his father knows, at last. He's got some kind of keeper now, a fellow called Bolsover. Follows him everywhere. Don't you go believing such rubbish."

Much as the idea of the marriage appalled her, to have it so lightly, so contemptuously dismissed, was a sting to pride.

"It is not rubbish. Or a daft idea. It is a serious proposal. Made by Sir Harald to my mother. I refused at first. Now I am going home to talk it over."

"Christ!" he said, and slapped the reins. "Do you want to do it?"

"I can't make up my mind."

"Then don't. You'd have the hell of a life, Hannah. That one isn't just daft, like Silly Sam, and harmless. He's *bad*. Look what he did to Jim Bateman. There're other nasty tales about, too. How do your people feel about it?"

"I don't know. Mother said it was for me to decide."

"There she was wrong, if I may say so." Unknowingly, Jerry Flordon agreed with Sir Harald. "You're too young to decide such a thing. It's for life, Hannah, and there's more to living than money and carriages and grand clothes. There's enough misery in this world without downright inviting it. I can't see why you should even give this cranky notion a second thought."

"Sir Harald seems so set on it."

"I daresay." Jerry thought he could see why. Sir Harald wanted his son married, and nobody in his own class wanted to give a daughter to a lunatic, so he'd fixed on this poor innocent, likely to be so dazzled by such an offer that she'd overlook the drawbacks. He could hardly say that to the victim. "He's a decent enough fellow, but daft in a way. About that young lout. If he wanted the moon, he'd try to get it for him. I should reckon the loony saw you somewhere and thought you were pretty. You *are*, you know. So he goes running to Papa saying he wants you for his wife and Papa sets out, like a good retriever."

"It was rather like that."

"Then for God's sake don't do it. Don't be persuaded or talked round. Look, if it's the future you're thinking of. . . . Reffolds is in the doldrums just now, but we'll warp out. We had a good season, I've got sixty pounds clear. I'll invest it, pay the rent and the bills if there are any. I'll work and get things going, and maybe take an odd job or two like I always did. We'd manage."

"I could work, too," Hannah said in a voice which gave her away.

"Of course you could. And if we grew more than ships wanted, we'd have a stall at Bressford, vegetables, butter, eggs, fowls. It wouldn't be luxury but we'd make a living."

For a second Hannah shared this glowing, rural dream; then it was overcast by the thought of Magnus Copsey and what he might do; wreck the stall, set fire to the house as he had to the hay. Then she remembered what Jerry had said about a keeper. Perhaps, after all, there was nothing much to fear.

"Talking it over like this has made me feel a lot better," she said.

✠═══✠═══✠═══✠═══✠═══✠

Mother was in the kitchen. She'd grown thinner and her hair was much more white than gray—prettier, really. Her greeting was warm, but agitated.

"This is a terrible situation, my dear. And before you go through there," she nodded towards the parlor, "I want to tell you that if you still say no, I shall support you. Sir Harald went behind my back and won your father over with all sorts of promises. Bribery no less. But it is for you to decide."

The very opposite of what Hannah expected. But there was no time to ask, what promises? what bribery? Father had heard the trap drive past the house and was calling. She went into the parlor, at this moment flooded with the bleak, aching light of the long drawn out Spring evening. It fell on the bed, pitilessly revealing his skeletal thinness. Yet there was about him a liveliness which had not been there when she said goodbye.

"There's my girl," he said, and kissed her warmly, then, holding her at arms' length, "My word, the Radmouth air suited you. You're bonnier than ever. A sight for sore eyes."

Just for a moment her mind veered again. Father had always been on her side, her best friend. She felt that she would walk into a lion's cage if it would ease his lot in any way.

But with lions it was quickly over, not a life sentence.

Back to the treadmill. And then, after supper, the serious talk which began with an air of sweet reasonableness and deteriorated into a row—the first that Hannah had ever seen between her parents.

At first Father did the talking. Mother mended a pillowcase; a man completely bedridden, to be kept dainty, was hard on linen.

"Now look here, my dearie, I want you to

understand that nobody's trying to *make* you do what you
don't fancy. But there's a lot to be said on the other side."
He said it all, much of it new to Hannah, since Martha's
letters had mentioned no details. The snug little house in
Bressford, the regular allowance, the manservant and
none of it an obligation, part of the family. "On the other
hand, upset Sir Harald over something he's set his heart
on, and where shall we be? The lease runs out come
Michaelmas. Nobody'd let an acre to a man with no legs.
It'd mean the workhouse."

Then Mother spoke.

"So this is what you call a fair discussion. It's mental
bullying! The workhouse indeed! Oh, I know about the
lease. I looked it up. But there are places other than Copsi.
Places where *I* could earn a living. I've given this some
thought lately. If we went to Bressford or Wyck and took
a house bigger than we need perhaps I could set up a small
school. Getting enough pupils would take some time, I
suppose; in the meantime I could let lodgings."

John's horror was quite unfeigned.

"What! A lodging house! Like Morley's. A doss
house for moochers and vagabonds and navvies. You
must be out of your mind."

"You know I mean nothing of the sort. I mean a
place where decent young men could live. If I provided
breakfast and an evening meal I should be free during the
day; pupils could come to me, or I could go to them.
Hannah could help, if we had enough boarders, or pupils,
or both. If not, she could find some employment."

"And what about *me*?"

"I could look after you, as I have done."

"The very thing I don't want. And you know it." His
voice became a kind of muffled roar; his face, blanched by
months of indoor living, turned crimson. "Twenty years
we been married and never once did you give me a
minute's *real* consideration. Oh, I grant you, there was
always food waiting and a clean shirt, but what do that
amount to, set against other things? When the boy died,
don't you think I was cut to the heart just as bad as you
was? Did you ever think: Poor John, and set yourself to
give me another? No, you thought: Poor Martha, and
locked yourself away with your grief. And fool that I was,

I let you. You'd be surprised if you knew what I been through, smoothing it over, pretending I didn't mind, talking about one of Frank's boys and feeling bloody *sick*." He was obliged to pause for breath, drew it raspingly and went on in a quieter voice, but with more edge to it. "Then take the girl, all I had. I was shaping her up nicely, learning her things. *That* didn't suit, did it? No, away to school she must go, and never mind how I missed her. And through it all I cared for you, give you what I could, spared you anything mucky. Now when there's a chance to get away from *everything* mucky you talk about taking lodgers. With you still tending to me. You that couldn't step on a hen's turd without washing your shoe!" He took another breath and then said the most terrible thing of all. "And I know why. Every time you do something mucky for me, you feel better; coming in here with that smile, gloating, being the good wife that you never was."

Sometimes Miss Allsopp came to Martha Reeve's aid. She did so now and recognized hysteria, a contagious thing, and Hannah, so pale as to be almost green in the lamplight, looked as though she might cry at any minute. In such a situation somebody must be calm. Miss Allsopp was so.

She said, "John, this is unfair to Hannah. How can she think lucidly after such an outburst? I may deserve some of the abuse you saw fit to heap upon me in this mood of—irritation, but that is quite beside the point. Hannah has to consider the future, not the past, and how can she do so when you are obviously so prejudiced?" She folded the pillowcase with precision, and in a different way said, "Jerry Flordon said he would look in and see you comfortable. Hannah, you should go to bed. You've had a tiring day. And the hot-water jar should still be warm."

"Good night, Father."

"Good night, me dearie. And if I said what I shouldn't have done, give it no heed."

But how not to? The future had still to be thought about, but the past was important, too.

In the past, until she went to school, Father had been her only friend. He'd paid a tinker to make her a little

hay fork, a perfect miniature, so that she could join in the
hay-making. He'd taken her—far too prematurely—to
market with him and bought her gingerbread and
marzipan. Once, coming home, she'd been sick and he'd
cleaned her with water from the ditch. "We won't say
nothing to your mother; she'd only worry."

There was the memory of waking with earacne in
the night, and Father's hand, warm as a plaster, hard as
wood, comforting the pain.

The ritual of the lantern on winter nights. Father
would come in and go out again, doing such jobs as could
be done by the faint light, until the glorious moment when
he blew out the lantern. That meant, to the watching
child, that he was now in for good, would sit by the fire,
take her on his knee and delight her with old tales and
rustic rhymes—often concerned with the weather.

> *If the ice in November'll bear a duck,*
> *There's nowt to come except mud and muck.*

About Candlemas Day,

> *If Candlemas Day be fair and bright,*
> *Winter will take another flight,*
> *But if Candlemas Day bring wind and rain,*
> *Winter have gone and will not come again.*

He knew hundreds of such homely sayings, and to
the end of her days she would remember them and believe
that a red sunset presaged good weather, a red sunrise,
bad; and would watch the weather on the first of March,
the month which if it came in like a lion would go out like
a lamb.

He'd been her friend, her first teacher, her loving
and lovable parent; and now he wished her to marry
Magnus Copsey. She could understand that and not hold
it against him. He wanted security and a man to do the
service he hated to accept from his wife.

The scene in the parlor, so sudden and so
revealing—a lightning flash—necessarily provoked some
thoughts about marriage itself. If two people peacefully if
not ostentatiously happily married for twenty years could

feel like that. . . . Granted, Father had shouted and made accusations, but Mother had been so cold and contemptuous. What hope would a couple, grossly ill-matched from the start, have?

Reffolds was on the very fringe of Sir Harald's domain, but because the land sloped down to the river and then up again, it was possible to see from Hannah's upper window the top of the castle, a tower, a bit of battlement, a cluster of chimney stacks above the trees. Hannah, who had made no move to undress, was crouching by the window, staring out, when Martha came in with a mug of hot milk. In her rather dictatorial fashion, she said, "Drink this. You only pecked at your supper. Your father was overwrought, you know. He has nothing to do all day but lie there and think and distort and exaggerate everything. I blame Sir Harald entirely. Dangling his promises. Yet another doctor! What good did the last one do? Comfort and security for life. I've never lived in idleness and have no wish to. And I am sure that if your father could get over this absurd sensitivity about such a simple thing, he'd be the last person to wish you to marry a lunatic—and a dangerous one at that."

"Aunt Hannah—mind she was very careful not to influence me in any way—seemed to think that marriage might improve him."

"If it did, it would be the first case in history. Do drink that milk while it is warm. . . . I, too, have been careful, leaving the decision to you, but since your father has said so much. . . . Hannah I am sure my way would be best. Shall I write to Sir Harald first thing tomorrow morning, refuse very positively, and at the same time give notice? So far he has made no threat but I think it unlikely that he would renew the lease, even if I wanted it, which I don't. It would be more dignified to give notice."

Abruptly, Hannah remembered Jerry Flordon's enthusiastic talk.

"Jerry seemed to think that he. . . that we could make a living here."

"As a stopgap it seemed a feasible idea. But it would be dependent on Sir Harald's good will—and upon Jerry's reliability. I think myself that like many men just back from a hard voyage he is inclined to favor the land.

That mood may pass. Then where should we be? And
there is another thing to be considered. Even if Sir Harald
were magnanimous and allowed us to stay, what might
that young lunatic do? I've never looked on myself as an
unduly nervous woman, but lately I have lived in dread. I
wake in the night and think I smell burning. I go down in
the morning, thinking about maimed cattle...." Poor
Mother, no wonder her hair had whitened! "In Bressford
with neighbors and with police, we should be safer.... But there again, don't be influenced by me. If the
thought of being Lady Copsey carries any weight with
you, say so and risk the consequences. But for God's sake,
Hannah, decide and put us all out of our misery."

The treadmill stopped. It was wonderful to have the
thing decided for her, not by an emotional outburst like
Father's, but by Mother. A kind of peace descended.
Everything taken out of her hands.

"Mother, the idea of a title and everything else never
did appeal to me. You know that. If they had, how simple
it would have been. Or if I were less of a coward.... Even
now, I dread him. He could do us a lot of damage between
now and Michaelmas."

"Oh, I shouldn't linger on here. I should move as
soon as I found a house. The cows will fetch a higher price
now than at Michaelmas. Now, Hannah, get into bed and
go to sleep. Your mind always has been made up to refuse,
hasn't it? I wish you to refuse. And I'm sure that your
father will think better of his little outbreak this evening.
Goodnight, dear." Mother being brisk and sensible,
being, in fact, Mother.

At Copsi there was a vast, remote apartment still
called the Armory though what armor remained was now
in the Great Hall. There nowadays in the mornings
Magnus and Bolsover often had sparring matches—with
gloves of course. Sir Harald approved; it was good
healthy exercise and it allowed Magnus to work off some
of his resentment against the man. Sir Harald noticed
how cunningly Bolsover fought, permitting Magnus to
land telling blows, exaggerating their effect, but always,

towards the end, when his wind was beginning to fail, becoming professional and dealing a punch that said: "I'm master, and don't you forget it!" Then Bolsover would give a curt word of praise: "Coming along very nicely. You'll floor me, yet." A sop to pride! In private Bolsover had promised never to hurt the boy, never to aim at his head. To himself Bolsover had added: Not that he's got any brain to rattle.

Sir Harald was watching one of these semi-friendly exercises when Martha's letter was brought to him. The final, definite refusal; and—the insolence of the woman!—giving notice. Never in all his time of power had such a thing happened. Copsi tenants knew how well off they were.

He felt his face flush and his neck thicken as the blood rushed to his head; his hand clenched, crushing the offensive paper. How dare she? He'd show her! Be calm. Breathe in, out; exercise control; careful on the worn, treacherous stone steps that led up from the Armory. By the time he reached the stableyard he had mastered his rage. On his way to Reffolds he could even feel a little sorry for the simpletons who had defied him. John Reeve, he felt, was a traitor.

In the field where the wonderful barley had grown, there was some activity. Sir Harald slowed down to see what was going on. Two men, the halfwit and another, not immediately recognizable, had dug over a patch of ground and were now making shallow grooves. What on earth?

Sir Harald called and the more active of the two came to the hedge. Ha! Widow Flordon's ne'er-do-well boy.

"Morning. And what are you up to?"

"Good morning. Planting peas."

"In a corn field?"

"It's too late for anything but vegetables, sir."

"I suppose so." Sir Harald sounded disapproving of an action which in other circumstances he would have found praise-worthy; somebody doing the best he could to retrieve a loss. But there was something about young Flordon which had affected him, much as something about Martha Reeve had always done. Misfits!

He rode on, dismounted and hammered on the front door. Martha opened it and felt her whole inside give a great tremor. He had not, as she had hoped, taken her letter as final. So there was another battle to be fought.

"Morning," he said, brusquely, and pushed past her into the parlor. There he greeted John in friendlier fashion. "Good morning, Reeve. I declare you look better. Having your daughter back has done you good, eh? Well now we can sit down and put all our cards on the table."

The abominable woman said, "But Sir Harald, I wrote to you."

"You did, ma'am. That is one reason for my visit. I hope," he said pompously, "that I have never yet failed in courtesy or respect to any female, but I am obliged to tell you that in giving *me* notice you showed ignorance. Your husband leases this farm from me. It is for him, not you, to end a tenancy."

John Reeve said, "Martha. You never!"

She had armored herself again.

"Yes, I did. Hannah made her decision last night and I wrote, early this morning, to inform Sir Harald, and to give notice."

"And not a word to me. I'm confounded. I reckoned I made myself pretty plain last night, and Hannah was going to think things over. And then you. . . ."

"I wished to put an end to an intolerable situation. Hannah does not wish to marry Mr. Copsey; we can no longer run Reffolds as it should be run. Last night I realized that further discussion with you would merely lead to more emotional scenes. So I wrote the letter which should have put an end to it all."

Brazen; there was no other word for it. And as good as telling him what to do.

"Well, we'll put that aside for the moment and start again. Where is your daughter?"

"I do not wish Hannah to be involved in further argument."

Sir Harald dearly would have loved to tell her that she was now in a situation where her wish was not paramount. John Reeve forestalled him by shouting, "Hannah. Come here."

Sir Harald had not seen her since she was a child and now he looked at her eagerly, curious to see what there was about her that had so violently attracted Magnus. Pretty enough—but then at her age all girls, unless they had some disfigurement, wore the bloom of youth. Good hair, rather remarkable eyes, but nothing appealing; rather hard and cold. Not at all to his taste. She held herself well. But certainly there was nothing here to send a young man off his head. A nasty little voice said: But the boy was off his head to start with.

"Now, if we may all sit down. I think it would be as well to assume that nothing so far, said or done, is of importance. I am here, this morning, to propose a marriage between your daughter, Reeve, and my son. How do *you* feel about it?" Ostentatiously he addressed himself to the man on the bed, ignoring the woman and the girl.

Acutely uncomfortable, John looked at Martha, at Hannah, back at his landlord.

"I got nothing against it," he said slowly. "But it ain't what I feel, sir, nor what Martha feel, thass how Hannah feel. And she's against it."

"And what exactly is your objection, my dear?"

The detestable woman interfered again.

"This is the kind of ordeal to which no girl should be subjected. Had the proposal been made to one of your neighbors' daughters, and refused, you would not demand an explanation. If you insist upon a reason, blame me. I have no desire to be grandmother to a pack of idiots."

It was a bombshell in the quiet neat parlor. Sir Harald gaped. John Reeve said, "Martha!" and looked at her with hatred. Hannah found it difficult to breathe.

"It pleases you to be offensive," Sir Harald said at last. She was obviously the stumbling block; demolish her and victory would be his. John Reeve was on his side and the girl could be discounted.

"I accept your notice, Mrs. Reeve. It was not for you to give, but it is legal—a wife's actions being presumably dictated by her husband. You have, I take it, studied the lease—the reciprocal agreement; I to be responsible for repairs, your husband to keep the land under cultivation and in good heart, or to pay compensation. Take a look. The arable land is untilled, and but for my intervention the pasture would be swamp. You may have considerable savings." He paused and John Reeve played straight into his hands. "Fifty pounds with the Pelican Insurance. Against my death."

"I'm afraid it would take rather more than that," Sir Harald said, almost gently. "I should have to strip you bare. Live and dead stock. Even the furniture, I fear. The compensation would be very heavy."

"Now," John said, "you see what you've done."

"I see. I could still make a living." Really, courage must be admired, even in an enemy! The woman was made of rock.

"May I enquire *how*?"

"You may not."

"Oh, Martha's got some bee in her bonnet. Teaching school, taking lodgers...."

Now addressing nobody in particular, rather as though talking to himself, Sir Harald said,

"I am not by many standards, a rich man. But ... disappointed in a sincere hope, verbally abused, I should retaliate with all I have. I will hound you down, wherever you seek a roof, I shall be there before you—even in London. I have friends ... I have influence, I'll ... I'll...."

The furious red tide of anger mounted again; worse this time because he was angry with himself. It was inconceivable that he should be saying such things, to a stricken man, a helpless woman, a girl hardly out of childhood. But here he was, saying them—and on the verge of a stroke into the bargain. John Reeve was the color of tallow, the detestable woman white as a sheet, the girl very pale. It was as though all their blood had drained into him, thundering away in his head.

Hannah broke the terrible silence. In a voice cool, light, false, modulated like Aunt Hannah's, she said,

"None of this is necessary, Sir Harald. Perhaps I have vacillated—but then, this was my first proposal. I changed my mind yet again, last night, *after* I had talked to my parents...." She knew that Sir Harald would find this a little hard to stomach and would think that his threats had brought about the change. "From my window," she said, "Copsi is just visible over the trees. I looked at it with new eyes. Such a beautiful place—and to be asked to live in it, a singular honor. I accept."

Even in his present condition the mere mention of Copsi as being beautiful, as being the decisive factor, worked with Sir Harald.

He said, with all the sincerity in the world,

"My dear, you shall never regret it."

Martha said, "You fool!"

John said, "That's my girl! I knew it all along."

<hr>

There followed a rather macabre, highly stylized performance, a dance with every step prearranged, every gesture premeditated. Sir Harald had caught Martha's remark about a neighbor's daughter and was determined that everything should be done, and as far as he could dictate, said, as though Magnus were planning to marry one of the girls of good family with whom he had tried in vain to tempt him. His own change of attitude came easily; he'd been horrified, had overcome his horror, seen that worse things could happen; so when he said that he was delighted he spoke the truth. And now that the dye was cast he had Copsey pride to fall back upon. Whom a Copsey chose to marry was automatically elevated. But everything must be done correctly.

Informed of Hannah's decision, Magnus said, "I'll go over there at once."

"You'll do no such thing! You will sit down and write a letter, asking leave to call upon Miss Reeve at some time convenient to herself. And to her mother."

"I hate that woman."

It was easy to think kindly of an enemy so totally defeated.

"You must endeavor to conceal such feeling. She is a good woman who has had much to try her. You will behave to her as you would in similar circumstances to Mrs. O'Brien or Lady Collins. Let that be understood. Put one foot wrong *now*, and the consequences will be very unpleasant—for you."

He was applying, though somewhat late, sound

tactics and they worked. His victory, the hope that all might yet be well, had thrown him into a state of euphoria which added to his self-confidence and bolstered his authority, an authority so far as his son was concerned, no longer undermined by too much affection or self-delusion. And presently, when the engagement was properly announced, though unkind things were said in private, the situation was accepted, in some cases even approved. Mr. O'Brien actually praised the choice. "He's a wily old bird. A good solid farm girl, with no nerves, was the only hope. Imagine that wild boy married to our wild girl. They'd have bred imps hot from Hell."

Magnus went to tea at Reffolds, behaved impeccably, said very little, and gaped at Hannah all the time. John, watching from the bed, was glad to see that the fear, so frequently mentioned, seemed to have vanished. Hannah looked calm enough; Martha was the one with the fidgets.

Sir Harald's determination to make everything seem ordinary and correct, in his somewhat old-fashioned way, did not, in this modest sickroom-parlor, quite influence things as it was to do elsewhere.

Magnus said, "Now that we are engaged to be married," a statement that showed how abnormal the whole thing was, no wooing, no proposal except by proxy, "you must have a ring. You can have a new one if you like. Or an old one. We've got a lot, up at the castle."

"I should prefer an old one."

"That's all right then. Come to ... I mean, could you come to tea with us tomorrow? And Mrs. Reeve, of course. Then you could choose. Dozens and dozens. The carriage will call for you. That's all right then. Yes."

Afterwards John said, "I can't see what all the fuss was about. He behaved all right. A bit shy, but no worse than Frank's Peter, or me when I was courting you."

Martha thought: If you can't *see* the difference, what can I say? She said nothing to John, saving her words for Hannah; one last appeal. "My dear, you cannot go on with this ... this masquerade. Even when on his best behavior, an impossible person. And Hannah, he looked at you as though you were something to eat."

"Mother, *please*. I made up my mind. I gave my word. Let's not argue any more."

━━━◆━━━◆━━━◆━━━◆━━━

The family—always the last to hear, of course; they hadn't known that Bolsover was a keeper until the old ladies took tea with Mrs. Barrington—were not informed, and all agog.

Lady Copsey whose reign had been so brief, and never, since her stepdaughter's return, unchallenged, said, "A girl from one of the farms! Times are certainly changing." And that was a cue for Madame le Beaune to say, "But how romantic!" She used the word in its debased sense; she'd been an ardent attendant at theaters in her youth and still read novels. This was the old Cinderella story. "Yes, a real-life romance."

"However you may choose to regard it," Sir Harald said, "it is my wish that Miss Reeve should be treated with the courtesy which would have been extended to any other young lady whom Magnus chose to marry. I hope that is understood."

It was understood; and both ladies were prepared to be civil, but patronizing. Cousin William, who prided himself on being shrewd, said, "My dear Harald, I think congratulations are in order. I hope in twelve months time to be able to congratulate you on being a grandfather."

A bit near the knuckle, Sir Harald thought, but he struck back.

"We're all getting on, William; some of us must look to the future."

Jonathan said, "A girl from a farm. How fascinating! If she is bonny and buxom enough, I might include her in my parody of the Graces."

Sir Harald said, "All I ask is that you should all be in the Long Gallery at four o'clock, so that introductions can be made."

Everybody, including Magnus, behaved perfectly. Lady Copsey, holding to her disapproval, thought both mother and daughter very affected and the mother's

manner disagreeable; Madame le Beaune considered
Hannah a perfect fairytale figure—Rapunzel of course,
with all that beautiful hair. Cousin William expressed his
opinion—a pretty little thing, not much to say for herself.
Jonathan was disappointed; paint her as one of the
Graces and the parody would cease to be.

After tea the family dispersed and Sir Harald led the
way around the pictures, pausing here and there with an
explanation or an anecdote. The woman seemed to know
about pictures and history, and to be appreciative. But for
the reason for her being in a place where never a tenant
had set foot before, Martha would have enjoyed herself.
Every now and then Sir Harald looked back, keeping an
eye on the young couple, and twice a man—not one of the
family or he would have been introduced, and yet by his
dress and mien, not a servant—entered the Gallery,
hovered, went out again.

They came to the huge oriel window at the end of the
Gallery.

"Now, my dear, Magnus has some pretty things to
show you. I hope you will find something to please you.
Let us sit down."

Magnus had hardly exaggerated when he said there
were dozens of rings, a collection varying greatly in age
and value. Not every ring brought by a bride or given to a
wife or mother was here—some had been given to
daughters or willed away as keepsakes; these were those
which had fallen into the Copsi net and now rated as
family jewels.

Hannah took her time. Martha longed to say again:
"Don't do it; you can't do it." But she knew that Hannah's
mind was set. Hannah chose the least valuable ring of
all—a cat's eye, a golden brown stone with a darker
streak, shifting in the light. It was prettily set in filigree
silver studded with small pearls, some dead and lusterless.

Sir Harald was disappointed; he would have liked
this curiously self-possessed little person to have chosen
something splendid—say the great emerald. Then he
could have taken her back to a portrait and said, "There
you see my great-grandmother wearing it."

"It's pretty," he conceded. "And it matches your
eyes." Then Magnus had to be prompted. "Come along

now, my boy." Hannah had extended a rigid hand, the ring slipped into place. Sir Harald said, with an assumption of heartiness, "Well there you are, formally engaged. And I claim my privilege." He dropped a light, father-in-law-to-be kiss on her forehead. "I wish you every happiness."

He wished he liked her better; he wished the wedding could take place at once; but there again, care was necessary; a hurried marriage would lead to talk. Even a three months' engagement was considered short. Three months of constant vigilance, for there was something most ominously wrong. Magnus, ordered to behave well, was acting like a zombie. Or like the mechanical man in *Frankenstein*. It was as though the necessity to act normally tied his tongue, shackled his limbs. Only his eyes seemed to be alive and aware, and they were fixed in a stare directed at the girl, who, give her credit, seemed undisturbed.

Jerry Flordon, digging, planting and, since there'd been no rain, carefully watering all his precious seeds, had seen Sir Harald come and go; then the idiot had come and gone—with his keeper hovering. Then the carriage. These things would have made the situation plain without John Reeve's sudden complacency and half-hints of wonderful things to come. Hannah had settled for wealth and a title—and marriage to a lunatic. And what was it to do with him? Nothing. Certainly he had never thought about marrying her himself. He'd never contemplated marrying at all. For one thing he'd seen his own parents, always on the wrangle and then, as he got out and about, realized that few couples did much better; a happy marriage was a rarity. Nothing he had seen of his sister's children had inspired any desire for fatherhood in him and he hated the idea of being tied down. Therefore it should have been a matter of indifference to him whether Hannah Reeve married, or whom she married; but it was not. He explained his concern by telling himself that she was a nice little thing who deserved better than a mad, bad boy. In fact he'd be sorry for any girl doomed to marry Magnus Copsey.

As his womenfolk entered the house, John Reeve called. Martha took no notice but went upstairs to change. Hannah opened the door and produced a smile, remembering how Mother had always entered the parlor smiling—and he'd misunderstood, called it gloating.

"Did you enjoy yourself?"

"I did indeed. It was all wonderful. And look!" She held out her hand. Her father regarded the ring with disfavor. He knew nothing about the curious stone, but he could tell silver from gold and he knew that all engagement rings should contain a diamond, however tiny. The one he'd given Martha had set him back a bit! Seeing his look, Hannah said swiftly.

"I chose this. There were so many. Like a jeweler's shop. Buy only this one cat's eye, and they're lucky. Alice Wentworth has one—not nearly so big. We used to borrow it if we needed a bit of luck."

"Well, so long as you're happy with it. . . . Where's your mother?"

He was sensible to the fact that since the evening when he'd let himself go Martha had been avoiding him. The tending was left to Jerry, and more often than not Hannah carried in a tray for two and some excuse for Martha not eating with them. And in the evening, she'd absent herself, too. There was so much clearing up to do. "Even your mother's clothes," she said.

"She went up to change," Hannah said, "and I must, too. I'll tell you all about it, the pictures and everything, while we have supper."

With another smile she slipped away and loneliness settled down again.

❦❦❦❦

Changed, into a plain dress and sensible shoes, Hannah went out into the field.

"Which tub, Jerry?" He had set up two, just inside the field gate. One contained plain water and one other a fertilizer made by a good shovelful of horse manure, stirred in and allowed to settle.

"Plain." For his watering he used a dipper, a metal cup with a lip and a long handle. Hannah used an old pewter teapot which leaked as well as poured.

She was deliberately inviting a confrontation which she rather feared. Not that Jerry Flordon or his opinion mattered much, but he'd been very kind and understanding, siding with her, as he drove her home from Radmouth. Now he must be wondering; she felt that she owed him an explanation. For no reason that she should explain to herself she did not want Jerry to think that she was either shilly-shallying or coaxed away by all that marriage to Magnus presented.

"I see you changed your mind," he said, when they had worked in silence for some time.

"Not my *mind*, Jerry." But as she said it she realized that she would be obliged to change her mind, to abandon the attitude that had made her choose the least valuable of many rings and accept Sir Harald's salutary kiss without a smile. "The alternative was too horrible. Absolute ruin for us all." She told him about the threats—and the promises. He listened, his hard face growing harder, his greenish eyes cold with hatred.

"Nobody should have so much power," he said when he had heard all. "Nobody can be trusted with it—even a decent-seeming fellow like him."

But he understood the necessity. The principle of the thing was all wrong, but Sir Harald was within his rights. There was nothing anybody could do about it.

"I'm damned sorry, Hannah.... When's the wedding?"

"June. I heard Sir Harald tell Mother that June was a month for *pretty* weddings." They both saw the irony of that.

"Well, I shall be around for a bit after that. Look, if that young brute lays a finger on you, apart from.... Unkindly, I mean, let me know and I'll come up there and pull him apart. I mean that."

Two words—apart from.... What a mental picture that evoked! The inward tremor shook her again; and again she wondered whether she would not have done better to have yielded that night at the Wentworths'. One submission to rape and all over and done with; now there'd be years of it. With some compensation, of course.

"It'll make things better for Father," she said, with seeming irrelevancy.

"I can see he hadn't much choice. But Christ! he might have the grace to be ashamed."

"He's done nothing to be ashamed of, Jerry."

"Well, I mean a little less pleased with everyting. As though *he'd* done something wonderful. Myself I'd sooner rot in the workhouse."

"I must go in now. Goodnight, Jerry."

"I shall be looking in."

After she had gone, looking so small and fragile— why the hell hadn't the loony picked on a real farm girl, capable, if necessary, of sticking up for herself?— Jerry took a hoe and methodically destroyed everything which would not reach perfection by June—all the winter stuff. Every swipe of the hoe was in effect aimed at Magnus Copsey, violent and destructive. Then he went in to do the final tending for the night for John Reeve who had had on the whole a disappointing evening. Martha had not come to supper in the parlor and Hannah, though she had chatted away, describing the Copsey family, with lively imitations, had not said what he *longed* to hear: Father, you were right.

Then Jerry Flordon came and his attitude was wrong, too.

"I reckon I can speak out now, Jerry. I'm gonna be in a position to pay a man to look after me. In Bressford. How about you? Would you like that?"

"I should loathe it."

"Why?"

"Being tied down."

"But you wouldn't be. I don't take all that much looking after. You'd have a lot of free time."

"All my time is free, Mr. Reeve. And I don't mean to spend it cooped up in Bressford."

"Whass wrong with Bressford?"

"Everything, as I look at it."

"I'm sorry. It means looking for another man. A stranger."

"You'll have no difficulty. Heave over so that I can get to your back."

For in addition to the detestable bottle and the even

more detestable pan, there was this humiliating business of guarding against bed sores. A rubbing with strong brine; sweeps were said to use it on the little boys they used to climb chimneys. It hardened the skin. Martha knew about it and had been so conscientious that John, at first heavy, and then very thin had never had any sign of a bed sore in his six bedridden months.

———————

There was a great deal to do. Sir Harald, having taken a meditative walk around his rambling establishment, decided that the best place for housing a bride was at the end of the wing where his own room, Magnus's and Bolsover's were. Mainly south-facing and all with relatively modern windows, the rooms which had been night and day nurseries, then schoolroom and accomodation for governesses and tutors, could be made into a perfect suite for Hannah: her own sitting room, bedroom and bathroom: Magnus could still use his own room—if things went well, mainly as dressing room.

At every point Hannah was consulted. Sir Harald was so anxious to please her that had she gone wildly modern and demanded that the centuries-old paneling should be ripped out and replaced with wallpaper he would have agreed without demur. She made no such absurd suggestion; in justice he was obliged to admit that she was easy to please; but she never *seemed* to be pleased. She'd study samples of chintz and velvet and say, "I like this," and having once decided, not change her mind as women were apt to do. But she never showed any awareness of the fact that had Sir Harald been preparing apartments for a princess he could have done no more. Now that the struggle was over and the pretence that everything was ordinary well under way, it would have pleased him to make a fresh start and to forget all past unpleasantness. He would have enjoyed indulging her fancies and humoring her whims—and did in fact do so as far as she had fancies or whims—but he would have enjoyed a show of appreciation, some smiles, a little gentle teasing. Hannah was altogether too matter-of-fact, and for his taste, too unfeminine. He could not know that often, when he said she must have the best, or asked if she *really* liked this or that, she was thinking about the brood mare remark. The brood mare was certainly going to have a beautiful stable!

John and Martha were to be well-housed, too. Sir Harald had bought a small, pleasant house in Bressford's Pump Lane, a quiet place within easy reach of the shops. Its chief drawback was that it was rather dark, an impression conveyed by a combination of small windows and brown paint. Easily remedied, Sir Harald said; french windows in the parlor which would be John's room, larger windows elsewhere, the brown paint scraped off and white put in its place. He sent men from the estate to work on the house, and a gardener to put the garden in order. John Reeve was interested and grateful and responsive; Martha was not. Invited to choose wallpaper, she said, "Let John decide; it will give him something to do." "But surely, Mrs. Reeve, you must have some preference—between say roses or sweetpeas." She said, "I like both."

In some ways the stipulated three months seemed a short time in which to do all that must be done; in another way it seemed long. Sir Harald was determined that Hannah and Magnus should never be alone together because even now, with the bargain struck, he feared that Magnus might do or say something offensive which would make Martha, and therefore Hannah, withdraw, despite all his threats. The more he came into contact with mother and daughter the more he sensed a strength of character, a fundamental independence which unfitted them for the role they were to play. One mistake and the whole thing might yet be ruined. And think of the scandal that would cause.

Still, on the whole Magnus was behaving well, Bolsover was being wonderful and so, surprisingly, were both the old ladies; as indeed they should, Sir Harald reflected, considering all that he had put up with from them in the past. Hannah never lacked a chaperone. Their attitudes varied: Lady Copsey looked upon Hannah as young, ignorant and pliable, somebody who must be gently initiated; Madame le Beaune still regarded her as a fairytale person. But the two attitudes converged, markedly where the wedding was concerned.

Lady Copsey said, "Dear Harry does so want everything to be done properly, but how can a *farmer*, poor at any time and now disabled, possibly afford white satin?"

"Muslin would be more suitable," said Madame le Beune, remembering the passion for the simple life which had distinguished the last years of the *ancien règime*. Even Marie Antoinette had worn muslin now and then.

"But dear Harry is set on a *grand* wedding. I know what I shall do. Offer my own wedding dress. It has been laid away in blue paper, hardly yellowed at all and with a few adjustments, well within the capacity of any competent dressmaker to make, it should fit her perfectly."

She scored a point there, for her stepdaughter, fleeing from France with what she could carry, had not thought her wedding dress worth the space it would occupy. But she was able to make an instant riposte. She was the daughter of the house and could say, "I think I could put my hands on my grandmother's wedding veil. I remember being shown it and forbidden to touch, it was so fragile. Venetian I believe and very old."

Of these well-meant arrangements John Reeve made nonsense.

"You're my daughter. And I ain't having you go to the altar in borrowed finery. I shall fit you out, same's I should hev done if you'd married in the ordinary way. Cash money I shan't hev till the cows are sold, but my credit's good. No Reeve ever owed anybody a ha'penny. So you go into Bressford and order what you want."

Sir Harald who thought her hard and unresponsive would have been surprised by her reaction to this. A warm kiss, an embrace, an "Oh *thank* you, Father." But how would he have felt about the brief conversation between mother and daughter only a few minutes later?

"Why should he waste his money, with so much rotting away there?"

"And he'll never know," Martha said, meaning that John would not be at the wedding. She almost said, "Poor man," but did not. She still blamed him for capitulating so easily and making Hannah take this calamitous decision. She still felt that if they had held together, put up a united

front, things would have been different. All around here
Sir Harald had power, possibly in Bressford, too, and
Wyck; but there were other places.... They'd have
managed somehow. And though she did not say so to her
daughter, Martha intended to be absent from the
wedding, too. To some extent she had been like her
namesake in the Bible; correctly dressed, well-spoken, she
had given Hannah all the support in her power, but in the
final hypocrisy—Whom God hath joined let no man put
asunder—she intended to play no part. It should be easy
enough to arrange to move on the wedding day. John was
now anxious to get away from the land on which he could
no longer work, the animals he could no longer tend, and
Sir Harald had promised to use all his efforts to find him a
manservant. Martha also looked forward to the move,
and had begun making plans. She intended to find
employment and not live on Sir Harald's bounty, which
was the price of Hannah's misery.

━━━━━━━◆━━━◆━━━◆━━━◆━━━━━━━

As Lady Copsey had remarked, dear Harry
intended the wedding to be grand; it must also be correct.
It was the prerogative of the bride to choose her
attendants. Hannah asked Alice Wentworth and Doreen
Adams. "Only two?" asked Sir Harald who had visualized
six, or at least four. She replied reasonably, "Alice and
Doreen were my *close* friends; to choose from mere
acquaintances would provoke jealousy."

Then there was the question: who giveth this
woman? Conventionally the nearest male relative.
Hannah's father couldn't move from bed and she had no
brother; but there were the Norfolk Reeves and Sir
Harald's passion for correctitude made him prefer the
presence of simple farmers in their stiff best Sunday suits
to the slightest hint that he was ashamed of his future
daughter-in-law's family. There should be nothing furtive
or hole-and-corner about this wedding.

The Norfolk Reeves turned shy, with some resentment in the shyness. Nothing had actually been said, but
there had been a kind of understanding; one day—no
hurry, they were not a hurrying family— one of their
younger boys would have married Hannah and succeeded

to the tenancy of Reffolds. Shooing an exceptionally venturesome hen off the table, Hester Reeve said, "I bet Martha Fine Airs is over the moon about this, even if the boy is wrong in the head." Frank Reeve and the son nearest to Hannah in age had occasionally stayed at Reffolds to visit an agricultural show or a cattle sale; one such visit had coincided with the shooting of Jim Bateman, when talk was rife.

"A pity. I always liked young Hannah," said her uncle who had three sons but no daughter. "Do we go?"

"We do not. It'd mean a lot of clothes. And just in the middle of haymaking. You write and say we're sorry we're too busy."

"Being asked, we gotta send a present." In his way Frank Reeve was as correct as Sir Harald. His wife considered this matter. The hen fluttered up again and she hit it with the porridge ladle. "*Your* mother," she said at last, "give me some house linen. There's tablecloths I never did use."

Rebuffed, Sir Harald tried to take counsel with Martha, awkward as she had been about making the list of wedding guests; there was, she said, nobody she wished to ask; and now she said there was nobody she could suggest as a giver-away of the bride.

So Cousin William must stand in. He seemed rather pleased to be chosen and actually bought himself a new top hat. Jonathan, of course, would be Magnus's best man.

Finally only one thing remained to be settled— where should the bride spend her pre-wedding night, her horrible mother having taken the wicked decision to go on the day before the wedding, John Reeve and his bed, her own bed and kitchen stuff on the day itself? Protest was quite useless. "I have already engaged the removal men." "But surely you *knew*, Mrs. Reeve, that I have wagons in plenty, and all at your command at any convenient time." To that Martha made no reply.

Lady Copsey came to the rescue. "Poor little girl! Imagine a *mother* behaving in such a way. Quite incredible! However, she can stay with me. It hardly counts as being under the same roof, does it? And I know that the bridegroom must not see the bride until they meet

in church. I shall be very careful." Thus, with everyone
except Martha being helpful and agreeable, everything
was arranged, and there were still ten days to go. Sir
Harald was blissfully unaware that his care for, his
hovering around, his expenditure upon the bride had
made people, some of them genuine friends, wonder why
the devil he wasn't marrying her himself.

Jerry Flordon had always been a very moderate
drinker; rum at sea to keep out the cold; ashore a mug or
two of ale. Now the rhythm of his life had changed. He
was tied to one place—Reffold. He tended John Reeve,
collected what was salable from the plot in the field and
took it down to the wharf where, as he had foreseen, it had
a ready sale. Had things been otherwise, he would then
have gone back and worked, digging more ground,
planting more stuff, but so far as he was concerned,
Reffords had no future; so having disposed of his spring
onions and lettuces, radishes, peas and beans, he had
nothing to do until noon, when he was due to tend John
Reeve again. He fell into the habit of dropping in at The
River Boat; a tot of rum, another. Then a bite of whatever
the landlady in her somewhat slaphappy fashion cared to
provide. Sometimes he had a chat, but never, if he could
avoid it, with locals because with them, sooner or later,
talk came round to that damned wedding; he talked to
men off the barges and coal cobs, men whose lives were
not centered around Copsi. With John Reeve made
comfortable again, there was the long idle afternoon for
one who had never been idle in his life and had no idea of
how to spend leisure time. Boredom added to his
moodiness and he was actually pleased when Martha
asked him to help with the packing and said dispiritedly
that she supposed the great press in what had been John's
father's room would have to remain there, since it was too
bulky to get out by door or window.

"Then how did it get in?"

"I don't know. I imagine it must have been
assembled in this room."

"Then maybe it can be disassembled. Shall I take a
look?"

It was so old that there wasn't a nail in it, no metal at

all; even the doors of its upper half swung on wooden spindles. Disassembled it made two spacious cupboards and two chests of drawers. Martha pasted labels for the information of the removal men. Downstairs left; downstairs right; landing. Jerry reckoned that she and he were the only people in Copsi who weren't talking about the wedding. John Reeve talked of it all the time. Pleased as punch. Hoping the good weather held and had Jerry heard that twenty-four little village girls had been provided with white muslin dresses and were to line the path between the church porch and lych gate and scatter rose petals? "That I shan't see, of course, but I'm to see Hannah in her wedding dress."

It was impossible to think, at one and the same time: Poor man, and, God, I could crack you across the head with this bottle. And I *would*, if it'd save her.

"Maybe it's the light," Father said narrowing his eyes, "but it don't look white to me. Sorta yellow!"

"Ivory," Hannah said. "The very latest fashion. But isn't it pretty?"

"Pretty enough. Yes, very pretty. It was just the color.... Ivory, you say. Ah yes, like the piano keys.... And that veil, Dearie, I don't want to find fault, but ain't that kind of flimsy? I did tell you to buy the *best*, didn't I?"

"And this is. With lace, the flimsier the better."

"Thass all right then. Yes, you look lovely."

"And this," Hannah said. "To hold the veil in place." She placed on her head, over the veil, a little jeweled thing, shaped like a horseshoe, diamonds and pearls alternating.

"Aah...." John gave a long drawn-out sigh of appreciation. "Like a queen," he said. He repeated the compliment. "Hev your mother seen it?" For surely, surely the sight of Hannah wearing such a costly trinket would convince Martha that he had been right.

"Not yet."

"I'll call her." He wanted to see Martha's face when she was confronted with such splendor; Hannah wearing the kind of thing that no amount of hard work, no amount of careful saving, could have provided for her, not in a thousand years.

"No. Don't. I think she is busy. I'll find her," Hannah said.

Apart from agreeing that it would be senseless to spend the cow money in advance when all that was necessary was ready to hand, Martha had shown no interest in the wedding dress, and Hannah had no intention of bringing it to her notice. However, in the hope that Martha would look in, John made an effort to detain Hannah. "Turn round. Let me see the back. A train! Fancy that!" Then he asked what the bridesmaids would wear.

"Very pale rose pink. With wreaths of rosebuds on their hair. Artificial ones because real ones wilt and to buy artificial flowers helps the poor women who make them, so Madame le Beaune says." Madame was happily ignorant of the fact that makers of artificial flowers were, if anything, more cruelly exploited than seamstresses and milliners.

"Alice'll look like a cow with a wreath on its horns." That was aimed at raising a smile, and Hannah dutifully smiled.

"Now I must take it off or it won't look new on the day."

Unwillingly he let her go and in the hall she ran into Jerry, coming to perform the last duty of the day. He stared, so thunderstruck that she said with forced lightness, "It's not a ghost. Only me."

Speaking as though with difficulty, he said, "I want to talk to you. Can you be in the garden in about ten minutes?" Hannah nodded, lifted the train and went upstairs.

The garden here, as at so many farms, was a happy mixture of orchard trees, rough grass, usually scythed once a year, but not this year, a bit of shrubbery, a few flowers. On this warm June evening the air was heavy with the scent of roses, honeysuckle and mock-orange.

Jerry was there before her; the wedding dress had to be folded very carefully, and as John Reeve had noticed with resentment, Jerry's attentions had lately become very brisk, thorough but off-hand, and no time for nice gossipy chat.

They sat down on a plank bench under an old pear tree.

Now that the moment had come Jerry's rum-inspired idea and his rum-boosted determination almost deserted him. He would have been unwilling to admit it to himself, but the sight of Hannah in all that finery had been awesome, making his idea seem absurd and his determination an impertinence. But when she said,

"Well, Jerry, what is it?" he rallied his weak forces and said,

"Hannah, I've been thinking. Day and night. And you could still get out of it, even now. *If you wanted to.*"

"How? Without ruining everything?" She knew it was a silly question and would get a silly answer. There was no possible escape now. But, as the day—and that inevitable night—grew closer, fear and repugnance had swept in, in successive waves, like the incoming tide at Radmouth. And she had had nobody to whom she could talk. Father here and up at the castle everybody seemed to think that everything was wonderful; Mother, having fully expressed her disapproval, had retreated into silence.

"Nobody," Jerry said, "can have two husbands at the same time. Suppose you married me. . . ." There, he'd said it and the earth hadn't opened and swallowed him up, nor had the sky fallen. "I could get a special license. I know I've got nothing to offer—except myself, but I'd work. I'd look after you all. . . . Hannah, I can't let you do this. I'm too . . . too fond of you. I'm in love with you."

Terrible, wonderful, terrible. And awkward beyond belief; a situation new to them both, the man's experience limited to hired women and a free but lascivious woman or two, here and there. Hired women were paid, hungry women obliged; he'd certainly never loved one. Hannah was even more at a loss, her experience limited to romantic stories and poems, broken into by Magnus Copsey's brutal, shattering approach in the Wentworth's barn. No man ever offered her love. And here was Jerry Flordon, saying that he loved her, offering her the sanctuary of marriage. Her very bones melted. How easy—how all too easy, to say: I love you, too; and run away, like the girl, snatched from a distasteful match by Young Lochinvar who came out of the west....

It just would not do! Look how Sir Harald had threatened to hunt them all down—and at a time when the whole thing was a secret. How much more ruthless would he be now? Made to look a fool? The jelly in her bones had turned, started to quiver. Thank God her head.... She could still think, see the risk. No home and a helpless, bedridden man; there was no question of eloping with Young Lochinvar.

But the cool head made one mistake—the worst of her life, so far, worse than that sudden decision in the parlor. What the head dictated sounded reasonable enough. "Jerry, I can't.... If it were just us. But there's my father.... And Sir Harald would hound us down. I gave my word. There's the house at Bressford and, and, everything.... I can't. If only I could...." To soften the refusal she put her hand on his arm.

Then they were in an embrace, mouth to mouth, his heart hammering in her body, hers shaking in his. Nothing frightening, nothing insulting in this; a shared moment of passion, part of the sunset's afterglow, one with the scent of flowers.

She freed herself and said in a terrible voice—far worse than a tearful one: "Oh, Jerry. It was bad enough. Now we've made it worse."

"And you're still of the same mind?"

"I have to be." She slipped away into the dark shadow of the house.

***

So the last days came and went; and everybody said it was the most beautiful wedding....

***

Sir Harald had not slept at all. Through what seemed an endless night, he'd prowled about, looking in on Bolsover. "Is he all right?" "Sound asleep. See for yourself." Bolsover had given Magnus a blow that had put better men to sleep; he had disentangled the net and removed it, heaved Magnus into bed and been watchful, until the blow-induced unconsciousness edged into sleep. Sir Harald saw for himself. And he listened. No sound from the bride's apartments.

"You go to bed, sir," Bolsover said. "You've had a hard day."

Bolsover was ready for bed himself. He'd locked the door between the two bedrooms, was prepared to lock the door which gave Magnus's room access to the corridor. Then even Lily could sleep. But after what seemed only a few minutes, there was Sir Harald, on the prowl again. "Everything all right, Bolsover?" "Everything all right; and how about a little whisky to help you settle?" A little whisky failed to do the trick. June nights were short and the birds chorused before dawn; the clock on the stable block boomed; four o'clock, and soon after birds began; and there was Sir Harald again. Poor old man!

"How about a cup of tea?" Bolsover asked, feeling that he could do with one himself. If you must be awake in the night, you might as well be comfortable.

"If you could. . . ." Sir Harald said; he was suddenly and incongruously aware that he had never, in the whole of his life, made a cup of tea. He'd been a fag at Eton, but the boy he served had not been a tea drinker.

Bolsover went away, soft-footed, and was away for quite a time.

"The fire was out," he explained. The tea was good, hot and strong.

"I'm worried about tomorrow," Sir Harald said. The hot tea cleared his head and brought tomorrow into sharp focus. Tomorrow! Today! The early birds were silent and the light was brightening. Today! "I had such high hopes, Bolsover. Now I am completely at a loss. How can I face her?"

"The thing is," Bolsover said, dismissing trivialities and going for the basic things. "He must be kept away from her, till he's learned to behave. I see a bit of hope, with Lily."

"Lily? Oh, yes, of course, your dog. I'm sorry Bolsover, I'm not at my brightest just at the moment. I fail to see the connection—if there is one."

"There is. He set about Lily—and he paid for it. He's never touched her since; plenty of opportunity, living in the same house. So he *can* learn. He set about the girl, but I can drum it into him, given a free hand, that she is not to be maltreated."

"How?"

"Twenty-four hours, locked in and nothing to eat. They say hunger'll tame lions."

"But how could it be managed—without a lot of talk?"

"Easy. You take the g...Mrs. Copsey out for the day. Natural excuse; her folks couldn't get to the wedding. Later on I'll make it look as though he's gone to join you. That'll take care of lunch. Later on...." What on a more mobile face could have been a grin, or a leer, merely shifted the under surface of Bolsover's. "Young couple, no honeymoon, entitled to a bit of privacy. Dinner alone in her sitting room, served by me. Then, early night for everybody and that'd bring us round the twenty-four hours. If that doesn't work, call me a Dutchman. And give me another day and night."

I'll tame that young brute if it's the last thing I do!

"Well, I suppose we must try.... He has behaved so well. Do you think I could say he was drunk? But that would hardly explain my extreme rudeness. I was so angry and disappointed I hardly knew what I was saying."

"Give her a chance. There's more in that g...in Mrs. Copsey, than you'd credit." He really must stop thinking of her as the girl.

Hannah woke from her drugged sleep, knew a moment of confusion, then remembered everything, going through the horror again. The one comfort was the promptitude with which Sir Harald and Bolsover had come to her aid as soon as she screamed. The whole episode had shamed her deeply, though she was in no way to blame. She thought about Jerry and his threat. He'd never know. Nobody must know. She went to her glass to examine the damage. She had instinctively tried to protect her face and it bore only one mark, a raised, discolored weal, high on her forehead; she pulled her hair forward to hide it. There were other marks, on her arms, on her neck—long sleeves and a dress high at the collar.

Bertie came in, and there began between them the embarrassment which was to spoil their relationship for some time.

"Good morning. How are you?"

"Very well, thank you."

"Did you sleep?"

"Oh yes, thank you."

"I'll just take a look at. . . . It might need redressing. No, young healthy flesh. I don't think it'll even leave a scar." Bertie went to the window. "It's a lovely day. *He's* locked in, so no need to worry. I know it's easier said than done, but try to forget it. I must go—we start shearing today."

Almost immediately the pretty little maid with the pretty name—Melissa—who had been assigned to Hannah, came in with morning tea. Sir Harald had chosen her with particular care; she was young and shy and came from Norfolk. No connections with either of the villages, less likely to gossip. Melissa had had some training—two years as second lady's maid. She was proud of her new position and pleased to find her new mistress young and apparently amiable. Old ladies tended to be crotchety and to have so much false hair which was difficult to arrange. What did Madam wish for breakfast? What did Madam wish to wear this morning?

Hannah was considering a visit to Bressford. After all, the carriage had always been at her disposal when she was only engaged. She wanted to get away from Copsi and she was anxious to see whether her vision had any basis in reality. Was there now happiness in the new house? Now that the thing was over had Father and Mother made it up?

While she was thinking, Sir Harald came, ashamed, apprehensive, prepared for tears, reproaches, sullenness. He had reached the age where a sleepless night showed and he looked haggard as well as shamefaced. Hannah, without forgiving him, was able to think: Poor old man! He had planned ruthlessly but last night had been more than he bargained for.

He also inquired how she was, how she had slept and, given satisfactory answers, cheered up a little and suggested the very thing she had in mind.

"I have a meeting in Bressford this morning. Would you care to drive in with me, and visit your parents?"

"The one thing I should like to do. And I should like to take some flowers. They were so beautiful."

"An excellent idea. We'll take some of everything that they missed."

* * *

He took the gig—carriages were for ladies and the elderly and infirm; they also had the disadvantage of the coachman's presence making real conversation impossible. He rather hoped that Hannah would offer him an opening, but apart from commenting on the good weather and saying how well the flowers had kept, she sat silent and in the end he was obliged to speak.

"I cannot tell you how abjectly I apologize for last night. Not only for the brutal assault, but for my own behavior. I said a most unforgivable thing to you."

"It was the truth. I have often thought so myself. Had I been more yielding it would have saved everybody a great deal of bother."

What an extraordinary, ungirlish thing to say! It struck him dumb for a moment. Then he tried again.

"For Magnus there is some slight excuse; he has always had an unreliable temper and he had been drinking. He probably did not know what he was doing...."

"I think he did. He has heartily disliked me ever since I repulsed him at our first meeting."

Sir Harald was sufficiently conventional to refute that.

"No. I am sure that you are mistaken. The attraction was genuine."

"I think you are mistaken. He is incapable of any normal human feeling. I never for one moment deceived myself. You did and what happened last night must have been a severe shock. Enough to warrant whatever you said, which I am quite prepared to overlook. The main consideration, for us both, now is the future. I know what you need, Sir Harald—an heir for Copsi. And that is the difficulty. I have heard of some strange things, but never of a child begotten by a riding crop."

Even from men, hardened veterans, Sir Harald had never heard such blunt talk.

Two flies were whirring about round the gig horse's ears. He flicked them away, eyes steady, hand steady. But his mind was in turmoil. He then looked at his daughter-in-law—a neat little figure clad in a dress suitable for gig riding, nothing fluttery, a brown and yellow pattern on a cream ground; severe, high in the neck, long in the sleeves. She wore a straw hat, firmly tied on with a brown ribbon, and cream colored gloves, on hands passively folded in her lap.

My ally!

Last night he had been routed, completely demoralized, hopeless. Now something, the possible retrieval of a desperate position, sneaked back. He said, "I can absolutely assure you that nothing of this kind shall ever happen again. He is being punished at this moment. He will never be allowed near you again until he is in a better frame of mind. You are right, of course, about the need for an heir. Hard on eight hundred years.... I was forced, much against my will, but forced...."

"So was I."

"Yes," he said, ashamed again. "I'm sorry. So far as it is in my power, I will make it up to you. I can't promise that he shall never molest you again.... But I still cherish a faint hope." He paused and then said, with a kind of suppressed violence, "Once there was an heir, or the prospect of one, I'd have him put under restraint."

"You may depend upon me to keep—to the best of my ability—my side of the bargain."

"You shall never regret it."

The gig had hardly stopped before the door opened and a stout, middle-aged somberly dressed man emerged.

"Ha, Wilson! Settled in all right?"

"I hope so, sir. May I take the hamper?"

"Yes. Go steady with it. There's a bottle of champagne."

"To be served now, sir?"

"Why not? Before it gets any warmer."

Had this business in Bressford this morning been of

a serious nature, Sir Harald would not have taken a drink
of any kind; but he had merely to attend a meeting of the
Almshouse Trustees before lunch and a Board of
Guardians meeting in the afternoon. Such dull but
necessary gatherings he had neglected in the last months,
dancing attendance upon Hannah. He had the pleasant
feeling of slipping back into routine.

The french window, now open upon the garden, and
the rose-flowered wall paper had made a great difference
to the room which had seemed dull; but as Hannah, her
arms full of flowers, stepped in she was aware of
something wrong. It was possible, she thought, that
Father didn't like Wilson, so very much the gentleman's
gentleman. In that case she would get him replaced.
Where such things were concerned she had power, now.

"My dearie," John said, "I wasn't looking to see you
today."

"Hannah and I thought that since you missed the
wedding, Reeve, we'd bring some of it to you."

"Very kind of you, sir."

Hannah put the flowers on a bare table which stood
against the wall, and went to the bed, kissed her father,
was kissed by him.

"You look well," he said. "I thought about you. Did
you hev a nice wedding?"

"Wonderful. Where's Mother?"

"Gone out."

"I," said Sir Harald, "have seen many weddings.
Never a prettier one, or a prettier bride." Dear Juliet,
wherever you are, forgive me; we had a miserable wedding
and I loved you not for your beauty.

The bed was near the window. A table covered with
a clean white cloth stood near its head and there were two
chairs. Sir Harald moved the lighter looking one with a
polite gesture and Hannah sat; then he lowered himself
into the more solid one.

"Wilson shaping up all right?"

"Couldn't be better. More than I ever hoped for."

Wilson, who understood the situation perfectly and
had heard nothing except wedding, wedding, wedding,
brought in the champagne and the little oblongs of dark,
rich cake.

"Perhaps," Sir Harald said, "we should wait for Mrs. Reeve."

"No use. She'll not be back yet. Tom, get yourself a glass. This is an occasion. We must drink to the bride."

The wine duly drunk, with appropriate words, Sir Harald looked at his watch and said he must be moving. He'd call for Hannah at four o'clock. "Have a nice day, my dear."

It was anyting but a nice day. As soon as he had seen Sir Harald out, Wilson, unbidden, brought in a large jug of water and several flower vases:

"You wish to arrange the flowers yourself, madam?"

"Yes. Thank you."

"Now," John Reeve said, "you set there, where I can see you." He indicated the solid chair which faced the window. Sitting there she would have the light on her face. She mustered what she hoped was a happy expression.

"Was everything all right?"

"Oh, yes. It was a wonderful wedding."

"Now don't *you* go dodging about. You know what I mean. Was him and you all right? Are you *happy*?"

"But of course, Father." Was this what was worrying him? She composed a smile and held it out to him, an offering.

The result was unexpected; he brought one hand down in a slap on the neat bedcover.

"There you are! I always knew didn't I? But there had to be all this carry-on and talking-against. . . . I begged her to change her mind and go and show you wasn't an orphan, and come back and tell me about it. But she wouldn't. Because why? Because I wanted it. I don't count no more, except to be gone against."

"Father don't say that."

"Why not? Thass true. You look around and tell me different. Think of our little old parlor; her chester-drawers with her work in it; her desk where she done her writing; her books on the shelves. You don't see them now, do you?"

"No. But the old parlor was overcrowded, difficult to clean."

"It ain't that. This room is twice the size. And the

only thing in it belonging to her is that clock—and that, she know, I hate. All her stuff is upstairs. I hear her moving about there, after she've looked in to see if I'm dead yet; and if I want anything, call Wilson. He's all right, strong and handy and civil, but she's my *wife*. And just when we could've been so happy, her with no rough work to do. Where'd you think she is now? Out, looking for a teaching job."

"But that is understandable, Father." Keep calm, keep sane in a mad world! "Mother was a very good teacher. . . . I wasn't very willing to learn, but even Miss Drayton said she'd never had a girl of my age with such a solid grounding. And here, with no dairy and with Wilson to see to things. She wouldn't want to feel useless."

"That ain't the point. She's punishing me for doing what was best for us all."

It seemed to Hannah that several people were being punished.

Magnus was being punished. He woke with a heavy, aching head. Too much to drink. When? Where? And how did a drunken spree connect with a lump just where his jaw joined his ear? He fingered it carefully and gradually, like things looming up out of a mist, he remembered. He thought of coffee and rang his bell. It was not answered because Bolsover had thoughtfully disconnected it so that the only result of the most vigorous pull was a loose wire wagging against the wall. All right, I'll shout, get all those lazy bastards off their backsides! Both doors locked. Locked in.

By this time Bolsover had carried out his plan with some precision. In the stable yard he said, with half a grin, "The bridegroom felt like taking a walk! I'm going to meet him with his horse. Then we're going in to Bressford." It had been a wonderful wedding and nobody felt very lively this morning; nobody showed curiosity or even interest. Leading Magnus's horse, riding the one he favored, Bolsover went some distance into Monkswood and there tethered the animals; then he walked briskly back to keep watch. When Magnus understood his position he had a fit of frenzy and began smashing things. Bolsover did not worry; this wing, though nearer the kitchen quarters than many parts of the castle, was remote enough; Melissa had tidied Hannah's rooms and Bolsover had taken the precaution of saying that he had done Mr. Copsey's, so no one would come and wonder why the door was locked. All he had done was to see that there was water in the ewer, and presently, when a thread of water crept under the door and into the corridor, Bolsover thought sardonically: Now you can go thirsty into the bargain! There was no chance of escape through the window, for in Magnus's room as in Sir Harald's and Bolsover's, the ancient windows remained untouched; three narrow lancet-shaped openings separated from each other by heavy stone mullions.

In Copsi a quiet day. Despite the hamperful of delicacies which Sir Harald had taken, enough cold stuff remained and only Cousin William and the old ladies were in the dining room for lunch. Jonathan had overcome his slothfulness and his dislike for riding and gone to Axworth in search of Alice Wentworth who was exactly the model he had hoped to find in Hannah. A substantial, graceless farm girl, in her pink bridesmaid's finery looking distressingly like a pink pig, just what he wanted. Naturally as best man he had been obliged to give the bridesmaids attention, but his to Alice had been so pointed that Mrs. Wentworth had begun to cherish inordinate hopes. If a milk-and-water girl like Hannah Reeve could make such a good match, why shouldn't Alice?

Cousin William issued a word of warning; he thought that even making allowances for the eccentricities of the artistic temperament, Jonathan was being precipitate. "Simple people like that might get totally the wrong idea," he said.

"I don't care about their ideas. I have my own."

Lady Copsey also had an idea of her own. Standing there in the church and seeing Magnus married, she'd suffered a pang of premonition. Dear Harry couldn't last forever and when he died there'd be a new Lady Copsey. The title mattered to her, the more so because it had been her chief weapon in the long-drawn-out battle with her stepdaughter. Twice she had been relegated to the dowager rank, but only for brief periods. Must one go through the same hoop three times? She thought not. For the first time she thought about the empty Dower House, so often a threat, now assuming the appearance of a haven. She decided to walk across and look at it, really *look* at it, this very afternoon.

In Bressford Hannah and her father lunched on remnants of the wedding feast. He ate well, but kept looking at the clock and seemed fidgety. She was glad when she could turn her attention to the flowers. Martha's room, immediately above the parlor, was Spartan in its simplicity; nothing new here, nothing that had not been Mother's own. An eloquent room in its way. Hannah put a vase of carnations—they lasted longer than lilies or roses—on the dressing table and then went to the desk and wrote:

"Dear Mother, just in case I should be gone before you return, I wanted you to know that everything is all right. Our fears were unfounded."

Well, in for a penny, in for a pound; go the whole hog!

"I am very happy. I am sorry to have missed you, but I shall come often. Sir Harald has promised me a pony-carriage of my own. I hope you like the flowers."

She considered propping this up against the vase of flowers, thought better of it and decided to hand it to Father to give it to Mother, who would read, perhaps be deceived; then they'd make it up. Oh God, let somebody come happy out of this muddle!

Martha had set about finding employment in a methodical way. The Wheeler family was scattered but she could remember some of their friends and had written letters before leaving Reffolds. Only on person, Mrs. Bettison, replied, saying that she was certain something could be done and inviting Martha to lunch as soon as she was in Bressford and settled.

Mrs. Bettison had changed little from the plump, garrulous young matron whom Martha remembered, the mother of children roughly contemporary with the Wheelers. She was blatantly, almost vulgarly curious about Hannah's marriage which had caused talk in the town as well as in the county; the near-rudeness of some of her questions was matched by the near-rudeness of Martha's terse and unrevealing answers. A wasted lunch, really; a tête-à-tête meal with the bride's mother should really have yielded more. However, at heart, Mrs. Bettison was a kindly busybody and had, as she said, plans.

"I know quite a number of people who would like to employ a resident governess but simply lack space. None of the new houses in the Avenues can really be called a *family* house. So I thought of old Mrs. Walpole in that vast barrack in St. Mary's Square. She is in very reduced circumstances—had you heard? Positively poor, and left saddled with the house, which she may not sell. She has actually let a few rooms, but the ballroom is so huge. Nobody could *live* in it. I am sure she would be glad to let it for about five pounds a year. You would have to see it and approve, of course."

"As a classroom?"

"That was my idea. Shall we walk round, presently?"

The ballroom was vast, and, built for its specific purpose, with windows so high that inquisitive outsiders could not look in, at first a discouraging sight. With so much other roof space to keep up Mrs. Walpole had obviously neglected this and the white and gold walls were discolored by rain that had leaked in. It struck cold, even on this warm June afternoon. It had one fireplace, midway in one of its longer walls. People here were expected to keep warm by dancing. The idea of a *class* here, instead of a few children in a cosy schoolroom, rather dismayed Martha; but Miss Allsopp came to her aid and saw the advantages. It was big enough to be both schoolroom and playground—a consideration in winter; and it had a separate entrance, designed for caterers and florists and musicians in the grand old days when Mrs.

Walpole had reigned here and made a very sharp distinction between townsfolk and county people. Mrs. Bettison derived a kind of satisfaction in doing that raging snob a good turn. And she thought that Mrs. Reeve might show rather more enthusiasm, but then a woman who could be so laconic about her own daughter's spectacular match.... For a moment Mrs. Bettison wondered if she had been wise in whipping up a putative class for the Miss Allsopp she remembered.

Miss Allsopp was thinking; Screens around the fireplace in winter; and the windows are so high that even ball games could be played, if we were careful; and what about lavatory accommodation?

"Well, if you think it feasible?" Mrs. Bettison said, with a slight grit in her voice. After all she had put herself about considerably.

"Yes, I think so," Miss Allsopp said.

"Then we'll go along to my young friend in Victoria Avenue. She has twins and they have friends."

Miss Allsopp went along too and faced not only the mother of twins but a number of other mothers whose presence must surely have been planned. All the young women stood in much the same relationship to Mrs. Bettison as Mrs. Bettison had once occupied in relationship with Mrs. Walpole. And most of them would not have cared much whether Martha were qualified or not, pleasant or not; just to get Charlie or Algie or whatever his name was, out of the house, occupied—one hoped happily—for a certain time each day.

"Read that," John Reeve said, handing over Hannah's letter which he had read, very slowly, twice, three times. His justification. Martha read it and thought: All lies! What could it be but lies?

Bolsover fetched the two horses, took them back to the entrance of the stable yard, gave them each a friendly smack on the flank and left them to find their own way. Then, with Lily just the stipulated four inches behind him, alert and suspicious, he went into Magnus's room, surveyed the wreckage and the mess and said, "Very nice, I must say!" The room was a shambles. Even Bolsover was amazed. Overnight he had removed anything which Magnus could have used as a weapon, even a pair of small nail scissors; yet the pillows and the feather bed had been ripped. He must have used his teeth! "Now you can start to clear up. Make a nice job of it and you might get a bite to go to bed on. I'll look in presently."

Bolsover then went through the elaborate pretense of serving dinner in Hannah's room. Dishes brought up and placed on what was called a dumb waiter just outside the door. Everybody in the kitchen thought: Do *him* good to do a stroke of work for a change.

Magnus for the first time in his life cleared up his own mess, ramming broken crockery and handfuls of feathers into the pillowcases and bed ticking. Nobody could be expected to pick up all the feathers. There was a place in his ribs which hurt when he stopped, the lump on his jaw throbbed,; he was hungry and thirsty. Every now and then he thought he could smell food, delicious, mouth-watering food, but when finally Bolsover came back he brought a mug of water and a single, small crust of bread and he said jeeringly, "Call that a good job? Well, I don't! Lick 'em up if you can't get 'em up any other way." Magnus was very near tears. Bolsover retired again, taking the miserable provender with him.

Sir Harald felt that he ought to just look in on Magnus, but Bolsover advised against it. "He's all right; coming along nicely. You need a good night's rest."

In the last light of the long summer day, Bolsover prowled softly about the castle looking for things which would make Magnus's room fit for a housemaid's attention in the morning. It was easy here, with so many rooms never occupied, seldom entered. By the time this task was completed, Bolsover was ready for bed, too, but still strong enough and outraged enough to speak very forcibly.

"Today was just a sample of what you can expect if you ever attack your wife again. Ill-treating women and children I never did hold with. I'll beat you to pulp and keep you on bread and water for a week. Get that through your thick head."

Magnus muttered that he never wanted to see the bitch again.

━━━━━━━━━━━━━━━━━━━━━━━━━━━━━━

Outwardly life went on much as usual; Magnus's indifference to Hannah, as great as his obsession with her had once been, made life much easier, since vigilance was no longer necessary; but it was, of course very worrying since it made nonsense of the whole thing. Sir Harald tested the indifference in various small ways, culminating in letting Hannah drive alone in the promised pony carriage to Bressford and then sending Magnus on an invented errand. Magnus could not possibly have guessed that Bolsover was shadowing him, just in case; but he passed his wife on the lonely, tree-shadowed stretch of road without so much as a sign of recognition.

So much fuss and bother, so much acting out of character—all to end in nothing!

━━━━━━━━━━━━━━━━━━━━━━━━━━━━━━

"If the worse comes to the worst," Bolsover said, in August—the marriage now two months old and not consummated—"there is stuff that'd do the trick."

"Aphrodisiacs," Sir Harald said with distaste. "Highly dangerous."

"Mostly taken by old men on their last legs. A cup of tea'd finish them off!"

"You think it safe?"

"In moderation."

"Then will you see to it, Bolsover? I am very ignorant about such things."

"It'll mean going to London." Bolsover doubted whether any country chemist had ever heard of such stuff, and he certainly didn't want to go buying them in a place where he was known. It was not, on the whole, an errand that Bolsover relished—though he had suggested it. And now that the conversation had reached such an intimate level he ventured to ask the question which had for months bothered his practical mind.

"There is another way out. And I've often wondered. Why don't you marry and get yourself a proper boy?"

Nothing to be ashamed of; an honorable wound sustained in the service of one's country!

"The bullet, Bolsover, did not stop short at my thigh."

He spoke in such a way that Bolsover knew he had offended. And he felt sorry for the poor sod. He did not however, apologize or sympathize.

"Nobody'd ever guess, sir." The words were well-chosen, but afterwards, thinking them over, Bolsover saw that they were not strictly true. He'd often thought that there was something a bit old-womanish about Sir Harald, a tendency to fuss about details, over-tidiness—and of course it explained a great deal about his soft attitude towards the boy. Widow's son!

"One would hope not," said Sir Harald stiffly. Then he relented. "Judging by the efforts made over the years to get me remarried, one may be reasonably certain, eh?"

"Dead certain. Well, we must make the best of what we've got. I'll go to London tomorrow." With his half-grin Bolsover remembered that the shop he had in mind sold other things.... He had the seduction of Melissa in mind and such affairs must be conducted with a degree of nicety; a cuckoo in a nest passed unnoticed, but so far as he knew and could guard against, Bolsover had never got a girl into trouble.

❡

In this, as in other things, you never knew quite where you were with Magnus Copsey, and the consummation of the marriage could have been due to the minute doses of a powder made from dessicated, pounded beetles, or to the thunderstorm, an exceptionally violent one which ended a sultry month. Thunderstorms had always affected Magnus; Sir Harald could well remember taking him, a tiny child, into his arms to comfort him during just such a storm; nothing to be frightened of, my boy, just a noise; and under his soothing hand the child's hair seemed to crackle, his whole body to vibrate.

Well, for whatever reason, it was done and now there was only to wait. Absurd as it might seem after such upsets, what Bertie had once said about marriage possibly being the makings of the boy, could have truth in it; all through September and October, Magnus behaved in a most normal way. And the girl was superb. Seeing them together, you almost thought that the wedding-night scene was something you'd dreamed.

Jerry Flordon, contrary to custom, to his mother's delight and his sister's disgust, spent the summer hanging about. He'd take any job in either of the Copsis or down at the wharf, but most nights he was back home, criticizing the behavior of the children and the quality of food served to his mother. His sister could not very well protest, he paid the rent, he paid for the food, but the cottage always seemed more overcrowded, the children more bothersome and the old woman less contented when he was at home.

He was hanging about, just in case; he was also earning less and spending more than was his habit. Casual labor, such as he had supplied in the past to remote places, paid much better than work nearer home. And he spent money at The River Boat. So far as he knew, keeping now a sharp ear for gossip, everything was all right up there—that was the castle and certainly Hannah *looked* all right. He'd seen her without being seen. Driving with Sir Harald, presently driving alone, driving with the madman she'd married. She *looked* all right. So what was he doing, hanging about? Waiting for something which, if it ever happened, would have happened in the first few days. God knew he didn't want it to happen.... He wanted her to be happy. He'd been a bit drunk that night in the garden at Reffolds.

And you are a bit drunk now, Jerry Flordon. In fact you've been a bit drunk, on and off ever since you fetched Hannah Reeve from Radmouth. You're acting the weakling, rotting your wits and your will. And unless you soon make up your mind about the season, you won't get a berth. Imagine a winter with little to do, at Copsi! So horrible a thought called for more rum. He was more than half-seas-over when Bolsover strolled in.

Jerry knew of his existence but he had never seen him close to. The dog was unmistakable. Only lately had Bolsover felt free to absent himself during the evening and then not for long, but he had already established himself as the kind of customer the landlady liked and seldom saw, civil, well dressed and a brandy drinker.

The easiest way to strike up an acquaintance with a dog-lover was through his dog. Jerry held out a hand and said, "Hi. Nice dog." Lily, usually so cautious of such approaches, hesitated for the briefest second, then sidled over and touched the outstretched hand with her muzzle. Bolsover followed and sat down beside Jerry in the little pew-like enclosure.

"Curious," Bolsover said. "She's not one to take kindly to strangers."

"I reek of sheep."

"Farmer?"

"Drover."

Bolsover was interested; drovers were usually rough in every way, rough of speech, rough of dress, and notoriously rough in their handling of animals, a fact that Bolsover deplored, having much the same feeling for dumb creatures as he had for women and children. The world was a hard place for those who could not use their fists. . . .

The conversation could have languished there, neither being a talkative man, but Jerry, rum-dazed as he was, saw in this keeper man a possible source of information. But it must be reached in a roundabout way; so he trailed a bit of bait.

"Just a day's work," he explained. "Miss Copsey up at Sheppey Lea had three pedigree lambs to go to a breeder the other side of Wyck. They needed careful handling, so she asked me."

"She's a nice woman. I worked for her for a spell. Very fair-minded."

"You're up at the castle now?"

"Yes."

"Then I wonder could you tell me...?" Not so drunk, after all. "The Reeves, they went to Bressford, didn't they? Did they settle in well?"

"No doubt about that. Happy as larks—or so I hear from Mrs. Copsey."

"That's the daughter?"

Just a shade too cautious. Bolsover had got his bearings now. Another poor sod!

"That's right, the daughter. She visits two, three times a week. And she always comes home happy. Her mother has started up a little school and her father has just the kind of manservant he always wanted."

"That should please her."

"It undoubtedly does." Administer the merciful *coup de grâce*. Put in the final punch. "So far as I can see," Bolsover said, after a meditative sip of the brandy which the landlady had brought without his asking, "they've all been damned lucky. She's got a devoted husband and a more than devoted father-in-law, her folks taken care of, her slightest wish, a command. What more could a g..., any young lady, hope for in this wicked world?"

"I'm glad to hear it. I used to work up at Reffolds now and again. I liked the Reeves and I always thought Hannah...." What a mistake! He was so off beam now that he couldn't even say her name as though it were just an ordinary name. "A pretty little thing." Pull yourself together. "And her father's accident was bloody bad luck. I was there when it happened."

I was there; I am here, tomorrow....

Could this man, a hireling, be trusted? Was he saying what he'd been told to say? With a drunken solemnity, Jerry studied Bolsover's face; hard eyes, hard mouth, and yet somehow the man gave the impression of being honest. Jerry was accustomed, at the beginning of each voyage, to sum up his mates. Honest? Likely to be reliable in an emergency? Sometimes such qualities went with a kind sympathetic nature, sometimes they did not.

Bolsover pretended not to know what he knew, pretended not to notice the scrutiny. And he could offer reassurance without betraying any confidences. His first meeting with Magnus Copsey had taken place at Peppo's club-pub-brothel. At least a dozen men had seen Magnus kick Lily and seen the instant retaliation so what he was prepared to say was nothing new—except in its presentation.

"Mr. Copsey and I," he said casually, giving the landlady the sign that his glass was empty, "started off on the wrong foot. He kicked Lily. I knocked him out cold. But he's improved since then. A bit thick-headed, but teachable."

Get it? How thick-headed are *you*?

The landlady came across, brandy in one hand, rum in the other.

"Not for me, thanks, Sylvie. I'm heading Rad-mouth—and that's along walk." He stood up, thinking: If I fail to find a trawler there, it'll mean a longer walk; Lowestoft or Yarmouth. He cursed himself for not having followed his usual custom and signed on when he signed off. Meaning to stay at Reffolds, helping out! And look how that had ended!

He was obliged to go back to the cottage for his gear and that brought him within sight of the castle; a dark, forbidding bulk. Was it possible that happiness could exist there? For Hannah, married to a madman? With Sir Harald who might be a more-than-devoted father-in-law, but was ruthless in his exercise of power? Also, now that he was out of Bolsover's presence, the feeling that he was to be relied upon began to fade. Relied upon in what way? To be loyal to his master?

Common sense and wanderlust combined to urge him to pack his gear and be off. Nothing untoward had happened to Hannah yet, his hanging about had been pointless. Still he had promised to be within reach....

First thing in the morning he'd go back to Sheppey Lea and ask Miss Bertie if she could give him a job—any kind of job.

Some of what Bolsover had said about happiness had apparent truth. In a way Martha was happy with her little class—rapidly growing as word spread that boys actually liked to go to school. The bleak ballroom had been transformed. The parent of one boy was a builder and decorator and sent men to see that the place was watertight, and to splash some fresh white paint on the discolored walls. Another father, a coalmerchant, had promised a ton of best house coal; unwanted chairs and tables had been contributed. Martha contributed Miss Allsopp, long laid away, like a garment sprinkled with moth-repellent things, brought out and shaken, as good as new.

For five mornings of the week Martha Reeve rose, ate a breakfast prepared by Wilson, had a few words with him about the day's program, looked in on her husband, and then stepped out into the invigorating autumn air.

Somewhere between Pump Lane and St. Mary's Square, she became Miss Allsopp, so very good with children, so resourceful. Martha Reeve had been a mother, so cruelly bereaved that she had wondered if she could ever like any living little boy again; Miss Allsopp was a different creature altogether.

And she could safely leave John with Wilson. Martha could never forgive Sir Harald, but it was only just to admit that he had found the right, the best man.

Wilson could not see why John Reeve—and himself—should be housebound. He somehow procured what was known as a bath-chair; lifted into it, a rug tucked around his useless legs, John, pushed by Wilson, could go anywhere; into the market, where he was recognized and greeted cordially, around the shops, to the theater and eventually to the Chess Club. Wilson said that anybody who could play checkers could play Chess if he really gave his mind to it. John gave his mind to it. Hannah came and went and always seemed to be all right, looking well and acting cheerfully. And even Martha seemed to have relented a bit; she'd come in and chat, almost like the old times. About how the school was going, and then, presently, about a new boy called Edward; Edward Fordham, six years old, straight from India, consigned to the care of his grandmother and sent to school without so much as a handkerchief, poor little boy. Very flimsily clad, too; Martha must look into that before the weather grew really cold and if nobody else undertook to replenish his wardrobe, she'd see to it herself. Admittedly Martha's visits to John were irregular and brief, more like those of a friend than a wife, but the bitterness had gone out of the situation and John was as happy as a disabled man could be. Far happier than he had been since the accident.

At Copsi all seemed well, too; all that Sir Harald needed for complete happiness was for Hannah to become pregnant; but it was early days yet. Nobody would have guessed that Lady Copsey would be the one to disrupt everything. She did it by dying.

She had held to her idea of occupying the Dower House and work on the place had begun; so every day, whatever the weather, she walked across the corner of the park to see how things were going, to admonish frequently, to praise somewhat rarely. The house, unused for so long, always struck chill, but she was a hardy woman, and even a slight cold did not deter her.

The best cure for a slight snivel was fresh air, she said, setting off in a fog early in November and breathing as deeply as her stuffy nose would allow. A slight pain in the chest; ignore it. Mere indigestion. Very well, she felt rather poorly; but a cold did pull one down; and what was the sense in sending for Doctor Fordyke? Just for a simple cold.

She died of pneumonia.

She had never been rich, her dowry had been negligible; but she had from time to time received small legacies and she had been thrifty. Foresighted, too; she had made a proper will, leaving everyting to Magnus when he became of age, until then in trust for him. Her everything amounted to a little over four thousand pounds, and the will was made when Magnus was a baby.

Four thousand pounds. With that in his pocket a man could have a good time in Naples. That carefree, corrupt city had seemed an enchanted place to Magnus; one of the places where he had been completely happy, with Mr. Mr.-What-was-his name? Garnet? Yes, got it! Garnet, taking care of all the troublesome things. With four thousand pounds a man could hire, if not Mr. Garnet, another man like him....

In vain Sir Harald explained, and Mr. Fullerton, the lawyer who had drawn up the will and was one of the trustees, explained, that the money was not immediately available. It would be his when he was twenty-one. A long time to wait for one who had exhausted all the possibilities of pleasure in his immediate surroundings and was bored. Everything, even a complacent wife, could be a bore, too tame, too much like any other woman.

For the fact that he could not take his legacy and go immediately to Naples, Magnus blamed his father entirely. Father the enemy. It all fitted; Father was always opposed to anything that Magnus wanted to do; Father employed Bolsover to spy upon him. Now Father was robbing him, more likely than not, intending to spend the money on Copsi.

The brief time of relative happiness was over.

"I wonder," Bolsover said, "whether it'd be better to give him *some* money and let him go to Naples. He's got that on the brain now just like he had Mrs. Copsey last year." Bolsover had never been to Naples but he knew London and several other cities well. A half-wit let loose with even fifty pounds in his pocket would soon be marked down for a bludgeoning; and that was in *England*; foreign places would doubtless be worse.

Sir Harald was thinking along the same lines, but with this difference—he minded what became of Magnus.

"He once went to Bristol. Alone. Just for a couple of days. He came home penniless, and without his horse and gig. He *said* he'd lost money at cards, but the innkeeper told the man whom I sent to recover the horse and gig a different story. He said that Magnus had been set upon and robbed. I'm inclined to believe that. I think he may have been knocked on the head. You may remember, Bolsover, that I particularly asked you, when sparring with him, to avoid any blow to the skull. I may be wrong, but after all the skull houses the brain, and the boy had a terrible birth, a forceps delivery and his head. . . ." Really too painful a subject.

"Born punch drunk?"

"It is possible. What is *not* speculation is that after the Bristol visit I noticed a distinct deterioration in his behavior."

"Could be." But Bolsover had heard about the shooting of Jim Bateman. And that reminded him of something else.

"If you'll be guided by me, sir, I wouldn't go shooting with him if I were you. Not while he's in this mood."

Sir Harald would have liked to say: "Ridiculous!" But he remembered the decanter.

"It might be wise," he said reluctantly. "Though rather awkward." And hard on a man who, since he could no longer hunt, found shooting his main winter pastime. And a man could hardly say to his friends: "I can only shoot over your ground if my son is not invited to make up the party." Or, "Do come and shoot at Copsi but I shall not be joining you." Still, better that than another accident. And he had his lame leg as an excuse.

A good host holding a shoot always provided a spare gun or two; so count them out, count them in again. Unobtrusively Bolsover made this his business and sure enough, early in December, there was a gun missing. Not Magnus's, one of the spares.

While Sir Harald, the family and three or four guests who had been invited to stay on were having dinner, Bolsover conducted a search. Worse than looking for a needle in a haystack; there were so many possible hiding places. Likely ones first, Magnus's room, Hannah's apartments, the Armory; Bolsover did not expect much sense or inventiveness from Magnus, but he was cunning. Empty rooms, which now included Miss Bertie's and Lady Copsey's. And all so difficult, just by the light of a hand lamp.

But Bolsover had faith in Lily who had more sense than most people and something else as well. "Gun, Lily, gun. I'm looking for a gun." She seemed to understand and joined in the hunt, sniffing under beds and in dark corners.

If hunting indoors in such a place was hopeless, outside was worse; acres of garden, the park, fields with thick hedges, the little coppices specially preserved for the sake of wild birds, the edge of Monkswood. Bolsover knew roughly what land had been shot over that day, but that, though fairly restricted, was a wide area. He deferred the search until morning, went to his room and was in the process of removing his boots when Lily gave unmistakable sign that Magnus, her *bête-noir*, was in the vicinity. Bolsover went to his door. Magnus entered his room and came out in a blink, shrugging his way into his topcoat, ran down the stairs and out by the door of the small hallway which served this part of the house. It took Bolsover half a minute to pull on the boot he had taken off, but that did not matter; however fast Mr. Copsey went, and however far, if Bolsover said, "Find him!" she'd be on his trail.

The moon was up, now and then hidden as a cloud, pushed by a brisk east wind, scudded across, but had the night been black as Newgate following Magnus would have been easy. In fact Bolsover was obliged to restrain

Lily; he did not want to overtake Magnus until the gun
was retrieved.

Cunning was right! The young rogue had left the
gun hidden in a young pine tree, upright against the trunk,
screened from sight by the boughs. He'd just got his hands
on it, pulled it clear, and there was that damned man, and
his damned dog.

"I'll have that," Bolsover said.

They entertained the identical thought. In a struggle
for a gun, it could go off. Accident. And good riddance!

Afterwards Bolsover told himself that he should
have taken the thing more seriously; been more prepared
for the next move. Maybe because he was not giving Sir
Harald and Copsi the whole of his attention. After all he
was not a eunuch and he had seduced Melissa. In
circumstances of some splendor. Most illicit relationships
were hampered by the problem of *where*? A good hayloft
could be luxury. But Bolsover reckoned that the most
private place at Copsi was the room that had been made
ready for a king. Even there, however, he was not
completely unmindful of more serious matters, and it was
from Melissa that he knew that Hannah's life was still
governed by the cycle of the moon. As was her own. She
wished it were otherwise. She thought highly of Bolsover
as a lover and had no doubt that should she become
pregnant he would marry her forthwith; he was such a
nice, good man. He wouldn't leave a girl in the lurch.

This however, was not one of the nights when
Bolsover had given her the secret sign and all Copsi was
asleep when Lily pawed at her master's bed and whined.
Bolsover woke and knew what she wanted. She was a very
clean dog, house-trained. Lighting his candle, dragging
on his dressing gown, fumbling for his slippers, Bolsover
said, "Hold on, old dear." He thought that much as she
enjoyed the bits of game bird too badly shot or too long
hung to be quite acceptable at table, she must be denied
them. Bad effect on the bowels. He opened his door and
Lily streaked down the stairs, but instead of making for
the outer door, swerved, halted outside the library and
looked at Bolsover with meaning. Then he smelled what
she had smelled earlier.

He tried the door. Locked. Outside, run around the

house, look in at the library window. A bit like London in a peasouper, the lamps hazy and seeming to cast no light. It was a casement window and latched on the inside, but it took Bolsover no time at all to break a pane and reach in. As he did so, and scrambled over the sill, something at the far end of the room, nearest the door, flared and through the smoke Bolsover could see Sir Harald huddled on the floor near the door, and the sofa nearby blazing.

Bolsover kept his head. The quickest way out of this inferno would have been through the door; but there was no key. Wind going, but muscles still serving, he hauled the far heavier man the length of the room and heaved him through the window. The smack of the sharp night air and the rough-and-ready treatment, all aimed at making him gasp, brought Sir Harald back to consciousness; a bit confused, not quite certain where he was or what had happened, but saying the correct thing. "I'm all right...."

"Breathe deep," Bolsover said and sped away, into the house again, across the hall, into the kitchen quarters, up the servants' stairs. By the time he had alerted that part of the house and organized a chain gang of buckets from the pump over the sink, the well in the stable yard, Sir Harald had concocted his story and although it was in a way incredible and made him look like a silly old man, he stuck to it. He'd dozed off, wakened to see the sofa smoldering and in his haste and confusion locked himself in and dropped the key. It was a hateful admission for a man who prided himself on being level-headed and it was not fully explanatory. A spark from the fire? The sofa—ugly, uncomfortable and seldom used but part of Copsi and therefore to be cherished—stood just inside the door, at least twenty feet from the fireplace around which in winter the room centered, another sofa, two high wing backed chairs, two smaller ones and a table. A curious spark, Bolsover thought to fly over such obstacles, take a righthand turn and still be lively enough to set a mass of velvet and horsehair smouldering. But what he thought, he kept to himself, and everybody else was too busy quenching the blaze to have any thought at all. Once going the fire blazed with fury, licking against the paneled wall, against the door. But Copsi was so solidly built that Hannah, in the same wing, but at the extreme end of it, slept undisturbed. Nearby Magnus dreamed, a thing rare for him. In his dream somebody came in and said, "Sir Magnus. . . ." And that was enough. At the opposite end of the house Cousin William and Jonathan and Madame le Beaune heard nothing. When he did hear about it Cousin William was irritable. "Damn it all, Harry, I could have handled a bucket!"

The damage was extensive, but confined to one end of the room and Sir Harald was philosophical about all but one thing—the complete loss of an ancient map of Copsi. It had been made in 1660 and drawn in such a way that one seemed to be looking down upon the whole estate, as with an ordinary map, but everything was three-dimensional. Every field and pasture and bit of woodland had its name, many of them spelled differently—Reffolds was Revves Fold; some names had fallen into disuse, a piece of ploughland now known as the Ten Acre was marked on the map as Luke's Knob. The map itself had lain for years, rolled up on a shelf, its edges worn and yellowing. Sir Harald had rescued it, had it properly mounted and hung on the wall above the ugly sofa. The fire had destroyed it completely.

"It is an irretrievable loss," he told Bolsover. In his present vulnerable state, it also seemed to be symbolic. Magnus had destroyed the pictured Copsi just as surely as, given his head, he would destroy the place itself.

"He came in and was very abusive—about the money, of course. And I was frank. I told him that he should have money and be free to go to Naples as soon as there was a prospect of an heir. That angered him still more and he accused me—perhaps rightly— of caring for nothing but Copsi. He then went to the door. As you know, I am now careful when alone with him to sit with my back to the wall and since I find it difficult to swivel in my chair, my view was partially obstructed by its wing. So I did not actually see. But he was smoking a cigar. . . . He paused by the map and said, "That's Copsi," as though he had never seen it before. Then he went out and after a time I smelt smolder. The sofa was burning. I thought I could extinguish it, but could not; I needed water. Then I found the door locked and the key gone. After that I remember nothing."

"But for Lily you'd have died."

"You acted promptly, too. You shall be rewarded. Everyone who worked to prevent greater damage shall be rewarded."

Bolsover dismissed this as irrelevant.

"The question now is, what do we do? Lock him up?"

For a moment Sir Harald seemed, by silence, to consent.

"It would make things easier for us all, but it would defeat my purpose. He's malicious and dangerous, but cunning, too. If his liberty were curtailed in any way, he would retaliate by refusing even to attempt his duty. As it is I have seen his interest in his wife decline in the last few weeks."

"Ever since he got Naples on the brain."

"Exactly. It may pass. We must be patient and hopeful. And of course, very careful. I have always held that he acted on impulse, in a fit of rage, but this was planned, deliberately, in cold blood. A most distressing thought."

An idea, very tricky and audacious, sneaked into Bolsover's mind. To put into action, even to get it started, he needed an ally—female, and who more likely than the girl's mother?

"I've got to go to Bressford," he said. "But you'll be all right with all the workmen about. Stay with them. Keep near people. I shan't be gone long."

He intended to go by the quickest way, on horseback, and that meant leaving Lily behind. Facts must be faced and there was no doubt about it she was showing her age; she could still keep up with a horse for a short distance, a couple of miles, but after that she flagged. As usual when obliged to leave her, he filled a bowl with water, cadged a bit of ginger cake of which she was very fond, and left the door of his room open. If she wanted to go out she'd have sense enough to make for the kitchen where if no door was open somebody would let her out. "You lay down," he said. "I'll be back soon."

Actually he had no notion of how long his errand might take. Mrs. Reeve might need some persuading. He made good speed, but had to ask direction to Brook

House in St. Mary's Square as he was unfamiliar with
Bressford's residential areas; having found it he made the
mistake of going to the front door and was told curtly to
go round the back. There was a large yard, no longer
much used; there were two trodden tracks on the weedy,
grassy surface. One to the back door of the house, the
other must be the way to the schoolroom. The lobby, the
passage, neither included in the redecoration, struck a
grim note on a December morning, confirming all that
Bolsover had heard about schools and making him glad
that he had never been forced into one. However the
classroom was different—very big. Bolsover had fought
in rings no bigger, but bright. The space around the
blazing fire was enclosed by screens and inside it were
twenty little boys all aglow from the singing and the
games with which Martha opened each morning session
in cold weather.

They knew each other's names, and a good deal else,
but they had never been face to face. Martha thought that
this neatly dressed, very assured-seeming man was yet
another importunate parent and was prepared to be firm
and say that twenty was her limit.

"I'm over Copsi, madam," Bolsover said. Martha
was holding a stick of chalk and it snapped in her fingers
as she said, "My daughter?"

"No need for alarm, *so far*. But I'd like a word with
you. My name's Bolsover."

"Oh yes." She gave a few instructions about old
boys helping new ones, and overlooked the shuffle of
changing places. Then she came through an opening in
the screen wall and said,

"What is it, Mr. Bolsover?" in a way that made what
he had come to say not only outrageous but worse—plain
ridiculous. He did not easily lose his composure but there
was a formidable woman. She must be softened up. It was
a process at which he was adept.

Martha had been against the marriage and had not,
at first, been readily deceived by Hannah's seeming
contentment and gaiety; but time had moved on, nothing
untoward had happened. Gossip had a way of seeping
through however careful people were, and since most lives
were dull, the tiniest bit of drama was eagerly seized upon,

exaggerated and spread. Men from Copsi came in to market; John and Wilson frequented public houses. She felt reasonably sure that had Magnus done or said anything outrageous some whisper would have reached her. John Reeve never realized that Martha's friendly visits to him were a form of spying and usually occurred on market days, or on days when Hannah had been expected. Martha would have known by his demeanor if anything were wrong. He'd favored the match, and would therefore have been all the more dismayed if it turned out badly.

Now she listened with horror to Bolsover's revelations, well calculated to induce such emotion in any decent woman even had her own daughter not figured in the story. "He'd have thrashed her to death but for Sir Harald and me.... But for my old dog we might all have burned in our beds."

He watched her carefully as he talked and saw her normal pallor change to gray. Going to faint! He shouted, "One of you boys bring a chair." A welcome break in routine, there was more scuffling; four boys brought chairs. "Two'll do," Bolsover said. One of the chair-bearers was little Edward who stared at Martha and began to cry as she slumped into her chair, "Oh, Mrs. Reeve, don't die! Don't die! Please!" He had seen death and suffered from its results.

"Of course not, Edward. How could I die when I haven't finished your scarf? Run along, now...." The effort had partially restored her and when she turned to Bolsover she spoke with some vigor, and said precisely what he wanted of her.

"I have always said Magnus Copsey was mad and should be locked up."

"I agree. And Sir Harald has come round to it at last. But there is a hitch..." Curiously, now that the outrageous thing must be said, it was easy to say. "He won't move till Mrs. Copsey is pregnant. And that's not likely the way things are. It didn't happen while the young brute was interested, so how can it now when all he's got on his mind is Naples and getting money? And killing people. But there is a way out, madam. There's many a child begot out of wedlock but legal in the sight of law."

She took that without flinching. Encouraged, he pressed on.

"If you think about it, there's a lot to be said for it. I, for one, wouldn't expect much of any child that lunatic fathered. Also, if there was somebody Mrs. Copsey *fancied*, it'd help. Also there is that old saying about children with two fathers tending to be boys."

"It is, of course, a preposterous suggestion, but the whole situation is like something out of a nightmare." She straightened up, pulling her spine away from the back of the chair. "I suppose you wish me to put it to my daughter?"

"I thought it'd come better from you."

"Very well. I'll do my best. You are going straight back?"

"Yes. I don't like to be away long."

"It would not delay you much to go home via Pump Lane and leave a message at my house. There—or if you meet her on the road, or if she is still at Copsi, tell her I wish to see her as soon as possible."

Pump Lane took a bit of finding too, and there he had to refuse a most cordial invitation to come in and take a drop of something against the cold. He missed Hannah because he could take a short cut through the woods, on a path not wide enough for even a pony carriage. She was hurrying in to forestall rumor about the fire; she knew how quickly talk spread and she did not want Father and Mother imagining Copsi burnt to the ground.

Bolsover entered by the door he usually used. All was bustle and activity in the library and in the hall to which books and busts and the lighter pieces of furniture had been carried and were now being cleaned of the greasy film left by the smoke. The estate carpenter had taken down the library door and placed it on a table, saying planing was easier on a horizontal surface. With infinite patience he was removing the layer of charred wood. Other men were washing down walls, mending the broken window pane. Sir Harald was busy, too, handing down more books. There was a good deal of noise which *might* account for Lily's behavior.

Never yet had Bolsover, having left her behind, come back without her somehow knowing; whether she recognized his step or scented him he couldn't say, but always, before he was half way to the foot of the stairs there she was, coming down more with the motion of flowing water than that of a four-legged animal. Then she'd whimper and flail her tail and generally behave, as he fondly told her, as though he'd been away a fortnight. This morning there was no such welcome. What with the bonfire stench from the library and the noise—and getting old, poor girl. What he'd do, Bolsover thought, mounting the stairs, was take her for a nice little walk down to The River Boat. She liked going through the woods and Sir Harald would be all right.

His door was more open than he had left it and just inside his room lay a bootjack—not his own. What he had intended to say—come on old girl, you getting deaf? Or lazy?—died unsaid. He pushed into the room and there was Lily, hanging from the rail of his bed. Bolsover let out an inhuman sound and pulled out his clasp knife as he leaped towards her.

She wasn't dead. She wasn't even unconscious. As he severed the cord and she dropped into his arms she made a feeble attempt to wag her tail and her pink tongue flicked out.

She hadn't died of suffocation because the idiot had put the noose so that the pressure fell mainly on the stout spiked collar; and she hadn't died of a dislocated neck because the idiot had underestimated her length. He'd knocked her silly with the bootjack and strung her up and as soon as she came round she'd instinctively scrabbled with her hind legs for a firmer hold on the counterpane. She was strained and stiff from holding an unnatural posture for so long, and she had on her high domed forehead a lump the size of an egg.

Bolsover knew the value of massage, what he called a good rub. He did not know that he was crying as he stroked and pummeled and promised venegance. "He'll pay for this, old girl. By God, he'll pay."

Lily sipped a little water, accepted the ginger cake and presently was allowed the hitherto forbidden privilege of lying on Bolsover's bed. He helped her on to it, noting that she was still a bit stiff. "Nothing to what he'll be, God give me strength," Bolsover said.

Casual now; know nothing! We've been neglecting our exercise lately, Mr. Copsey.

There was a lapse of time. The workmen were just knocking off for their midday meal when Bolsover, holding a small valise and followed by Lily, went into the library again and said in a way that made Sir Harald instantly suspect intoxication. "I'm leaving."

Blow upon blow.

"You can't."

"I don't see what's to stop me. The strain is too much. My nerves won't stand it."

"Bolsover, I should have said you were without nerves."

"There's a point where we all crack. If you like to lock him up for good and all and give me full charge, just let me know. I shall be at The River Boat. And if you want him, he's in the Armory. Not a pretty sight."

Because Copsi was built on a slope, the Armory, though below ground floor level for the rest of the building was not actually underground. It was reached by a flight of worn stone steps and well lighted by three tall windows. On the stone floor in the unkind light of a winter midday, Magnus lay on his back. Not a pretty sight. Sir Harald, of course, had seen worse and his chief thought, once he had assured himself that Magnus was alive, was how to conceal the truth? Almost callously he dragged his son to the foot of the stairs and laid him in such a position, sprawled, face downwards, as to give the impression that he had fallen. Then, very calm and controlled he went up and said, "My son has had an accident. Bring that door. It will serve as a stretcher."

The estate carpenter, his son, and another man carried the heavy four-inch-thick door to the head of the Armory stairs and the estate carpenter looked down sideway, measured with his eye and said, "Sir, it'd only go down and sideways wouldn't be no use coming up. A rug'd be better."

"Very well, then. A rug."

Sagging on the rug and at a pace horribly reminiscent of the slow march at military funerals, Magnus was carried to his room and laid upon his bed. Sir

Harald felt that it would be wise to be alone while he investigated for other injuries than were on the boy's face—they included what looked like a broken nose—so he dismissed the men and undressed Magnus himself.

He had been right. Several red patches which would turn into bruises. But a nightshirt would conceal them. Struggling with the heavy, inert body, Sir Harald cursed Bolsover, a deserter if ever there was one! Running away just when he was most needed. And he had not only deserted, he had given offense. For so long as Sir Harald could remember no member of his household staff had ever left voluntarily. Jim Bateman and the other silly young men were in a different category.

He turned his attention to the facial injuries. Nose definitely broken. (Bolsover, looking down after Magnus fell for the last time had thought viciously: You'll never be handsome again, you young bastard!) Would a fall, face downwards, on the treacherous stairs account for a broken nose, what would soon be two black eyes and a swollen ear?

Bolsover, disloyal wretch, would probably have known how to set the nose; Sir Harald, despite his army experience, did not. He must, however unwillingly, send for Doctor Fordyke.

By this time Sir Harald was beginning to worry about the length of Magnus's unconsciousness. A knock-out blow, like the one on Magnus's nose, which at the moment seemed to be the worst, might stun a man for a time, but it was now well over an hour. Had a lady swooned in his presence Sir Harald would have suggested smelling salts, burnt feathers; but he had no faith in them, regarding them as devices to keep other women running about and so not swooning themselves, or becoming hysterical. And brandy, such a good restorative, was useless when a man couldn't swallow, it could even be a danger, making the unconscious fellow choke.

He rang the bell. Gordon answered. Seemingly in full control, Sir Harald said,

"Send a man in to Bressford for Doctor Fordyke. Say it's urgent. Then tell Fincham that I am ready for lunch. You come back and sit by Mr. Magnus while I am away."

Actually, what with one thing and another, he had

little appetite, but in this as in other matters, discipline counted. A man who had been through such shocking experiences as he had suffered since last evening needed sustenance. Going off one's fodder wouldn't help.

It was Fincham who came; and Sir Harald had time to think: Good loyal fellow! before Fincham, looking as though he were on defaulters' parade, said, "Sir, while in no way wishing to appear disobliging we all—that is Thomas, Gordon and I—and Jacky— feel that nursing is outside our duties."

Sir Harald's eyes bulged slightly.

"D'you stand there and tell me that you all refuse to obey an order?"

"It is our hope, sir, that no such order will be given." Fincham was a man of archiepiscopal dignity of mien and speech, and having delivered the message entrusted to him had regained his poise.

"A request then."

"I am sorry, sir. I am not prepared, none of us are, to accept the responsibility."

Sir Harald thought, even when he comes round he'll be stiff and sore and need to be helped to the bathroom. He was due—rather overdue, in fact, for a visit there himself.

"Then who will?"

"If I may suggest, sir, such persons can be hired."

"So can butlers and footmen and jacks-of-all-trades," Sir Harald snapped.

"As you say, sir."

What the devil had got into everybody? Last night so active and eager and helpful; today so recalcitrant.

"Sorry as I should be, sir, to terminate my association with Copsi which has lasted for thirty years...."

"Get out of my sight!" Sir Harald spoke more rudely than he had ever spoken to a servant, or a soldier, in his life. "No, wait! Send me something on a tray."

"It is here, sir." Thomas and Gordon carrying heavily laden trays, the food in double dishes filled with hot water and lidded; behind the two footmen, Jacky with fuel for the fire. Safety in numbers! Sir Harald noticed that they carefully avoided looking at the bed. What the devil?

Little things. How could a spark fly so far and take such a crooked course? And where was the key to the door? It had been searched for last night because had the library door been open water would not have had to be carried out of the house, round a corner and handed in at the window. It had not been found this morning and the estate carpenter—an unquestioned authority on such matters—said that it could not have melted; it took more heat than that to melt iron; and even if it had melted it'd still be there, a lump. Then there was the man who had helped to carry Magnus up; he was old enough to recall the time before Sir Harald forbade prize fights; and he said that to him it looked as though Mr. Copsey had taken a real pasting. And there was Bolsover, too angry to be discreet. Jacky, the runner of errands, the doer of odd jobs, had been down to the wharf to buy fresh fish, if a boat had just arrived, and coming back he'd met Bolsover, walking a bit slower than usual, keeping pace with his dog, limping a bit. Magnus Copsey had strung up his dog, so he'd knocked him out cold and quit.

Few people in or outside Copsi would have hesitated to give a dog a kick or a clout, but there was a difference; hanging a dog up to die slowly smacked of torture, a thing everybody was against. The estate carpenter went so far as to say that if he'd known that a few minutes earlier he'd have made certain that going up the stairs the young ruffian's bum got a good bump. It was all rather mysterious and being mysterious the more fearful; everybody felt sorry for Sir Harald, but not to the extent of being willing to relieve him in his watch over his son.

Left alone, Sir Harald made a check on Magnus's tongue. There was always a danger with unconscious people that the tongue might slip back and choke them. He then used the slop pail and sat down to his lunch. Sitting, his eye was more on a level with Magnus's dressing table and there he saw a key, lying between a silver-backed brush and a bottle of Macasser oil. He knew what key it was, but the long habit of being just, of not jumping to conclusions even over matters one was certain of, made him heave himself up and take a closer look.

Copsi had many doors and most of them had keys, all with permanent labels made of metal. Some ancestor of Sir Harald's, with a similar attention to small things, had grown tired of paper labels written in ink. The paper tore or the ink smudged, so he had ordered copper tags with engraved lettering. This one belonged to the library. Would anybody but a born fool, an absolute idiot, have done what Magnus had done and then tossed the key on to his own dressing-table?

And still the habit of concealment held and Sir Harald hoped with all his heart that nobody else had noticed it. He put it into his pocket and resumed his lunch.

Outside the fog came up as it sometimes did on a clear winter day. If you were out-of-doors you could see it, coming in from the sea, following the course of the river and then spreading. He thought, with unaccustomed spitefulness, of Cousin William who having made his protest at not having been roused to carry a bucket, had gone off to shoot at Fowlmere; and of that young ass Jonathan over at Axworth, painting that great lump of a girl again. Then he remembered Doctor Fordyke who should by now be setting out from Bressford.

Bressford, further inland, was merely hazy, but Doctor Fordyke knew how rapidly it could thicken, and how, with the coming darkness, it could become impenetrable; so he threw into his gig a small valise containing his nightclothes and razor and warned his wife that he might be obliged to stay at Copsi. Not that she would have worried.

The groom who had brought the message seemed ill-informed; he simply said that Mr. Copsey had fallen downstairs and that the carpenter, who knew about such things, said there were no bones broken. Doctor Fordyke tended to disregard this—ignorant laymen didn't recognize a broken bone unless it stuck through the flesh. At the bridge which formed a boundary between town and country the fog thickened and the groom shouted, "I'll go ahead, sir. The horse'll find his way home."

⊱━⊰⊱━⊰⊱━⊰⊱━⊰⊱━⊰

"He is suffering from a severe concussion, Sir Harald. The broken nose would hardly account.... Ah, yes...." the sensitive, probing fingers found what they were searching for, a bump, a laceration, both slight, at the back of Magnus's head. People—as a rule elderly or drunk—did fall downstairs, the elderly doing real damage, the drunken on the whole getting off lightly with a few contusions. But Doctor Fordyke in his considerable experience had never known of anyone falling downstairs and suffering injuries of such variety, in such diverse places. An acrobat in a deliberate tumble could hardly have broken his nose, bruised both eyes, hurt his ear and given himself a crack on the back of his skull. The injuries were far more consistent with an attack. However Doctor Fordyke was neither policeman nor coroner. It would be merciful to set the broken nose while the patient was unconscious. The unconsciousness was deep enough to warrant the word coma. And for that there was nothing that he could do except issue a warning; don't try to rouse him, don't try to administer any liquid, keep constant watch. . . .

About Magnus Copsey Doctor Fordyke knew little. An overworked man, he had no time or taste for gossip in which his poorer patients would gladly have indulged; his richer patients would never have dreamed of discussing the vagaries of one of their own kind. And like everybody else in the neighborhood the doctor had respect for Sir Harald, a faithful Friend of the Hospital, trustee of the almshouses, a member of the Board of Guardians, and on a more personal level, so energetic on behalf of John Reeve. But he did remember being consulted, years ago about, what was it? Suppressed epilepsy, of which the chief symptom had seemed to be fits of reasonless rage. Now, looking down at the young man on the bed, Doctor Fordyke thought it possible that Mr. Copsey—perhaps in a rage—had come up against somebody certainly in a rage and come off worst. Of his thoughts his manner gave no indication.

"How long is he likely to remain in this condition?"

"It is impossible to say. The external injury is slight, perhaps because of the thickness of his hair. Unfortunately we have no means of assessing the inner damage."

"I shall need a male nurse. Do you know of one?"

"I know three. None very reliable. And all engaged at the moment." Doctor Fordyke then looked at Sir Harald and thought he seemed tired and haggard, aged since he had seen him last at the Hospital Committee. "Actually," he said, intending to comfort, "very little is needed in the way of *nursing*. Somebody in attendance, of course. Any servant...."

Sir Harald could not face the humiliation of having to admit that what amounted to mutiny had broken out among his staff.

He said, "Of course." He thought: William and Jonathan will have to help; damn it I've fed and housed them all these years!

"Don't be alarmed," Doctor Fordyke said, "if, when he regains consciousness, he is somewhat confused."

Confused? Good God, he's been confused all his life.

The fog outside the windows was now so thick that the room was almost dark, but Sir Harald for once failed in the most basic courtesy—that of offering hospitality. Oh well, Doctor Fordyke thought resignedly, his horse would have to find its way home, and there'd be little danger of colliding with anything, nobody with a grain of sense would be out in *this*.

The mutinous brutes would still answer bells; they'd fetch and carry, but they all acted as though Sir Harald were in a tiger's cage, with the tiger pretending to sleep. Gordon, of course, had seen the library key and reported. "Yes, I *am* sure," he said. "I can read. I had two years at a dame school."

Sir Harald sent across to the other side of the house demanding Cousin William to come to him at once. And Cousin William sent back a polite but firm negative; he was fully occupied with Jonathan who had arrived home in a terrible state. Sir Harald did not even enquire what state, he was preparing to make his vigil as comfortable as possible. He wanted his own armchair, his dressing gown, his slippers, his cigars, his whisky, and presently his dinner. If a man had to camp out it was his duty to see that he was as comfortable as possible.

The fog had not quite reached Axworth when Jonathan said, "That's all for today, Alice. Thank you very much."

He had first of all made rather mysterious sketches,

back in the summer, for a picture which so far nobody but Cousin William had seen. A powerful sardonic parody of the Three Graces. Mrs. Wentworth was not content; she wanted, she wrote—she was the scribe of the family—a picture of Alice in her bridesmaid's clothes. And Jonathan felt that he owed the family that. So he pained a picture, pretty as an apple tree in full bloom against a blue sky. He, who hated prettiness, thought it hardly worth signing, but even Mr. Wentworth, a hard, practical man, thought it beautiful. So did neighbors. Several of them thought that anybody who could make Alice Wentworth look so pretty could do better with their daughter, and had he been interested in, or in need of, money, Jonathan could have made what country people called a pretty penny. But he was comfortably housed, well fed and not prepared to paint to order. He refused all commissions and did not think of Alice Wentworth again until he conceived the idea of a parody on the Muses, with Alice, graceless girl, as Terpsichore, with the blind girl who sold penny chapbooks as Euterpe, and so on and on.

Mrs. Wentworth and Alice were deceived by this revival of interest. Mr. Wentworth was not; his code was simple and stood the test of time. A man with serious intentions declared himself. None of this dilly-dallying about. "I'll ask him downright," Mr. Wentworth said in his uncouth way. Mrs. Wentworth begged him not to; the gentry, she said, had a different way of going about these things. Mr. Wentworth said, "Maybe. But though he make monkeys out of you two, he don't fool me. Nobody made a monkey outa me yet."

Nonetheless his confrontation with Jonathan was accidental. Jonathan was on his way back to Copsi, anxious to get home by dusk and Mr. Wentworth who was weatherwise was making his way home with what less than an hour's shooting had provided for the pot. Two cock pheasants and a hare. Half way along the lane which connected the Wentworth farm with the high road Mr. Wentworth stepped through a gap in the hedge and Jonathan's horse shied. The mutual faith which should exist between horse and rider was nonexistent; Jonathan sat in the saddle as though it were a chair, a dangerous and rickety chair, and when Mr. Wentworth, looking very large and solid and appearing so suddenly, frightened the horse, there was none of the reassurance, from hand, from voice, or knee that a frightened horse needed.

"I'd like a word with you, Mr. Winthrop."

Jonathan had been almost unseated. Settling himself into the saddle he asked, with a marked lack of graciousness,

"Yes? What is it?"

"I reckon it's about time I knew your intentions towards Alice."

"I intend to make her immortal."

It sounded flippant; but he meant it. Look what artists had done for ordinary females. That fat baker's wife with the nasty smile, La Gioconda; Emma Hamilton. Jonathan's belief in his own genius, though with so far little to encourage it, was limitless.

"You're putting daft ideas in her head. And her mother's. So now I'm telling you straight. Either you do right by Alice or clear off."

Mr. Wentworth carried his gun on his right hip, his right hand supporting the barrel which pointed, correctly, downwards. It looked casual enough, but it was a ready gun. By chance or design he shifted it slightly, and Jonathan thought: *A shotgun marriage!* One heard of such things. Fathers took guns and said, "Marry my daughter or I'll shoot you dead." Such a position, forced upon him, so utterly neutral where women were concerned, was enough to provoke a nervous giggle. He suppressed it.

"Mr. Wentworth, I *assure* you that I have never taken the slightest liberty with your daughter. And if you mean marriage, it is ridiculous."

Mr. Wentworth had himself said that a number of times; now, perversely, he changed.

"Whass ridiculous about it?"

"How could I possibly marry? I have no home, except Copsi. I have no money except what my cousin gives me."

"Easily remedied. Look across there." He jerked his head towards the stackyard beyond the hedge. A number of neat stacks and what looked like a badly made one, but with a door and two windows. "Done up a bit, it'd be just right for you and Alice. Rent free." Fond as he was of

Alice he did not wish to share his home where his wife would give Jonathan all the attention. "Alice could help her mother, and you. . . . You don't look hardy to me, but work in the open'd soon put some brawn on you. Alice'll hev a bit of money and I'd pay you. . . ." There was a brief struggle in which Mr. Wentworth's fondness for his wife and daughter got the best of his sense. "A pound a week!" Just twice the wages of a farm laborer with experience and with brawn.

The mere prospect made Jonathan hysterical.

"I'd sooner die!"

"Then bugger off and stay away. If I see your pasty face around here again I will shoot you. So help me God!"

Jonathan rode off quickly; he could already smell fog which always affected his chest.

Mr. Wentworth stood stock still for a moment. What to say? His wife would blame him entirely; hasty she'd say, and clumsy. And how would Alice feel, told that that foppish young fool would die rather than marry her? He was not an inventive man, but the desire to protect inspired him and he gave a perfect performance.

"Mr. Winthrop tell you his plans? No? Well maybe he only made up his mind when he smelt the fog. Can't stand it, it seem. Something wrong with his lungs. Gotta go abroad where there ain't no fog."

Alice wanted to cry, but pride forbade.

Mrs. Wentworth said, "Well, I always thought he looked delicate." And who wanted a lunger in the family?

Alice did cry that night, while across the passage her parents discussed other possible suitors. A bit of time had been wasted, but a girl like Alice, so pretty and with a bit of money, wasn't likely to be left on the shelf.

Hannah arrived at the Pump Lane house in time to share the guard against cold weather which John and Wilson had offered Bolsover, a concoction of sherry, hot water, honey and a pinch of mixed spice.

"I came early," she said, "because I didn't want you to hear about the fire and think the worst." What fire? Oh, nothing much, just a spark in an old sofa. "I didn't even know about it until this morning."

"I gotta message for you, dearie. Your mother wants

you to go round to the school. And don't you stop long. 'Less I've lost my weather sense we're in for a fog."

At Brook House a meal which was both picnic and lottery was in full swing. There had been some bother at first. The young, that is boys under six, were supposed to go home for lunch and stay there; older boys who lived nearby were supposed to go home to lunch and then return. Boys who lived at some distance brought a picnic meal—as Martha herself did. But, considering that they all came from roughly the same strata of society, the discrepancy was amazing and distressing. Boys with careful, loving parents, or served by good hirelings, brought a delicious food; the less fortunate were fobbed off with almost anything. Martha Reeve had seen the unfairness of it and wished she could provide something between the two extremes for all. But that was obviously impossible. Miss Allsopp had come to her rescue. Everything must be pooled and shared—even her own neat sandwiches. But how to assure that the largest and most aggressive did not come off best? Miss Allsopp had an answer for that too,—an answer which, incidentally, helped with arithmetic. A slip of paper, one for each boy, and numbered, dropped into an old soup tureen. Youngest to take his chance first, go to the table and take his pick.

Curiously, no boy resented this arrangement—how could he, when Mrs. Reeve herself was last of all, left with what nobody else had wanted?

After the meal, Martha went to the piano again and they played Musical Chairs, or Living Statues, or Sheep, Sheep Come Home. Before midterm all the boys were bringing their lunches.

Today however there was something missing, the vitality and enthusiasm which made everything such fun. High-spirited Miss Allsopp had gone, leaving Martha Reeve, preoccupied and deeply troubled behind. Little Edward kept a dubious eye on Martha, and another boy whose mother had a headache whenever anything happened to displease her, enquired, "Does your head ache, Mrs. Reeve?" "No, thank you dear. I just have something to think about."

Something to think about! Self-blame: I should

have taken a firmer stand; defied John and brought more
pressure to bear on Hannah herself, sent her away, if
necessary. Useless to think in that fashion now. It's done.
Think about the immediate things, what you are going to
say to Hannah! Think about that man Bolsover's
monstrous suggestion; absolutely immoral—but sound
common sense. If it could be managed. Of course it could
be managed; anything can be managed if the will is strong
enough. Rubbish! Your will was strong against the
marriage in the first place, and look how you were
defeated. Somebody she fancies. How can you know? By
deliberate action you've really cut yourself off from her,
content with secondhand information from a tainted
source; of course John would say that Hannah had been
in and looked fine and bonny; and of course I was only
too glad to believe it.

Think about something quite different. Think about
the gun.

She'd brought it, a rigid core in a roll of blankets,
from Reffolds to Bressford and it now stood in her
wardrobe, quite harmless. She'd known why John had
asked for it, and by lies and cunning she had prevented
him from committing suicide. Had that been altogether
wise? Balance the self-invited death of a hopelessly
disabled man in a desperate state of mind, against the life
of a young girl with everything to live for? I may have been
wrong there, too!

But she knew how to use the gun. During those first
quite happy years at Reffolds she'd often shot rabbits. For
them a more merciful death than being beaten to death by
the children who gathered in any field where harvest was
in progress and the scythes made steady inroads into the
standing corn until no sanctuary was left. She'd shot
pigeons, too, they were so terribly destructive and so
contemptuous of scarecrows.

Martha Allsopp, what are you planning?

Hannah came in, and she looked as John had
always said, and as Martha knew for herself from the
times when she had been at home when Hannah visited,
fine and bonny.

Hannah thought Mother looked very poorly, dead
pale and worried. She could have heard about the fire. . . .

"I'm all right, Mother," she said hastily, "it was only a small fire, quickly put out. I slept through it."

"So I heard. Bolsover called on me this morning. Hannah, I know *everything*." With four words she demolished the pretence that he existed between them since the wedding.

Theirs had been an unusual relationship; Martha so cool, so withdrawn, so almost unfriendly during Hannah's formative years; then, when disaster struck, so firmly and sensibly and entirely on Hannah's side. But with Hannah's decision things had changed again; Martha's repudiation of the marriage seemed to include her daughter. It was not the best basis for an intensely intimate conversation such as this was bound to be—if Martha took Bolsover's advice seriously.

Hannah had turned pale, not red, with anger.

"Bolsover had no right," she said. "I shall have something to say to him when I get home!" She was surprised. Bolsover had always seemed so closemouthed, the last person to come here, gossiping and worrying Mother.

"He acted as he thought best," Martha said. "Let me just settle the boys."

She drove them out into the part of the room called the playground, set them to games, quiet, but not silent; this was one conversation no word of which must be overheard.

Inside the screens, by the fire, and seated, Martha said,

"Bolsover, I suppose, was not exaggerating?"

"Far from it. But what good he thought he could do, coming here with his babble, I fail to see."

"He enlightened me and set me thinking about what to do."

"What could anybody do? Magnus is mad, we knew it from the first, didn't we? There seemed to be a slight improvement, but only while his venom changed direction. It is now directed against Sir Harald."

"I am desperately sorry for you, Hannah."

"I chose my fate."

"Has Sir Harald ever said anything to you about putting him under constraint—once you became pregnant?"

"Oh yes. That was understood almost from the first. Copsi must have an heir! He seems oblivious, poor man, to the fact that it might be a girl, or another idiot."

An opening of which Martha could take advantage.

"Sex, of course, is a matter beyond our control, but if you chose a sane, healthy man as a father...."

There! It was said. Rather like a tooth extraction, dreaded beforehand and over in a second. Hannah did not even look shocked. Her eyes had narrowed a little.

"Is that Sir Harald's suggestion?"

"Good gracious no! How could it be?"

"I merely wondered. You see, in his way, he is unbalanced too. Sane in most ways, he is quite mad about Copsi. Magnus and I were married in June; after the wedding night he didn't come near me again until late August. In November he got another bee in his bonnet and has avoided me in that way since. So I had two months. It did just occur to me that Sir Harald could have decided that I was barren and decided to get rid of me. And how better than by making such a suggestion and then catching me out in an act of adultery?"

Martha *was* shocked. By the complete cynicism, the total acceptance of disillusionment. In a girl so young, as age went, barely out of the schoolroom. What she must have suffered to learn so much in so short a time.

"It has nothing to do with Sir Harald—in fact he must never know." Better not mention Bolsover. "It is an expedient to which many women in your position, my poor dear, have resorted, often successfully."

"I shall think about it. Of course a good deal depends upon the attitude Sir Harald takes to last night's little prank. I suppose Bolsover told you all about *that*."

Martha nodded. "I realized then that some action must be taken. Think what might have happened. Of course there is an alternative—I could shoot him."

"Mother!" Hannah's carefully cultivated imperturbability gave way at last. "What a fantastic notion!"

"Actually not. Magnus Copsey must have made many enemies but I am not acknowledged as one, so what motive could I have? I should come to spend the evening with you at Copsi; what more natural? I should bring your father's gun hidden inside one of the screens you so kindly provided. I should be returning it as unsuitable, far too light; in fact one of them is, mere bamboo. . . . Ladies still retire from the table, leaving gentlemen to their port, do they not? I should shoot him then, from the outside, and drop the gun into the lake. I can move swiftly if I have to. I should be inside again before anyone knew what had happened."

"And everybody would say how fortunate that you were there to comfort me in my sad loss." The flecks in Hannah's eyes danced; but she put out her hand and took Martha's in a gesture more meaningful than a kiss. "I know you would, Mother and I'm sure you could. But it shan't come to that. I would sooner commit adultery."

Here we sit, two completely respectable, ordinary women, talking about choosing between two crimes as though they were hats.

"I am inclined to think," Hannah said, "that when Sir Harald fully realizes what last night meant, he'll take some action. I shall press for it. I never have before, but this evening I shall be able to point out to him that Magnus is not only a danger to me, and to himself, but to Copsi. That should stir him."

Suddenly that part of the vast room which was not lighted by the flickering fire, darkened as the fog rolled up. One little boy shouted, "Mrs. Reeve, it's gone dark." Another said, "Only fog, you fool." Little Edward who had never seen an English fog and whose new world, based on Martha, had tottered a bit that morning, began to wail, "It's the end of the world."

"I must comfort him," Miss Allsop said, shouldering Mrs. Reeve aside. And make arrangements for the others. How bad would it be? Would those who lived at a distance be stranded, sleeping on the floor? Supping on what? Could she, if the worst came to the worst, fumble her way to the nearest cook shop and buy pies? She snatched a moment to embrace Hannah and say, "If it's thick beyond the bridge, turn back and go to the house. Edward, leave go of me. A fog is nothing to be scared of. Hannah, let me know. *Keep me informed.*" Little Edward had started a panic in which older and more experienced boys had joined. Shouting was useless and exhausting; Miss Allsopp went to the old battered, secondhand piano and brought both hands down on it making a noise that sounded like the end of the world. In the resultant silence, Mrs. Reeve said, "Get into line; go into your places and sit with your arms folded. In all my life I have never seen such a display of silliness. I'm utterly ashamed of you."

Beyond the bridge the fog was worse rather than better, but Hannah's pony plodded placidly along and Hannah made no attempt to hurry him. She felt vaguely sick, probably because she had had no lunch, or because the fog seemed to smell of fish oil. Resolutely, she ignored the nausea, for to put it coarsely, you couldn't be sick with nothing to be sick *on*. Sick in mind, yes. Mother, always so sensible and logical—and *right*— suggesting adultery, planning murder. Yet, neither idea should be summarily rejected because, fantastic as they sounded, they dealt in a very real world, with realities.

Think. If Bolsover's dog hadn't alerted Bolsover last night and Sir Harald had died, where should we all be? Imagine Copsi with Sir Harald dead and Magnus in full control. Quite apart from my own situation, left without any protection, it would mean the end of Father's happy state—and of Mother's; for with the allowance withdrawn and Wilson gone, Mother would have to give up the school. Had she thought of that and concocted these two desperate remedies? Murder, of course was unthinkable. What of the other?

A sane, healthy man as father.... Inexorably her thoughts came round to Jerry Flordon, the only man for whom she had ever had any feeling of *that* kind. The only man with whom the act could be performed without the deepest repugnance. But could one possibly go to a man and say: I refused your offer of marriage; would you now give me a child?

That was unthinkable, too. In fact the only hope for them all was that Sir Harald could be made to see that while Magnus was at large neither he nor Copsi was safe. She began mustering the arguments.

Melissa was all agog with talk. Gordon said he had seen
the key to the library door on Mr. Magnus's dressing
table. Jacky said he'd met Bolsover and Bolsover said Mr.
Copsey had hung his dog up to die by slow torture and
he'd knocked him down flat. Mr. Copsey was now in his
bed, quite senseless. The doctor had been. None of the
male servants would sit by the bed and what the men
daren't do you couldn't expect women to do, could you?
On and on and on, while Hannah changed from her
fog-dampened clothes, into a plain day dress.

Melissa, who once could not speak of Bolsover
without a heightening of color and a softening of voice,
now made no difference between his name and that of any
other man. Bolsover had turned out not to be nice at all;
he'd told her plainly that he was not a marrying man. She
so evidently thought otherwise, and dropped so many
hints that bluntness was necessary. Melissa was quite
brokenhearted for a full twenty-four hours and then took
comfort in the thought that she was young and pretty and
could do better for herself; a farmer's son—Tim Sawyer
for instance—was more eligible than Bolsover, who for all
his fine airs, was only a servant.

Hannah took from the drawer of her bedside table a
small paper packet and holding it concealed in her palm,
went along to Magnus's room, where boredom had added
itself to Sir Harald's other miseries. He longed to go down
and see what progress the workmen had made. He longed
for somebody to talk to. He wanted to go across to the
other side of the house and find out whether Jonathan
were genuinely ill. He'd have liked to study a book which
he had discovered behind all those on the very top shelves
of the library, and which he did not know existed; an
account book for Copsi, 1689-1702. Over the years he had
carefully set aside all such things with the vague idea of
one day sorting everything and perhaps compressing and
correlating all the information into a definitive history.

He could perfectly well have gone out, locking the
door behind him, but his exaggerated sense of duty
forbade him to do that. Something could happen during
even a moment's absence.

He was pleased to see Hannah. And looking so
unruffled.

"I suppose you know what happened, my dear."

"Yes. Melissa told me. I have been to Bressford."

"All well there, I hope."

"Very well, thank you."

"Did the fog inconvenience you."

"It slowed us down." Unlike everybody else she managed to look at Magnus whose appearance was not enhanced by the white plaster snout which held his nose in position.

"Is that the worst injury?"

"No. When he fell he struck the back of his head. That caused the concussion."

Speak now? No. Poor old man, he looked so harassed.

"I will sit with him while you change and have your dinner."

"I should not dream of allowing it. Greatly as I appreciate the offer. He might come round at any moment and Doctor Fordyke warned me that he might be confused. We know—what that might mean."

"It would be all right. I have the pepper."

"Pepper?"

"Yes." She showed him the little packet. "It was Miss Drayton's idea. A girl was once attacked on a train. Miss Drayton thought, after that, that any girl obliged to travel alone, should carry a little pepper."

And I, he thought, despised—no, that is the wrong word. . . . I thought her unworthy to take my mother's, to take Juliet's place. God forgive me!

"No, my dear. My place is here. If you would like to do me a service you could go across and find out what has happened to Jonathan. And then perhaps—I know I handed the books out carelessly and it may be hard to find in the general muddle—a rather small book in a mottled cover; handwritten. An account book. If you *could* find it. . . ."

Jonathan was being cared for with tenderness and assiduity, Cousin William, his man, and Madame le Beaune all in attendance. A kettle was belching steam from the hearth, Madame had brewed what she called a *tisane*, and Cousin William and Parker had rigged up an inhalation tent, a large towel inside which Jonathan was wheezily breathing the healing fumes of Friar's Balsam. Cousin William was holding the bowl and Parker was supporting the invalid in a sitting position. "Let him out long enough to drink this while it is hot," Madame was saying. "One more good deep breath, my dear boy. There!" Red-faced and perspiring slightly, Jonathan emerged and coughed in a weak pitiable manner. He was going to make the most of, actually enjoy, this attack, the first he had suffered since Lady Copsey's demise. She had pooh-poohed coddling and advocated open windows and boiled onions. And look what had happened to her! The same thought was in all their minds. Cousin William had another reason for making the most of Jonathan's indisposition; Parker had by this time assessed and reported the situation on the other side of the house. Cousin William had not the slightest intention of helping, or of allowing his man to help.

Going back through the frigid corridors, Hannah modified the gloomy tidings she was entrusted to carry; poor Sir Harald had enough to worry him. In the hall that served the other side she paused and remembered the book. Some books, wiped clean, had been replaced on the shelves, also wiped, but a good many remained in unsteady piles. The hall was lighted by two lamps on tall stands, but the lower part of the piles was in shadow. She set her hand-lamp on the floor and went down on her knees. She found what looked like the book Sir Harald wanted and, with a tiny feeling of satisfaction, stood up with it in her hand, just as Thomas went to the door in answer to the bell which rang in the passage behind the baize-lined door. She had not heard it.

"I want to see Mrs. Copsey." It sounded like, it *was*, Jerry Flordon. Before Thomas could say his piece, asking the name and promising to see if Mrs. Copsey was at home, she was at the door,

"Jerry!"

"Good evening," he said, sounding stiff and stilted.

"Take this, Thomas," she thrust the hand-lamp into the footman's hand, transferred the little book from her right hand to her left and reached out.

"Come in. I am so *glad* to see you...."

Thomas, thus assured that the visitor was a welcome

one, remembered his drill and took charge of Jerry's top coat and hat, both slightly rimed, for the fog was beginning to freeze.

"My sitting room is upstairs," Hannah said, and led the way into the room which was like the heart of a rose, and faintly scented too. Once, in the library, a log of applewood had burned and Hannah had sniffed it and said it smelt nice. Ever since then it had been one of Sir Harald's small pleasures to see that her fire burned nothing but apple wood. He'd taken one ride, dedicated to spying out ailing apple trees and commandeering them ruthlessly—but always giving a replacement; because where an apple tree had once grown, there an apple tree must grow forever and forever.

"Do sit down, Jerry," Hannah said, indicating the rose-colored sofa, behind which stood a rose-shaded lamp. She sat down on a little low chair on the other side of the hearth.

"I had to come, Hannah," he said, using her name for the first time. "You know how tales spread. And how people exaggerate. A tinker came to Sheppey Lea early this afternoon. . . . Is it true that he tried to burn the place down?"

"Half true. He tried, but thanks to Bolsover and his dog, he failed."

"Yes, the tinker had some garbled story about a dog being half hanged, and Bolsover bashing him silly and walking out. I thought I'd better come and see for myself. I told you I'd keep watch, didn't I?"

"I know. I'm grateful."

"Where is he now?"

"In his bed. Knocked, as Bolsover said . . . silly. The doctor called it concussion."

"I wish to God I'd done it!" Bashing Magnus Copsey would have been some minute compensation for all this tedious, and, he could see now, pointless hanging about. Last night Copsi could have been well ablaze and Hannah injured before he could reach her. That was not the kind of trouble he'd foreseen when he decided to stay in the vicinity, sacrificing the profitable fishing season. Bloody fool!

"You're still at Sheppey Lea, Jerry?"

"Yes. As soon as the trees were planted we started building, stables, outhouses."

"Did you tell Miss Copsey what the tinker said?"

"No. I thought I'd make certain first."

"You can tell her no real harm was done, thanks to Lily. But for her Sir Harald would almost certainly have died."

And serve him right, Jerry thought, keeping the lunatic about the place, pretending everything was all right, forcing Hannah into marriage.

It was a difficult conversation because neither of them was giving it full attention; the thought of that flower-scented June evening kept intruding. Hannah had another preoccupation, too. Mother's suggestion. She realized that she could have searched the world over and not found a man with whom she would more willingly have gone to bed, or one more likely to beget the kind of child that was needed, sound in mind and body. But the thing was impossible. No man, leave alone Jerry Flordon, should be *used* in such a cold-blooded way.

"Drink some wine with me, will you? Or whisky, if you prefer it. I have only to ring the bell."

"Is the wine handy?"

"Yes. In the corner cupboard."

"I'll get it." Two heavy cutglass decanters with silver labels around their necks; sherry, madeira. "Which do you like?"

"I haven't yet learned to distinguish between them."

He poured sherry, and back on the sofa started the conversation on a different tack.

"What's going to happen now? Even Sir Harald must *see....*"

"He's willfully blind. But I intend to have a serious talk with him."

Poor little dear, did she really think that anything she could say would influence a stubborn old man?

"Let's hope he'll take heed. Or that young brute dies."

The conventional, automatic, "Oh Jerry, what a thing to say!" came from her lips, but somewhere within her there was a small explosion. If Magnus should die...and she could consider that possibility with an icy detachment, for never once, even when they were sharing a bed, had he said or done anything to endear himself to her, anything which would make her feel one pang of grief or remorse. She'd be free! She'd go straight to Jerry and say.... Another small explosion, leaping to the surface of her mind, Mother's fantastic suggestion about shooting. If Mother could so calmly contemplate and plan murder, couldn't she? And in a far more easy, less dramatic manner. A pillow held firmly over that hated face....

Jerry stood up. "I'll be going. I just wanted to see.... And Hannah, remember, if there's anything I can do...."

My dear, my darling, not now, not yet.

She said, "I know." She stood up, too, and for a second they were in dangerous proximity, both of them magnets, both of them the metal susceptible to magnetism. The scene in the garden was almost repeated, clamored for repetition, with a happier conclusion. But both were wary now. Jerry said he could let himself out; Hannah went along with the book Sir Harald wanted. And, fortified by sherry, to talk, if necessary to plan action. It occurred to her that madness, like many other things, was contagious. We're all mad!

Magnus lay as he had lain except for the brief period when Doctor Fordyke examined his head, flat on his back, breathing rather noisily, as people did who slept with their mouths open. Almost anybody else in that state would have been pitiable. Magnus was not; just slightly more revolting, just slightly less dangerous than usual. "I found the book," Hannah said, proffering it.

"Thank you, my dear. And what news from the other side?"

"Jonathan breathed in some fog and has a cough. Nothing serious. But he is keeping them all busy."

"He would!"

"I do most sincerely wish that you would let me take my turn here."

"Nonsense, my dear. I am perfectly capable. Go and have your dinner. I have ordered mine." Again without appetite, though saddle of mutton was one of his favorite dishes. Still, he held to his code; dinner would be eaten. Watch would be kept.

"How long will he be like this?"

"Nobody knows."

"And when he comes round, what then?"

"We'll worry about that when we come to it."

"You are fully aware of what he tried to do last night?"

"He tried to kill me. Not his first attempt."

"Don't you think you should . . . take precautions?"

"I do take such precautions as circumstances permit. I shall continue to do so."

"Last night made no difference?" He had become quite fond of her; he admired her spirit; he remembered that she was the only person in Copsi who had offered to relieve him; but he lost patience with her, standing there with that governessy look—her mother's look.

"We both know the one thing that would make a difference. Run along now to your dinner. I hear mine arriving."

Fincham *and* Thomas; as though the room were too dangerous for one man to enter alone. Yet they were prepared to allow him to sit here, unrelieved and unsupported. Let them wait. He'd sack them all; make a clean sweep.

※※※※※※※

"The point is," said the carpenter to whom everybody looked for guidance, "He can't sack us all. All we gotta do is stick together. ain't gonna go near Mr. Bloody Magnus, asleep or awake. And anyone of you that does I'll never speak to again. Disregarding all this," he looked around the havoc at this end of the library, "I ain't forgot Jim Bateman."

There was only one voice, not dissentient exactly, but argumentative. It said, "Well, we ain't been asked to yet."

"It'll come, this day. Mark my words. Forewarned is forearmed and I'm warning you. Just stick together."

As so often, the carpenter was proved right. During what seemed an endless night, Sir Harald had reckoned what might be called his reserve forces and was prepared to call upon them.

He'd had a horrible night; little snatches of sleep

from which he woke with a guilty start. Mental anguish and some physical pain for his wounded thigh resented the chair, easy as it was. It demanded to be laid out, stretched between smooth sheets, eased of all weight. He'd tried lying on the floor and that was worse. He'd walked up and down, better slightly, but not good. The chair again. And in Magnus no change, except that the open mouth looked parched. Unconscious people couldn't drink, but Sir Harald moistened a sponge and passed it over the dry lips, dribbled a drop or two—very cautiously—on to the tongue. No ill effects. The moisture seemed to be absorbed. He applied the sponge at regular intervals and a part of him stood off and asked Why? There were a number of answers; under all conditions one must do one's best; while there was life there was hope, and always the possibility of a miracle. Miracles were very rare, but in this long night, brushing the damp sponge across his son's mouth for the eighth or ninth time, Sir Harald remembered one to which he had been a witness, long ago in India, a soldier, a gunner made stone deaf when an ill-laid gun exploded. Stone deaf was useless to the army and the man was about to be shipped home when he got drunk and fell down and hit his head and was restored. Was it just possible that it could be so in Magnus's case? The skull housed the brain and the brain governed all. Magnus's had been injured at birth; was it possible, likely, that the damage inflicted by the forceps had been corrected by the blow on the back of the head—like setting a clock right. Fantastic thought, but now, well into his second sleepless night, Sir Harald was not fully answerable for his thoughts.

Morning came at last. No change; but presently an urgent need. In all ways Sir Harald was a creature of habit and he had a disciplined bowel. He had said himself, many times, "a fine thing if in the middle of a parade, or a battle, a man had to go and squat!" Now, in the gray dawn he must.

He took himself—and the slop pail which had served a lesser need—to the bathroom. He took care to lock Magnus's door; an unecessary precaution, the boy had not stirred. Sir Harald tried to remember how long life could be maintained without water. Magnus had been knocked down on Tuesday, it was Wednesday now: it would soon be twenty-four hours; but Magnus was not making any physical effort, he was not exposed to the heat of the sun. To judge from the state of the bed, which Sir Harald had inspected with conscientious regularity, all his physical functions had been suspended. Except that his heart was beating and he still breathed.

Sir Harald rang the bell and then went to the window and looked out upon a scene of phenomenal beauty; the fog had frozen overnight and every blade of grass, every twig was encased in semi-translucent glass. For once he was indifferent to the loveliness of it all, and turning back gave his orders snappily; he wanted hot water and his shaving tackle, and then, after ten minutes exactly, his breakfast. He also wanted a word with the head carpenter as soon as he arrived.

A wash and a shave restored him slightly; the interview with the carpenter cast him down again. The carpenter, like Fincham yesterday, was sorry; he was speaking for them all, they could not take the responsibility. Yellow-bellied cowards! Sir Harald longed to say, "Then go home, all of you and starve!" But that would mean the cessation of work on the library and would be a shocking break with tradition. He contented himself with saying as brusquely as possible, "Get back to your work."

His breakfast was always a simple meal—no porridge, which he held to be fattening; one slice of toast, half of which he ate with whatever the main dish was, the other half spread with marmalade. A pot of coffee. Thomas could easily have brought it up on one tray, but he came with the eggs and bacon and toast, with Gordon close behind, bringing the coffee and marmalade.

"Still hunting in couples, I see," their master said nastily.

─────◆─────◆─────◆─────◆─────

On the other side of the house, Jonathan, upon whom all the palliatives had worked well and who had had a quite reasonable night, was careful to speak in a weak, hoarse voice and produce an occasional wheeze. Cousin William suggested sending for the doctor and

Jonathan said, with an invalid's understandable petulance,

"What could he do? He can't alter the *climate*! The English *winter* is what ails me."

He had said the same thing in much the same words, many times before. As a very young man, in circumstances of extreme penury, he had spent two years in Europe, Paris, Rome, Venice, all places congenial to an artist. He longed to revisit them, with Cousin William's purse to draw upon. Every winter he dropped heavy hints, but the most Cousin William would ever say was that he would think about it. He had good reason for not doing anything; he still enjoyed hunting and shooting; he disliked the idea of disrupting his easy carefree life; but most of all he dreaded the effect upon the relationship which existed between himself and Jonathan. In places where there were other artists Jonathan might well drift away....

But the state in which Jonathan had arrived home the previous day, coughing, wheezing, on the verge of collapse, had momentarily ousted selfishness and fear had taken its place. Better share Jonathan with a congerie of fellow artists than have no Jonathan at all. So instead of saying that he would think about it, and then doing nothing, Cousin William prepared to do soething. And Madame le Beaune, hearing the magic word, *Paris*, immediately proposed that she should go too. She was intensely Francophile, yet she had never gone back; fearing to find things so greatly changed, fearing loneliness since so many old friends had vanished, fearing the effort which the arrangements for travel involve. But with William taking charge, with him and Jonathan for company, the visit might be delightful.

⬤━━━◆━━━◆━━━◆━━━⬤

Thursday was a very long day and by mid-afternoon Harald was beginning to doubt his staying power. It was all very well to think of this vigil in military terms he'd been a young man then and always hopeful that the enforced wakefulness was serving some purpose. Now he was older and unless Magnus soon came out of what the doctor had called coma, he'd die, and all this effort, all this watchfulness would have been wasted. His head was woolly, his eyelids lined with grit. Mustn't rub, it simply added to the inflammation. All the same he rubbed, grinding the grit into his eyeballs.

Hannah looked in from time to time, offering to relieve him; stubbornly he refused such offers. She was his contact with the other side of the house and she reported that Mr. Orde, Mr. Winthrop *and* Madame le Beaune were contemplating a prolonged holiday on the Continent.

"Rats deserting a sinking ship," he said as fiercely as his depleted vigor allowed.

He was at his lowest ebb when Magnus stirred and spoke.

"God blast you all," he croaked. "I can get out of this strait-jacket. I saw it done at a fair." He began to struggle against the bedclothes.

Confused? Really no more so than was to be expected after such a blow on the head and more than twenty-four hours' unconsciousness. Sir Harald's very mixed feelings shifted like the colors in a kaleidescope, but the habit of fond fatherliness obtained the upper hand. He bustled about, water first, then food. Magnus said he was unable to sit up; the strait-jacket was too tight. Sir Harald assured him that he was not in a strait-jacket, he was in bed.

"Tied down then, damn you. What's the difference? I can feel the cords across my body."

"You're rather stiff and bruised. You had a slight accident."

He could see by the blankness of the boy's expression that he remembered nothing. Perhaps it was just as well. Despite his long fast Magnus took the water and presently the cold chicken which was the only food readily available at half past three in the afternoon, with marked suspicion, muttering about poison.

"I know you. You're in the plot. You drink first." Sir Harald drank, and when the chicken came, ate some of that, too. Magnus's talk was rather more rambling and incoherent than usual, but granted the premise that his father was his enemy, not senseless.

At one point Sir Harald remembered that he was alone in a room with his son who had twice tried to kill him and that on the marble-topped washing stand there were two razors. He moved furtively and slipped them both into his pocket where they clinked against the key.

"That's right," Magnus said, "you're a pickpocket. But you can't deceive *me*. I came up against one in Bristol and Naples was full of them. Mr. Garnet knew that. And where is he? I know." He proceeded to describe Mr. Garnet's whereabouts and activities in terms so extremely coarse that even Sir Harald was shocked. Common troopers sometimes used such words but only among themselves. Quite horrible. The miracle, he thought dismally, had not happened; if anything Magnus had emerged from his coma rather worse. It was a relief when he fell silent as he was until Sir Harald suggested a little walk to the bathroom. That he knew could be a test of physical strength, for physically Magnus was more than his match, especially now when he felt so exhausted and so lame. But the alternative was coolie work of the worst kind.

Magnus refused to move. Coolie work must be done.

On the other side of the house, Jonathan, too, was making the most of his supposed weakness; but he was far more amenable and dropping back into his bed, drove the spur home: "My dear, unless I get away soon I shall die."

"Parker rode down to Radmouth yesterday, Johnny. He booked provisional passages for us all on the *Mary Rose* bound for Calais. If you are sufficiently recovered to bear the journey, she sails on Friday afternoon." Jonathan, cosseted and fussed over, would be quite recovered, fully prepared.

Sir Harald thought; What of the night? Must vigil be kept? Magnus was now in no danger of choking on his own tongue or getting out of bed in a dazed condition and falling down. The worst was over now; as for thinking or planning for the future, he was simply incapable of it. On Monday night he had almost died, roused himself to take part in the salvage of the library and then, in bed, had in the early hours of the morning been tortured by thoughts; all told asleepless night; add Tuesday and Wednesday, day and night. With this thigh gnawing like a rat. Could the most ruthless commander demand more of a man; could any man demand more of himself? He thought not, and despised himself for it. Lock the boy in, see to it that the fire was out, that no lamp or candle remained in the room, and what harm could he do? Sir Harald thought with something of a drunkard's lust for liquor of the black bag which stood on the top shelf of his wardrobe. It contained, amongst various other things, a bottle of a dark, viscous liquid, unequaled as a pain reliever. The regimental surgeon had prescribed it for him when his wound was raw and agonizing. Powerful stuff and potentially dangerous; five drops, no more, in water and only to be taken when necessary because there was always the danger of becoming an addict. Sir Harald had been so sparing of it that the bottle was still more than half full. He needed it now. Walk across the corridor, measure out the careful dose, go to bed, feel the pain ease off and sleep. Sleep. Sleep. . . .

Breaking a long silence, Magnus said, "I'll hang that bitch." At first hearing it seemed that he could be talking about the dog, Lily, whom he had tried, ineffectually to hang, but the talk drifted off; some girl in Bristol, or Naples who had attempted to deceive him. "I gave her something to think about, and no mistake." Sir Harald's mind, clinging desperately to sanity despite sleeplessness and pain, fixed on the word *hang*. Magnus he thought, was quite capable—not of hanging himself—but of making a pretense to and such pretenses often went wrong and became realities. Could a room be stripped of everything potentially dangerous in that way? The bell rope, curtain cords, towels, belts? It would be a difficult task, and suddenly he was overcome by such a wave of bone weariness that he felt incapable of doing anything at all and dropped into his chair so heavily that he jarred his aching thigh. He could still think in a muddled way, and made up his mind that he must have a very light dinner, and drink no wine. That should make keeping awake easier. Keep awake for what? The futility of the whole thing suddenly struck him; tomorrow and tomorrow, keeping watch so that Magnus should not harm anybody else, or himself. He reached out and tugged the bell-rope savagely. Thomas, with Gordon not far behind, appeared promptly. But the effort of getting up and unlocking the door was so immense that Sir Harald knew he had taken a wise decision.

"Go down to The River Boat," he said, addressing the younger, spryer man. "Tell Bolsover I want him, at once."

<hr>

Gordon did not take the short cut through the woods; it was already dusk and queer tales were told about Monkswood. He held to the road, but made good speed, spurred by a feeling of guilt. Sir Harald looked to be on his last legs—and he'd always been a kind, good master. He'd been let down by Mr. Fincham, by Thomas, by Gordon himself, by Jacky. Trotting a few paces, then walking, and trotting again, Gordon made up his mind that if Bolsover refused to come—as he almost likely would, for how could he dare?—he would suggest that *two* of them might take over for the night.

However, Bolsover was not only willing, but ready. He had been awaiting this summons.

"We'll take the shortcut," he said.

"It's nearly dark, Mr. Bolsover."

"Lily knows her way."

<hr>

Despite the muddled talk, Magnus's cunning set to work. It had noticed that the door was locked. Why? If he'd just had an accident, as Papa had said, why must he be locked in? Then that word, Bolsover. In the opacity of his mind a little crack opened. Bolsover, of whom he'd always been slightly scared and who by this time would know what had happened to Lily. There were other things, too. The library and the Armory.... But one thing was enough to think about. That had always been his way. One thing at a time...and cunning. Cunning.

He said, in the reasonable way which had deceived people so often,

"There's someting wrong with this bed."

Sir Harald, roused from the half-somnolence, largely induced by the thought that soon, soon, Bolsover would be here, said, "What?"

"The canopy is loose. It creaks. Listen." Magnus threw himself about in the bed and there was not merely a creak but a crack and on one side the curtain sagged and rattled.

"We'll soon see to that," Sir Harald said and rang the bell again.

He couldn't have sworn that he had not dozed off for a moment.

"Send the carpenter to me," Sir Harald said.

There was some consternation in the library, where work was just ending. Disputes with employers were very rare in rural districts, but when they occured it was always the ringleader, or the spokesman who was sacked.

"Better say you'll do it if you can take a mate," somebody suggested.

"If I must," the carpenter said, looking sullen.

Sir Harald admitted him and deliberately refrained from locking the door, thinking that the man might need some tools other than those he carried in his apron pockets. He indicated the lopsided bedhead and the carpenter thought: Worm, or a peg gone. Mr. Copsey looked to be still asleep, though his position had changed and he now lay on his side. The carpenter advanced and pulled at the curtain which impeded his view of the damage and quicker than a snake Magnus's hand shot out and snatched the nearest of the assembled tools, which also happened to be the heaviest and most dangerous; a big chisel. With it in his hand and looking triumphant, fiendish and defiant, Magnus flung back the bedclothes and swung his legs over the side of the bed.

"Making for his dad, no question about that," the carpenter said later, telling the tale that was to be told and retold. "and me, like a fool, getting in his way."

What he actually did without thinking about it in the moment of shock, was to say, "Hi," and attempt to take the chisel away. Magnus plunged it into his neck, just above the collar bone. Blood shot out in an arc. The sight of it was too much for the man, he fainted and fell with a thud, between Sir Harald and his son who said, "Come on! you next!"

That was a terrible moment—less than a moment, an agonized flash of time. Sir Harald knew the difference between the slow, dark red blood that issued from veins and the bright red spouting that came from arteries. Unless someting was done to help Ransom immediately all his blood would pump out and he'd die. And unless Magnus could be disarmed more people would die, himself first. Unless some crumb of reason remained in the demented mind.

"Put it down," he said. "You shall have anything you want."

"That's better," Magnus said and gave a maniacal laugh. Master of all—at last! With this splendid weapon in his hand he could do anything he wanted to, obtain everything he wanted without anybody's consent.

Sir Harald was not unfamiliar with steel in enemy hands, swords, sabres, bayonets. He did not, even now, doubt his ability to disarm the mad boy and was quite prepared to suffer some injury while doing so; he was more concerned for poor Ransom for whom something must be done, and soon. He roared, "Help! Help!" The workmen, lingering about near the library door, waiting to hear what Sir Harald had had to say to the carpenter, heard the cry and stood irresolute, nobody caring to make the first move as without the carpenter they lacked leadership.

The carpenter's body lay between father and son; either to reach the other must step over it, or sidle around, so that the swift, headlong attack was out of the question. Sir Harald had time to call again. This time he was answered, a clatter on the stairs and Bolsover stood in the doorway. The awe Magnus had felt for his keeper had vanished; armed as he was he felt he was a match for him.

Bolsover muttered something and Lily understood; she'd been Bolsover's dog for eight years and inbred in her was the hunting instinct—hares, rats, all best tackled at the back of the neck. She slithered around the bed like a shadow.

"Come to see the fun?" Magnus asked with another high cackling laugh. Then Lily had him by the back of the neck. Her teeth were not what they had been, but good enough, and once she had a hold she flung her whole weight forward so that Magnus, a second ago so proudly defiant, fell forward. Bolsover took the chisel and administered one punishing, temporarily disabling punch to the stomach. he turned to the carpenter and pressed the gushing gap with his fingers. "Get me an egg and be quick."

There were plenty of messengers for once Bolsover had gone up the stairs—three at a time—the workmen had followed.

The egg, firmly pressed into the hollow just above the collarbone, acted as a tourniquet; no ordinary one could be applied to a wound in such a position. Sir Harald himself helped to tear a sheet into strips and Bolsover did the bandaging. Sir Harald then supervised the removal of Ransom to one of the unoccupied rooms nearby, and sent for his wife.

Hannah had been to tea on the other side of the house and had stayed longer than usual because the three would-be travelers had so much to tell her about the wonders awaiting them. Madame le Beaune was bubbling with enthusiasm, which Cousin William's deflating remarks did nothing to lessen. He warned her that she would find everything greatly changed—and not for the better. When she said, kindly patronizing, that she would think of Hannah in January, the month when it usually snowed, Cousin William remarked that snow had been known as far south as Sicily. How did he know that? Somebody had told him, adding the information that cold weather in such places was far more uncomfortable than in England since few houses had fireplaces and most floors were tiled. Cousin William was, in fact, regretting his hasty decision, though when Jonathan coughed as he did rather regularly, he reflected that he had been wise.

Magnus's door was half open; as she paused by it, she could hear Sir Harald's voice, extremely weak and then—could it be—Bolsover's?

"...spend a night in such a shambles," Sir Harald said.

"It'll do for tonight. We'll make other arrangements in the morning. You get to bed, sir."

Hannah pushed the door and went in; she managed six words. "Oh Bolsover, I am so glad...."

"Go away, Mrs. Copsey; this is not sight for a lady."

"Bolsover is right, my dear. Go away. I will tell you everything, later."

Magnus lay sprawled on the disordered bed, but now his eyes were open. And there was blood everywhere. On Magnus's white plaster snout, on his night shirt, on the bedclothes, and a great pool on the white fur rug by the bedside.

Feeling sick again! And with good reason. She pressed her hand to her mouth, willed the nausea to pass.

"Who was hurt?"

"Never mind. Go away. Everything's all right now," Bolsover said.

Making the final, supreme effort, Sir Harald took her arm and said, "Come my dear. I will take you to your room."

"I had better take you to yours," Hannah said. He was shaking so violently that the touch of his hand set her quivering too. "Come along, you're exhausted."

As they crossed the corridor a woman, carrying a big bundle wrapped in what looked like a table cloth, and followed by two small children came up the stairs.

"Where is he? Where is my husband?"

Sir Harald just, but only just, managed to say, "Mrs. Ransom," and indicate the door of the room to which the carpenter had been taken. Then he could do no more. He allowed himself to be steered into his room.

Bolsover ordered dinner for two, a sumptuous repast. Not that he and Lily hadn't eaten well at The River Boat but there were things which Copsi could provide which the simple landlady of a humble inn had never heard of. What Bolsover didn't eat of the two dinners, Lily enjoyed. She'd saved the situation and deserved the very best. Magnus received a cup of water and, great concession a crust of bread. He was, he realized, in the hands of the enemy; two pair of hostile eyes, Bolsover's icy gray and the dog's greenish, watched his every move. But he'd killed the dog; so this was another dog, or Lily's ghost? Too difficult to sort out. Everything had gone wrong; he was tired of trying to think things out; leave it till tomorrow.

Bolsover regarded his charge's passivity with suspicion. The young devil was planning something. He poured himself a drink and smoked, with leisurely enjoyment, one of Sir Harald's cigars. Then he moved into the corridor anything that could possibly serve as a weapon, the bootjack, boots on trees, crockery from the washing-stand, even the silver-backed hair brushes and every bottle.

"You make a sound or a move while I'm away and you'll answer for it when I come back," he said, and taking the lamp with him, went out, locking the door and putting the key in his pocket. He looked in first upon Sir Harald, sound asleep. The carpenter was awake, weak and slightly befuddled. Sir Harald's last words to Hannah had been, "See that Mrs. Ransom has everything she wants," and Mrs. Ransom shared the almost universal belief that red wine could replace lost blood. She had drunk some herself; after all she had had a bad shock, and was now doomed to spend the night under the same roof as a dangerous lunatic. The first thing her husband had said when he could speak was that Mr. Copsey had stabbed him with his own chisel. Bolsover tested the egg which seemed set in place, and that meant that the blood had gone sticky. He loosened the bandages slightly and said, "You'll do, I reckon." The two children, of an age to fall asleep in any position, at any time, were curled up together like puppies in an armchair; they'd had an enormous supper and just a sip or two of the wine. All well in this part of the house. Bolsover set out on his prowl. He knew what he wanted and had an idea where he could find it.

◄━━►◄━━►◄━━►◄━━►

Sir Harald, vastly restored, woke in the morning and immediately accused himself for gross dereliction of duty; he had not thanked Bolsover for coming so promptly and dealing so cleverly with poor Ransom's wound; he had not apologized to Ransom's wife and had left it to Hannah to make arrangements for her comfort—and that of the children. He'd simply abandoned everything and gone to bed. He hadn't even taken the pain-killing dose; just shed his clothes and lain down. Weakling!

In this mood of self-abasement he was in no state to resist or even to argue with Bolsover's clear-cut decision.

He did make one feeble protest; he glanced at the bed where Magnus lay, not asleep but completely withdrawn, and said, "Perhaps, Bolsover, we should not carry on this discussion in the presence of the person most nearly concerned."

Bolsover said callously, "What difference does it make? He'll know sooner or later. Just leave it to me. I'll see to everything. Stands to reason, we can't go on like this, can we? And I for one don't mean to."

"Very well. Do what you think best."

What Bolsover thought best was Miss Bertie's old room, now empty and stripped bare. It had the inestimable advantage of having it's own latrine, in the adjoining tower, part of the original castle. Bolsover had no intention of doing coolie work.

Ransom's son, eighteen years old and always overshadowed by his father, came into his own, vested with a brief authority. There was much to be done, all in a hurry. A plain wooden table to be fastened down to the floor, and a chair at just the right distance to make eating possible, also fastened down. Most significant of all, the big window to be barred. "On the outside," Bolsover said, "allowing a clearance of six inches so that the window can be opened." Young carpenter and those told to help him were busy preparing a place for a lunatic. Other men were busy making the empty room next door fit for Bolsover. Sir Harald had told him to do as he thought best and he had taken that as permission to take what he wanted and now he commandeered many things which, as he went about the huge place, had attracted his admiration and made him think: If I were a rich man. . . . The carpet he chose had been woven in Isfahan, silky and though colorful, not gaudy, very different from the now fashionable Turkey carpets, all harsh blues and reds. Since Lily's mishap Bolsover had taken against four-posters and chose for himself an elegant small French bed, its head and foot curving inward, gently, like a shell, and embellished with cherubs. Two very easy chairs, velvet covered; a Chinese cabinet, scarlet and gold, a table of marquetry. Even Lily was provided for luxuriously; for her a chaise-longue, it's cushions beautifully embroidered with roses and peonies.

The move was made without any trouble, though Bolsover was ready for it. He knew a hold, not strictly a prizefighter's trick, but very effective. Just above the elbow on what was known as the funny bone. It was painful and partially paralyzing. "And one squeak out of you and you'll get a rabbit punch," Bolsover said, just as a precaution, though it seemed to be unnecessary. Magnus appeared to have relapsed into real idiocy. Better so.

***

"Bertie, I had no choice. I hope you, at least, understand that. Setting fire to the place and attacking Ransom...."

"I'm terribly sorry, Harry. If I'd only known I'd have come and kept watch."

"I managed. And Bolsover is now in charge. What bothers me is what to *say*.... To people. Bolsover made it very clear to me this morning that he would not agree to half measures."

"He was right. It should have been done... before... before so much damage was done."

"I clung to hope, Bertie."

"I know."

"One of the doctors said that there was a change every seven years...."

"Have you ever known of one?"

"I must admit, no."

"Nor I. You may not remember, Harry, but a long time ago, before we even knew *how* demented he was, I suggested that you should marry again. You were displeased with me. It's still not too late. Look at Walter Hillborough, years older than you."

"For me it has been too late ever since Waterloo."

Surprisingly, her eyes filled with tears.

"You poor man." She turned slightly and looked out of the window, blinking angrily. When she could trust her voice she said, almost lightly, "In a story it would read as though we were cursed. The curse of Copsi. Not even a collateral branch.... Well, there's one thing, you need not worry about what people say, or think. Everybody regards you with respect and affection." She deliberately omitted the word sympathy. "There'll be talk, of course, but everyone will think that you have acted wisely in locking him away."

A thought occurred to her, so fantastic that she dared hardly examine it. But she did, while Sir Harald tried to change the subject by saying what a difference the newly planted saplings made. She said, yes, in a couple of years her wonderful view would have a frame. Dare she say what she was thinking? Would he be irretrievably shocked and disgusted? Perhaps this was not the moment. Perhaps better not to mention it to him at all but talk to Hannah directly. Dreadfully embarrassing, but she could bring herself to it.

"If I were you, I'd have some old, tried friends to dinner and tell them the facts. Blame the fall."

As usual, Bertie's advice was sound, and although she had offered no actual comfort—how could she, for what comfort was there?—he left her feeling slightly less abject.

———————————————————

The transfer had been made by the time he reached home.

"Quick work," Sir Harald said. "I'm sorry I wasn't here to help."

"No trouble at all," Bolsover said cheerfully. "Everything went smooth as oil."

"Should I just look in upon him?"

"I wouldn't," said Bolsover, beginning as he meant to go on. "Give him time to settle down. The sight of you might upset him. Bear in mind it was *you* he was after. Poor Ransom just got in the way."

"Ah yes, poor Ransom. I must look in on him."

The carpenter's family had rallied round; Mrs. Ransom's sister was there, with two children, Ransom's sister with one. The unaccustomed space had goe to their heads and the corridor was bedlam. The children all looked as though they had shared Ransom's accident, strawberry jam all over their faces. They'd taken the trees out of Magnus's boots and were clumping about giggling. Trying to push each other over. Sir Harald's appearance at the top of the stairs brought a hush, little bobs from the bigger girls, a pulling of the forelock from the bigger boys.

Sir Harald said in his habitual, benevolent way, "That's right, enjoy yourselves." Inside the sick room Mrs. Ransom was holding court, dispensing tea and plum cake. Tea was still something of a luxury and she ordered it almost every hour.

Ransom lay high, propped on many pillows—Bolsover's suggestion—and though he still looked pale he seemed to be suffering no discomfort.

"I seen my boy, sir and told him how to rehang the door. I reckon he can manage."

"I'm sure he can. But you should not have bothered, Ransom."

"I'm still in charge, sir." That was the trouble between father and son. Young Ransom, well trained, sternly disciplined, rarely praised and frequently upbraided, was a wonderful craftsman, but the time for him to take his father's place was not yet.

Day followed day. Sir Harald had taken Bertie's advice and sent dinner invitations to his nearest neighbors. He prepared for the occasion very carefully, but in deep gloom. Even a visit with Fincham to the cellar was disheartening; he'd hoarded some precious vintages for Magnus's coming of age, for the christening. No point in saving them any longer; let this dismal gathering be remembered for the good wine as well as for the official, slightly deceptive statement he intended to make.

And now he really must *see* the boy. He had allowed Bolsover to put him off too easily, because he was weakly willing to be put off, not wishing to see Magnus in solitary confinement, necessary as it might be. He'd face it this morning and this evening be able to tell his friends—with a clear conscience—that the boy was in good health and comfortable.

Bolsover was not there. Well, of course he needed some air and exercise; and it was a bright clear morning. Listening outside Magnus's locked door, Sir Harald could hear sounds of some movement within, nothing very definite, a thud now and then, a kind of scraping, a grunt or two; all very faint, for the door was thick. Waiting, Sir Harald remembered that outside the windows of the three rooms in this corner of the house, part of the original castle wall jutted in a kind of terrace, wide enough to take two men abreast. Bolsover's door was locked, so he went into the third, empty room, edged his way through the window and walked along to the barred one. At first he could see very little, the morning was so bright and the room by comparison, so dim; and he could not, because of the bars, put his face to the glass and cup his eyes with his hands. However, his eyes presently adjusted and he could see Magnus, wearing a dressing-gown, but no slippers, crouched by the door. He appeared to be scraping or picking something from the floor and eating it. Like an animal. Sir Harald watched, with horrid fascination, then backed away and re-entered the house. Bolsover, whistling jauntily, was just unlocking his own door.

A glance informed him where Sir Harald had been, and that he was not very pleased. He got his word in first.

"Better in health than in temper this morning, I'm afraid, sir."

"Why is he eating from the floor, Bolsover?"

"He hurled his porridge at me. I was temporarily blinded. Lucky Lily was there."

Magnus took all his food from a wooden bowl, and the only implement he had was a blunt wooden spoon. All his meat—rather strictly rationed—was chopped before-hand and made into a mash with the vegetables. That was his midday meal. His breakfast was porridge and his supper some kind of soft, spoonable pudding.

That morning, as Bolsover placed the wooden bowl on the table and backed away, Magnus said,

"You bring me any more of this pap and I'll chuck it at you."

"Chuck away," Bolsover jeered, confident that even an idiot had sense enough not to waste his breakfast. But he was wrong; the bowl of porridge came hurtling through the air, well aimed. Bolsover had not been temporarily blinded; he'd caught the bowl and dropped it to the floor and said, "Now you can lick it up."

Sir Harald accepted Bolsover's version of the story, but persisted with something that was not quite a complaint, not quite an inquiry.

"And he had nothing on his feet."

"Oh? Well, he has a pair of slippers. If he didn't choose to put them on, that's his lookout. I can't be expected to dress him until he's calmed down a bit."

The calming down, the taming process was taking rather longer than Bolsover had anticipated, but it must surely come.

"Perhaps," Sir Harald said, blaming himself again, "I have asked much of you, Bolsover. Shall I look about for an assistant, somebody with experience in handling...difficult people?"

"If you think you can find somebody to do better...." Bolsover said, and left the sentence hanging in the air. "In that case don't count on me. I shouldn't feel easy, sharing the responsibility." He spoke with mild reasonableness, but his cold hard eye issued its challenge and Sir Harald said, hastily,

"Oh, no, no, Bolsover. Nothing like that. I was merely wondering if you needed help."

"I don't. All I need is time."

❦❦❦❦❦

Bertie had finally made up her mind to make her preposterous suggestion to Hannah and had asked her to lunch. She was nervous and had made the mistake of taking more care than usual about the food, the wine, the service; anxious to show the girl that she was an honored guest, even though something dishonorable was about to be proposed to her. Hannah had been to Sheppey Lea before and enjoyed Bertie's casual, haphazard hospitality; the change of atmosphere made her vaguely uncomfortable. Both women took refuge in an unwonted garrulity, Bertie elaborating on her plans which included a heated greenhouse in which she hoped to establish a cutting of the Copsi Everlasting Rose—Hannah had brought her two blooms—and Hannah enlarging upon the invasion of Copsi by the Ransom family. "Cousins and second cousins now, all with children, of course. Bolsover says Ransom could go home, in the carriage, but Mrs. Ransom thinks otherwise. I suspect that she intends to keep Christmas at Copsi. Not that I should blame her; it is the noise I find so trying."

This kind of talk could go on forever, with the tension growing. Abruptly, Bertie said, "Hannah. I beg of you, don't take what I am about to say amiss; you know that I like and respect, admire you.... *Has* it ever occurred to you that you could have a child by another man?" There it was done and Hannah's face had not whitened with shock, or reddened with anger.

"That has been suggested to me before."

"By my brother?"

"Indeed no. He'd be the last! But by a responsible person. I can see all the advantages, but I don't think I can do it. You may think this stupidly sentimental, but I happen to be in love. And that makes the idea of going to bed with just *any* man repugnant to me. At the same time I respect the man whom I love too much to treat him as a stud animal."

"I can understand that. Yet, forgive me if I sound prying.... You did, or at least it is believed that you did bed with Magnus."

"Yes, I did. But I had bargained to do so—before I realized anything about being in love. It was a hard bargain to begin with—you may not know it, Bertie, but Harry can be very ruthless. To save my parents, not merely from eviction but from downright persecution, with father so utterly helpless, I agreed. Then I ... then he ... Well, we realized, which made it harder for me. But I held to my word. I kept my side of the bargain, to the last letter. I do not feel that I owe Copsi anything."

"My God, no!" It was Bertie who was appalled. She had always considered Harry, apart from his deliberate blindness over Magnus, as near perfection as a man could be; honorable, chivalrous, kind. That he could have used his power to coerce.... In one sense incredible, in another logical as night following day. Another illusion shattered, she thought, as, having seen Hannah off, she went in search of distraction, to see how the stable-building was getting on. Almost immediately she missed the most energetic worker of the gang, a man who always seemed to labor with a grim intensity as though being driven by an inner demon.

"Where's Flordon?" she asked.

"Gone," said the foreman. "Didn't turn up on

Monday. They say he's gone back to sea. He never was one to stick anything for more'n five and twenty minutes."

━━━◇━━━◇━━━◇━━━◇━━━◇━━━

Sir Harald's little party began with the deliberate heartiness which defeated its own purpose. Everybody was so sorry for him in this, his final facing of facts. Everybody knew that the mad boy had run amok with a chisel, practically killed a carpenter, threatened everybody else, including his own father, and was now confined behind bars. Everybody had, of course, said that this was bound to come, but now that it had there was great sympathy for Sir Harald, good decent man that he was.

Gradually, under the effect of the excellent wine, hilarity became more genuine and Sir Harald began to dread the moment when what he must say would shatter the jovial mood. He'd always despised what was known as Dutch courage, but now he thought, from moment to moment, that another sip, another glass would make it easier. Finally he decided that the best moment would be when that most excellent port had made its first round.

Two of the company—Sir Walter Hillborough and Sir Henry Collins—had known Sir Harald all his life but it was left to Mr. O'Brien, still by Suffolk standards a newcomer, to speak for all. He had taken enough wine to affect even his hard head, and his warm Celtic nature took charge.

Apropos of nothing, he said, "Copsey, dear man, we all know of your trouble and our hearts are scalded for you. It is a great sorrow you are bearing and we share it, one and all."

Sir Harald almost broke down, but he still had a small duty to perform, so he pulled himself together and said with enormous dignity,

"Some very lurid stories are going around, I have no doubt. I would like my friends to know the truth. Magnus had a fall which gave him severe concussion and left his mind confused. He had no intention of injuring the carpenter, Ransom himself says so. I have taken steps to see that no similar accident can ever occur."

Everybody murmured; yes, yes; of course; truly sorry; hope for the best. And pass the port.

Edward O'Brien said to his wife, "Anything more like a wake I never did see until I broke the spell. After that it was merry."

"If I am knowing you," she said fondly, "you'll dance at your own wake."

* * *

After the porridge-throwing, Bolsover no longer bothered to go into the prison room. That midday he opened the door just wide enough to allow him to retrieve the bowl. He put the rather unappetizing looking mash into it and unlocked the door, opened it a little and slid the bowl in on to the floor.

"When you've finished, put the bowl back there."

At supper time the bowl was not there and Bolsover said, "Please yourself. Go without." Magnus pleased himself and went without, missing breakfast next morning; but by midday he had come to his senses and the bowl was waiting.

Bolsover adopted the same method where washing was concerned. Another, slightly larger bowl of water, a towel and a cake of soap slid in and were presently retrieved. It didn't look as though they had been used—but whose fault was that?

For Bolsover, life was easy and pleasant. He was on excellent terms with the landlady of The River Boat, middle-aged and plain, but good in bed and married. Her mornings and evenings were busy but she took a little rest in the afternoon. The inn, like Copsi, had several entrances and exits; Bolsover's comings and goings were not noticed.

During the week before Christmas, Sir Harald was extremely busy, resuming those civic duties which he had so much neglected. Even in his present melancholy state of mind he derived some satisfaction from planning the gifts and treats associated with the season of goodwill; flannel petticoats or shirts, tea or tobacco for the almshouse inmates, beef instead of the usual pork for the workhouse dinner; for the hospital an innovation, turkey; boots and a packet of sweets for the pupils at the Ragged School. From such cheerful activities he went home to the aching emptiness of Copsi, an emptiness emphasized by the departure of the Ransom family. The carpenter was not by nature a sociable man and as soon as he felt well enough to assert himself insisted upon going home, to the house where he was indisputably master and where lack of space and limited supplies controlled hospitality.

Hannah was very good. Few girls of her age would have accepted such a dull life, so placidly. She made efforts to keep conversation going at the dinner table—now so much too large. Mother, she told him, had asked little Edward to spend the whole Christmas holiday at the Pump Lane house because his selfish old grandmother was going away and proposed to leave him in the care of servants; Wilson had won a Chess tournament and had tactfully attributed his victory to having played with Father so much. Father had had his small triumph, too; on the market. Somebody, to raise money for Christmas gifts for the poor who were not in the workhouse or the hospital, had donated a pig for a Guess Its Weight Competition, threepence a guess. Father had guessed to within a pound and won the pig, of no use to him, so he'd asked the auctioneer to sell it and give the money to the fund. Everybody had thought that extremely generous. And John Reeve, who had never had much opportunity to be generous, had basked in the general approval.

So much of this was what, if Sir Harald had not actually planned, he had hoped for. The best for all concerned. For all except himself.

He said, "This is a very dull life for you, my dear."

"It suits me," she said.

<hr>

All this time he had not been unmindful of his own; blood of his blood, bone of his bone, demented and locked away.

"Is he warm enough, Bolsover? I know he isn't to be trusted with a fire, but the weather has turned sharp."

"I gave him a fur rug yesterday."

"And he is eating well?"

"On and off. Sometimes, if he's sulky, he won't eat."

Bolsover had protected himself from any possible blame by drawing attention to the uneaten food which

Thomas or Gordon carried away after Magnus had had his allowance and Bolsover and Lily had eaten their fill. Lily had the lurcher's inbred ability to live on almost nothing and still keep going, or to live on the fat of the land without getting fat. And Bolsover, though a hearty eater, was choosy; he hated fat and always cut it away; meat that ran red when cut affected him unpleasantly; he'd dealt in a bloody trade, but who wanted a reminder on his plate?

Sometimes it seemed to Thomas and to Gordon that there was almost as much food to be carried away as there had been to carry up. Yet, try to lighten the task by missing out a dish and Bolsover was sharp to notice and reprimand, and worse, to send for it.

On Christmas morning Sir Harald presented Hannah with a sable jacket and having thanked him, she said, "Your present is in the library. Come and look." Just for once there was about her something of the girlishness, the animation and warmth which he had so often found lacking in her. In the library he could see nothing that had not been there the previous evening.

"On the wall," she said. And there on the wall above the more elegant sofa which had replaced the ugly one—young carpenter had said he *could* restore that, make it as good as new, but Sir Harald never wanted to see it again—hung the map. He was dumb with amazement.

"It may not be entirely correct," she said. "I had to rely on my memory. And on what I could learn by walking around."

It was, apart from all else, a beautiful piece of work; she hadn't even used white paper, just that slightly buff shade which the original map had acquired from age.

"It is ... wonderful," he said when he could speak. Then, to his horror and shame he felt tears in his eyes. Copsi, his Copsi.... The map so beautifully duplicated, the estate running down to its end. And this girl, so thoughtful, so kind, so clever.... Oh dear, if only things had been different! He blew his nose fiercely.

Now this morning he really must see Magnus. He took with him the only gift he could think of, a box of chocolates. Finding something for Bolsover was easy. The man was inclined to be a bit of a dandy and a pair of cuff-links, too ornate for Sir Harald's taste and therefore never worn should please him.

Mollified by his present and also running out of excuses, Bolsover said,

"Very well, sir. But careful's the word. Lily!"

Magnus knew his real enemy. He had dozens of them; all men were enemies, all in the plot against him. Bolsover was bad; his dog was worse; but worst of all, the archenemy was Papa. Let him once show his face!

The missile, cunningly constructed, cunningly concealed for so long was anything but deadly in itself. A pair of carpet slippers tightly wrapped into a nightshirt, the sleeves wound about and knotted. It was well aimed and hit Sir Harald on the cheekbone, just below his left eye; rather more damage was done because the impact, slight as it was, made Sir Harald's head jerk and strike the edge of the door. Bolsover said, "Back!" Lily snarled. Then they were all safe outside in the corridor.

"It's nothing," Sir Harald said mopping the thin trickle of blood from his temple.

"Nothing," Bolsover agreed. "But it just shows." He'd had presence of mind enough to snatch up the bundle and now examined it. "Cunning," he said "That's why he hasn't been wearing his slippers. I often wondered."

Bolsover was kind; he made Sir Harald sit down in the most comfortable chair, gave him a glass of brandy. But nothing could obliterate from the father's mind what he had seen in the half second between the opening of the door and the throwing of that pitiable bundle. Thin, unshaven, dirty.

"He's deteriorating, Bolsover."

"They do," Bolsover said. "But apart from this little flurry he is calming down. Soon I'll be able to go in and give him a clean up."

"He certainly needs that. . . . And there are slippers, without heels, or soles. Just felt or velvet."

"I daresay he had a pair. I'll look, Don't you worry, sir. I'm sorry about it, but there it is."

Sir Harald became aware that through it all he had retained his clutch on the box of chocolates. Ludicrous! He said, "I seem to remember that Lily liked chocolates." He laid the box on the marquetry table. "And now it is time for church."

Giving the old boy his due, Bolsover thought with the grudging admiration he had accorded in the past to an opponent who struggled up after a knockout blow, only to take another, he's tough! And some of that inherent toughness was in the lunatic he'd bred. Anybody else shut away, with no occupation, scanty food, not a hope in the world, would have given in by now. But even that thought did not cause him to relent. What Magnus had done to Lily, to Hannah and to Sir Harald, and to the carpenter—in that order, took a lot of expurgating.

In fact, after that Christmas morning, Magnus seemed to change. He no longer looked towards the door when it opened and often he left his food untouched. He no longer banged with his wooden bowl or yelled curses. He had calmed down. Bolsover was still wary, and rightly so, but he was now daring to plan the cleanup he had promised. He did not propose a trimming of hair and beard yet since that would involve a pair of scissors, but he would either make the lunatic wash himself, or wash him. On New Year's Day, an apt date, he began to assemble what was needed. Magnus had thrown out his worn nightshirt and Bolsover had thrown in a clean one, but that was a week ago, so he laid ready another, a fresh dressing-gown, the wash-bowl, towel and soap. For the first time since Sir Harald's last attempt to face his son, the door was fully opened. The room stank like a ferret's cage and there was evidence that lately Magnus had not bothered to use the latrine.

Magnus lay huddled in bed; nothing new in that, it was his best refuge against the cold. He took no notice of Bolsover's entry. With Lily alert beside him, Bolsover carried the bowl of warm—not hot—water to the table, set it down and placed beside it the other things.

With just the slightest possible lessening of hostility

in his manner, Bolsover said, "Come along now. You're going to have a wash."

The taming process appeared to be complete. Magnus rose from the bed, advanced towards the table and stood behind the chair. Then, with maniacal strength, he wrenched off its back. A solid wooden chair which Bolsover himself had chosen after testing it in every possible way. The movement was so sudden, and the whole thing so incredible, that even Bolsover was taken unawares and the ragged, splintered edges of the ripped-out chairback hit him full in the face as Magnus lunged across the table. The fact that the table was between them mitigated the power of the thrust and prevented Magnus from following it up with a more disabling blow. It was, in fact, the attack of a lunatic, cunningly planned, but ill-executed. Bolsover and Lily were out into the corridor and the door slammed and locked while Magnus was still on the far side of the table.

Vain and skilful, Bolsover had always taken care of his face, and now an idiot had marred it. The damage was superficial. Nothing, as Sir Harald had said of his trivial hurt on Christmas Day. Nothing, Bolsover said to himself as he saw to his wounds and realized that his eye had been missed by half an inch. While he was dealing with his damaged face Bolsover heard the smash and tinkle of broken glass and realized that another action that he had not foreseen had been committed. Magnus was breaking his window.

It would avail him nothing in the way of escape, for young carpenter had done a sound job on the bars. Unless... well, who would have believed that the idiot could have torn a solid chair apart? For once in his singularly self-sufficent, self-confident life, Bolsover felt that he was not infallible and realized that he had made another mistake in ordering the bars to be placed outside the window rather than inside.

Some of that broken glass would have fallen inward, or within Magnus's reach, between the window frame and the bars. Bolsover remembered how he had netted Magnus on his wedding night; but Magnus had then been armed only with a riding crop; a whole armory of broken glass was different.

He rang his bell and when Gordon came, grudging, unwilling—what now? Still a good two hours to lunch time—sent a message that he wanted to see Sir Harald, at once.

Bolsover apologizing was something entirely new. But there it was, Bolsover saying, "I'm sorry, sir. I reckoned without the window and I'd never believed he could break that chair. Nobody in his right mind could have done it. So now he's in there, armed with a lot of broken glass. I don't intend to go near him again. Not even to open the door. He could be behind it, with glass in his hand, ready to blind me—or Lily."

Sir Harald received the news, and what sounded like an ultimatum, with dismay and he almost said: If you won't, who will? Then he remembered his military training. No officer should ever ask a ranker to do something which he was not *willing* to do himself. Ability counted less. Willingness was all.

"Then I must," he said.

"And that I can't have, either," Bolsover said, putting a protective hand over the pocket in which he kept the key. "He'd simply *slaughter* you."

"Then what do you propose should be done?"

"What you once said, sir. People accustomed to handling difficult cases. I scorned the idea then. I thought I could manage. I *was* managing—and God damn me, I clean forgot the blasted window. I am sorry."

Sir Harald had often felt that Bolsover was a trifle too cocksure, but to see him in this mood of self-abasement did not please him at all.

"I should have thought of the window. I am equally to blame, Bolsover. And perhaps we exaggerate the danger. Using the window glass as a weapon may not have occurred to him."

"Tearing the chair apart did."

"Yes, but with him.... Anyway, I'll go along and inspect the damage."

Out by Bolsover's window this time, a shorter walk to the barred one. Almost every pane in the lower half of the tall window was broken; shining jagged pieces still clung to the frame, the space between the window and the bars was thickly littered, a few pieces had even traveled further outward and crunched under Sir Harald's feet. It was probably the noise which brought Magnus to the window.

On this not-so-bright morning it was easier to see, and perhaps the lack of glass made seeing easier. Magnus was stark naked, in a room already frigid and now open to the cutting northeaster that threatened snow. He was skeletally thin, like the pariah dogs of India. Clotted hair mingled with clotted beard. He came gibbering and grimacing to the window. Like a caged animal; and despite the broken window and the wind, the stench came with him. Unlike any caged animal, he was armed, just as Bolsover had expected. He'd wadded something around his hand to protect it, and he held a sizable piece of glass. When Sir Harald sat down, later on, seriously to think, he gave that fact weighty consideration—not for the danger implied, though that was evident, but for another reason.

He went back into Bolsover's room where Lily was licking her master's face. Another, if minor, nasty sight.

Fixed upon the immediate!

"Bolsover, do you think that is altogether wise? Dogs nose about in filth."

"They lick their own wounds," Bolsover said, "and they heal. And there's something, if I remember rightly, in the Bible about dogs licking sores. All right, old girl. That'll do. Well?"

"The window is much damaged and he is holding almost half a pane in his hand. I think it would be dangerous to open the door. But...he could be fed through the window. Until...until I can make some other arrangements."

But what arrangements?

He thought of the window. How could that be mended except from the inside, which nobody would dare—and which he was not prepared to ask anyone to dare; or from the outside, which meant removing the bars which again would constitute grave danger?

As for people trained and experienced in dealing with the dangerously insane, he had really no clear idea of where they were to be found. He had once mentioned finding some such person to help Bolsover, but that had been impulse, almost casual. In this area, in fact, there

was no lunatic asylum from which experienced keepers
might possibly be bribed away. Bressford and Wyck and
the countryside which they served in so many ways had
never known the need for a Bedlam. There were village
idiots, sometimes teased, but more often cherished—
especially by their mothers; and there were a few old
people, witless because they were senile, in the
workhouse, tended by people only slightly more sensible
than they were. The nearest proper asylum was in
Colchester, miles away. Would the governor of it know of
experienced keepers? And what sort of men would they
be? He'd need two to do the work which Bolsover had
been doing, and until now, doing so well.

He spent the two hours before lunch in troubled
thought and when his own meal was served, had no
appetite and too little self-command to force himself. The
savory odours were all tainted by the stink of that
dreadful room; and between him and everything he
looked at was the vision of Magnus. Keeping up the
pretense of correct behavior, he said, "Keep my food hot.
I shall not be long." He went upstairs again, running into
Thomas, whose turn it was to carry up the meat course;
two mutton cutlets apiece, mashed potatoes, carrots,
cabbage, red currant jelly.

"It's a bit of a problem," Bolsover said. "His bowl is
still in the room and even if it wasn't it's too big to go
through the bars."

Sir Harald looked about and spied one of the little
decorative objects which Bolsover in his magpie search
for things to beautify his room, had chosen, a little
sweetmeat bowl, a nymph, lightly clad, beautifully
colored, proffering a bowl no more than four inches wide.

"That would do," he said. Bolsover agreed that it
would, though he was fond of his nymph and knew he
would never see her again. Under Sir Harald's watchful
eye he chopped the meat of one cutlet, added vegetables, a
little less haphazardly than usual, and crowned all with a
dab of ruby jelly.

"I'll take it," Sir Harald said. Now it was Lily's eye,
reproachful. She was always fed first.

"Later, old girl. We'll both wait."

Sir Harald went along to the window. Magnus, still

naked, was sitting on the bed and made no attempt to respond when called by name.

"Here is your lunch. Come along Magnus. It's getting cold." He was coaxing now, as he had often done in the past when the child Magnus had known that one sure method of drawing attention to himself and getting his own way was to refuse a meal. "It's a nice lunch, Magnus. Come along, you *must* eat." Magnus never even turned his head. The food grew cold, and so did Sir Harald, exposed on this windy ledge. Finally he put the pretty bowl down in the space between the window and the bars; and he had hardly got back through Bolsover's window before the gulls which he disliked came wheeling and screaming down.

"He wouldn't take it, Bolsover. He wouldn't even look."

"It's often that way when he's sulky."

"What is to be done?"

Bolsover, always so ingenious, said, "Nothing."

"But we can't let him starve."

"He'll eat when he feels like it."

"I'm worried about the weather, too. He's wearing no clothes. The wind blows straight in. And it will snow before night."

Bolsover thought: Who cares? Where there's no sense there's no feeling!

He said, "He'll get into bed when he feels cold." Then feeling for Sir Harald, not for the lunatic, made him add, "Maybe they could rig up a bit of sackcloth. Tack on to the bars."

"Yes. That must be done at once. I'll see to it."

It would take two men, one to hold the flapping sailcloth while the other nailed. And they'd see Magnus in his shocking, shameful condition. Everybody knew, of course, but it was one thing to know, quite another to see. There was a vast difference between Mr. Copsey, kept under control and looked after by Bolsover, and a hairy naked ape surrounded by its own ordure.

He thought about it all the time he pretended to eat his lunch, pushing the food about. He sent word along to the carpenter's shop that young carpenter and another man should stand by with a stack cover, as he might need them later in the afternoon.

Bolsover went along and retrieved his nymph whose bowl the gulls had somehow managed to clear so thoroughly that it looked unused. He did not place her back on his overmantel, but in a cupboard for her own protection. He had noticed that though Magnus sat as though he were paralyzed, he still held a big piece of glass. Not that it mattered; he suddenly felt completely divorced from it all. He'd done his best, he'd failed, and he was finished. He went down to The River Boat.

Sir Harald, this time wearing his top coat and a hat, went out through the window of the empty room. The bowl had disappeared though Magnus appeared not to have moved. He resumed his coaxing talk this time with the object of persuading Magnus either to put on some clothes or get into bed. "Some men are coming to rig up a shield from the cold. I don't want them to see you like this. Come along now, Magnus. Listen to me. Put on your dressing gown or get into bed. . . ." On and on, fruitlessly. And yet at last Magnus seemed to become aware of his presence and came to the window, making noises that were not words, not human. He still held the piece of glass in his right hand, around which he had wrapped a piece of his nightshirt; he put his left hand through one of the empty panes and grasped the bar, testing it. It was an agonizing moment for Sir Harald, not that he feared that the bar might give, but because the empty pane was fringed with jagged splinters. The boy might cut himself.

"No, no! Don't do that. You'll hurt yourself, Magnus."

Magnus made some more indescribable sounds and Sir Harald thought he had better withdraw.

Magnus had not hurt himself—he had enough sense for that; and enough sense to protect his hand from the glass.

Granted that amount of sense left. . . . For the first time Sir Harald looked at the whole business, not as an outsider, however loving and sympathetic, but from Magnus's own standpoint. How did it feel to be Magnus? How did Magnus feel when a flicker of sense broke the general obscurity? Locked away as dangerous, filthy, degraded, completely demented for most of the time, but not yet quite incapable of thought? Too far gone to realize *why* he was in the condition that he was but not yet—would he ever be?—a happy, resigned, vegetablelike idiot.

Sir Harald was not an imaginative man but it was as though now, in the rapidly gathering January dusk, all the unused imagination of a lifetime swept over him swamping every landmark, every guideline of conduct, everything that had made him what he was. He sat down in his library, close to a heaped fire, but this exercise of the imagination so affected him that he shivered, and then sweated, like a man in the grip of malaria. When he was back in his own skin, in his own mind, he knew that there was only one thing to be done and that he must do it. Now! Now while the house was virtually deserted; Hannah in Bressford, Bolsover down at The River Boat, no servants about. He might not succeed of course but at least he would have tried to save Magnus from the living Hell which he had briefly shared. He set about doing his best in a methodical manner.

Bolsover, smelling of rum and also of some faint cloying scent—how sensitive one's nose could become!—came back on the stroke of four. It was beginning to snow lightly, a few desultory flakes, but the landlady said it was too cold to snow properly, it'd have to wait for a change in the wind.

And here was Sir Harald, lurking about. More anxious now than he had been since the move was made. This would have been intolerable had not Bolsover decided that he had done with it all.

"I think, Bolsover, that something has happened to him. I looked in just after lunch and again more lately, trying to persuade him to put on some clothes before the carpenter and his mate. . . . And then again, just now. In the last light. So far as I could see, he is lying on the floor, near the bed."

Well, what did it matter? Except that the poor decent man looked so hag-ridden.

"Probably asleep, sir. Floor or bed, he can't tell the difference."

"But in this cold, Bolsover. . . . I did not have the screen erected because I did not wish him to be seen in that state. I was, in fact, making a last reconnoitre before calling upon the carpenter and his mate, when I saw that he was on the floor."

"Foxing," Bolsover said.

"How can we know? It is so bitterly cold. I think that he should at least be covered. Where is the key?"

"You mean you're going to go in and look?"

"Go in and pull a rug over him. That at least. . . ."

It sounded valiant; it was the kind of almost mystical thing, called leadership, which could make a number of men follow one man to almost certain death. Bolsover could not know that it was an illusion, as deceptive as any ever staged at Drury Lane. He simply felt that Sir Harald was being brave and daring, and that he, although he had finished with the business, must also be brave, or live ashamed for ever.

"I'll come with you. We'll need the lamp. I'll carry that," he said. "Lily, you wait. Wait!"

Lily, at least shouldn't be harmed. And if the lunatic made one move, he'd get the lamp, flame, oil and all, straight in his face.

Magnus made no move. With what struck Bolsover as singular recklessness, Sir Harald advanced and Bolsover, his heart thumping, went with him.

"Careful, sir! Careful!"

Magnus lay crumpled on the floor and the dangerous piece of glass lay nearby. At the sight of it, Bolsover became bolder, but still ready for anything. Sir Harald knelt down, felt for heartbeat, for pulse and then said in a completely expressionless voice.

"He's dead. Poor boy"

"You sure? Here, take the lamp. . . ." Yes, dead as pork! And what a mercy. But you couldn't say that to his father. "I'm sorry, sir. He's dead all right. But why? Strong enough this morning to rip the back off that chair. And if he'd felt the cold he'd have got into bed. I just can't understand it." The thought of suicide presented itself. A lunatic with a pane of glass; but there wasn't a scratch on him. No blood. "I just can't understand," Bolsover said again.

"Possibly Doctor Fordyke will offer some explanation," Sir Harald said in that same flat way. "And I should not wish him to see . . . my son as he now is."

"I know. Just leave everything to me. I'll manage."

Then something unnerving happened. In the next room Lily set up a banshee howl. At the sound even Sir Harald seemed to lose some of his unnatural composure.

"It's only Lily. She can't bear being left. You go and send for the doctor—and have a stiff drink, sir. I'll see to everything."

Despite the snug closed carriage sent to convey him to Copsi, Doctor Fordyke arrived in a bad temper. The coachman knew nothing, didn't even know who needed medical attention. The smallest child, from the lowest slum, generally managed to say something which gave a clue if only so little as: "It's me mum; she gotta bad pain in the belly." Here nothing except the message that he was wanted at Copsi. And the carriage sent a silent assumption that he would go. As indeed go he must. An influenza epidemic raging and there'd been two difficult childbirths; he was short of sleep; he'd almost forgotten when he last had a decent meal. In the carriage he went to sleep and was only half awake when he stood by the bedside of one whom neither he, nor any man living, could aid.

Death had been kind to Magnus. Except for the slight bend in his nose—I didn't do a very good job there, the doctor thought—his face had taken on something of its old handsomeness. And if as Sir Harald said he had been so confused ever since his fall that he had been confined to this one room, he had been most carefully tended; dying, in fact, as he had lived, in the lap of luxury.

"What happened exactly?" he asked.

"That we do not know," said Sir Harald. "Nothing *happened*. He was alive and well at about half-past two."

"He was all right when I went out," Bolsover chimed in.

"I looked in from time to time."

"And when I came back on the stroke of four, he was dead."

In other circumstances the emaciation of the dead man might have aroused suspicion, but not here with a bowl of fruit and a silver-lidded biscuit barrel on the table, well within reach. Bolsover saw the assessing glance and said,

"He had been a bit off his food lately, I noticed."

"So did I," said Sir Harald. "And both footmen complained that they carried down almost as much as they carried up."

"Anorexia." Doctor Fordyke knew the word. It was usually a thing which afflicted young women, a prey to hysteria anyway; but it could affect a demented young man. Still the final cause of death was in every case heart failure. There were a myriad diseases and afflictions but a man was alive while his heart beat, and when it stopped he was dead. So far as he was concerned Magnus Copsey had died of heart failure, in a most elegant bed, spread with fine linen and with cherubs clustered around the head of it. Slightly macabre, for this bed had been designed for the living, not for the dead. But there it was. Nothing anybody could do about it.

Doctor Fordyke was the first of the many to treat this as an ordinary bereavement.

"You have my sincere sympathy, sir," he said.

<hr />

Everything was done correctly. Up went the old pretenses. Poor Sir Harald had lost not an always unsatisfactory and lately insane son, but his only child and his heir. Letters of sympathy were phrased on that assumption. Usually letters of that kind contained rather fulsome praise for the dead, but it was difficult to eulogize Magnus. Mrs. Barrington made a gallant effort: "I shall always remember him as such a handsome little boy." In fact she would remember him as the dreadful little boy who had gone berserk at a party and smashed her chairs. Mrs. O'Brien wrote about the long friendship between Magnus and her own boys and certainly that friendship had enabled Ross and Barry to make the Grand Tour at little cost to their father.

The estate carpenter tottered down to oversee and exasperate his own son over the making of the coffin; the

Copseys were always buried in Copsi-grown wood.

Sir Harald, having conducted his own court-martial and pronounced his own sentence, enjoyed by day the complete resignation of despair. He went about, doing all that must be done with the demeanor of grief borne with dignity which was exactly right. In the days before the funeral he visited Mr. Fullerton's office and made a new will designed to provide for Hannah. He had very little to leave. As soon as he inherited the title he had used his own modest legacy to bolster Copsi's ailing resources and he had never bothered to retrieve anything; he was Copsi and Copsi was his. He could see now that he had been imprudent, but he had not then visualized a daughter-in-law, widowed, and unprotected by any marriage settlement. He left Hannah all that he could; the freehold of the Pump Lane house and the money which safely invested at five percent provided her father's security; the money in his personal account, after the servants' legacies had been paid; and all his personal effects. He was relieved when Mr. Fullerton pointed out that as Magnus's relict, she would eventually inherit Lady Copsey's money. She'd be all right. Almost certain to marry again. There remained Bolsover. For his swift, single-handed work on converting something like a jungle ape into a presentable corpse, Bolsover must be rewarded; fifty guineas, my wardrobe and the pick of any horse from the stables.

That business disposed of he turned to lighter things.

"By the way, this argument about the allowance to the almshouse people. I know my great-grandmother stipulated a shilling a week, but where does a shilling go these days? Next Friday, at the meeting, I shall propose doubling it; the Trust is accumulating money. Can I count on you to support me?"

"Most certainly, Sir Harald." What a man, to think of such a thing at such a time.

What else was to be thought of? Boots.

"I was obliged to be in Bressford today," he said, after accepting the bootmaker's condolences, "and thought I'd snatch the opportunity."

Then, positive inspiration. The gunsmith's. Condolences again; received in the proper way, and matched by an inquiry about the gunsmith's family. Then an inspection of what was on offer.

"I wanted a Locksley. Of all my guns my Locksley is my favorite but it is no longer reliable. Getting old, I suppose. I've had it since I was sixteen."

"That is no age for a good gun, sir. I'm sure a repair.... If I could take a look at it."

Locksley's had been making the best guns for more than a hundred years, but the firm had been taken over recently by someone with new and most inconvenient notions about giving credit. Sir Harald always paid bills promptly, but he was the exception.

"I should be much obliged. I'll send it in."

What with this and that, the days were all right. It was the nights. Sleeping or waking it was the same; that last scene would be lived through again, either in nightmare, or in deeply branded memory....

Here I am by the library fire, knowing, knowing that death would be preferable to that death in life. I go along to where unused silver is kept in a display cabinet and I select the right thing, a christening cup, narrow, with two handles. I tip the stuff in. More than five *drops*, dangerous, ten held to be lethal. I put in more than that, much more. I top it with the best, ripest, richest port wine and stir well. I know that he is strong; so I loop and tie, tie and loop a stout piece of sashcord, through both handles, around the base, leaving one long stretch with a loop, through which I slip my hand. I go along, speak enticingly: "Magnus, I have brought something nice; port wine, Magnus."

The worst moment, then when it happened, and afterwards in nightmare and in memory, was the macabre tug of war, after Magnus had drunk, noisily, smacking his lips, obviously enjoying it. Then he began to pull. Sir Harald pulled too, thankful for the loop around his wrist. For if the cup were found in the room then Bolsover would know. Doubtless he'd be discreet, but Bolsover's connivance was one thing Sir Harald did not desire. Finding tugging useless, Magnus began to gnaw at the cord. The action of an animal, but of a rational animal. Since Sir Harald's action had been dictated by pity for the poor boy who had little flashes of sense, it was absurd to

be so horrified by this flash of sense, to think: Perhaps I
was wrong; too hasty. But it was too late now and he
continued to haul upon the cord with such vigor that
when Magnus suddenly released his hold, he lost balance
and almost fell over the edge of the terrace. He recovered,
went back to the window and spoke to his son for the last
time. "Go to bed, Magnus. Bed. Bed!" And from the
position in which the body had been found it looked as
though for once in his life Magnus had tried to obey.

Night after night. He went to bed drunk, he went to
bed sober; it made no difference. That last half hour of
Magnus's fated life must be lived through again and
again. He was surprised at his own reaction. He'd killed
before in battle and out of it. Once in charge of a firing
squad he'd been obliged to administer the *coupe de grâce*
with a pistol. Was this so different? Once, near the North
West Frontier in India he'd used his sword on one of his
own men, badly wounded; the women of that area were
notorious for their slow mutilation of any captured
enemy. Was this so different? Putting somebody out of
misery, surely an act of mercy. Arguing with himself,
seeking self-justification, he always ended with the feeling
that he had been too quick to despair; hadn't slept on the
matter, been a little too sensitive to what two men nailing
up a tarpaulin might see, might think. Then his mind
would veer and he realised that half his trouble was the
fact that memory of Magnus in that shocking condition
was being overlaid by how Magnus had looked when
dead and cleaned up.

A good general test of past conduct was to answer
the question: In the same circumstances would you do the
same again? And he was doubtful about the answer.

Everybody at the funeral—which was well attended—thought that poor Sir Harald looked very stricken.
Magnus was interred with due ceremony, inside the
church. Nearby lay a crusader Copsey in stone, his
crossed feet resting on a little dog; on a wall above, a
memorial like a stone stage, peopled with stone figures,
commemorated a late Tudor Copsey, with his wife and
five children, all in vast ruffs. After that the dead were less
ornately chronicled. Slabs on the wall. . . .

Strange to think that by this time next week I shall be one with the dead; even stranger to feel nothing about one's own demise. None of the drill—church-going in childhood and during schooldays, church parade in the army, setting a good example to tenants—had ever meant anything to him, apart from the dutiful performance of certain actions. Faith, could he have attained to it, would have helped when Juliet died, but then, utterly bereft, he had come to the conclusion that the ability to believe was either in you, or not; like the ability to play the piano by ear or reckon three colums of figures simultaneously. He felt the same now. An incapacity to visualize the resurrection, about which the parson was speaking so confidently. Equally inconceivable, to him, was the idea of reward or punishment hereafter. At the very moment of committal he thought: And that is the end of us. The end of Copsi.

And then a very curious thought struck him— perhaps because he was in church where he had often repeated the Commandments. "Thou shalt have none other gods before me." That commandment he had flagrantly disobeyed: Copsi had been his god and this was his punishment! But meted out by whom?

>|=====>|=====>|=====>|=====>

The funeral, on account of the uncertain weather and the shortness of the days, was held in the morning. There was the afternoon to get through. He changed into riding clothes, the wide band of black crepe already on the sleeve of his tweed jacket, and went round the estate, not saying goodbye to it—that had been a mental exercise at the moment of self-condemnation—this was a further putting up of defenses against any suspicion that might damage Copsi's name. His visit to Cowfield was typical of the others. "Mrs. Cowper, I understand that you have a leak in your roof."

Face to face with him, a man so bereaved whom she had last seen, sorrowful and dignified, that very morning in church, Mrs. Cowper felt embarrassed.

"Well, the rain did come in a bit, sir and you always said let you know in good time.... So Cowper did, but

I'm sure the last thing he'd want, me neither, would be to bother you about such a little thing at such a time."

"Life must go on, Mrs. Cowper."

"So it must, sir. I've buried four. I wonder now, would you accept of a glass of my elderberry?"

Mrs. Cowper made exceptionally good elderberry wine. Unkind people said that at one point she put a *live* rat into her brew. Not a nice thought, and of course nobody knew for certain, a trade secret as it were; the result was good.

"Extremely kind of you, Mrs. Cowper." But when she handed it, in her best glass, up to him, it looked too much like. . . . "Now if you would just show me where the fault in the roof is." She turned and pointed and he quickly tipped out the contents of the glass.

"Thank you, Mrs. Cowper, delicious. I'll send a couple of men along first thing tomorrow morning and I'll come in the afternoon to see that the job is well done."

A most natural and convincing performance. He had no idea that as he made his last ride, seeing to this triviality and that, he was gathering laurels for himself, and that other people would think, as Mr. Fullerton had thought: What a man to think of such a thing, at such a time.

❖❖❖❖❖

The wind had dropped and there was that hushed, waiting atmosphere which presaged snow; the sky was full of low, sagging clouds, dove gray; yet to the extreme west there was a kind of glow, with no sunset colors about it, just a luminosity. Against it Copsi stood, stark and stripped amongst its leafless trees. Most people preferred it in a softer season—he'd loved it the year round. Now he viewed it without feeling; he had no feeling left, except in two tiny areas; he was anxious that everything should seem ordinary and in order, and he had thought of a way of adding something to Hannah's resources.

Back in his library he rang his bell and ordered a fire and lamps in the gun room. Then he had a little talk with Bolsover—surely a good witness. Bolsover, between the death and the funeral, had not been much in evidence; he'd moved back into his old room to sleep, had looked in on Sir Harald from time to time, "You all right, sir? Anything I can do?" Sir Harald was always all right and there was nothing for Bolsover to do, so contact had been brief and slight.

Now Bolsover couldn't have said anything more useful than what he did.

"You won't, I take it, be needing me any more."

"There you are mistaken, Bolsover. I shall need you. You may remember that at our first meeting, my sister told me that it was your real ambition to be a valet."

"That is so."

"So far I have managed without any man's full attention. But, Bolsover, I have now reached a point where *my* needs must be given some consideration. I need an ... an amanuensis, that is somebody prepared to deal with anything that may crop up. Seeing to my clothes would be the least of it. The truth is, Bolsover, running an estate is a burdensome business—and we none of us get younger."

"Well of course, anything I can do, sir."

"You'd better start by riding round with me tomorrow, get to know the tenants and their peculiarities. Act as a sort of agent for me at times."

Next to being a landed gentleman being a landed gentleman's agent was a most enviable position, usually reserved for members of the family. Bolsover congratulated himself.

Before dinner Sir Harald went through the family jewels and was pleased to find two items of value which through some oversight had not been listed. He could, he supposed, give Hannah almost anything, but when a whole estate by the process of escheatment went back to the Crown, it was likely to fall into the hands of some pettifogging little officials, anxious to dot every i, and it might be embarrassing to the poor girl if somebody suddenly asked what had become of such-and-such.

During all this troubled time she had endeared herself to him by the absolute correctitude of her demeanor and by her acceptance and understanding of bizarre situations. When he had told her, "My dear,

Magnus died this afternoon," she made neither a false display of grief nor a callous hardihood. She said, "I am sorry for *you*. He was your son. For him it must be a happy release."

And even now, as they sat down to dinner, alone together—for the last time, but she, of course—could not know that—she made an effort to entertain him.

"I had a letter from Marie this morning. She did not know what had happened, of course. She wrote from Grenoble where," Hannah made that little pause which gave the next words weight, "they were snow-bound."

She had thought that this might cheer him on a dismal day, and it did, after a fashion, though he no longer cared. His sister and Cousin William and Jonathan had all been part of Copsi; their desertion had hurt him a little just as the idea of their being snowed in at Grenoble amused him a little.

"I always felt that William was persuaded into this excursion," he said "and I'd venture to guess that snow at Grenoble will give him a splendid excuse for turning back. We'd better have their beds aired."

What could be more ordinary? More forward looking?

Hannah sat on his right; away and beyond stretched the starched damask, shining like silver in the candlelight. To his left two jewel cases, one oblong and dark blue, one square and mulberry-colored, lay like dark islands.

He chose his moment well. Fincham and Thomas were both in the room when he said—and he hoped this would be remembered, too—

"My dear, if I live to be ninety, I shall never forget how you, and you alone, offered to watch with me. It has been a most trying time for us all. I'd like you to have these, a mere token of my affection and esteem." He snapped open both cases and pushed them towards her. The oblong case held a string of pearls, shimmering in the light, the square case a diamond brooch, shaped like a star, sparkling with rainbow colors.

"Thank you," Hannah said. "They are beautiful. Beautiful."

She made no move to do anything about them. And a man with so little time left was impatient.

"Try them on," he suggested.

Then she mocked him and all the rules of correct behavior to which he had always been enslaved.

"Pearls" she said, "may be just permissible. But no gem stones for at least a year."

Now that he was so shortly to be free of it all he could afford to make light of the chains he had worn all his life,

"Nonsense," he said, "Magnus will not be less dead in a year's time than he is now. Well, if pearls are permissible...." He rose, a little awkward, but gallant, lifted the pearls from their nest and placed them about her neck, fumbling a little because between the silvery upswept hair and the neckline of the stern black widow's dress, her nape looked so childish and vulnerable.

He thought: I have managed badly again! I should have sent her away. Tomorrow she will wake and be told about my accident and there'll be nobody but servants. Not that his death would mean anything to her, she had no real fondness for him, and why should she have? Still, he should have organized things better, sent her to her mother, asked Bertie to stay. Too late to think of such things now.

The shining cloth was withdrawn, the shining table revealed, dessert set out with the decanter of port wine of which ladies might take one glass before retiring. Fincham, dense idiot that he was, still had to be reminded that Sir Harald no longer drank port wine, hadn't done so for a week, saying that it provoked gout.

Everything in good order. He refused to succumb to self-pity and think: This is the last time I shall raise a glass to my lips; this is the last time I shall speak into a living ear with my living voice. Yet even the denial was an acknowledgement. In the refusal to think, he was thinking.

Hannah said, "I was waiting until we were alone. I have something to tell you. I waited until I was absolutely sure...." That had been essential because, unlike so many girls, Alice Wentworth for one, regular as the moon, she'd been easily set off course; going to school, after all that tug-of-war between Father and Mother, and the adjustment to a new way of life, had made her miss two months;

she'd missed again over Father's accident and Magnus's persecution and her exile to Radmouth. But now it was more than two months, in fact it was three and there'd been all those times when she felt sick, the mornings when she had been. She felt safe in saying,

"I am going to have a baby."

She had expected him to be slightly surprised, but delighted; surely delighted. The prospect of a living child must offset the death of a dangerous lunatic. But if she'd shot him across the shining table the effect could not have been worse. For half a second he gaped at her, eyes bulging, mouth half open, but issuing no sound. His face turned the color of a damson, then he slumped forward, knocking his head on the painted dessert plate and overturning the decanter of port.

Something happened to time; everything slowed down. Slowly, slowly she tugged at the bell-pull, went back to the table and lifted Sir Harald's head, holding it against her waist, close to the place where in darkness and secrecy, seed of his seed had germinated. In the long time before Thomas came she had time to wonder whether this reception of her news was due to shock and suspicion, whether Bertie had been indiscreet; whether her own delay—three months *was* a long time. But she'd been so anxious not to raise false hopes. She remembered that Sir Harald had once told her that he tried not to lose his temper or get excited about anything because most male Copseys who lived past fifty died of apoplectic strokes. After an age Thomas arrived and she said calmly, "Fetch Bolsover. Then send for the doctor."

Another age while she held the man she believed to be dying. Then Bolsover came, brisk and confident, snapping out orders to the servants who had gathered in the doorwway.

"Get some ice. One of you relieve Madam."

Bleeding, once routine, had lately been frowned upon, largely because it had been so often used on those who had no blood to spare—women after childbirth for example, but Bolsover had seen it used effectively. A blazing hot day in Nottingham; twenty-five rounds against a real bruiser; he'd won and a heavy, red-faced fellow blundered forward and hit him on the shoulder. "I won fifty pounds. I'll buy you. . . ."and dropped as though he'd been poleaxed. Somebody in the crowd had stepped forward and bled him and by nightfall he was sufficiently recovered to keep his promise.

Somewhere on the hand. But where? Finger or thumb? Bolsover took out his pocket knife and made a little nick in the congested vein which showed between the thumb and first finger of Sir Harald's left hand.

"Look the other way," he said to Hannah who after handing over to Fincham had gone back to her own chair and seemed on the verge of collapse. Bolsover reached for a crystal finger bowl and as the slow dark blood dropped into the scented rose-water, the sound was answered by the plop of the spilt wine running over the table's edge on to the floor.

Gordon brought the ice. "Put it in a napkin, make a kind of cap of it," Bolsover ordered. "One of you give Madam a little brandy. And clear up that mess." Even without that brief conversation with its mention of the magic word *agent*, Bolsover was in command of the situation.

Quite perceptibly the ominous color began to ebb from Sir Harald's face. Bolsover pressed his thumb to the little cut and staunched it. Then he set about transferring Sir Harald to bed, propped high in pillows as Ransom had been. "You did right," he told Hannah, "holding his head up. Now you'd better get to bed yourself. Must have been a shock for you."

"It was. I'd just told him something I thought would please him. I'm going to have a baby."

"Oh." Bolsover took it for granted that the suggestion he'd made to Mrs. Reeve had been acted upon. *Who*, he wondered, and remembering how he had guessed Jerry Flordon's secret, he hoped *he* had had the pleasure. "I congratulate you. And I'm sure that when Sir Harald comes round he'll be beside himself with joy."

"You think he will recover?"

"Almost sure. His face hasn't even gone lopsided."

"Is that a sign of damage?"

"Sometimes. And if you're . . . as you say, all the more reason to go to bed. When is this happy event to be expected?"

"In August, I think."

Reckon backwards. November then; so it could be all above board. Or she might be very cunning in which case she would have Bolsover's full support, since the cuckoo in the nest had been his idea.

Hannah said she would wait until Doctor Fordyke came. But for once Doctor Fordyke could not answer any call, however urgent; he had caught influenza himself, and overworked as he had been was laid very low indeed. "Never mind," Bolsover said, "we'll manage."

━━◆▶◀◆▶◀◆▶◀◆▶◀◆━━

When Sir Harald came round there were too many people. It took him a little time to realize that there seemed so many because he was seeing double. He squeezed his eyelids together and tried again. Still two of everybody.

The double Bolsover said, "You're all right, sir. Just a rush of blood to the head. You'll feel better tomorrow."

That needed no answer and he did not bother with it, but to the double Hannah something must be said. My dear what joyful news. He said it, and it came out sounding foreign language. But what language? School had given him a workable knowledge of Latin, a mere smattering of Greek; in India he'd picked up a few essential words from the widly varying tongues; but what came out of his mouth when he tried to speak to Hannah resembled nothing he had ever heard. He saw the various duplicated people look at each other, dismayed, questioning. Only Bolsover seemed unperturbed.

"You're having a little difficulty with your speech, sir, but it'll pass. Don't worry. You'll be all right tomorrow."

Sir Harald nodded vigorously and swung a confident smile around all faces; then he reached out for Hannah's hand and gave it a little eloquent pressure. She bent and kissed him.

━━◆▶◀◆▶◀◆▶◀◆━━

He slept well and woke in the morning to find only one Bolsover by his bed. A great improvement, but when he said, "Good morning, Bolsover," the words came out mangled. He thought; If that is all that is wrong with me, I can bear it easily enough. He lay for a moment thinking about what Bolsover had called a rush of blood to the head. That could mean apoplexy which often left people disabled or disfigured. However when he made a move to get out of bed—Bolsover hovering but not obtrusively— he was as sound as he had been yesterday; and happier than he had been for years. Copsi was saved! As resolutely as he had set his face against acknowleding Magnus's mental condition, so he ignored the possibility that something might even yet go wrong, that Hannah might miscarry or produce at the end of it all, a girl. Life, he knew, played some funny tricks, often dirty tricks on people, but he'd had his bad times; by the simple law of averages he had good times to come.

He had never regarded conversation as one of life's pleasures and, he now discovered when he had an excellent excuse for retiring, his public duties had been boring on the whole. Now he could give his whole attention to Copsi and to Hannah whom he cherished in a fatuous way, acting as though she were some very fragile exotic plant unlikely to survive unless kept under glass and watched every minute. She was no longer allowed to drive to Bressford in the little pony carriage; something might happen. The mildest pony might shy, any pony might lose a shoe. She must be driven, in the carriage.

This wish, and almost every other wish he expressed, had to be conveyed through Bolsover who very quickly mastered the art of understanding the garbled talk and became virtually a translator. Hannah never understood a word, but he could write and she could read. Bolsover alone understood and sometimes he said, "I'd like that in writing, sir." He said it when Madame le Beaune, Mr. Orde and Mr. Winthrop came back, all with heavy colds.

"They are not to come near Mrs. Copsey," Sir Harald said. They were welcome back but they were tokeep to their own apartments. And come to his table when invited, not otherwise. Bolsover said he would like that in writing, and Sir Harald wrote.

He'd been an exceptionally easygoing landlord; strict but kindly, now he was more strict and less kindly, especially about arrears. People blamed Bolsover, sitting there on a horse and saying: "Sir Harald says." A few hardy delinquents ventured to question Bolsover's translations and were soon quelled. "He'd like that in writing," Bolsover would say and Sir Harald would produce his writing pad and his pencil and confirm what Bolsover had said. Losing his speech had made Sir Harald very arbitrary, everybody thought; in fact he had always been arbitrary but he had always—except in the case of the Reeves—exercised immense control over himself; now he no longer felt the need to do so, no need to pretend.

John Reeve received Hannah's news with simple joy. He had, after all been right. Martha, just for a moment, shared Bolsover's thought and determined that if the baby should be born even a shade too late she would swear that Hannah and her husband had had one night together at whatever would seem the appropriate date. Bertie was prepared to do the same.

August, the harvest month, came and the next Magnus Copsey, with that regard for punctuality and consideration for others which were to distinguish him all his life, slipped into the world with the minimum of fuss. Martha was there; she had brought little Edward with her because school was closed and his grandmother was taking a cure at Bath. Also at the ready was the midwife from Bressford whose proud boast was that in twenty-five years she'd never bungled a birth yet. A mother or two had died, but always later and for varying reasons. Sir Harald chose her for her record of success and because she did not hold with surgical interference. She and Mrs. Reeve were fully agreed on one subject—keeping on the move until the last possible moment made for easier and safer confinement; that was why poor women did better than those who could afford to loll about on sofas. Martha's judgement was based on experience, she'd been busy up to the very day; the midwife had never borne a child herself, but had had ample opportunity to observe.

So on the second Saturday of August Hannah was taking one of her gentle little walks when the first warning came. "I think I had better go in," she said. Two hours later she was safely delivered.

It was a time of acute anxiety for Sir Harald and in his new state of mind he made no effort to conceal his feelings. Bolsover was anxious, too, but mainly on Sir Harald's behalf; one stroke, however slight, could be a forerunner and it would be too cruel if in this moment, the culmination of so much hope, so many fears, so many schemes, the poor old gentleman should be struck again. This time, however, Sir Harald was prepared for joy and when Martha came down and said, "We have a grandson, Sir Harald," he took her arms and kissed her on both cheeks.

He wept when he first viewed the baby, not only a boy but a beautiful, healthy-looking one; and not only that but a proper Copsey, born with hair of a sandy shade. He wasn't going to risk his speech with the midwife, but he touched the reddish fluff and then his own grizzled hair. She said birth hair always rubbed off and might grow again any color. That did not please Sir Harald and he toyed with the idea of giving her a guinea less than he intended to. By evening he was planning the christening which was to supercede all others. He would ask Lord Hornsby to be one godfather; that should heal the slight breach. And Bolsover must be the other.

"I'd like that in writing, sir."

Sir Harald wrote: "I wish Daniel Bolsover to be sponsor to my grandson. But for his prompt action I should not have lived to see this happy day."

Lord Hornsby accepted the honor, and because Withinstone was so far away, spent a night in the splendor and supreme discomfort of the King's Chamber. Hannah was allowed to select the godmother and chose Miss Drayton; so rank, good sense and scholarship stood by the font when the name Magnus was bestowed on the child. Only Bolsover questioned the choice of name, saying sternly, "You ought to consider her a bit. The name can't hold any happy memories for her, can it?"

Sir Harald retorted—and was prepared to put it in writing if Bolsover chose not to understand—that the firstborn male Copsey had always been Magnus. Not that it mattered. Young Magnus was so often called my boy, my dear boy that he identified himself with the name and called himself, and was called, Boy until he became Sir Magnus, and was still after that, known as Boy Copsey to his friends.

※━━━━※━━━━※━━━━※━━━━※━━━━※

Nothing, of course, was too good for Hannah who had proved her worth in so many ways. She could never be Lady Copsey, but she must have her place in the Long Gallery, and despite the dislike Sir Harald felt for Jonathan's work, on the whole family solidarity forced him to offer the commission to Jonathan, who could paint properly if he wanted to. Admonished, through Bolsover, and through many written instructions with much underlining, Jonathan produced another infuriating portrait. In it Hannah had dignity—upon that Sir Harald had insisted, underlining the word so fiercely that he broke his pencil point—but it was a dignity imposed upon a girl so young, so frail-looking that it seemed to be assumed. It was the picture of a very young girl given access to some magnificent jewels and finding them a burden. The great emerald ring looked too heavy for the delicate hand, the neck seemed only just able to support the weight of the piled-up, silver-gilt hair and the tiara upon which Sir Harald had insisted. As for the eyes. . . .

Partly in words, partly in writing, for even Bolsover lacked understanding in some spheres, Sir Harald kept up a long grumble. Mrs. Copsey looked nothing like that; so damned unhealthy; look at the way she'd recovered from childbirth; look at the sense and resilience she'd shown during those difficult months! If, as Jonathan claimed, he painted real people, why had he caught no glimpse of the good sense, the wry, almost caustic humor and all the other sturdy qualities which Sir Harald so much admired in his daughter-in-law?

Beware of provoking another stroke! Bolsover said mildly that in some ways it was a good likeness; look at the silvery gleam of the hair! In other ways it was an exaggeration, but then anybody who could draw exaggerated.

All right! Sir Harald was not willing to quarrel with the one person who seemed—if only partially— to understand him, but where did exaggeration stop and distortion begin? The poor girl looked starving and miserable, and look how happily she romped about with her baby, now at the crawling stage.

Oh, granted, Bolsover said, the baby was a great joy to her.

"But there's another side to it, sir. She's what, sixteen? seventeen? It wasn't much of a marriage, was it? And now she's a widow. If you think of it, it's enough to make any woman feel sorry for herself."

Once, making his will, Sir Harald had thought about the possibility, the near certainty, of Hannah marrying again. Then it had seemed to be the best thing, but that was when he had contemplated, quite calmly, the end of Copsi and the end of himself. Since then he had not given so peripheral a matter a thought. Everything centered around the baby.

※　　※　　※　　※　　※

Then it was Spring again, with drifts of snowdrops, followed by primroses, and with catkins dancing in the hedgerows. Sir Harald had ridden round with Bolsover and had a very happy day and as he mounted the stairs he looked forward to its culmination— seeing young Magnus, now seven months old, taking his supper. There had been alterations on this floor; Bolsover had moved into the room which had been Magnus's, and Sir Harald had moved into Bolsover's; the room which had been briefly occupied by the carpenter, Sir Harald's room and a small dressing room had been made into a palatial nursery suite. As he approached the door of the day nursery Sir Harald heard a male voice and his heart began to flutter. The doctor? Something wrong with the child? The one thing of which he lived in mortal dread. He flung open the door and entered hastily. Nurse Baxter, a paragon of her kind, sat in the rocking chair by the fire with Magnus's little nightshirt warming over her knee. Hannah with the child on her lap was at the table, removing the top from a boiled egg, and also at the table was a man, his big, tanned hands employed in the delicate business of cutting bread and butter into strips.

Jerry Flordon.

Sir Harald faintly disapproved of him, largely because he had so early broken with the Copsi tradition and followed what might be called a perapetetic life; here today and gone tomorrow. One could set against this that he was good to his old mother and always paid her rent regularly. And you could set against that the fact that his sister was a disgrace. And his own manner tended to be free and easy.

Of course he and Hannah were acquainted, John Reeve had employed him; but did that justify this intimate, almost family scene, with Jerry Flordon helping with the baby's supper?

These thoughts sped through his mind as he made the unintelligible noise meant to be: "Evening, Flordon." It was one of those rare times when he felt his disability to be a disadvantage; so much could be conveyed by *tone* of voice.

Jerry said, "Good evening, sir," and offered his chair. Before taking it, Sir Harald patted Hannah on the arm and stroked Magnus's hair, which, defying the midwife, had grown again in the true Copsey color and was now curly.

Hannah said, "Wait in my room, Jerry. I shall not be long."

Sir Harald forgot everything in the delightful business of dipping strips of buttered bread into the egg yolk and feeding the avid little mouth. Young Magnus could already distinguish between people and when being fed by these could make a game of a meal, turning his head away pretending to refuse the proffered morsel, and then turning it back again and laughing. He never tried such tricks on the other one. Nor with her did he attempt to take the mug of milk himself. At one point in this performance, Sir Harald looked at Hannah and was incensed with Jonathan again; how could he possibly have so misrepresented this happy young woman with the wildrose color in her cheeks and the laughing eyes?

"Jerry really wanted to see *you*," Hannah said when Nurse Baxter moved in with a dampened face cloth to remove smears of egg. "Will you come to my room or shall we come down?" We?

He'd feel more at ease on his own territory, so he pointed down the stairs.

"It's partly about Luke's Knob," Hannah said, using the old term for the ten-acre field which had been hired by the tenant of Squirrel's Hall for years but was now just that bit too much for him. He was getting old and his son had been one of those who had prefered voluntary exile to living under Magnus—an echo of the Jim Bateman affair. "And partly about something else," Hannah said. "But they are connected. I hope you will give him patient hearing."

And when had he ever denied patient hearing to anybody? To the most trivial complaint, the most demanding request, he had always lent a ready ear and done what he could. Only once in his life had he been grossly unfair and the result of that lapse was the splendid little boy now being bedded down in the night nursery.

What Jerry Flordon said was pretty shocking. He wanted to hire Luke's Knob because he wanted to marry Hannah and did not wish to look like a kept man.

"Given Luke's Knob at a reasonable rent, I could do with it what I once hoped to do with that field at Reffolds. I'm prepared to live here"—Good God! Jerry Flordon, prepared to live at Copsi!—"because naturally you want the boy here, and Hannah wants to be with her child. But I must pay my way."

Had Sir Harald not suffered an impairment to his speech he would have been dumbstruck. Then, and after a moment's goggling silence burst into angry speech saying offensive things. As it was he simply stared, his eyes bulging. A danger sign! Hannah went quickly across and perched on the arm of his chair, putting a soothing hand on his arm, smiling, coaxing. Employing indeed all those little feminine tricks in which he had once found her so lacking.

"You are surprised," she said lightly but with a certain trenchancy, enough to warn him that surprise was about the only emotion he must show, here in his own library, face to face with Widow Flordon's fly-by-night son who was condescending enough to visualize making his home at Copsi. Proposing to become one of the family; stepfather to that beloved child! Insufferable impertinence! Blasted impudence! "I was surprised myself," Hannah said, "to see Jerry this afternoon. He's been on a very long voyage this time. All the way to Iceland. I was growing worried."

Jerry watched this little performance with a cool, sardonic eye. He knew exactly what Sir Harald felt; he'd warned Hannah that the old gentleman would be obstructive and she had said, "Why should we care? Look what he *owes* me."

He had remained standing, looming large against the sunset-lighted window.

"I know how you feel about it. A man groveling about in the soil and peddling what he grows and then coming back here. There's no shame in honest labor let me tell you and dirt washes off. This siutation was none of my making—except that I was slow. Waiting till I had someting to offer and then too late. . . . But I love Hannah and she loves me. And I'm doing my best to be reasonable. I have money saved. Hannah and I could go and live anywhere—but there is the child to be considered."

Sir Harald made some gargling sounds and reached for his pad. He wrote fiercely to the peril of his pencil again. "*Think*. Is this what you *really* want?"

"But of course. Yes. Yes."

The red tide of anger had had time to recede and Sir Harald had had time to think. An attractive young widow like Hannah could have chosen anybody *and taken the child with her*. And after all, had he not by the exercise of his will forced everybody to accept the farm girl? Could he not do the same again? Of course he could. He and Copsi had withstood some hard knocks.

He wrote: "You have my blessing."

It went, actually, as much against the grain as using his power to enforce that earlier marriage had done. Both acts out of character and both rewarded.

For Sir Harald the halcyon days began; the happiness engendered by the love match seemed to brim over and affect everybody in the house, changing the whole atmosphere. Young Magnus grew, lively, intelligent, goodnatured, and he not only loved his grandfather but understood him. Between the speech of a child experimenting with language and that of an elderly man whose pronunciation had gone wrong, there was great similarity. The two had long conversations, punctuated by laughter and presently Bolsover was not the sole translator. Boy would say: "Grandpa says...," and he was invariably right. Martha said that Boy was growing up bilingual and that was good, making for flexibility of mind.

There was another link, too; they walked at about the same pace, Sir Harald slowed down by his limp and the gathering years, Boy stepping out manfully but handicapped by the shortness of his legs. They walked in the garden, and in the maze, and often in bad weather in the Long Gallery where their shared history hung mute on the walls. Unlike that other little boy whom Sir Harald had striven in vain to interest, this one listened attentively, regarded the painted people as real and was equally ready to hear a new story or the repetition of an old one. Sir Harald had always enjoyed showing off his family portraits, but he had never had quite such an appreciative listener as his grandson to whom he could tell, in their own private language and in bits and pieces, the long, long history of Copsi.

ABOUT THE AUTHOR

The name NORAH LOFTS is familiar to all readers of women's fiction: she has long been one of the grande dames of the historical novel. For forty years she has made the past live vividly and romantically for millions of women. One critic observed that, "Norah Lofts has the almost uncanny gift of writing about olden times as if she has lived them." Uncanny, too, is the unflagging energy Ms. Lofts brings to her craft. *Books In Print* currently lists thirty-eight of her titles in hard and soft covers. Her previous novels have included *Uneasy Paradise, Hester Roon, Jassy* and *The Lute Player*.

A Special Preview of
the opening pages of a sweeping
new novel of reckless passion
and profane love.

THE HELLIONS

by
George McNeill

In this latest saga of the Deavors family, which
began with THE PLANTATION and RAFAELLA,
a brother and sister are threatened by their twisted
heritage.

in his manner, Bellever said, "Come along now. You're going to have a wash."

Prologue

Natchez, 1840

... At The Columns, Rafaella left the carriage on the house road. On foot, she crept up the big front lawn, shivering with the cold. She sensed that she was being followed, as she had been on the frantic ride out from town.

The big house was dark and quiet. She crossed the veranda and passed through the huge white columns. After one creaking step in the front hallway, she was able to move upstairs without making a sound. The nursery door stood partly open. A black woman was sleeping on a cot near the double crib. Rafaella slipped into the room. She snatched up a vase and smashed it against the woman's head.

Then she picked up a down pillow and moved toward the crib. The twins were fast asleep. . . . Clayton and Cynthia, Storey had said they were called. They should have been named after her father and mother: Roger and Sarah.

As she lowered the pillow, she heard a voice.

"Raffles!"

The voice chilled her. She dropped the pillow and wheeled to face him.

Wyman Ridgeway stood in the doorway. His face was hideous, twisted, scarred. Part of his left ear was missing.

Rafaella shrank away from the sight of him. "Wyman? My God! What are you doing? Oh, Wyman!" Involuntarily, she stared at the ever-present sword in its scabbard at his side.

"You were going to kill the children."

"Yes, yes, so I was . . . But why should you care? A man like you?"

"I'm their father, Raffles! And I told you you'd pay with your life if you tried to harm them."

"Their father! You . . . and Lucinda! Oh, God!"

Ridgeway made a swift movement. His naked rapier suddenly glinted in the candlelight. "I had hoped the last swordsman would kill me. But the scoundrel lacked the ability. How appropriate. Now we can die together . . . beloved husband and wife."

"No!" Rafaella screamed. "No! I won't . . . I'll do anything. I didn't know. Oh, Wyman . . . They killed my father!"

He moved toward her, his rapier high. She screamed again and threw a silver vase at his head. He ducked, laughing.

Rafaella ran into the hall, down the stairs, screaming incoherently. Ridgeway followed. She ran out the back door of the house, oblivious to the voices from the quarters, to the lights blinking on in the small cabins.

"No, no!" she screeched as she reached the edge of the swamp. "No . . . Daddy . . . Save me, Daddy!"

Rafaella turned to beg Ridgeway. He cut off her right thumb. The index finger dangled by a thread.

She lurched, screaming like a wounded animal, into the swamp. He followed . . .

1.
Natchez, January 1860

The twins stood in lantern shadow at the veranda's edge and argued about kissing and responsibility. Chessie was upset because her brother was leaving the party early for a rendezvous with some woman and Clayton was annoyed because he had seen his sister being kissed on this same veranda earlier.

As usual with the Deavors twins, discussion resolved nothing, and five minutes later they returned to the crowded parlor of the Clarence T. Pugh mansion, where the raffle was about to begin.

The Hellions

The party was the first of many being given in honor of the twins' mother, Lucinda, who was marrying Anthony Walker. Mrs. Pugh, a widow of uneasy social standing who was scarcely tolerated by Natchez's most prominent families, had set up an unusual entertainment—a raffle of expensive and unusual items, including a "surprise," to make her party different and to lure Adams County aristocrats to her home.

Chessie glanced at the long table. Slaves were setting out items ranging from rococo silver sconces, a crystal chandelier imported from Bohemia, and a bolt of black Italian silk to a pair of chattering monkeys. Chessie touched her own raffle ticket, safe in the pocket of her blue silk dress, and wondered what she would do if she won the monkeys.

The ten-piece orchestra stopped for a rest, and as the Deavors twins crossed the parlor, the young people who had been dancing gravitated toward them. A young Natchez doctor and two Adams County planters looked eagerly toward Chessie but, as usual, since his return from school in the East a few months earlier, Clayton received more attention than Chessie from both men and women.

For Clayton was charming as well as handsome. As Chessie listened, he amused the group with a humorous story about a Yankee peddler being swindled by a Mississippi horse trader. Then he quickly drank two double whiskeys. Chessie dreaded her mother's reaction to Clayton's leaving early and hoped he would be discreet about it.

When the music began again Chessie danced first with the Natchez doctor and then with a handsome young planter named Dunbar Polk. Protesting weariness, she declined an invitation from the other planter and walked toward her mother, who was standing near open French doors at the far end of the room talking to several elegantly dressed ladies.

Lucinda Deavors smiled at her daughter and motioned for Chessie to stand at her side. The ladies' talk was light, mostly gossip, and Chessie tried to seem interested, but her mind drifted away. The wind was cool and brought the damp, sweet smell of japonicas from the garden. The smell was provoking, exciting . . .

it stirred her senses, made her feel restless. She sighed. Then she realized that it was raining again. Had there ever before been so much rain in January?

Some of the ladies excused themselves and others joined the group and started another conversation, asking about the Grand Tour to the Continent planned for the twins right after their mother's wedding.

Yes, Chessie told the ladies, she and Clayton were very excited about going and had studied both Italian and French to prepare. Chessie was particularly looking forward to the chance to sketch the Roman ruins.

When the talk turned to the raffle and the surprise promised by Mrs. Pugh, Lucinda stepped closer to Chessie.

"I hope nothin's seriously wrong with your brother, Chessie," Lucinda whispered.

Chessie Deavors had been christened Cynthia Susannah, but called Chessie ever since a house slave named Cellus had declared she was too small a baby to carry such a big name.

"Wrong?" Chessie asked. "What do you mean, Mama?"

"Clayton told me he's not feelin' too well and that he plans to leave shortly."

"Oh, I . . . I think he's just . . . It's nothin', Mama. Just all this constant partyin' and all, so soon after the holidays."

"I hope he hasn't had too much to drink," Lucinda said. "Sometimes I think your brother became too fond of whiskey in that Eastern school, Chessie."

"Oh, Mama, don't worry. Clayton doesn't drink all that much." Chessie's was an automatic response, an unconscious defense of her twin brother although she increasingly resented having to lie for Clayton. It wasn't at all fair. The way Clayton took pleasure in confessing his affairs and all the while claiming that if she so much as let a boy kiss her that she was next thing to a fallen woman.

"Well, I hope you're right," Lucinda said. She shivered.

"Are you cold, Mama?" Chessie asked.

"A bit. There's nothin' colder than a damp cold," Lucinda said.

"I'll ask one of the slaves to close the windows," Chessie said.

"No, no, it'll be too stuffy in here," Lucinda said. "I'll send Myrtis out to the carriage for my shawl."

Lucinda turned and called to a young Negro girl who was standing in the shadows against the wall. Myrtis was fifteen. Her mother, who was Chessie's personal maid, was sick with diphtheria and this was the first party that Myrtis had attended.

Chessie had always been fond of Myrtis, even thought of her as a little sister. Myrtis was slim and lovely and very shy around strangers.

"Myrtis, please fetch my shawl from the carriage," Lucinda said.

Myrtis glanced from Lucinda to Chessie. She licked her lips and glanced at the floor quickly, then back at Lucinda.

"Well, child, what's wrong?" Lucinda asked.

"Are you afraid to go out there to the stables alone, Myrtis?" Chessie asked.

"Yes'm, Miss Chessie," Myrtis whispered.

"Now, I'll hear none of that," Lucinda said. "You march yourself right out there, Myrtis. You hear me?"

"Yes,'m, I'm goin', Miss 'Cinda," Myrtis said.

She walked away and Chessie turned back to her mother.

"You look lovely tonight, Mama," she said. "Ever since you brought that damask home from New Orleans I've been longin' to see it on you. It's perfect, Mama. It flatters your hair!"

"Why, thank you, dear," Lucinda said. "The dress has brought me any number of compliments. I only hope Anthony likes it. But . . . do you think the dressmaker made it too . . . ? Well, is it too young lookin' for somebody my age?"

"Oh, of course not, Mama," Chessie said. "It suits you and you look beautiful in it."

Her mother did look beautiful in the green damask gown but Chessie had private reservations. The gown was cut so low and fit so tightly that her mother's breasts were clearly defined. In truth, it was a dress more suitable for a woman younger than Lucinda's forty-two years.

Chessie could never say so—it would hurt her mother's feelings, but since she had met Anthony Walker, Lucinda had changed both her style of dressing and her behavior. Perhaps it was because Anthony was a bit younger—only thirty-five—but for whatever reason, it embarrassed Chessie to see her mother in provocative dresses, blushing and radiant like a young girl in love.

"I wonder what's keepin' Anthony," Lucinda said. "His note said he'd be here by ten and it's half past already."

"Well, didn't his note say that something had come up at the docks?" Chessie asked. "From what I understand, bein' a shipowner means one has to keep irregular hours."

"Oh, I know, Chessie," Lucinda said. "Anthony has great responsibilities. But it's just . . . I find myself missin' him, I reckon."

They talked to the other ladies about the trip to Europe, then Chessie danced with a lawyer from Natchez and a banker from New Orleans. She talked briefly to Clayton and his crowd of admirers, then returned to her mother.

"Just look how that woman is fillin' up the table for the raffle," Chessie said.

"Yes, she's got everything up there but Adam's offox," her mother said. "Lord, she must have spent a fortune on this raffle."

"I wonder what the surprise is," Chessie said.

"I don't have any idea, but leave it to Spoony to come up with something you wouldn't . . . Oh, there's Anthony!"

Chessie glanced toward the door and saw Anthony talking to Mrs. Pugh. She looked back at her mother and read in her expression the mixture of emotions: happiness, relief and anxiety. Lucinda looked so vulnerable Chessie was almost afraid for her. She put out a restraining hand. Was her mother actually capable of running across the room and flinging her arms around Anthony's neck?

As they watched, Anthony took his time chatting with their fat, fawning hostess.

2.

Myrtis walked slowly from the house. She paused at the back of the veranda and looked into the deep shadows in front of her.

She glanced over her shoulder and saw all the white people dancing and talking and she heard the music and laughter. Miss Chessie was dancing with Mist' Dunbar and she thought of sneaking back inside and begging Miss Chessie not to send her out to the stables alone. But she shook her head at the idea. If Miss 'Cinda found out, she would be furious.

And so would her own mother. Her mother was forever scolding her for being so afraid of the dark, for fearing every night sound. And she had the responsibility of taking her mother's place tonight. It was important. It was the first time she had ever attended a party, one of the few times, in fact, that she had left the security of The Columns.

Myrtis moved off the veranda with quick, uneasy steps, and half a minute later she left the halo of light from the brightly lit house and walked down a path through a rose garden, toward the stables.

She hummed a song she had heard from the driver of a New Orleans guest at The Columns. She thought of the shiny new shoes that Miss Chessie had bought her in Natchez. But her heart thumped and she glanced from side to side at the shadows, and even the familiar sounds of crickets seemed menacing.

The stables loomed in the distance but they looked so far away. Myrtis heard a fiddle from the quarters, heard laughter. The drivers would be dancing, she knew, gossiping, sneaking drinks of whiskey or beer. She hated it when slaves got drunk. Then, men she had known all her life seemed different, seemed to threaten her as they looked up and down her body with strange expressions on their faces.

Finally, she neared the stables and the dozens of

carriages parked around them. She glanced about, looking for the Deavors' carriage, but she was also looking for anyone who might be lurking in the shadows.

Two minutes later she located the carriage. She found the shawl and turned to run back to the house.

Myrtis stifled a scream. A huge black man loomed over her.

The man laughed and she smelled whiskey on his breath.

"You must remember old Scaggin, girl," he said. "I'm Miss Spoony's lead driver, met you out to The Columns at a party, few weeks ago. We had us a dance together."

"I've got to get back to the house," Myrtis said.

A chill raced down her back. She did remember Scaggin. He had been rough and had used bad language and other slaves said he was a man to avoid when he was drinking whiskey.

"Let the white folks wait," Scaggin said. "They not goin' to miss you for a while. Come on, let's have us some fun. I got me some whiskey good as the white folks drink. Come on, girl, dammit, don't shy away from me like that!"

"No, don't touch me!" Myrtis gasped. She bolted from his hand and ran among the carriages.

She glanced over her shoulder. She couldn't see him. But when she stopped a moment she heard the sound of his feet on the gravel as he moved toward her. She turned and started running again, clutching the shawl to her breasts as though it would protect her.

Finally, Anthony left Spoony Pugh and came over to Chessie and her mother. He kissed Lucinda's cheek and gave her a smile that always annoyed Chessie, a smile she considered patronizing. Anyone with eyes could see how much her mother loved Anthony Walker —she just hoped he was worthy of her.

"Darling, I'm sorry to be late," Anthony said. "But the rain had damaged several crates of that last shipment from Africa and I had to try and salvage what I could. I've been so anxious to be with you. You look ravishing in that shade of green!

"And you, Chessie," he added quickly. "I trust

you're well this evening. I like your blue frock. But not nearly so much as your mother's gown."

"Thank you," Chessie said. "I'm fine."

"Darling, did you see Myrtis when you arrived?" Lucinda asked. "I sent her out to fetch my shawl."

"No, I didn't see anything of her," Anthony said. "I was much too eager to be with you."

Lucinda blushed as Anthony flattered her. Chessie felt her embarrassment mount and she could have kissed a Woodville planter for asking her to dance.

When the dance ended, Spoony Pugh announced that it was time for the raffle and everyone crowded around the long table. There was an empty space in the center of the table between a pair of caged thoroughbred hunting dogs and a set of jewel-studded silver goblets. A strapping young black man, bare to the waist, ran into the room and climbed onto the center of the raffle table.

The man wore skin-tight white satin pants that clung to his genitals and muscular thighs. After a moment's silence, there was a chorus of gasps and murmurs as the guests realized that he was the grand prize, Spoony Pugh's surprise.

"Well, I think it's shockin'," Dunbar Polk said. "I mean the way that boy's dressed—with women present. And the idea. Rafflin' off a nigger just as though we were at a slave auction when many of us disapprove of slave tradin'."

"Yes, it is unusual . . . and rather despicable," Chessie said. Like Polk, the Deavorses were strongly opposed to slave-trading and they never sold their own slaves.

Excitement mounted as the guests' numbers were called and they received their prizes—Chessie won an ivory brush and comb set—and soon only the slave was left on the table. Everyone glanced around the room, trying to remember whose number had not yet been called.

Then number twenty-seven was called.

Frannie Deavors rose from a chair at the side of the room and walked slowly through the crowd to claim her prize.

Chessie glanced at her mother and her mother shook

her head. Frannie had married into the Deavors family many years earlier, had married some granduncle named Lavon no one ever had anything good to say about, and she was never so much as acknowledged by the family now. In addition to everything else, Frannie had the worst reputation in Natchez, as far as men were concerned, and it was said that the men weren't always white.

People whispered as the slave climbed down from the table and Frannie, a big-breasted woman in a tight lavender dress, left the room with him.

The orchestra played a waltz but no one moved to dance. Everyone talked, gossiped, compared their prizes and accepted fresh glasses of whiskey and cherry cobblers with straws.

Chessie began to feel melancholy and she took a glass of punch. As she put the cup to her lips she saw Clayton at the door. Their eyes met and he winked, then walked out.

By watching, Chessie seemed to condone Clayton's behavior, but she truly resented it. It was unbearable—outrageous—that he had the audacity to wink at her knowledge of his little rendezvous.

Chessie flushed with anger as she gulped down her punch and, for the first time in her life, she ordered a whiskey.

3.

Half an hour later Chessie was both angry at Myrtis and worried about her. She had sent her driver to the stables but he had not found the girl. Now Lucinda and Anthony had left the party, and Chessie felt that Myrtis was her responsibility, though she very much wanted to leave and Dunbar Polk had offered to escort her home.

"It happens all the time, honey," Spoony Pugh told Chessie between sips of whiskey. "Niggers, they reach that age, their juices get to flowin' like only nigger juices can flow, and they get so irresponsible they not hardly worth their keep."

"But Myrtis isn't like that," Chessie said. "She's just a girl. She's shy, responsible, hard-workin'. And she blushes and hides her head if a man so much as looks her way."

"Well, then she's the exception," Spoony Pugh said.

"Maybe I don't know her as well as I thought," Chessie said.

"She's all right," Polk said. "She's young. And you did say she never leaves the plantation. She probably met some young buck out there and forgot all about the time. She'll be back before we leave, I'm sure."

Chessie let herself be talked into another dance but despite the swirl around the room and her light talk with Polk she continued to worry about Myrtis. She considered asking Polk to search for the girl, considered sending her driver again, then decided that she would feel better if she simply went out to find Myrtis herself.

Chessie made an excuse to Polk and left the parlor. She hesitated on the veranda, listening to the fiddle music from the slave quarters. That's it, she told herself angrily. Myrtis was down in the quarters, dancing, having a good time. The girl had completely forgotten her duties. As Chessie walked down the veranda steps she vowed she would punish Myrtis.

The path was dark and shadowed from minute to minute by fast-moving clouds that slid across the full moon. Chessie hurried along the path through a rose garden. In her haste she walked too fast and stubbed her toe on a large stone and nearly fell. She caught her balance and started to move off again.

A sound from the darkness to her right stopped her. Something was thrashing on the ground. Chessie feared it was some preying night creature that was devouring its catch. She shivered.

The shivers became a shudder: Those were human sounds! Someone was moaning, whimpering. Another, deeper voice was cursing and there was erratic, labored breathing.

Chessie glanced around at the big house blazing with lights, back in the darkness. She was afraid to go toward the sounds but she sensed someone needed help. She was about to turn and run back and get Polk when the clouds cleared the moon.

Chessie gasped. There, on the ground in the moonlight, lay Myrtis, her face bruised and bleeding. A huge black man was ramming his body between her quivering thighs.

Chessie was immobilized and made speechless by the horror of the scene and for what seemed an eternity she could only make little mewling sounds as she watched the man's savage thrusts at Myrtis' body.

Myrtis' eyes met Chessie's a moment later and Myrtis' mouth opened. No words came out, only a barely human moan of agony that snapped Chessie from her trance.

"No, no!" Chessie cried. She ran, half stumbling, toward Myrtis and her attacker. "Myrtis! Oh, Myrtis . . ."

The man craned his head around. His face was distorted with passion and hatred. Chessie stopped. She screamed.

He staggered up, his penis still erect. He lurched toward Chessie, his enormous hands doubling into fists. She staggered backward and screamed hysterically.

There were shouts from the house and the quarters. But the man had nearly reached Chessie. He towered over her . . .

But he ran past her and disappeared into the darkness.

Chessie trembled with fear and relief. Her legs were rubbery. She felt faint.

A whimper reminded her of Myrtis. Chessie fell to the ground beside the girl. Tears swelled in Chessie's eyes. She hesitated, gathering her strength and courage, then touched Myrtis' cheek.

Myrtis tensed and cried out.

"It's me, Myrtis," Chessie said. "It's all right now . . . I'll take care of you, Myrtis . . ."

Chessie could barely bring herself to look at Myrtis. Her face was cut and bleeding and her left eye was swollen shut to a shadowy purple mass of pulp in the moonlight. Her dress was torn open, baring her small, dark-tipped breasts which were scratched and bruised. Below her waist, Myrtis' skirt had been ripped apart and a stream of blood trickled between her thighs.

Slowly, with obvious difficulty, the girl turned toward Chessie and opened her eyes. She swallowed hard and her body shook.

"Miss Chessie," she whispered. "Oh, Miss Chessie . . . He's done hurt me bad . . . He done ruined me . . . I want to die . . ."

Chessie took Myrtis in her arms and tried to soothe her, stroking her soft, thin shoulders.

There were shouts all around Chessie now and people ran up, both white people and slaves, and Dunbar Polk was the first to reach Chessie.

"My God!" he said. He sank to his knees. "Chessie, what in hell happened? Are you all right? The girl . . ."

"He raped her," Chessie mumbled. "And he hurt her so badly. Why did he have to hurt her this way, Dunbar?"

"Someone send for the doctor," Polk said as people crowded around.

A gray-haired slave woman knelt beside Myrtis and covered her body with a cloak.

"He'll hang for this!" a man in the crowd said.

"Yes, he will," Polk said. "Who did this?" He looked up at a male slave. "Dammit, boy, don't you think about not tellin' me or I'll have your hide from here to sundown!"

"Honest, I wasn't nowhere 'round when it happened," the slave said. "We was all in the quarters or in the house tendin' to the party."

"It was Scaggin," the gray-haired woman said. "I seen him runnin' away. And it ain't the first time he done somethin' like this to a girl."

"Whose nigger is Scaggin?" Polk asked.

"He belong to Miss Spoony," the woman said. "He her pride and joy, her lead driver, can't do no wrong in Miss Spoony's eyes."

"Where did he go? Is he still on the place?"

"No, I reckon he done runnin' far as he can get, seein' as how he done raped hisself a Deavors nigger."

"You, boy, ride into town and fetch the sheriff," Polk said.

"They dogs on the place here?" a man in the crowd asked. "Good trackin' dogs?"

"They no decent dogs to this place," the woman said. "Miss Spoony, she don't care nothin' 'bout no trackin' dogs."

"Who's got the best dogs, Dunbar?" the man asked.

"Crane Whindle?" another man suggested.

"No, Anse Felson's got the best dogs," Polk said. "And they're nigger dogs, too. Mean as a snake but best dogs in the county for trackin' down a nigger. You, boy, yes, you there, you go find Anse Felson and tell him to bring his nigger dogs."

The slaves left. Polk asked that everyone leave Chessie and Myrtis alone and the crowd began to drift away, whispering and glancing back as they disappeared.

Polk and the old woman stayed with Chessie and Myrtis. The woman mopped Myrtis' forehead with her kerchief. Chessie stroked the girl's hair and cried softly.

Chessy and her brother, heirs to the plantation, go to Rome to escape the temptations of their home, only to find their lives forever haunted by Rafaella, who is bent on revenge for the sins of their father.

Read the complete Bantam Book, available June 1979, wherever paperbacks are sold.

BRING ROMANCE INTO YOUR LIFE

With these bestsellers from your favorite Bantam authors

Barbara Cartland

☐	11372	LOVE AND THE LOATHSOME LEOPARD	$1.50
☐	10712	LOVE LOCKED IN	$1.50
☐	11270	THE LOVE PIRATE	$1.50
☐	11271	THE TEMPTATION OF TORILLA	$1.50

Catherine Cookson

☐	10355	THE DWELLING PLACE	$1.50
☐	10358	THE GLASS VIRGIN	$1.50
☐	10516	THE TIDE OF LIFE	$1.75

Georgette Heyer

☐	02263	THE BLACK MOTH	$1.50
☐	10322	BLACK SHEEP	$1.50
☐	02210	FARO'S DAUGHTER	$1.50

Emilie Loring

☐	12946	FOLLOW YOUR HEART	$1.75
☐	12947	WHERE BEAUTY DWELLS	$1.75
☐	12948	RAINBOW AT DUSK	$1.75
☐	12949	WHEN HEARTS ARE LIGHT AGAIN	$1.75
☐	12945	ACROSS THE YEARS	$1.75

Eugenia Price

☐	12712	BELOVED INVADER	$1.95
☐	12717	LIGHTHOUSE	$1.95
☐	12835	NEW MOON RISING	$1.95

Buy them at your local bookstore or use this handy coupon for ordering:

Bantam Books, Inc., Dept. RO, 414 East Golf Road, Des Plaines, Ill. 60016

Please send me the books I have checked above. I am enclosing $_____ (please add 75¢ to cover postage and handling). Send check or money order —no cash or C.O.D.'s please.

Mr/Mrs/Miss_____

Address_____

City_____State/Zip_____

RO—6/79

Please allow four weeks for delivery. This offer expires 12/79.

Barbara Cartland

The world's bestselling author of romantic fiction. Her stories are always captivating tales of intrigue, adventure and love.

☐ 02972	A DREAM FROM THE NIGHT	$1.25
☐ 02987	CONQUERED BY LOVE	$1.25
☐ 10971	THE RHAPSODY OF LOVE	$1.50
☐ 10715	THE MARQUIS WHO HATED WOMEN	$1.50
☐ 10975	A DUEL WITH DESTINY	$1.50
☐ 10976	CURSE OF THE CLAN	$1.50
☐ 10977	PUNISHMENT OF A VIXEN	$1.50
☐ 11101	THE OUTRAGEOUS LADY	$1.50
☐ 11168	A TOUCH OF LOVE	$1.50
☐ 11169	THE DRAGON AND THE PEARL	$1.50
☐ 11962	A RUNAWAY STAR	$1.50
☐ 11690	PASSION AND THE FLOWER	$1.50
☐ 12292	THE RACE FOR LOVE	$1.50
☐ 12566	THE CHIEFTAIN WITHOUT A HEART	$1.50

Buy them at your local bookstore or use this handy coupon for ordering: